Elizabeth Chadwick lives in ̲N̲o̲ ̲̲ ̲̲ ̲̲ ̲̲ ̲ nd two sons. Much of her research is carried ̲ ̲ ̲ ̲ ̲ ̲ ̲ber of Regia Anglorum, an early mediaeval re-enactment society with the emphasis on accurately recreating the past. She also tutors in the skill of writing historical and romantic fiction. She won a Betty Trask Award for *The Wild Hunt*, her first novel, and was shortlisted for the Romantic Novelists' Award in 1998 for *The Champion*, in 2001 for *Lords of the White Castle*, in 2002 for *The Winter Mantle* and in 2003 for *The Falcons of Montabard*.

The Scarlet Lion is the second of two stand-alone novels about William Marshal, Earl of Pembroke and regent of England.

For more details on Elizabeth Chadwick and her books, visit www.elizabethchadwick.com

Praise for Elizabeth Chadwick

'Blends authentic period details with modern convention for emotional drama'
Elizabeth Buchan, *Mail on Sunday*

'One of Elizabeth Chadwick's strengths is her stunning grasp of historical detail . . . her characters are beguiling, and the story intriguing and very enjoyable'
Barbara Erskine

'Prepare to be dazzled'
Nottingham Evening Post

'The best writer of mediaeval fiction currently around'
Historical Novel Review

'Elizabeth Chadwick kno ̲ ̲ ̲ ̲ ̲ ̲ ̲ ̲how to write convincing and compe ̲ ̲ ̲ ̲ ̲
M ̲ ̲

Also by Elizabeth Chadwick

THE SCARLET LION

Elizabeth Chadwick

sphere

SPHERE

First published in Great Britain in 2006 by Sphere
This paperback edition published in 2007 by Sphere

Copyright © Elizabeth Chadwick 2006

The moral right of the author has been asserted.

*All characters and events in this publication, other than those clearly
in the public domain, are fictitious and any resemblance to real persons,
living or dead, is purely coincidental.*

A CIP catalogue record for this book
is available from the British Library.

ISBN 978-0-7515-3659-1

Papers used by Sphere are natural, recyclable products made from
wood grown in sustainable forests and certified in accordance with the
rules of the Forest Stewardship Council.

Typeset in Baskerville by Palimpsest Book Production Limited,
Grangemouth, Stirlingshire
Printed and bound in Great Britain by
Clays Ltd, St Ives plc

Acknowledgements

I would like to take a page to say thank you to the various people who have helped me during the writing of *The Scarlet Lion*. First and foremost, I couldn't have written the novel without the research help of my good friend Alison King, who has found for me unique details concerning the lives of William Marshal, his wife Isabelle and the people surrounding them. Any faults in the interpretation of these details are entirely my responsibility. My thanks also go out to Professor Gillian Polack for her insights into thirteenth-century life and Tamara Mazzei for helping me to piece together the difficult issue of Alais de Béthune and William de Forz.

My agent Carole Blake is always there for me and I'd like to say a huge thank you to her for her efforts on my behalf, and her support as a friend. Thank you also to my lovely editors: Barbara Daniel, Joanne Dickinson and Sheena-Margot Lavelle at Little, Brown. Also Richenda Todd, who must have suffered many a headache sorting out the mish-mash of alternative dates and seasons left in the course of several drafts of the manuscript!

Online, I must thank the members of Penmanreview

and Friends and Writers for their support, friendship and fun. There are not many places where a writer can speculate on the state of Thomas Becket's undergarments and not be thought strange!

Offline, I send my love to my husband, Roger, for being my own safe harbour and giving me the space I need to write my books.

KINGS OF ENGLAND

THE CONTINENTAL DYNASTIES
1066–1216

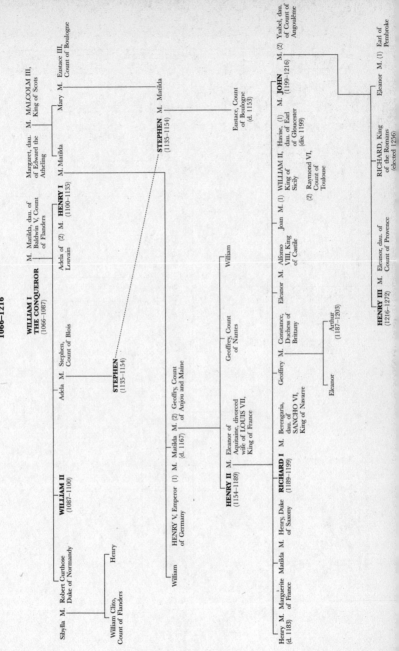

MARSHAL FAMILY TREE

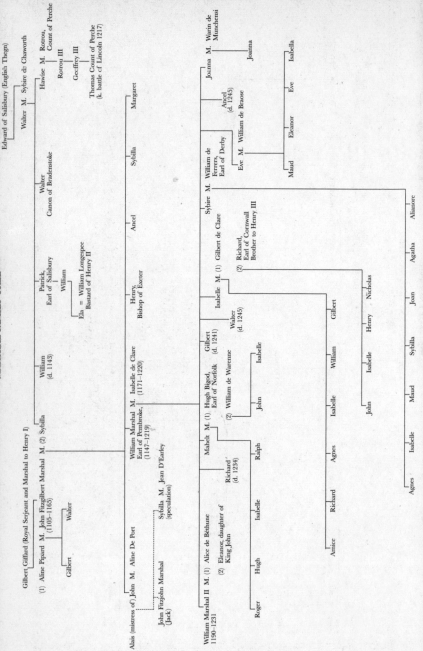

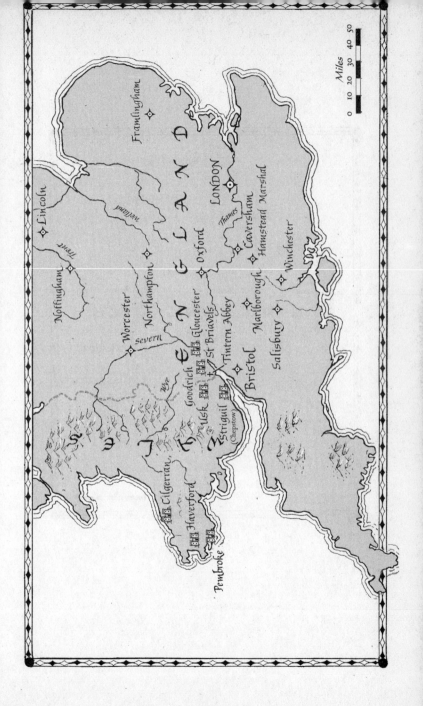

Carrickfergus

I R E L A N D   ◇ Dublin

Glendalough
                    ◇ Wicklow
Kilkenny
OSSORY   ◇   ◇ Glasscarrick
                    ◇ Wexford
Tintern Parva ◇   ◇ Waterford
              New Ross
              (NewTown)

Miles
0   10   20   30

1

Fortress of Longueville, Normandy, Spring 1197

Isabelle de Clare, Countess of Leinster and Striguil, wife to King Richard's Marshal, was in labour with their fourth child.

'Arse first,' announced the midwife, wiping her hands on a length of towel after examining her patient. 'Bound to be a boy, they always cause the most trouble.'

Isabelle closed her eyes and reclined against the piled bolsters. Throughout the morning the contractions had become steadily more frequent and painful. Her women had unbraided her hair so there would be no bindings about her person to tie the baby in the womb, and the thick, wheat-gold strands spilled over shoulders and engorged breasts to touch her mounded belly.

'He' was already late. Her husband had hoped to greet his new offspring before setting out to war ten days ago, but instead had had to bid Isabelle farewell with a kiss at arm's length, her pregnant belly like a mountain between them. It was May now. If she survived bearing this child and he lived through the summer's campaign, they would see each other in the autumn. For now, he was somewhere deep in the Beauvaisis with his sovereign, and she was wishing she was anywhere but this stuffy chamber undergoing the ordeal of childbirth.

A contraction started low in her spine and tightened across her womb. Pain bloomed through her lower body, causing her to gasp and clench her fists.

'Always hurts more when they come tail first.' The midwife looked shrewdly at Isabelle. 'It's not your first; you know what to expect, but infants that enter the world by their backsides have a dangerous passage. Head comes last and that's not good for the babe. Best pray to the blessed Saint Margaret for her help.' She indicated the painted wooden image standing on a coffer at the bedside surrounded by a glow of votive candles.

'I have been praying to her every day since I knew I was with child,' Isabelle said irritably, not adding that the overdue birth of a baby in the breech position was hardly a happy reward for her devotion. She was coming to abhor the statue. Whoever had carved it had put a sanctimonious expression on its face that fell little short of a smirk.

The next contraction wrung her in its grip and with it the urge to push. The midwife signalled to the girl assisting her and busied herself between Isabelle's thighs. 'You should summon your chaplain to christen the child, immediately,' she announced, her voice muffled by the raised sheet. 'Do you have a name?'

'Gilbert for a boy, and Isabelle for a girl,' Isabelle gritted through her teeth as she bore down. The contraction receded. Slumping against the bolsters she panted at one of her women to fetch Father Walter and have him wait in the antechamber.

The next pain seized her, then the next and the next, fierce and hard, no respite now as her body strove to expel the baby from her womb and into the world. She sobbed and grunted with effort, tendons standing out in her throat, her hands gripping those of her attendants hard enough to leave lasting weals on their flesh.

There was a sudden gush of wet heat between her thighs and the midwife groped. 'Ah,' she said with satisfaction. 'I was right, it is a boy. Ha-ha, fine pair of hammers on him too! Let's see if we can keep him alive to have use of them, eh? Push again, my lady. Not so fast, not so fast. Go gently now.'

Isabelle bit her lip and struggled not to push as hard as her instincts dictated. Taking the baby's ankles, tugging gently, the midwife drew his torso up and on to Isabelle's abdomen. As the mouth and nose emerged from the birth canal she wiped them clear of blood and mucus, then, watching intently, controlled the emergence of the rest of the head with a gentle hand.

Propped on her elbows, Isabelle stared at the baby lying upon her body like a drowned, shipwrecked sailor. His colour was greyish-blue and he wasn't moving. Panic shot through her. 'Holy Saint Margaret, is he . . . ?'

The woman lifted the baby by his ankles, swung him gently and applied a sharp tap to his buttocks, then again. A shudder rippled through him, his little chest expanded and a wail of protest met the air, uncertain at first, but gathering momentum and infusing his body with a flush of life-giving pink.

Righting him, the midwife turned to Isabelle, a smile deepening the creases in her wrinkled cheeks. 'Just needed a bit of persuading,' she said. 'Best have the priest name him though, to be on the safe side.' She wrapped him in a warm towel and placed him in Isabelle's arms.

The cord having been cut and the afterbirth expelled and taken away for burial, Isabelle gazed into the birth-crumpled features of her newborn son and, still deeply anxious, watched his shallow breathing. A baffled, slightly quizzical frown puckered his delicately sketched brows. His little hands were tightly clenched as if to fight the world into which he had been so brutally initiated. 'Gilbert,' she said softly. 'I wonder what your father is going to make of you.' She blew softly against his cheek and gave him her forefinger around which to curl his miniature hand. After a moment, she lifted her gaze from the baby and fixed it on her chamber window and the arch of soft blue sky it framed. Her own ordeal was almost over and, God willing, if she did not take the childbed fever, she would soon be on her feet. Saint Margaret could be thanked with an offering and packed away in her coffer again until needed. Now she would concentrate on prayers for her husband's safety and ask God to bring him home in one piece to greet their new son.

The assault on the castle of Milli was not going well; indeed, it was a shambles. Eyes narrowed, William Marshal stared across the ditch towards the castle walls and cursed under his breath, his gaze clinging to the serjeants and soldiers toiling their way up the rungs of the scaling ladder like ants on a twig. Several of these ladders had been concentrated at one part of the wall as King Richard's forces attempted to storm the castle and seize it from its rebellious constable.

'Make haste, in God's name, make haste!' Jean D'Earley, William's former squire, now a knight of his company, danced from foot to foot, chewed his lip and clenched and unclenched his fists.

The defenders on the battlements strove desperately to dislodge the ladders from the walls while the weight of their enemies was still sufficiently low down to make it feasible. Crossbow bolts, arrows, stakes and boulders

4

rained down on the attackers. Stricken men tumbled from the ladders into the ditch, some in silence, others screaming.

'It's going to fall, Christ help them!' Jean's voice was anguished as the defenders succeeded in lodging a crowbar between one of the ladder ends and the wall and began levering.

'My shield.' William beckoned to his squire with a flick of his left hand.

The ladder slipped sideways and toppled, smashing its burden of soldiers into bank and ditch. The cries of the crushed and maimed rose in chilling twists of sound to join the clamour of battle. A few fortunates crawled and hobbled to safety, but many more lay broken and dying amid the splintered remnants of the siege ladder. Cheers of abuse and a fresh barrage of missiles pelted down from the walls in a lethal rain.

William thrust his hand through his shield grips. The legendary green and yellow Marshal colours faced the embattled walls, the painted scarlet lion clawing the foreground. Something had to be done and fast. If they didn't gain those wall walks, they were going to have to choose between sitting down to starve the bastards out or retreating to lick their wounded dignity . . . and King Richard had neither the patience nor the temper for either. He couldn't afford to wait and he couldn't afford to lose. William snatched a glance along the embankment to the royal standard. Standing beneath the wind-rippled red and gold banner, King Richard was plucking his auburn beard with one hand and gesticulating vigorously to his mercenary captain Mercadier with the other.

Armed with a fresh ladder, a group of serjeants and mercenaries charged across the makeshift bridge of planks spanning the ditch, prompting an increased storm of missiles from the walls. Most fell short or bounced off shields, but one serjeant was hit in the chest by a crossbow quarrel and another by a sling stone that struck his hand, shattering his fingers. Undeterred, the others planted the ladder's feet into the soft turf of the bank and slammed the end down on the wall.

A vigorous effort led by the Flemish knight Guy de la Bruiere was on the brink of success and the battlements boiled with activity at that section. William took his open-faced helm from his squire and settled it on his head, adjusting the nasal bar until it was comfortable.

'God's bones, the whoresons have got a pick,' Jean spat.

William swore. Two defenders were leaning through a crenel space, manipulating a large siege pick, intent on using the vicious iron beak to snag themselves a victim. As he watched, they succeeded in hooking the front of de la Bruiere's surcoat, threatening to yank him from his perch. The burdened ladder thrummed ominously against the stonework, in serious danger of following its companion into the ditch.

William gave a peremptory signal to the knights of his mesnie. Covering himself with his shield, he ran across the ditch planks and scrambled up the bank to the new ladder. Ordering aside the serjeant who had been about to set his foot on the first rung, he began climbing himself. He refused to think about the defenders above him and what they might be doing to try to dislodge the ladder, or topple him from it. He needed to take that section of the battlements and seize control of the situation before it became a debacle.

He felt the vibration of the men climbing behind him, adding their weight and stability; gambling their lives as he was gambling his own. His breath roared in his ears, muting other sounds. He didn't look down, just kept

6

climbing rung to rung, gripping the rough ash staves, feeling their pressure against the soles of his boots. Grasp, step, grasp, step. Closer, closer. Almost there. As William readied himself, he felt the stave shudder under his hands and realised with a wallow of his gut that the defenders were in imminent success at prising the ladder off the wall. The detail galvanised him into a burst of harder effort and his lungs began to burn. Reaching the final rung, he launched himself at the crenel gap, gained it and leaped on to the walkway. He used his shield to beat aside the soldier trying to dislodge the ladder and drew his sword. Breathing harshly, he dealt with a serjeant brandishing a spear and brought down another man who took a wild swing at him with a spiked club. A glance showed him his own men scrambling on to the wall walk. Leaving them to secure the ground, William ran to tackle the defenders wielding the pick. A serjeant jabbed a glaive at his face. William beat the weapon aside on his shield and downed another soldier on the backswing of his sword. A gasping Jean D'Earley dealt with a second assault from the glaive. On the ladder, de la Bruiere had managed to cut himself free of his snagged surcoat; having gained the battlements, he was laying about with his sword.

The fight on the wall walk boiled like a cauldron over a hot flame as Milli's garrison made a desperate effort to repulse their attackers. Another ladder smashed into the ditch but two more went up in its place. William was aware of Jean fighting doggedly at his right, and his standard-bearer Mallard to his left. 'Marshal!' roared Mallard at regular intervals. 'God aid the Marshal!'

The cry drew a breathless chuckle from William as he realised Milli's constable Guillaume de Monceaux had arrived on the battlements to fight beside his men. God could not have aided him any better.

'Marshal!' William bellowed to Mallard and sprang upon Milli's constable with all the vigour and determination of a young knight with a reputation to carve, rather than the experienced veteran he was. Monceaux's gaze widened in shock. He flung up his shield, but William swept it aside as if swatting a fly off his dinner, and brought his sword down on the constable's helm with the full strength of his right arm. Finest steel of Cologne, the blade hewed through the helm and arming cap and opened a gash in Monceaux's scalp. The shock of the blow dropped the constable like a stone at William's feet. William snatched the sword from Monceaux's hand and sat on him to make sure he stayed down. Besides, William needed a respite after the fierce exertion of his ladder climb and frantic battle on the wall.

The fight raged around them as the defenders strove to reach and rescue their castellan, but Jean, Mallard and the Marshal knights, aided by the Flemings, kept them at bay, until the defenders realised they were beaten and began throwing down their weapons and crying surrender. Mallard waved William's standard triumphantly aloft and further along the wall the leopards of England replied.

De Monceaux was beginning to turn purple. Easing to his feet, William stood back, but kept his sword levelled at his captive's throat.

'God's bollocks, Marshal, what in the name of all that's holy did you think you were doing?' The voice was deep with a harsh metallic timbre sharpening the edge.

'Sire?' William turned, bowed, then looked questioningly at his King. Richard's complexion was scarlet beneath his helm; runnels of sweat streaked his face. His grey-blue eyes were ablaze with battle fire and as always with Richard the line between laughter and rage was so fine it was difficult to tell which side of it he stood. Behind him, his mercenary captain Mercadier was watching the exchange and smothering a grin behind his mailed fist.

'You're a commander, not a young glory-hunter. Why didn't you stay back and leave the heroics to youths like these?' He made a peremptory gesture towards a gasping Jean D'Earley, who was cleaning his sword blade on the surcoat of a fallen defender.

William's shoulders stiffened with affront. 'Sire, the assault was failing. I took a commander's decision and acted. You have your castle and the surrender of its constable.' He forbore to add that the King was a fine one to talk. Richard's penchant for leading from the front was legendary. 'I am not so far into my dotage that my will outstrips my strength.'

Richard grunted. His gaze flickered to the castellan whose windpipe remained mere inches from the steady point of William's sword. 'I saw you sitting on him,' he said and his narrow mouth suddenly twitched. 'That either means you were keen to make sure no one else took him for ransom, or you were too exhausted to stay on your feet.'

'Or that I was rendering him *hors de combat*,' William retorted calmly. 'A good commander is capable of doing more than one thing at a time.'

Richard yielded his irritation to an open grin. 'I cannot argue with that, Marshal. For what you've accomplished I would let you have this one's ransom even if he was worth ten times the sum you'll get for him. Nevertheless, I value your counsel too much to enjoy seeing you take such risks. Your wife is too young to be a widow and your sons too small to lack a father. If anything happened to you, I'd never hear the end of it. The Countess has an Irish temper.'

It was William's turn to grin. 'Isabelle is as sweet as honey if you know how to handle her,' he said.

'And, like my mother, she stings like a bee when provoked,' Richard retorted and, chuckling, moved on. Arms folded, Mercadier started to follow him, then paused in front of William, his dark eyes sparkling with amusement.

'When he saw you running up that ladder, he was fit to burst,' he said in a low voice, glancing to make sure Richard was out of earshot. 'If he's annoyed with you it's because he saw de la Bruiere dancing on the pick too and would have gone to his aid had you not beaten him to it. We had to pull him back – we couldn't risk both of you on the same ladder. The moment he saw you gain the wall walk there was no stopping him.'

'Better I should take the risk than him.'

'He didn't think so.' With a nod to William, Mercadier strode after his paymaster.

William sheathed his sword. He had answered Richard with robust assertion but, in the aftermath of hard effort, he was aware of aching, strained limbs and of the fact that before long he would mark his fiftieth year on God's earth. The sweat chilling on his body made him shiver. Stooping, he hauled the dazed constable to his feet and gave him into the custody of Mallard, telling the knight to keep him under close but courteous guard and attend to his scalp wound. When he turned round, Jean was holding out a cup of wine, his expression studiously blank.

William took the offering with gratitude, drank thirstily and wiped his mouth on his gambeson cuff. 'When I was newly knighted and still wet behind the ears, I was involved in a street battle at Drincourt,' he said reflectively. 'The commander told me to stay back and let the experienced knights do their work – said I was too young and a hindrance, but I ignored him and forced my way to the front.' He leaned on one hip, his left hand resting on his sword hilt, and drank again, this time more slowly. 'I lost my horse, took a nasty shoulder wound and impoverished myself into the bargain because I demanded no ransoms from the knights I put down. But we won and I lived to tell the tale.' He gave a self-deprecatory smile. 'I was a whelp then; I'm an old dog now, and unlikely to change my ways.'

'I'm wise enough to leave that kind of persuasion to the Countess,' Jean said with a straight face.

William laughed and started towards the stairs leading down to the bailey. 'She'll boil my hide in oil when she hears about today's battle,' he said over his shoulder. 'Tell the men not to exaggerate too much for my sake.'

'I'll do my best, my lord,' Jean replied with a rueful grin.

Isabelle set the final stitch in the scrap of linen on which she had been working, secured the thread and snipped it with her small silver shears. 'There,' she said to her fidgeting three-year-old daughter. 'He's finished. What do you say?'

Mahelt's little face lit up as she took the representation of a swaddled baby from her mother. It was the size of a man's thumb; the body made from whittled wood and fleece purloined from the spinning basket, then wrapped in a strip of linen. 'Thank you.' Mahelt gave her mother a smacking kiss and a fierce hug before dashing back to the corner where she had been playing with her *poupées*. Isabelle smiled with tender amusement. Mahelt might be little more than an infant, but already the maternal, nurturing soul was as fierce within her as the warrior spirit was in her older brothers. She possessed a moppet made of soft cloth to nurse and cuddle, but this new, smaller addition was for her 'family' of *poupées*, each one the size of a small tent peg. They dwelt in a small carved chest

11

by Mahelt's crib-bed and she played with them most days. The child would chatter to them as brightly as a magpie and make up stories about them. They had briefly fallen out of favour when her baby brother had been born, but, fascinated as she was by Gilbert, once the immediate novelty had worn off, she had returned to her toys. Now she tucked the baby *poupée* gently against the arm of the mother one who sported a rose-coloured gown and long golden braids like Isabelle's.

Isabelle brushed threads from her lap, rose to her feet, and went to look at Gilbert, now almost five months old. Despite his awkward birth, he was thriving and showed no ill effects, either of body or disposition, the latter being remarkably sunny. Providing he was fed, kept dry and played with, he made few demands, unlike his two older brothers who at seven and six were into every scrape imaginable and frenetic with energy from the moment they woke until the time they were sent to bed, Richard in particular. She could hear his voice now through the open shutters, raised in a shriek of excitement, and his brother's yelled reply.

Isabelle frowned. Their training in weapon play must have finished early, or else Eustace, their tutor, was letting them have a moment to run wild. But the shout of masculine laughter that followed their exclamations was not from Eustace and it caused her heart to kick in her breast and her breath to shorten. She ran to the window arch and looked out. Eustace was standing on the sward, hands on hips, a broad grin on his face as he watched her sons blithely attacking their father and Jean D'Earley with their wooden practice swords. Behind them, the knights and serjeants of the Marshal coterie were making their way towards the hall, shields slung at their backs, arms filled with baggage rolls and equipment.

Gathering her scattered wits, Isabelle turned from the window and began issuing swift commands to her women. She didn't know whether to laugh or be furious that William had not sent heralds to warn of his arrival but had chosen rather to sweep in like an autumn gale and take her unawares. Once the matter of a bath and food had been set in motion, she sped down to the hall, checking her wimple and smoothing her gown as she ran.

A son bundled under either arm, William was entering from the courtyard as she emerged flushed and breathless from her chamber stairs. Composing herself, aware that all eyes were upon them, but only having eyes for William, she went forward to greet him. His cloak and boots were pale with dust from the road but he himself was tanned from his summer of campaigning. He looked lean, fit and dangerous.

He saw her and released the boys. 'Go to,' he said, tousling their hair. 'Let me greet your mother fittingly.'

Nudging each other, grinning, Will and Richard stood aside. William went to Isabelle, lifted her right hand in his and formally kissed it. He had grown a beard whilst away in the field and his whiskers tickled. The expression in his eyes filled her heart and liquefied her loins. 'My lord, welcome home,' she said with equal formality, although the look she returned him was incandescent. 'If you had sent word ahead, we would have been better prepared to greet you.'

'And that would have been a pity. I wanted it to be a surprise.' He turned to take the welcome-cup of wine presented by the hall steward. Having taken a formal sip, he passed it on to Jean D'Earley who also drank and in his turn gave it to another knight of the mesnie.

'Your supper will be a surprise too, depending on what supplies we have to hand,' Isabelle answered, but she was laughing. She felt giddy, a little drunk on his presence. It was always the same after so long a parting. Appetites that had been suppressed of a necessity were suddenly brought into sharp focus, both the physical and the intellectual.

'After the rats' tails and boiled worms we've been eating, anything will taste like manna,' he said with a wink to his sons, and headed for the tower stairs. All around the hall wives, sweethearts and children were greeting their menfolk and the sound of voices raised in pleasure and merriment filled and warmed a room that had been too long empty.

'That bad?' Isabelle said.

'Some of the time,' William answered evasively. Entering the chamber, he acknowledged the curtseys of Isabelle's women with a nod and went over to the cradle at the bedside to gaze down at the slumbering baby. He had received news in the field of Gilbert's birth and baptism. A third son to vouchsafe the bloodline.

'He chose to come feet first into the world and frighten everyone into thinking he might be stillborn, but he's behaved himself ever since.' Isabelle joined him in his scrutiny. 'From the tales I have heard of your days as a squire, he takes after you.'

He looked amused. 'In what way?'

'It was said that you did naught but eat and sleep and earn yourself the nickname "Guzzleguts".'

'Unfair,' William protested. 'I liked food and sleep when I could get them – what youth of those years does not? But I had to work for them.'

'Still, the name suits him. He's already got a tooth and he's started eating pap.' She looked at him through her lashes. 'I employed a wet nurse last week.'

William said nothing, but his body reacted instantaneously. Isabelle liked to suckle the children herself for a time at least, viewing it as both a maternal pleasure and an obligation. Her offspring were of de Clare blood and it was only fitting they were nourished from that source, at least until they were ready to begin weaning. However, the Church declared it a sin for a nursing woman to have carnal knowledge of her husband. While he and Isabelle sometimes ignored the strictures, the burden of guilt in disobeying them added furtive worry rather than piquancy to their marriage bed. It was always a relief when the time came to employ the wet nurse, especially following a long, dry summer.

He became aware of another presence at his side and, looking down, met the wide solemn gaze of his three-year-old daughter. Her bottom lip was caught in her teeth as if she wasn't quite sure who he was and what her response ought to be. He squatted on his heels so that his gaze was on a level with hers. Her eyes were winter-deep like his own and her hair was rich brown with coppery lights. Freckles peppered her dainty nose and there was a smear of dust on her chin. He raised his hand and gently thumbed it away.

'And how goes it with you, young mistress?' he asked solemnly.

Mahelt made a face at him and giggled. She presented him with some of her *poupées* to admire, including two he hadn't seen before: a swaddled baby and a knight with a surcoat and shield of green and gold.

'Who's this?' he asked.

'It's you,' she replied, eyeing him as if he was a lackwit.

'I thought you already had one of me,' he said.

'Yes, but that's when you're my papa at home. This one's you when you're gone. Mama's going to make me a king next.'

He bit his lip to avoid laughing, and at the same time felt a little sad. He swung her up in his arms. 'Well, I'm home now, sweetheart.'

'Yes, but you'll go away again.' She touched the rich braid edging the neckline of his tunic.

'Not for a long while yet . . . plenty of time to make kings and queens and princes.'

'And another baby?' she asked, eyes wide.

He spluttered. 'You'd have to ask your mother about that,' he said with a grin at his wife.

Tucking a towel around his waist, William stepped from the bathtub. Isabelle dried his torso and conducted a careful scrutiny. Apart from the scars of wounds taken in his youth, of which there were very few given his career in the tourneys and on the battlefield, she was disturbed to notice one or two recent additions, mainly of bruises fading to yellow. Since he was a senior commander and overseer of campaigns these days, there should not have been any bruises at all.

'What?' he asked warily as she moved from his back around to his chest.

'We heard a preposterous tale about the siege of Milli.' She handed the damp towel to a maid and folded her arms. 'Apparently you ran across the ditch, led an assault up a scaling ladder and fought single-handed on the wall walk.'

He shrugged. 'You should know by now not to listen to tales, my love.'

'It depends who's telling them. When it's one of my own messengers who was in camp and witnessed the event, I tend to yield him credence.'

He caught her round the waist and pulled her against his damp body. 'I'm not in my dotage yet, and I'll have neither my king nor my wife putting me out to grass.'

16

Isabelle set one palm against his chest and with the fingers of her other hand traced the outline of his freshly shaven jaw where the ghost of his beard lingered in the outline of lighter, untanned skin. 'I harboured no such thoughts, but I am bound to think of your safety. Besides,' she added mischievously, 'when old warhorses are put out to grass, it's usually to stud.'

His eyes narrowed at the remark. 'And those in their prime can usually manage both the battlefield and the breeding stall.' He gestured towards the bed. 'Draw the hangings and I'll prove it to you.'

Isabelle laughed and blushed, aware of the proximity of the children and grinning, wide-eared servants. 'I already have the proof . . .' she said with a nod towards Gilbert's cradle, and a glance at their other offspring who were chasing each other round the room, wild with excitement at having their father and his entourage home. '. . . of both.' Her fingers were rueful as she ran them over his bruises. The towel did little to conceal the detail that he was perfectly capable of proving his point, but decency was swiftly restored by the garments which had been warming at the fire: loose linen braies, chausses, and a tunic of soft dark-blue wool. Nonetheless, the look William exchanged with her promised the matter would be attended to at a more appropriate and leisurely moment and caused Isabelle to shiver with luxurious anticipation.

'We took Milli and captured the Bishop of Beauvais, so Richard was mightily pleased.' William sat down to drink wine and eat a platter of honey pastries. 'And we turned back the French – for now at least. Richard's short of money again but that's nothing new. He's talking about raising the taxes in England to gain more revenue. I daresay his chancellor will do his best to accommodate him and squeeze where necessary.'

17

Isabelle made a mental note to have a word with their stewards and clerics. She and William would pay their dues and even a little more than their dues because it was useful to keep royal favour. There were often occasions when they would lend Richard money from their own revenues, but they were able to do that because they were astute and kept an eye on their own interests and purse strings. It helped that much of their English revenue was based on the wool from their Welsh Marcher estates, of which Flemish looms could not get enough.

William sat Mahelt on his knee and shared a pastry with her. 'Prince John acquitted himself well,' he remarked.

Isabelle couldn't prevent herself from making a contemptuous sound.

'Mama doesn't like Prince John,' announced seven-year-old Will, who had been listening and watching the parental exchange and unconsciously absorbing the nuances. 'She says that an ermine is still a stoat under the season's changes.'

William helped himself to another pastry. 'Your mother is right to be cautious,' he said. His tone was casual, if not the warning look he cast at Isabelle. When he spoke again, his words were as much for her as for their son. 'But for the moment I have no quarrel with him and he is the King's brother.'

'Do you like him?' Will asked with the raw candour of childhood.

William licked his fingers. 'He's a competent commander and good company round the fire at night.'

Isabelle noted his evasive answer. She knew William and Richard worked well together and, despite past frictions, their relationship was one of mutual trust and the liking that William declined to admit for Prince John.

Isabelle's antipathy for John went much deeper than her husband's. She sometimes thought that if the Devil walked the earth in the shape of a handsome and charming man, he would look and act like the King's brother.

'He is Richard's heir,' William added with quiet emphasis. 'One day he might be King. He's also our overlord in respect of your mother's Irish lands.'

Not wanting to begin an argument within an hour of William's return, Isabelle bit her tongue and busied herself chivvying the maids to empty the bathwater and take away the dirty items of baggage to the laundry. Her Irish lands were a sore point, and one which could only be resolved by putting time and effort into them – time and effort that William was too busy giving to Richard and Normandy.

The shutters were closed against the night, but the ceramic oil lamp suspended from the bed canopy had cast enough light to see by and enhance desire and pleasure. Isabelle held William close, savouring the sensation of his hard body upon and within hers: the thunder of his heartbeat, the catch of his breathing, the relaxation of muscles which a moment ago had been bunched with tension. They had been married for eight years; some times were invariably better than others, and this occasion, fed by a season's built-up appetite, was one of them.

'Is that proof enough for you?' William gasped against her throat.

Isabelle arched her neck. 'It is certainly proof,' she replied in a sultry murmur, 'but whether it is enough . . .'

'Is that a challenge?'

'And if I said yes?'

He nuzzled her throat. 'I can still race up a siege ladder and have the stamina remaining for a long campaign.'

19

Isabelle answered the sally with soft laughter. 'Maybe so,' she said, enjoying the banter, 'but in me you have met your match.'

He rolled to his side, pulling her with him. 'Ah, Isabelle,' he said tenderly, and drew his hand through her thick tawny hair. 'I thank God for it every day.'

'So do I . . . and that's why I worry for you.'

'Now that I'm getting older?' His tone was still light but Isabelle didn't miss the sardonic nuance.

'Your age has nothing to do with it.' She gave him a nudge. 'Were you three score and ten, I suspect you'd still be leading your men from the front rather than staying back to command.'

'I know what I'm about. As in all things there's much to be said for experience.' He nibbled the inside of her wrist. 'Truly, I am not in search of glory these days.'

Isabelle wasn't so sure, but let the matter drop. She feared that King Richard involved William in too many scrapes, but saying so was pointless and would only create a vicious circle compounded of her worry and his exasperation. It did not mean, however, that she was finished with skirmishing on other matters close to her heart. 'Did you speak of Ireland to Richard and John?' she asked.

'Yes,' he said diffidently, 'I mentioned it.'

'And?'

He sighed. 'The King agreed in principle to give me leave to go, but for the moment he needs me to command in Normandy.'

'And what did John say?'

'Very little.'

'He would,' she said tartly. 'He's our overlord in Ireland and he doesn't want us stirring our spoon in his cauldron lest we dredge up things that he doesn't want us to see.'

When he didn't reply, Isabelle raised herself up on her

elbow to look at him. 'You think I am being foolish about John, don't you?'

'No, my love, I don't. A trifle zealous in your dislike, I admit, but you are right. John doesn't want us interfering in Ireland, but it's a moot point anyway because I cannot spare the time to go.'

Isabelle exhaled impatiently. 'We have been wed as long as Richard has been a king, yet not once have we crossed the sea to Leinster. When *will* you be able to spare the time?'

'As soon as it is right on all counts, I promise.'

With an effort, Isabelle restrained herself. She didn't want to quarrel on his first night home. The privacy of their bed might be the place, but it wasn't the time. She suspected that William was as reluctant to visit Ireland as Richard and John were to see him go. She had long realised that while the tranquillity of retreats such as Caversham in England or this keep at Longueville were necessities to his wellbeing, he was uncomfortable when away from the hub of the court for too long. He had dwelt in its glow for most of his life, so that leaving it for the distant periphery of Ireland would be an almighty wrench. Then there was the sea crossing. He abhorred travelling by ship and the passage to Ireland was no calm day's sail. Still, she intended holding him to his word. He was always insisting that it was by her auspices he held the land and only in trust for their children. Let him put his actions on the same level as the courtesy of his words and give them substance.

'I was born there.' Her voice took on a wistful note. 'Half my blood is of that land. I have a longing to see it again . . . and my mother. I was little more than a child when we parted and now I have children of my own. Even if we were never close, I desire to speak to her one woman to another, and she has a right to see her grand-children.'

'I always keep my promises,' he said with the assertive reiteration she had heard him use to difficult vassals and pouting children alike.

She sighed. 'I know you do.' For a while there was silence as Isabelle tried to put her concerns aside and focus on the pleasure of having William's warmth in the bed beside her. 'You will give it serious thought though . . . ?'

William's voice was filled with wry humour. 'I haven't been asked to think about so many things in a long time, and I've not been home a day yet.'

'I suppose there are many things you haven't done in a long time,' Isabelle said, leaning over to kiss him. 'What were you saying about stamina?'

2

Longueville, Normandy, Spring 1199

Isabelle sat at her embroidery with her ladies. Pulling away from winter, the season's light had a pale clarity that meant more intricate sewing could be undertaken. Bending an attentive ear to the chatter, she was glad to hear a lively note in the women's voices, for that too, like the return of the sun and the sight of birds building their nests, was a sure sign spring had arrived.

Jean D'Earley's young wife Sybilla was stitching an exquisite design of silver scallop shells on to a tunic band. Embroidery was her particular skill and her husband was the best-dressed knight of William's mesnie. Sybilla was William's niece, daughter of his deceased elder brother. The young woman possessed a quiet disposition, but Isabelle believed the creativity and dedication exhibited in her sewing were indicative of a rich internal life that didn't need gossip and socialising to sustain it.

'How are you feeling now?' Isabelle asked her. The young woman had been unwell for three days running with a queasy stomach, and Isabelle had her suspicions, compounded by the way Sybilla kept looking at the cradle holding the newest addition to the Marshal family, three-month-old Walter.

'A little better, my lady. The infusion of ginger has helped.' Sybilla looked pensive. 'I . . . I think I may be with child, although I am not yet certain.'

Isabelle patted her arm in reassurance. 'I suspect so too. It is good news for you and Jean if it be the case.'

Sybilla looked dubious. 'He has been much absent with the Earl and we haven't bedded together often of late; it may be a false alarm.'

Isabelle sent a rueful glance towards the cradle herself. 'William only has to look at me and I quicken.'

'Aye, well, you and the Earl have had plenty of practice,' teased Elizabeth Avenel, wife to one of William's knights. She was always eager to talk of matters bawdy or sexual when the bower ladies were gathered over their sewing, although in mixed company she was less bold. 'Everyone knows that unless a wife experiences the same satisfaction as her husband, her seed will not descend to mix with his and she will not conceive.' She chuckled at Sybilla. 'If you're feeling full enough for the sickness, my girl, then your lord must have discovered the art of pleasuring you in bed.'

'Elizabeth!' Isabelle spluttered with a look at Sybilla who had flushed bright pink.

'Well it's true!' Lady Avenel defended herself. 'Even some priests say so. The ones who don't are juiceless old prunes who've never had a good fu—'

She bit off her words as the chamber door opened and William flung into the room. He glanced swiftly at the circle of women, said, 'Isabelle, a word,' and strode over to an embrasure further down the room. Sweeping aside a motley assortment of children's toys, he sat down on the cushioned chest under the window splay, two vertical frown lines etching the space between his brows.

Isabelle's mirth faded. Abandoning her sewing, she left her women and hastened to William's side. 'What's wrong?'

He breathed out hard and rubbed his neck. 'Ach, nothing out of the usual. I don't even know why I am surprised. Is there any wine left, or has the sewing party drunk it all?'

Something had riled him; he didn't usually make acerbic comments about her women. 'No, there is plenty left to drown your woes,' she said sweetly and fetched the cup and flagon herself, exchanging eloquent glances with her ladies as she did so.

Having taken a long drink, William rested the cup on his thigh and sighed out hard. 'I've just been talking to a messenger from Baldwin de Béthune.'

Isabelle sat down beside him, plumped a fleece-filled cushion at her back and looked at him expectantly. Baldwin de Béthune, Count of Aumale, was William's closest friend and currently with the King. Even when William was absent from the court, such contacts kept him well informed. Whatever the news was, it had certainly put a burr in her husband's braies.

'Prince John is under suspicion of conspiracy and Richard's in a quarrelsome mood. I tell you, Isabelle, sometimes I want to knock their heads together until their brains run out of their ears – not that it would make any difference except to my own satisfaction.'

'What do you mean, under suspicion?'

He eyed her sombrely. 'Philip of France claims to have letters implicating John in treason. John's supposed to have asked for Philip's aid in mounting a rebellion against Richard – who is not best pleased.'

'It was only a matter of time,' she said.

His nostrils flared. 'Why is everyone prepared to believe

25

the worst of John and not allow that he might just have learned his lesson and matured?'

'So you don't believe it is true?' She managed to school her voice to calm enquiry, avoiding the flat note that usually entered it when they spoke of Richard's brother.

'Of course it isn't,' he said impatiently. 'Philip's as wily as a fox and false rumours like this are a fine way of creating discord. John might be devious and self-seeking, but he's not mad and he would have to be insane to go conniving with Philip. The last time he dabbled in conspiracy, Richard was locked up in a German prison. John won't risk anything with Richard close enough to breathe down his neck.' He drank again, his movements swift with displeasure. 'Whatever his flaws as a man, John has been a model of loyalty to Richard these past five years.'

'So what will happen now?'

'It's already happening. John's gone off in a fury at being accused and God alone knows where.'

'Perhaps to Paris,' she said with pessimism. 'Perhaps the King of France has succeeded anyway.'

William shot her an irritated look. 'I sincerely doubt he'd turn to Philip, but he might just be sufficiently annoyed to go and plot some mischief by way of revenge.'

'Has Richard done anything about it?'

'Not yet, from what Baldwin says. He's decided John probably isn't guilty, but he's not entirely sure. Why would he leave court unless he had something to fear? If ever our sons start behaving like Richard and John, I will drown them, I swear I will.' He heaved a deep sigh. 'Richard is going on campaign in the Limousin to work off his anger and hunt for gold to fill his coffers. Some vassal of Aymer de Lusignan has dug up an ancient hoard on his lands and he's refusing to give it up.' He picked up one of Mahelt's *poupées*, the one of himself as a warrior in the

26

green and yellow surcoat, and eyed it thoughtfully. 'Richard needs funds and the idea of a spring campaign to make the sap rise appeals to him.'

Isabelle's stomach lurched. 'You are not going with him?'

'No, I'm still due to sit on the Bench of Justices with Hubert Walter at Vaudreuil. De Braose, de Burgh and Mercadier are attending on Richard. He says John can wait until his return . . . I'm not sure he can, but it's a decision for Richard's cup, not mine.' He put aside the *poupée* in the surcoat and picked up the one of himself in court garb of red twill embroidered with silver thread. 'Jesu, another tunic,' he said with a shake of his head, making it clear which of the two figures he would rather be. 'I am in danger of becoming a fop.'

Isabelle's heart lightened with relief that King Richard was not summoning him on yet another campaign. 'Sybilla made it for her. She's so quick and skilled with a needle that it takes her no time.' She lowered her voice and added, 'Sybilla thinks she may be with child.'

'So that's what you were gossiping about when I came in?'

She smiled demurely. 'More or less.'

He grunted with amusement. 'Lady Elizabeth has a loud voice,' he said. 'It is good news for them. Jean will be pleased.' He rose to his feet and stretched. Isabelle was glad to see the tension had gone out of him; glad too that he had come to her to ease and share his burden. Not all marriages were thus.

'I suppose if I am leaving for Vaudreuil on the morrow I had better find my two eldest sons. I promised them a jousting lesson.' A regretful expression crossed his face. 'It doesn't seem a moment since I was their age and my father was teaching me my sword strokes at the pell.'

'While doubtless your mother looked on with her heart in her mouth.'

'Not in the least. She knew the only way I was going to make my way in the world was by learning to use the tools of my trade. Besides, she had already had her moment of anguish when I was five years old and King Stephen almost hanged me from a gibbet.'

Isabelle shuddered. Whenever William mentioned the episode from his infancy when King Stephen had taken him hostage for his father's good behaviour, she felt cold. His father had gone back on his word and in retaliation Stephen had threatened to string William up in full view of the besieged garrison. 'And no surprise. If any man tried to do that to one of ours, I would bar his way with a naked sword,' she said with a curl of her lip.

He looked wry, 'I do believe you would, my love. I know their marriage almost foundered when my father told King Stephen to go on and hang me – that he had the anvils and hammers to get more and better sons than the one he lost.'

Indignation shone in Isabelle's eyes. 'If I had been wed to your father, I would have killed him.'

He gave a humourless smile. 'I think my mother came close to it on occasion. He lived very close to the edge . . . Died in his bed, though, and of old age.' He kissed her cheek. 'Don't look so worried. No one is going to take our sons as hostages.' Leaning past her, he picked up the representation of Isabelle from Mahelt's collection of *poupées*. 'New clothes for you as well, I see.' He pursed his lips in assessment. 'I like the cloak.'

'It's Irish plaid,' Isabelle said, eyeing him.

'I noticed – even if you think I don't know anything about Ireland. When Richard returns from his campaign

28

I'll ask his leave to visit Leinster. You have waited long enough.'

Isabelle stared at him. Then she flung her arms around his neck and kissed him on the mouth. 'Thank you!' she gasped. 'Thank you!'

Grinning, he squeezed her waist. 'I intend to thoroughly exploit your gratitude,' he said. 'Be warned.'

She watched him leave the room, his tread buoyant now that he had shared his burden with her, then she turned back to her women, her face flushed and her eyes alight.

Elizabeth Avenel was waiting to pounce. 'Jesu, I see what you mean about him only having to look at you and you quicken,' she quipped. 'You look like a woman who has just been thoroughly pleasured.'

Isabelle laughed and clapped her hands. 'I have. We're going to Leinster!'

The expression on Lady Elizabeth's face was priceless.

3

Vaudreuil, Normandy, April 1199

William eyed with relief the servants bearing covered dishes and salvers into the room. It seemed an age since he had broken his fast on bread and honey following mass at dawn and his stomach had been growling for hours. He and the Archbishop of Canterbury, Hubert Walter, had spent a long morning sitting in judiciary session; dealing out what William hoped was fair justice, although he was not certain some of the plaintiffs agreed. The mental exercise involved had given him a numb posterior, a throbbing skull and a savage hunger.

The Archbishop appeared to have worked up an appetite too, for he blessed the food in short order and signalled to the attendants with the fingerbowls. William washed his hands in the perfumed water, dried them on the proffered embroidered towel and immediately set to. Even if it was still Lent and the fare somewhat short on variety, the poached salmon was moist and succulent and the spiced frumenty laced with almond slivers and raisins was a pleasure on the palate. A sinful dish of pale primrose butter stood beside a basket of crusty wheaten loaves and William reached for it eagerly. He would do penance for gluttony on the morrow.

Hubert Walter shook his head as he watched William spread butter on the bread with the back of his knife. 'I see you still indulge in rustic English habits,' he remarked.

William shrugged. 'I was born an English rustic and a man should know where he comes from as well as where he hopes to go.'

Hubert smiled thinly and conceded the point with a wave of his beringed right hand. He too had risen to an eminent position from less exalted beginnings, although the peculiar English habit of putting butter on bread had not been part of his upbringing.

Whilst they ate, the men forbore to discuss the cases they had been judging. Hubert, a consummate lawyer, would have been happy to do so, but William preferred to use the time to refresh his mind for the following session.

'Your family is growing swiftly,' Hubert said between mouthfuls of salmon. 'How many is it now?'

'Four boys and a girl,' William replied. 'Will's nine, Richard's seven, Mahelt's five, Gilbert's almost two and Walter was born at Christmas.' He could recite the names and ages by rote and had made of a point of doing so ever since William de Braose had confessed one day at court to not remembering the names and ages of several of his sixteen children.

The Archbishop looked thoughtful. 'Any of the boys destined for the Church? You could do worse than put one of them in Holy Orders.'

'If they show the aptitude, then certainly,' William said, 'but they'll be trained in general terms first. I am my father's fourth son, but it would have been a disaster for myself and the Church if I had taken vows. My brother Henry was far more suited to the priesthood.'

'Ah yes, the eminent Bishop of Exeter,' said Hubert

Walter, his impartial tone more eloquent than words spoken with feeling.

William seldom had dealings with Henry, who had risen high in the Church by courtesy of King Richard's favour towards the Marshal faction. William preferred to keep a cordial distance from his brother, who was patronising, finicky, and would not have dreamed of eating buttered bread. Occasionally, when they encountered each other on formal occasions, they associated, but out of fraternal duty rather than personal choice.

William was cutting into a curd tart dappled with ground cinnamon when one of Hubert's messengers arrived. The man was covered in dust and dried mud from his journey and his eyes were inflamed from lack of sleep. As he knelt to kiss the Archbishop's ring, he was already producing from his satchel two letters bearing King Richard's seal. 'They are fair copies of each other, my lords,' he said, giving one to William and one to the Archbishop.

Hubert Walter nodded and dismissed the man. Waving away the table attendants, he wiped his eating knife, cut the tags and opened out the vellum. William cleaned his hands on a napkin and looked at the Archbishop expectantly. On occasions like this, it was a nuisance not to have the skill of reading. He had tried to learn, but the letters remained so much spider scrawl to his eyes.

Hubert Walter's expression gave little away, but William noticed the tensing of his lower lids. 'Trouble?' William's first thought was that the King's brother John had been caught with his fingers in the treason pie again.

The Archbishop raised his head and glanced around to ensure that no one but William was within earshot. 'The King has been wounded,' he muttered. 'A crossbow quarrel in the shoulder.' He frowned at the lines of brown ink. 'This is the work of a scribe but I hear Richard's words in my head, so he must have been competent to dictate it. He says that as a precautionary measure we've to secure the treasury at Rouen but to say nothing for the moment.'

William looked hard at the Archbishop. 'Secure the treasury for whom?'

'He doesn't say – probably hasn't decided yet. He wouldn't write to us if the wound was a mere pinprick, but this is still probably no more than a precaution.'

William took his own letter and pushed it through his belt. He'd have his chaplain read it over to him as he prepared to ride, and he would send a messenger to Isabelle. 'Should it prove serious, no one currently knows the whereabouts of Prince John.'

'I dare say he can be found swiftly enough if necessary.' Hubert's offhand manner immediately informed William that the wily prelate had his spies out. Hubert cocked a look at William from beneath his brows. 'Have you ever suffered battle wounds, Marshal, beyond the usual scratch and scrape?'

William nodded. 'In the same place as the King, but not a crossbow quarrel, thank God. A Flemish mercenary put a gaff through my hauberk when I was a newly fledged knight and I still bear the scar. Then in Poitou I took a spear through the thigh. I might have died from that one, but God was merciful.' Memory sent his hand to his leg where he felt the ghost of the pain beneath his fingertips.

The Archbishop wiped his lips on his napkin. 'I saw men die of their wounds in the Holy Land,' he said. 'Acre was full of death, even from a gnat bite or an insignificant graze, but Richard was strong and survived all of those – the camp fever too.'

William frowned. 'It is only a precaution that we go to Rouen.'

'Let us hope it is, but there is no harm in making preparations.' He sent William an eloquent look. 'The race is to the swift, my lord Marshal, and it would be foolish of us to squander our head start.'

Stripped to his shirt and braies, William sat wearily down on his bed and stared at the irregular soot mark above the candle in the wall sconce. It had been three days since the letter had arrived from the Limousin and no word since then – which might mean that either the King was making a good recovery or that his condition had deteriorated. Without news they were in limbo, but perhaps it was preferable to the hell waiting to heave up beneath their feet should Richard die.

Hubert Walter's informants reported that John was in Brittany, visiting Arthur, his twelve-year-old nephew, who was the other nearest claimant to Richard's throne. Whether John's sojourn was purely social, or involved dubious plots and mischief, was open to conjecture, but if Richard succumbed to his wound and Arthur chose to assert his own claim, John was in serious danger.

Heaving a troubled sigh, William lay down. Beyond the door, he could hear his servants talking in the antechamber as they prepared for sleep. In the light from the candle flame, he raised then bent his right arm and scrutinised the powerful swell of muscle and corded sinew. He still had the strength and tone of a man holding on to his prime, still retained a fierce appetite for life. Knowing it could be snatched from him at any moment made that appetite all the keener. He had spent most of his adult existence travelling in the company of various Kings of England – had watched them die one by one, whilst he journeyed on, feeling ever more exposed. Richard was forty-one, ten years his junior, a survivor of crusade and imprisonment. It would be ironic if he succumbed now because of a grubby little dispute over treasure.

The marshal of the Tower had discreetly offered William the comfort of one of the castle whores. He had declined, but admitted to himself that the warmth of a woman in his bed would have been a welcome distraction tonight. 'Ah, Isabelle,' he said softly. He needed her here so that he could talk to her about the situation with Richard and, in so doing, find a way through, before losing himself in the pleasure and comfort of lovemaking. He wanted to look in the cradle and watch his infant son sleep in milky bliss, to play-fight with the older boys and teach all the songs he knew to Mahelt. He wanted to live to see his offspring wed and bring children of their own to the feast table.

Restlessly, he left the bed and, kneeling on the floor, prayer beads looped between his fingers, prayed to God to grant him the grace of such a future in these precarious times.

Outside, the murmur of the servants ceased. He heard the outer door open, then another voice, the tone urgent. A moment later came the knock on his own door he had been expecting and dreading. 'Come,' he said loudly, already reaching for his tunic and thrusting his feet into his boots.

Osbert, his chamberlain, poked his head round the door and ushered one of Hubert's messengers into the room, a young monk, his fingers brown with ink stains.

'My lord.' He bowed. 'The Archbishop summons you to his presence at once. There is urgent news from King Richard's camp.'

He was dead then. The news of Richard's recovery

would have been cause for smiles and relief and a different atmosphere. Nodding acknowledgement to the monk, William pinned his tunic at the neck and, after a brief hesitation, reached for and latched on his swordbelt. He knew it was foolish, but he felt as if he needed something to arm himself against the trouble that was coming. He bade his squires fetch Jean D'Earley and Jack Marshal from the hall and have them meet him in the Archbishop's chambers at le Pré. 'And do it quietly, lads,' he cautioned. 'Men will be settling to sleep and there is no cause to wake them just yet.'

Across the Seine at le Pré, the Archbishop's apartment was ablaze with lamps and beeswax candles, the sweet honey smell permeating the air and creating a soft heat haze. Indeed, the level of industry made the room not unlike a bee skep at the height of midsummer. The room resonated with the scratching of quills on vellum. Every scribe, priest, attendant and cleric capable of holding a quill had been set to work drafting the letters and writs that would soon be winging to every prelate and magnate, informing of a royal death.

Hubert Walter sat at a lectern himself, reading a document. He was dressed in his robes of office, although his mitre was perched on the bench beside him and his tonsure was covered merely with a plain dark bonnet. An ornate crosier lay along the edge of the trestle, the shepherd's crook fashioned of ivory carved with the image of the Lamb of God. He looked up as William was announced and handed what he had been reading to the scribe at his side. 'Good,' he said. 'Make a dozen fair copies.' Then, folding his hands, he turned his attention to William. 'Grievous tidings from the Limousin,' he said and indicated a creased sheet of vellum lying beside his mitre.

36

'I knew the moment your messenger came for me.' William too pointed at the vellum sheet. 'Queen Eleanor's seal,' he said.

Hubert nodded. 'She was at Fontevrault, but she reached him in time, riding day and night. The wound festered and poisoned his body. He was dead even before we received that first message.'

'God rest his soul.' Feeling numb, William crossed himself and with his eyes still on Eleanor's seal, thought this would likely kill her. Of the five sons she had borne, Richard had been her favourite: great, golden, magnificent Richard, the child on whom she had lavished her hopes, her dreams and most of her maternal affection. Four sons were dead now; only the lees of the cup remained. 'Did Richard name his successor?'

The Archbishop cast him a shrewd look. 'Supposedly, but there are doubts. Everything hangs in the balance, and you and I, Marshal, hold the weights to tip the scales.' He passed his tongue over his lips, but whether in relish or trepidation, William could not tell.

'If you say he named his successor, what is there to doubt?' he asked sharply.

Hubert unclasped his hands and opened them towards William. 'As with many making their end, perhaps he didn't want to admit how close death rode him until it was too late. This letter tells me that William de Braose was the only man near enough to hear Richard name John as his heir, but do we take de Braose's word for that nomination?'

'Is there reason not to?'

The Archbishop's upper lip curled. 'De Braose is as scant with the truth as he is at washing before he eats.'

William wondered what Hubert was pushing at. De Braose was William's neighbour in Ireland and the Welsh

Marches. As such he kept on working terms with the man, who was bluff, crude and self-serving, but nevertheless amicable and an ally. 'Queen Eleanor believes him.'

'It is in her interests to do so,' the Archbishop said drily. 'John is her son.'

'Indeed, but I see no reason for conflict.' William waved his hand. 'Look at the matter in a practical light, my lord. That letter is all we have for the moment and it says Richard named John his heir. You cannot question de Braose until he returns from escorting the body and that will be some days hence – we do not have such time to spare.'

His expression less than sanguine, the Archbishop nevertheless had to admit the truth of their predicament. William pressed his point. 'John is a grown man, the son of a King, and a proven warrior these last five years. He knows these lands and the people; he has been born and bred to them. Supposing Richard did name Arthur as his heir, what do we have? A malcontent beardless boy with no knowledge of England, Normandy or Anjou, and living in the pocket of the French. Do you really want to be ruled by a puppet child controlled by Philip of France?'

'Yes, Marshal, but we can wean the boy away from such influences. We can break and train him like a young horse, whereas John . . .' Hubert let the words hang in the air where they grew in potency. 'We have both had enough dealings with him to know his nature. Your own brother was his man and came to grief because of it.'

William compressed his lips at Hubert Walter's manipulative reference to his elder brother. John Marshal had died defending the keep of Marlborough when the Prince had raised revolt in England during Richard's absence.

'My brother knew his road when he took it.' An edge to his voice warned the Archbishop not to pluck that particular string.

Hubert steepled his hands under his chin. 'We must think hard on our own road, Marshal. We have this one chance to change things and it will be gone by the morning.'

William hesitated, but not because he was deliberating over his decision, which had never been in doubt. Rather it was a pause to gather his mental strength. 'Seven years ago I was faced with a choice between Arthur and John. Richard was on crusade and the Bishop of Ely was trying to make a case for Arthur's right to rule us, should Richard die. I refused then, and I refuse now because John has the better claim.'

'You have your feet on a very slippery ladder,' the Archbishop warned.

Hubert's words made William think of the siege ladder at Milli. He almost smiled, although there was no reason for humour. 'I hope I have enough experience by now to stay attached.'

Hubert pursed his lips, deliberating, then sighed and threw up his hands in capitulation. 'As you wish, Marshal, but I suspect you will never regret any decision more.'

'But you agree to it?'

'I accede to it, which is a different matter,' the Archbishop said darkly. 'You have vast goodwill and influence with the English barons and if you put your weight behind John's cause, they will cleave to him, because of you. The Normans will take John over Arthur because they do not trust the Bretons and the French. Better the devil they know. I cannot swim against two such forceful tides.' He gestured an attendant to replenish the cup at his side and fill one for William. 'The choice is made and we have now to decide how to steer a course between dangerous shoals.'

The wine was sugared hippocras, of which the Archbishop was fond. The pungent scent of the spices stung William's nostrils and the polite sip he took almost made him gag. 'We have to get John out of Brittany,' he said after a valiant swallow. 'As soon as the Bretons hear of this, they'll do all in their power to stop him from reaching Normandy.'

Hubert was unperturbed. 'I have two of my best men with horses saddled up and ready to ride. They'll find John and get him safely away before the Bretons can move against him.'

William set his cup down, his palate cloyed almost beyond bearing. He pitied any man who was an enemy of the powerful, ruthless Hubert Walter. Should the decision have gone the other way, those saddled horsemen would be riding to Brittany with a message for Prince Arthur and John would never see the sky beyond a prison window again.

It was late at night, all the candles extinguished save one, burning on a tall iron stand at the bedside. Cradling Walter in the bend of her left arm Isabelle suckled him at her breast. It was pleasant to have this time with her son, to sit and be quiet and enjoy the moment. Walter was at the enchanting stage where he was beginning to smile and respond. One small hand was wrapped tightly around a tress of her hair and his eyes were focused on her smile as he drank. He was going to have fair hair and blue eyes like herself rather than William's winter-hazel. She sang softly to him, an Irish lullaby that she could remember Aine, her nurse, singing to her and her brother in their childhood. She did not know what the words meant but they were soft and the tune was gently wistful.

'Crid hé
Daire cnó
Ócán é
Pocán dó.'

A week ago, she had been buoyed up by the thought of their imminent visit to Ireland, but all that had changed with William's first terse letter, and then his return this morning on a lathered courser. Ireland was again to be pushed away into the mist as William prepared to go to England instead, and alone. All day he had been consulting with his clerks and the knights of the mesnie, making plans, arranging details. He hadn't stopped since riding in from Rouen. She had packed his baggage chests and made sure he had sufficient travelling provisions. She had spoken to their stewards and chamberlains and prepared herself to govern their estates in his absence.

'Crid hé
Daire cnó
Ócán é
Pocán dó.'

William entered the room, prowling on the balls of his feet like a cat, his edginess almost as tangible as the tension in her hair when she combed it vigorously enough to hear sparks. He was always like this when there was a campaign in the offing, whether of diplomacy or battle. She hoped he had the energy to sustain him through this particular one. He still possessed a young man's vigour and zest, but Isabelle had not forgotten how the squabbles over England during Richard's absence on crusade and subsequent imprisonment had drained that vitality perilously low.

Walter had fallen asleep at her breast. Gently she prised him from the nipple and went to lay him in the fleece-lined cradle. Then, lacing up her shift, she turned her attention to William. He had sat down on the cushioned bench before the banked hearth and removed his shoes and tunic. Isabelle went to pour wine for them both, cutting her own with spring water.

'The royal *esnecca* sails on the noon tide tomorrow.' He rotated the cup in his hands. 'I have to be gone by dawn.'

'Then you are not going to get much sleep,' she said. 'It's already the darkest part of the night.'

He shrugged. 'I am not tired. I'll sleep when I have the leisure. If the sea crossing is calm, then I can snatch a few hours in the deck shelter.'

Setting her drink aside, she came to stand behind him and began slowly kneading his shoulders. His muscles were so tight with tension that it was like pressing her thumbs into stone, and she was certain he must have a savage headache.

'Am I doing the right thing?' he asked.

She heard the need for reassurance in his voice and pitched her own to the same lazy rhythm as her movements. 'Do you believe you are not?'

He laughed sourly. 'When the Archbishop of Canterbury shakes his head and my own knights and members of my family look at me as if I've turned into a dribbling lackwit for supporting John, then I wonder.'

'If you supported Arthur, you would probably have received the same looks,' she murmured. 'It is not an enviable choice.'

'No,' he said, the one word serving to express the surfeit

42

of burdens caused by the dilemma. Closing his eyes, he gave a soft groan. 'Ah that's good.'

'You and William de Braose will make John a king,' she said thoughtfully. 'It was de Braose's word at Richard's deathbed that named John the heir, and it is your influence on the English barons that will bring them to accept him. He will owe you.'

He made a non-committal sound.

Isabelle kneaded his shoulders in silence. The fire ticked softly in the hearth and the baby snuffled in his sleep. 'At the least he should confirm you in the rest of my father's lands,' she murmured. 'Ask him for Pembroke. My grandsire was the Earl, but my father was never granted the title or given the lands. I would have it restored to where it rightfully belongs.'

She felt his muscles tighten again, and waited, fingers gently massaging. Finally he released the tension on a deep sigh. 'I cannot deny that I have sometimes thought on the matter.' He reached up to take one of her hands and draw it down to his lips.

'Pembroke should be ours,' she said. 'And Cilgerran. The soil is rich and fertile; there's a fine port and good sea crossing to Ireland . . . If you ask him for nothing else, beloved, ask him for this.'

William slid his hand up her arm and pulled her round and down onto his knee. 'You are ambitious, my love,' he said, smiling.

'And you are not? I only want what is ours by right – for you and for our sons.' Her tone sharpened. 'If we are going to have John for King, then we should have some recompense.' She pushed herself out of his lap. 'Are you coming to bed?'

He shook his head. 'I'm not tired.'

'You don't have to sleep.' When he started to grin,

she made a face at him. 'I meant you could just rest awhile.'

Still grinning, he followed her to their bed. As Isabelle drew back the covers she felt his hands on her shoulders, turning her, pulling her into his arms, dextrously untying the ribbon on her chemise. 'Rest be damned,' he said.

Sensitive warmth flooded Isabelle's loins. 'I am still feeding Walter,' she warned breathlessly. 'And it's Lent.'

'Then I'll confess my weakness in the morning,' he muttered against her ear. 'Be sweet, Isabelle, I need you.' He pushed the chemise off her shoulders, his mouth seeking hers. Suddenly weak with desire herself, she let their bed catch the bend of her knees, and falling upon the coverlet of embroidered wool, drew him down with her.

Later, she lay quietly beside him as the few remaining hours of darkness counted towards dawn. Despite his declaration that he was not tired, he was heavily asleep, one hand grasping her hair as Walter had done. She was the wakeful one. The possibility of attaining what until now had been a dream, the full restoration of her father's de Clare inheritance, filled her with anticipation, but also made her queasy with fear. The higher the climb, the longer the fall, and she had no illusions about the danger of embarking on such a path.

4

Northampton Castle, May 1199

Ranulf de Blondeville, Earl of Chester, threw the dice, cursed at the score and moved a pawn on the chessboard. 'I learned never to play this game with John,' he told William, who was sitting across the trestle from him. They were occupying the window embrasure of a private chamber above the great hall, their game illuminated by cresset lamps and candles. 'He cheats.'

William scooped the dice into a small ivory cup and gave them a shake. 'Mayhap, but all men do their best to help fate along in some way.'

Chester conceded the point. 'True, Marshal. I wouldn't put using loaded dice beyond my stepson either. He's a brat.'

William arched his brows. The brat to whom Chester was referring was Prince Arthur, Chester being married to the youth's mother, Constance, Countess of Brittany. It was not an amicable match and the couple lived apart; indeed, an annulment was in the offing, mooted by the lady, so rumour ran, although no one was going to ask the proud and touchy Earl of Chester for the intimate details. Still only twenty-nine, he was one of the most powerful magnates in the realm with his own strong sphere of influence.

Chester's thin upper lip curled in fastidious aversion. 'Even if there are issues between myself and John that have to be resolved, I would rather a hundred times serve him as King than see that obnoxious child put his backside on the throne and be guided by his poisonous bitch of a dam. At least John's mother is an asset to him.'

William threw the dice and moved his own chess piece. 'Constance is as ambitious for her son as Queen Eleanor is for John,' he said. 'Without her striving, Arthur would not be the threat that he is now.'

'Mayhap not,' Chester said, 'but she is still no Eleanor. I'd have every respect for her if she was because there is a woman of truly noble heart and spirit.'

'Amen to that,' William agreed vigorously as he thought of the ageing Queen Mother, who even now was embarking on a progress of her lands, calming the turbulence left by Richard's death, the son who in her own words had been the 'staff in my hand and the light in my eyes'.

Ranulf eyed William astutely. 'You, the justiciar and the Archbishop between you seem to have the disaffected lords eating out of your hands.'

William laughed. 'Not quite, my lord. The only thing we can be pleased about is that they haven't bitten our hands off yet.'

Ranulf rattled the dice cup. 'It helps that men respect all of you. You may serve John, but you are not his creatures. If he had sent de Burgh, de Braose or Faulkes de Breauté to do his courting, there might have been a different outcome.' He threw the dice on to the table, calculated, and moved a bishop. When he spoke again, his voice was hard and uncompromising. 'The peace will hold, Marshal, providing John honours the promises you have all made on his behalf. If he reneges and plays false, then there will be bloody rebellion. Men want justice. They want what is theirs by right.'

'It is not John's fault their lands and privileges have been undermined and abused; the blame lies with his father and brother,' William defended him.

'Yes, but unless he mends the damage . . .' Chester let an eloquent shrug of his shoulders serve for the rest.

William wasn't certain that John had it in his nature to grant some of the demands, but having laid the groundwork for negotiation, he had accomplished his own task. His duty now was to return to Normandy and escort John to England. The prospect of more sea crossings, even in calm weather, filled him with trepidation. 'That is up to him. I have done what I can.'

'Then God grant it is not in vain,' Chester replied darkly.

Aboard the royal galley, John, uncrowned King of England and inheritor of all that he had so long coveted, watched the coastline of Normandy recede into haze. 'You were always my brother's man, Marshal,' he said to William, who was standing beside him at the mast. 'Faithful as a dog.'

Watching the gulls wheel above the undulating swell of the waves, William hoped the wind would bid them a swift voyage and allay his suffering. He didn't want to puke in front of John, who had the gift of a steady gut even on a rough crossing. William would have liked to make the voyage with Isabelle and their household, but John had specifically requested his presence on the royal nef and it wouldn't have been politic to refuse the soon-to-be King of England. 'I gave him my oath, sire, as I gave my oath to your father and your brother Henry before that, God rest their souls.'

John flicked a speck from the ermine border of his cloak. 'Men's oaths are always for sale. My brother purchased your fealty with Isabelle de Clare and Striguil. What would you have from me?'

William looked at him steadily. 'Sire, I give my fealty to you because it is your right to inherit your brother's crown.'

John flashed a mocking smile. 'I am sure you do, just as I am sure that ambition spurs you as hard as any man. Don't be embarrassed, my lord. Name your desire, let us have it out in the open between us: no hidden rocks on which to founder.'

William thought drily that having a matter out in the open must be something of a novelty for John, whose dealings were frequently twisted with intrigue. 'Then, sire, I would have my wife's paternal inheritance restored to her family. I would have Pembroke and Cilgerran.'

'Hah!' John's mouth curled with the pleasure of a cynic proven right. 'Your wife been at you, has she?'

'No more than usual, sire.'

John laughed. 'It's always the women who push the men for more. Ask de Braose. That wife of his is like a bucket with a huge hole in the bottom. After sixteen children she probably feels like one too when he swives her.'

William said nothing. Maude de Braose was no beauty and it was true she was ever pressing her husband for grants and privileges to support their enormous brood of offspring, but the remark was cruel and unnecessary. His gut lurched with the next heave of the boat and he tightened his lips. Across the waves he could see the galley carrying his family, but too distant to make out the figures on deck. Isabelle would be enjoying the salt spray and the brisk breeze. She loved sea crossings. He sometimes teased her that she had the blood of Viking sea-reavers in her veins. Perhaps she did. If so, he hoped she had passed it on to their children in her breast milk, for suffering *mal de mer* was a wretched affliction.

'I knew you would ask for Pembroke.' John wafted his hand with gracious nonchalance. 'Well then, take it, I grant it to you freely, and the right to call yourself Earl – which is something that my great and glorious brother never did. You should think on that.'

'Thank you, sire.' William swallowed the urge to retch and knelt to John. The deck was hard beneath his knees, the sea a dragon's roar under the keel as he bowed his head.

'Get up,' John said in a smiling, almost scornful voice. 'Save your oath for England and my coronation. More privileges will follow providing you know where your loyalties lie.'

William lurched to his feet. 'Sire, I have sworn my fealty to you, and my oath is binding unto death.' He wondered how many times he would have to repeat his loyalty to John before John was convinced. It stood to reason that a man who broke his own promises as easily as they were made would have difficulty believing that some men kept theirs.

'I trust you as much as I trust any man, Marshal.' Suddenly John's expression was closed and dangerous. 'And that is less far than I can throw you.' He turned towards the canvas pavilion pegged at the stern of the nef. 'I would ask you to join me, but you are green at the gills and I would be doing neither of us a favour. Besides, you wouldn't approve of the company I keep.'

William watched him duck into the shelter and received a brief glimpse of several gaudy court whores, and a select

49

company of John's bachelors – knights beholden to him for their earnings. Grimacing, he leaned against a barrel and willed the coast of England closer. He had his earldom and hoped the price would not beggar him. He suspected his current queasiness was as much a reaction to his conversation with John as it was *mal de mer*.

5

Westminster, May 1199

It had been several years since Isabelle had attended the court. Richard and Berengaria, his Queen, had led separate lives and his gatherings had been of the military, masculine kind with little thought for women. Besides, Isabelle had been too preoccupied running the affairs of her estates and bearing children to have time for a life in the royal train.

John's coronation and the feast that followed were a different matter and Isabelle had been delighted at the opportunity to don fine garments and attend a grand formal event. Her gown was of salmon-coloured silk, embroidered with seed pearls and beads of rock crystal. Her gauze veil was edged with pearls too and the ends of her fair braids were bound with fillets of beaten silver. Being between pregnancies, the lacing of her gown showed off a slender waist and full curves at bosom and hip. With not a little feminine vanity, she had been pleased to see heads turn, not least her husband's.

As was customary, the feast itself was segregated, with the men fêting the King in the great hall and the women in the smaller White Hall on the south side. With no queen present, Isabelle and the wives of the other magnates were the highest ranking women present, and thus afforded a position on the dais at the far end of the hall. Although separated from William for the feast, Isabelle had stood beside him at the coronation and watched as the newly crowned King had officially belted him with the title Earl of Pembroke. Their two eldest sons had been present to witness the moment and as Isabelle had watched, an arm at each boy's shoulder, her eyes had filled with tears of pride and triumph.

Will and Richard were not attending the feast, but had been taken back to the Marshal lodging houses at Charing, there to await with their younger siblings their parents' return from the post-coronation festivities. Mahelt had a new set of *poupées* robed in royal finery and Isabelle had promised the children she would bring them some almond marchpane, purloined from the subtleties at the end of the feast. She had noticed one on the sideboard, fashioned to resemble the Tower of London where she had been held as a royal ward before her marriage. To break off a few crenellations would be extremely satisfying.

William being high in John's favour, many of the barons' wives were seeking hers, twittering around her like sparrows in search of crumbs. Isabelle found herself rather enjoying the admiration and flattery after so long away from court. Nevertheless, she did not allow it to turn her head because most of it was a means to an end and she was adroit at sifting wheat from chaff. However, there was one woman who had no time for compliments and fuss, and was abruptly direct in her approach.

'You and your lord are to be congratulated, Countess,' said Maude de Braose. Her deep-set eyes were mocking. She had a ruddy complexion netted with broken veins, and bushy, almost masculine eyebrows, which she plainly scorned to pluck. A once magnificent figure had slumped gradually southwards during the carrying and bearing of sixteen children until her breasts were at her waist and her belly rested on her thighs like a bag pudding. Her mind, however, was muscular and honed for battle. 'The Earl of Pembroke, no less. That was a title your late father couldn't wrest from the Angevin grip.'

Isabelle smiled pleasantly at Lady Maude. Courtesy cost nothing, and the de Braose family were their natural allies in Wales and Ireland. De Braose and his wife had been married for thirty years and although they bickered a great deal, they still shared a common ambition and obviously liked each other well enough in bed since their youngest child Bernard was only two years old. Isabelle admired Maude for her endurance and the fact that all of her children were healthy and thriving – no small feat. Whatever face she presented to others, Maude de Braose was known to be a proud and doting mother. 'Thank you,' Isabelle said. 'Your own husband has been rewarded too.'

Maude showed her teeth in a yellow smile. 'Indeed, but then our husbands are responsible for putting John on his throne. Without them, our new King would be whistling for his kingdom. He is in our debt for his golden crown and, if we are shrewd, we may reap yet more benefit for our services.'

Isabelle felt her spine prickle, as if something dangerous stalked in the periphery of her vision. 'All I desire is my rightful due: the restoration of my father's lands.'

'Opportunities arise and you take them,' Maude said with asperity. 'Your husband understands this well, or he would still be a common hearth knight bedding down in the straw near the hall door instead of the great magnate he is now.'

Curbing a sharp retort, Isabelle murmured the excuse that she had to visit the privy and gratefully freed herself of Maude de Braose's abrasive presence. On her return, she was quietly misappropriating the top turret of the Tower of London and a small boat fashioned of coloured sugar paste from the subtlety on the sideboard when Ida, Countess of Norfolk, arrived, intent on a similar mission for her own offspring. Within moments the women were giggling together as conspiratorially as girls.

Crenellations and sundries purloined and secreted into napkins, the talk naturally turned to children in general terms, although with exploratory undercurrents at work on both sides for it was never too early to begin investigations and enquiries concerning marriage alliances. Isabelle had noted the Norfolk heir standing beside his parents at the coronation: a tall, graceful youth with light-brown hair and vivid blue eyes. Isabelle's delicate enquiries drew forth the information that no, young Hugh was not yet betrothed and his parents were open to negotiation – should a likely bride present herself.

It was past the hour of midnight matins when Isabelle and William returned to their houses at Charing by barge. William was to attend the new King's council in the morning, but for now John had retired with his latest amour: a London merchant's daughter with fat golden braids and breasts the size of cow udders.

Isabelle listened to the rhythmic plash of the oars in the water as the two bargemen leaned forward and pulled back. A lantern shone at the prow, and glimmers of light answered from other travellers late on the river. A wistful smile lit her face as she thought of another boat journey she and William had made ten years ago on the way to their marriage at the cathedral of St Paul. The time had flown so fast that it seemed not a moment since he had come to claim her from the Tower where she had been lodged as the King's ward. The memory of their wedding prompted her thoughts, and she turned to him. 'I was talking to Ida of Norfolk earlier,' she said.

He gave a reminiscent smile. 'I remember when she first came to the court as the King's ward. She was as delightful as a kitten and even if she had claws, they didn't hurt. Everyone wanted to play with her, but it was inevitable she'd end up curled in the King's bed, and even more inevitable that he'd get her with child.'

Isabelle gave him an assessing look. Ida's son, born of that liaison before her marriage to Norfolk, was William Longespée, the young Earl of Salisbury and Marshal kin by marriage. 'Did you ever wish she was curled in yours?' she asked, her question prompted by the timbre of his voice as he had spoken of Ida.

He flashed her a grin. 'Roger of Norfolk's a very lucky man,' he said, 'but not as lucky as I am.'

Isabelle acknowledged his diplomacy with amusement-filled eyes. 'Roger of Norfolk has a rather hand-some son,' she said mischievously. 'I think several of the women tonight would have enjoyed "playing" with him too.'

'Yourself included?'

She gave him a teasing look through her lashes, let it linger a moment, then sobered. 'No, like you, I value what I already have beyond measure, but I appreciate beauty when I see it. In seriousness, I was thinking about Mahelt. A marriage bond with the Bigods would be useful, especially as Ida's firstborn son is the King's half-brother.'

William shifted on the bench. 'Worth considering,' he said in an offhand way, 'although perhaps not yet.'

'No, but for the future.' Isabelle gave him a knowing look through the lantern-lit darkness. William adored Mahelt and she him. As their only daughter she held an unchallenged place in her father's affections and it would be as difficult for him to see her go to a husband as it would be for Isabelle to watch her sons leave the bower to become knights and soldiers.

The oarsmen altered stroke and began pulling in towards a landing stage, its weed-covered struts glistening in the lantern's light. 'I didn't see John's wife at the feast today,' she said to change the subject. 'I assume he does not intend making her his Queen?'

William shook his head. 'He married Havise for her lands; they've never shared a bed. De Braose says John's going to set her aside and look to Portugal or Spain for a consort. He needs to protect his southernmost borders and what better way than an alliance with such kingdoms?'

Isabelle wondered what Havise of Gloucester was feeling. Since Havise and John had only paid lip service to their marriage, Isabelle could not see her being distraught over an annulment, but she might regret being denied the opportunity to be Queen.

The barge bumped against the jetty. 'I suppose we'll be returning to Normandy,' she said with a resigned sigh.

William stood up, legs planted wide to keep his balance. 'It has to be secured for John, and Anjou as well, but I will ask his leave to go to Pembroke and Leinster, I promise.'

Isabelle forced a smile as she took his extended hand. She knew he was honour bound to serve in Normandy first. It was the reason John had clasped the gilded belt of an earl at William's waist, and why they had Pembroke at all, but she wondered if they were ever going to see it, much less use its port to sail for Ireland. Perhaps she ought to have their own cook build her a castle of marchpane with an Irish sea of whipped and coloured egg white and, after populating it with Mahelt's *poupées*, make do with that.

6

Lusignan, Poitou, Summer 1200

The July heat had settled into balminess as night fell and William was sitting outside enjoying the slight breeze rustling through chestnut and lime. Crickets chirred softly and moths performed dances of death around the lamps and torches lighting the trestle tables set up in the castle gardens. He drank the rich red wine, nibbled candied fruits and watched a group of dancers weave the steps of a carole to the lively music created by lute, pipe and tabor. He might have joined them, except he felt lazy tonight. It had been a long day in the saddle, the same as yesterday, and the exertion would likely continue on the morrow. A royal progress by its nature entailed a different destination almost every night. Much of John's travelling through his lands had been a show of military strength, a display of the power he could bring to bear should it become necessary. William had sweltered each day in his hauberk, sword girded at his hip, even though he wasn't expecting to fight. The only women in the entourage were courtesans and laundresses. No wives were present on what was essentially a military parade.

They had arrived at Lusignan late in the afternoon to

find the castle grounds aflower with gaudy pavilions, stalls, entertainers and folk clad in their richest garments, however the festivities were not in John's honour. Hugh le Brun of Lusignan was celebrating his betrothal to the daughter of his neighbour, Count Aymer of Angoulême. Since the houses of Lusignan and Angoulême were traditional enemies, it was an auspicious occasion – although not for John, who had relied on the antagonism to play one off against the other. United they were a danger to him.

William had no love for the name of Lusignan and would rather not have accepted hospitality from one of their number, but a courtier's diplomacy enabled him to restrain his aversion. In his youth, his uncle had been murdered before his eyes by a Lusignan and he himself had been wounded and imprisoned. Time had created distance, but he had never forgiven or forgotten. The slick scar tissue on his right thigh was a constant reminder.

John was sitting on an arbour bench beside Aymer, talking earnestly and smiling a lot. Aymer was listening with arms folded, a look of deep interest on his narrow, sun-browned features.

'Fine night for making plans and trysts,' remarked Baldwin de Béthune, Count of Aumale, joining William at the trestle and refilling his cup from the wine jug standing there.

'If you're of that mind,' William agreed with a smile. He and Baldwin had served together as young knights in the mesnie of King Henry's eldest son, had ridden together on the tourney fields of France and Flanders and carved reputations for themselves. Both were now established as powerful lords with retinues and young knights of their own. 'Aymer and the King seem to have plenty to discuss.'

'Bound to now that Aymer's set the fat in the fire by

59

betrothing his daughter to Hugh of Lusignan. Hardly in John's interest, is it?'

'It's awkward,' William agreed. 'If the houses of Lusignan and Angoulême unite instead of fighting each other, they'll create trouble for John.'

'Very awkward, although our King doesn't appear unduly bothered.'

'Oh, he's bothered,' William said, eyeing John. 'I've seen him approach women at court like that when he's intent on seduction. You'll notice de Braose is keeping Hugh of Lusignan occupied while his master makes his play.'

Baldwin glanced towards de Braose's large striped pavilion, its interior luminous with lanterns and loud with the noise of hearty masculine camaraderie. 'John's going to have to offer a lot to make Aymer of Angoulême sell his virtue.'

'He can but try. What does he have to lose?'

Baldwin grunted.

'How's your daughter?' William replenished his cup.

'Thriving,' Baldwin said with a shrug, 'or I suppose so from the little I know of infants.' He made a reciprocal gesture. 'And your own new little one?'

'A typical woman already.' William grinned at the mention of his second daughter, born nine months to the day from John's coronation. 'Seducing you with her eyes one moment, and bawling at you the next. Named for her mother who's an expert at both.'

'I will tell your wife how you malign her,' Baldwin threatened with a chuckle.

William sobered. 'I may tease, but she knows her place . . . as the light of my life.'

Baldwin laughed again but looked envious. 'I am glad you and Isabelle have that kind of harmony,' he said. 'I rub along with Hawise, but neither of us pines much for the other. Then again, at least we don't hate each other to perdition like Ranulf of Chester and his wife.'

'No,' William agreed wryly.

A group of youngsters entered the garden from the direction of the keep and William's attention was caught by a girl who was as light and leggy as a young cat. She was just beginning to develop a figure: breasts the size of green apples were outlined by her close-fitting silk gown but her waist and hips were still flat and boyish. Her rich golden hair was tamed in a single braid woven with silver ribbons and she had large, wide-set eyes that in daylight were probably blue but just now looked almost black. She flickered William and Baldwin a startled look as she met their scrutiny, twisted to avoid the young squire who was trying to tag her in the game, and bumped into John, who had risen from his discussion with Count Aymer.

The girl obviously knew who John was, for she gasped and swept him a graceful curtsey. John raised her to her feet, and taking her right hand, lifted it to his lips and kissed her fingertips. He studied the gold ring she was wearing. 'That's a pretty bauble, sweetheart,' he remarked.

'It is my betrothal ring, sire,' she replied breathlessly.

'Is it now?' John's voice was a caress. 'How would you like to exchange it for a crown?'

She widened her eyes at him and gnawed her underlip uncertainly. 'We were playing chase,' she said, clearly feeling such a remark was safer ground than that of her ring. She looked over her shoulder at her young companions who were watching her with apprehension.

John's smile showed the merest glint of his fine teeth. 'One of my favourite games,' he said, and with a sardonic

61

glance towards William and Baldwin, stood aside to let her pass.

The court stayed a second day at Lusignan and John went hunting with the lords Hugh and Aymer. The latter's daughter remained in the bower with the women, shut away from masculine eyes, but out of sight did not mean out of mind. William was not fond of hunting himself, but joined the pack because it was expected of him. However, his indifference to the chase gave him plenty of opportunity to observe the different kind of pursuit being played out between King John and Count Aymer with Count Aymer's absent daughter as the bait, and all under the nose of the unsuspecting bridegroom.

That evening after dinner, William sat in John's chamber, drinking wine and playing dice with Baldwin de Béthune and William, Earl of Salisbury. The latter was married to William's cousin, Ela. He was John's bastard half-brother, and his mother was Ida, Countess of Norfolk, with whom Isabelle had struck up a firm friendship at the coronation. Salisbury had his mother's beauty but rendered in a strong, masculine version, enhanced by vigorous dark curls and eyes of changeable green-hazel fringed by soot-black lashes. He was known as Longespée because he used a sword several inches longer than usual. Rumours abounded that the appellation didn't refer to his sword alone and Salisbury, a glint in his eye, had done nothing to curb them.

Throwing up his hands, he pushed away from the table. 'You've wrung me dry, Marshal, my pouch is as flat as an old whore's tit.'

'It was hardly virgin plump to start with,' William retorted. He scooped the small pile of silver into his palm and gave it to his squire. 'Here, lad, find my almoner and tell him to give this to the leper hospital.'

John strolled over and joined them, cradling a cup of clove-scented wine. 'Lost again, brother?' he needled Salisbury. 'That's another mark you'll be asking me to lend you.' He flashed a sour smile at William. 'Not content with Pembroke, Marshal, you fleece my coffers through my foolish brother who lacks the abilities of a sheep when it comes to such games.'

'Would you care to win it back, sire?' William gestured to the dice.

'Not after you've given it to lepers,' John declined and took a long swallow from his cup. Then he looked at the three men, dropped his voice and said nonchalantly, 'I am thinking of taking Aymer's daughter to wife.'

The news was no surprise to William after the way he had seen John looking at the girl yester eve, and the manner in which John and Count Aymer had been circling each other during the hunt. A glance exchanged with Baldwin confirmed that the latter had been expecting it too. Salisbury, however, stared, his mouth open. Then he shook his head.

'The girl's very young. She won't be much support to you as a queen.'

John waved his hand in negation. 'She's old enough to say the vows; she'll grow into the role fast enough. Richard's Queen spent most of her time living in seclusion and it didn't harm him.'

Salisbury voiced the obvious: 'But she's already betrothed.'

'Christ, Will, are you sure you're the fruit of my father's loins?' John scoffed, causing Salisbury to flush. 'You're far too innocent to be one of us! Any betrothal can be broken and a marriage annulled if the price is right. I cannot afford to let Angoulême and Lusignan unite. Aymer's salivating at the chance to have his daughter crowned Queen of England. He'd certainly rather get into bed with me than with Hugh de Lusignan – and I'll be delighted to share the night with his delectable daughter!'

William said impassively, 'You will earn the undying hatred of the Lusignans, sire. Personally it doesn't worry me to see them slighted, but they are accomplished warriors and know how to stir up trouble.'

'I can deal with the Lusignans,' John said shortly. 'If I marry the girl, my father-in-law will continue to keep them in check as he has always done.'

'I agree it will be awkward if Angoulême and Lusignan unite' – William nodded – 'but as Salisbury says, the girl is perilously young – and she's narrow in the flank for childbirth. Has she had her first flux?'

'Not yet, but she's ripening fast.'

The notion of a girl so young in John's bed made William uncomfortable. Twelve years old. He didn't want to think of Mahelt in such circumstances, but the match itself made sound political sense. Many men would wait on her ripening, but he had seen the look on John's face when the girl was in the room. Besides, it was necessary for a king and the last direct male of his line to beget heirs as soon as he could.

'You must weigh up whether this marriage will be more useful than the Portuguese one you had in mind before,' he said by way of a caveat. 'Perhaps you should find another husband from among your barons for the heiress of Angoulême.'

'The girl's father would not cooperate,' John said. 'As far as he is concerned, it is either England for his daughter, or Hugh of Lusignan.'

William succeeded in maintaining a dispassionate expression. 'Then you must do as you see fit, sire.'

'Oh, I intend to.' John gave a lazy lupine smile and raised his cup in toast. 'I thoroughly intend to, my lords.'

In the guest house of the nunnery at Fontevrault, William bowed over Queen Eleanor's hand and pretended not to notice the dark splotches and the tremor of old age. Her nails were still tended and polished, and her fingers adorned by gold rings. She might be approaching eighty years old and have retired to dwell amongst nuns, but she still had her vanity. The full wimple that framed her face was a flattering soft shade of blue; her gown, although plain, was thrice dyed and her prayer beads were fashioned of smooth, polished amethysts, topazes and sapphires.

'Madam,' William said. 'As ever your presence lights up the chamber.'

Eleanor's eyes, once golden like John's, were muddy with the weight of years, but a spark kindled in their depths. 'Do I, my William? I suspect these days that it's the light of another world – probably hell if my second husband was right. He always said he would see me there.' She gestured him to be seated on a bench by the hearth and, with the aid of her stick, eased herself slowly down into a chair facing him. 'Old age is not to be recommended,' she said wryly.

'I heard that you had been ill, madam, and I was sorry to hear it.'

She made a dismissive gesture. 'Naught but the spirit overtaxing a worn-out body. I am better now and glad of my visitors.' She glanced around the room, which was busy with the knights, clerics and courtiers of her son's household. Her rheumy eyes fixed on John and the golden-haired child-bride standing nervously at his side.

'Did you counsel him to marry her?'

'No, madam. He had already made up his mind when he told me, but I thought it no bad policy.'

'Policy you say?' Eleanor snorted. 'Well, mayhap, but aided and abetted by more than a seasoning of lust.'

William winced. The new bride's name was Ysabel and it disconcerted him to hear John render the name with husky desire in his voice. They had been married for three weeks and the girl was never away from his side, at John's behest, not hers. He had seen the nervousness in her eyes and the way she steeled herself when he touched her. 'If the houses of Lusignan and Angoulême had united, it would have made matters difficult.'

'Uniting Anjou and Angoulême won't necessarily resolve things either,' Eleanor said. 'A Portuguese alliance would have served us as well in the long term. My son has gambled and I am not yet sure that he has won the throw.' Her eyes filled with melancholy. 'Who would have thought I would still be living after near four-score years and all my sons but one would be dead.' She gave a deep sigh and closed her eyes. 'I am tired, William. The world no longer holds the savour it once did. I am too rusty to dance.'

'I do not believe that, madam.'

'You should, because it is the truth. I am content to dwell with my nuns and find my peace – or at least try.'

Not just with her nuns, William thought, for Fontevrault housed the mortal remains of her beloved Richard.

She opened her eyes. 'And you, William, what will you do now?'

'Once the Queen has been crowned at Westminster, I have permission to visit Pembroke and Ireland, madam. I have been promising Isabelle for so long that I don't think she believes me.'

Eleanor eyed him with a mingling of severity and

humour. 'It is never wise to make promises to a woman and then delay them beyond her expectations,' she cautioned. 'Your wife is forbearing and fair. Do not take her for granted or you will lose her trust.'

'I don't, madam.' He made a face. 'If not for love and respect of my wife, I wouldn't be contemplating a crossing of the Irish Sea in late autumn.'

Eleanor laughed, but the sadness in her eyes deepened. 'Have a care, my William. I have been far in my life, even to Jerusalem like yourself, but I have never seen Ireland, nor will I now. Count it as a blessing and an opportunity to investigate pastures new.'

'In your honour, madam,' he said, feeling chagrined at her words.

'In my memory,' Eleanor responded with pointed amusement.

Taking her hand, William bowed over it again, deeply saddened at the sight of a dying flame.

7

Pembroke, South Wales, October 1200

A bitter wind whipped down the estuary and out to sea, capping the waves with white surges of foam. Water and sky were the colour of a sword in motion: changes of light and cloud creating pattern-welded moments of sharp silver and dark, quenched steel. Standing on the deck of the trading galley the *Sainte-Marie* as the rowers pulled past Pembroke dock and out into Milford Sound, Isabelle was exhilarated, for finally they were on their way to Ireland. If she felt queasy, it was due to anticipation rather than seasickness. Last time she had trodden Irish soil, she had been twelve – little older than Will and Richard, who were making the voyage with her and William, as was Mahelt. Gilbert, Walter and the baby had remained behind at Pembroke in the care of their nurses. William said that they were too young for the rigorous sea crossing, and should anything happen to the ship, then at least two sons and a daughter would survive to carry on the family line.

William stood at her side, his expression grim as he watched Pembroke Castle recede into the distance. By squinting Isabelle could still make out the scaffolding around one of the towers and the mounds of foundations and earthworks, with labourers and masons swarming over them like ants. To exert his power in South Wales, William needed an impregnable base from which to operate and as soon as they had arrived had embarked on a building programme to modernise and improve the defences. She curled her arm around his. 'Did you drink the horseradish tisane?'

'Yes, for what good it will do.'

Isabelle marked the irascible note in his voice and the lines of tension creasing his face. Sea crossings were one of the few occasions when William's good nature deserted him and he became a complete trial to be near. 'It will be all right,' she said in the same low pitch she used to soothe the children when they were fractious or upset.

'There is no need to coddle me,' he growled.

'I was offering comfort, not coddling,' she answered tartly. 'I suppose you'd rather be at court fêting King John and his new Queen?'

William glowered. 'Now you are being foolish.'

Isabelle bit back a retort about the state of his temper and watched the sleek heads of seals pop up on a wave crest then just as rapidly submerge. She had attended the coronation of John's bride and had felt deeply sorry for the slender girl put on display like a newly bought young filly at an exclusive horse fair, and struggling to come to terms with the harness of expectation and duty. John had apparently sworn that he would not get her with child until her body was capable of birthing an infant, but such an oath did not prevent him from indulging in debauched and lecherous practices that would not lead to pregnancy. Isabelle suspected William was also braving the swells and troughs of the Irish Sea in order to escape the moral laxity of John's court.

As they headed into open water, the wind freshened and gusted. Isabelle tasted salt on her tongue and exulted in the sight of the dark waves bursting against the sides of their ship. The children were wild with excitement and she had to warn her women to keep an eye on them. Richard in particular had to be watched like a hawk for he was fearless and ran amongst the crew, clambering on barrels, swinging around the halyards and scampering everywhere like the Bishop of Winchester's pet monkey, until William seized him by the scruff, shook him and threatened to lift his hide with a whip. Richard was quieter after that, prudently keeping out of his father's way by going to talk to the steersman.

The crew shipped oars and lowered the strake shields to cover the oar ports. The coast of Pembroke fell away to be replaced by a heavy grey swell, stretching from horizon to horizon and meeting a sky of similar hue. For a while an escort of gulls wheeled above the *Sainte-Marie*'s linen sail, occasionally settling on her mast, or harpooning into her white wake after fish, but as the ship ploughed on into mid-ocean, they ceased to follow her.

The wind increased, blowing hard from the north and hitting the galley beam on. To Isabelle it felt like riding a boisterous new mount. When she said as much to William he snapped that it was nothing of the sort; he'd ridden plenty of wild horses in his time, but none like this. Lips compressed, cloak huddled around his body, he retired to the deck shelter. Isabelle remained in the open a while longer, but as the gusts strengthened and the swell grew choppy, she too sought the deck shelter and summoned the children within. Mahelt's teeth were chattering with cold and she was beginning to look wan. Will too was quiet and pale. Richard remained exhilarated. Cheeks red, eyes sparkling, he regaled them with details culled from the sailor at the steerboard.

'He says the ship's made to twist with the waves and not break her back if the seas grow very big and wild,' he informed his parents in a cheerful voice.

'Well, that's reassuring,' Isabelle murmured with a glance towards her husband who was swallowing convulsively.

'He showed me a gold ring from a ship wrecked off Waterford when he was a boy. He said he pulled it off a severed hand that washed up on the shore.'

'I will hew off his own hand with my sword, once I have cut out his tongue,' William snarled. 'And perhaps I'll cut off your ears for listening to such nonsense.' He gave up fighting the surges of nausea that had grown apace with the screw and twist of the ship and vomited into the bucket. Richard eyed his father and with a pragmatic sigh lay on his stomach and peered out between the flaps of the deck shelter. 'It's raining,' he announced. 'The clouds are black with it.'

Jean D'Earley, who was not afflicted by *mal de mer*, sat down cross-legged beside Richard and stared out with him. 'Best stay quiet, lad,' he murmured. 'Your father keeps his promises . . . or he does when he's well enough, and I'd hate to see you and the steersman mutilated.'

Isabelle smiled faintly at Jean, who returned the gesture. They were the same age and had known each other since he was a squire and she a young bride. Their relationship was one of respect, understanding and solid friendship. That such traits had never developed beyond those values owed much to their mutual love for the man currently retching into a pail beside them.

Isabelle was beginning to feel queasy too, but tried to put on a brave face for the children's sake. It was her desire that had brought them here and she felt responsible. Mahelt fell asleep in her arms, her skin ghost-pale against her rich bronze-brown hair. Isabelle tucked a corner of her cloak tenderly around her daughter's narrow shoulders and stroked her wan little face.

Towards dusk the weather worsened. Isabelle had experienced some rough crossings between England and Normandy but the plunging and yawing of the *Sainte-Marie* in the crests and troughs of the Irish Sea far outweighed them. The wind screamed like a wild creature howling for blood and souls and the ship kicked and shuddered as if she had been seized in its dripping jaws and was being ground between its fangs. Savage gusts hurled great slaps of water over the strake shields to spew across the open deck. The linen canvas of the shelter had swollen and tightened in the deluge but still the fibres didn't keep out the rain and sea water. The pale sides of the tent trickled and dripped until the occupants were soaked and shivering. The shouts of the sailors were lost in the roar of the wind and the tremors of the ship as every beam, strut and caulked seam was battered by the ferocity of the storm. Isabelle could tell from the wide eyes and clenched knuckles of her women that hysteria was not far off.

Mahelt woke and began to cry, but her sobs were no competition for the inhuman scream of the wind. Will was vomiting now and even Richard had grown quiet and pale. William was curled in a shivering, foetal ball, eyes closed, lips pressed tightly together, complexion deathly. They dared not light a lantern and as nightfall engulfed what remained of the light, their world closed down to the terror of Armageddon. All sense of time vanished before the harrowing rise and plunge of the *Sainte-Marie* as she battled the Irish Sea for her survival.

The family's chaplains, Eustace and Roger, knelt with hands clasped and led prayers for the ship's safe deliverance, but the voices of the suffering passengers were snatched by the storm and cast into oblivion.

The ship's master spared a brief moment to visit them, bellowing that he was going to reduce the sail and try to run before the storm. He nodded with grim approval at their prayers, shouted something about being fortunate if you were born in the caul and returned to his crew.

'What's "born in the caul"?' Richard wanted to know.

'It means that you are born inside the bag that held you in the womb,' Isabelle told him, 'and that you'll never drown.'

There was a hesitation while he digested the information, and then came to the logical conclusion. 'Does that mean we're going to drown?'

'Of course not,' she said with more hope than conviction. 'God will help us if we pray to him.'

William dragged himself up from his prone position and Isabelle groped for his hand. His palm was clammy and the usually strong, dependable grip weak and shaking. Fear swept over her, not for their wider peril, but for William. Was it possible to die of seasickness? He swallowed and strove to speak. Isabelle leaned closer to him, trying to hear what he was saying.

'If we . . . if God spares us . . . I make Him an oath to build a church where we make landfall to thank Him for His mercy.' He gulped, gulped again and retched.

Isabelle squeezed his fingers with her own to show she had understood.

Throughout the night, the passengers prayed as the fierce gales and high waves continued to pound the *Sainte-Marie*. The crew fought to keep her running before the wind without broaching, which would have sent her straight to the bottom. The chaplains' voices grew cracked and hoarse. Everyone huddled together, exhausted, terrified and frozen to the marrow.

At last, as dawn broke, the wind dropped and changed direction, veering to the east. A pearlescent sun rose through dissipating indigo clouds ragged as witch's hair and the sea calmed to a sullen grey swell. The *Sainte-Marie* wallowed on the water like a dockside whore after a night with new sailors in port. Her mast sported a deep crack; her sail was shredded to rags and her timbers waterlogged where the caulking of moss and pitch had sprung leaks. Her exhausted crew were taking it in turns to bail the lake of water sloshing in her bilges, but she was alive – just. William was in no state to do anything but lie and shudder under a blanket, but Jean D'Earley and a couple of the knights were fit enough to assist with the bailing, and Richard too, his fear rapidly receding in the face of daylight and improved weather. Given a clay cooking pot as a bailer, he set to with a will.

It was dusk of that evening and the wind threatening to get up again when the *Sainte-Marie* finally limped into the deep-water channel of Bannow Bay and beached up under the cliffs. Staggering ashore more dead than alive, William knelt and, seizing two fistfuls of the gritty sand, renewed his vow to found a church in gratitude to God for the safe deliverance of the ship, her passengers and crew. Everyone else followed his example, although Isabelle was the last to kneel, for she was preoccupied and over-whelmed by the physical reality of setting foot in the land of her birth for the first time in seventeen years. Suddenly it was real. The sea journey had completed the transition from 'One day' to 'Now', and as she finally sank to her knees, her face was streaming with tears.

* * *

Guarding a crossing over the River Niorte, Kilkenny Castle was an unprepossessing timber fortress protected by a palisade and a stout set of wooden gates. It had been burned down during a skirmish twenty-eight years ago, and subsequently rebuilt, but never improved upon as a defensive site.

Still recovering from the ordeal of the crossing, William was as weak as a kitten. The nausea had ceased, but his stomach muscles were torn from the constant retching, his throat was raw, and the thought of food still made him gag. In such a state, he noted the condition of the stronghold and its deficiencies, but with a passive eye. Something would have to be done, but not now when he could barely manage to sit a horse, let alone think about taking up the reins of government. Dismounting was slow agony to his tender gut, but he insisted on doing so unaided, irritably waving away his knights when they tried to help.

His deputy, Reginald de Quetteville, was waiting in the courtyard to greet him. William had sent him to Leinster to oversee the lands more than ten years ago, knowing full well that the man could no more handle the situation than a mongrel pup was capable of running down a wolf. It had been a token gesture to fill a gap. Like the fortress itself, de Quetteville was of sound construction, but not adequate to the purpose.

De Quetteville's welcome was anxious. He spoke too rapidly and stammered. Barely comprehending, William replied in monosyllables.

'Whatever measures you have provided for us, I am sure they will be satisfactory,' Isabelle intervened with a diplomatic smile at the man. 'For the moment, all we need is warmth and rest.' For emphasis, she set her arm around Mahelt, who was ashen-faced and shivering.

'Yes, my lady, of course . . .' Ears burning with embarrassment, he led them towards a long timber building with a thatched roof and low eaves. It resembled an old-fashioned English manor hall, the interior supported by wooden pillars between which the spaces had been divided off into living quarters. A fire of peat turves glowed in the centre of the room and an aroma of roots and onions wafted from the cauldron suspended high over the embers. Servants and retainers ceased their business to make obeisance as de Quetteville led the visitors to a partition wall at the end of the hall and took them through a door into a private chamber. Turf braziers warmed the room. A linen band of embroidery depicting a scene of invasion and battle went all the way around the white plastered chamber walls. At the back, between two brightly painted pillars, an alcove held a bed piled with wolfskins and surrounded by red woollen draperies.

De Quetteville started to speak, then stopped and hastily bowed. 'My lady,' he murmured.

William turned to look at the woman who had entered the room. She was of a similar age to himself with a fair complexion, limpid blue eyes, a small, sharp nose and full lips. Her breathing was rapid and her complexion flushed as if she had come at the run. Her right hand was pressed to her heaving bosom, the other clutched her cloak and gown to hold them above the floor rushes. A veil of ivory silk covered her hair and artfully draped her throat. Even without de Quetteville's salutation, William would have known he was looking at Aoife McMurrough, daughter of King Dermot of Leinster, Isabelle's mother and grandmother to their children.

Her gaze flickered over her visitors, paying cursory attention to William, dwelling briefly on the children, then settling hungrily upon Isabelle. Then, uttering a small cry, she ran to her daughter and grasped her in a fierce embrace, a torrent of Irish pouring from her lips between kisses and weeping. Isabelle, not normally given to excesses of emotion, burst into tears and clung to her mother.

Finally Aoife collected herself and, dabbing her eyes with one of her sleeve ends, stood back, altering her language to strongly accented Norman French. 'I don't suppose you remember your mother tongue after so long,' she said, her voice tremulous with tears and a hint of reproach. 'Your father would never let you speak it anyway.'

Isabelle swallowed and shook her head, tears shimmering down her face. 'A few words, no more,' she said in a watery voice.

Aoife turned to William. 'My lord Marshal, your reputation precedes you.' Now her smile did not reach her brimming eyes, nor did she embrace him, merely extended her hand for him to kiss.

He bowed over it, noting the gold rings, the carefully tended nails. A faint aroma of rose water and lamb fat set his queasy stomach churning again. 'Not much of a reputation at the moment except for seasickness, madam,' he said.

A flicker of disdainful amusement kindled. 'Unlike Isabelle's father, you did not have ancestors who were sailors and Vikings, my lord.'

'No, madam. Their skills were with horses and the mustering of a military household on the move.'

'Useful for Normans, I imagine,' she said dismissively. Her gaze fastened on the three wide-eyed children and her chin quivered. Isabelle swiftly pressed them forward.

'William, Richard and Mahelt,' she said, lightly touching each head in turn. 'We left Gilbert, Walter and Belle at Pembroke. My lord thought them too small to make the crossing this time, and he was right.' She gave William a look of apologetic admission. He managed a smile in response and forbore to comment that had he known what the crossing would entail, he would have stayed behind too and played nursemaid.

Will and Richard bowed deeply to their grandmother as they had been taught and Mahelt swept a perfect curtsey before backing up to William and seeking the security of his hand. Aoife was so overcome that she had to utilise her sleeve again. 'Ah, I am a fool,' she sniffed, her voice quavery and choked. 'What is there to weep about? My daughter is home at last and brings me the gift of a son-in-law and fine grandchildren . . . if only my father the King could see you all.' She made a gesture of apology. 'I am neglecting my duty. Come now, into the hall. There is food and drink laid out, and honeycomb for the children. You like honeycomb?' She smiled at Mahelt and held out her hand. William felt the reluctance ripple through his small daughter, but she was brave and, after a brief hesitation, let go of his hand and dutifully went to Aoife. He felt a pang of pride at her courage and her ability to see that duty mattered.

'Good girl . . . how pretty you are, just like your mother.'

All William wanted to do was lie down on the wolf-skin-covered bed and sleep, but he had received the impression that the lady Aoife had a cordial contempt for Normans and was reserving her judgement on him. Besides, she couldn't show off her daughter and grandchildren if they all retreated into this chamber and shut the door for the rest of the day. Digging within himself, he found the fortitude to follow her into the hall.

'How long will you stay?' Aoife asked Isabelle.

It was late evening. The children were abed, and

78

William had retired with them to recuperate, leaving mother and daughter to catch up the distance of years over a jug of mead.

'I do not know.' Isabelle sipped the brew which was sweet and tart at the same time. She had only been allowed it as a special treat when a child, and this brimming cup seemed almost too much even now. 'Until the spring at least. William won't risk another sea crossing in midwinter.' She looked rueful. 'Were I to mention one to him now, I think he'd vow to remain here for the rest of his life rather than take his feet off firm ground.'

'Aye, well, all to the good since he owes this land more than his passing fancy.' Aoife raised her cup to her lips. Isabelle was astonished to see how swiftly the mead slipped down her mother's throat. She had already consumed three measures as if drinking water. Obviously she was accustomed to downing it in some quantity. 'Tell me,' Aoife said, replenishing her cup, 'what kind of man is your husband?'

Isabelle eyed her mother. 'Have you not heard the tales?'

Aoife sniffed. 'Sure, and many tales cross the sea to Ireland, but who is to say what is truth and what is not? I hear tell he is a great warrior whose men would follow him into the jaws of hell should he ask. Your father was like that too, but that was not always to the good. Is he of your father's ilk?'

Isabelle noted the tension in her mother's wrist as she lifted the refilled cup and what was almost hostility in the sea-blue eyes. 'In some ways, perhaps, but then I remember little of my father. I was very young when he died.'

The drawstring lines at Aoife's mouth puckered. 'He was always bound to die,' she said scornfully. 'You marry a warrior: it comes as part of his baggage.'

'But he died in his bed, I remember that . . .' The silence, the tiptoeing around, the terrible sense of dread growing in her stomach. Standing at the bedside, having her hand taken in a fever-hot grip. Her father's gaunt, red-starred cheekbones and fogged eyes. The terrible smell of corruption. Women wailing and cutting off their hair . . . Oh yes, the memory was there, just waiting to be dredged up from the deep where she had consigned it.

'Yes,' Aoife said scornfully, 'of a leg wound taken in battle that never properly healed. One day it festered too far, poisoned his blood and made me a widow within a week. Still, your man looks as if he'll be robust enough once he's over the seasickness; certainly he must have plenty of steel in his lance to have given you six children.' Her tone was ambivalent, perhaps slightly censorious.

Isabelle reddened. 'I cannot tell you what William is like,' she said, striving for dignity. 'You will have to find that out for yourself.'

Aoife tossed her head. 'Well, I hope he is cunning, astute and prepared to nail his courage to the mast. Many lords will baulk at being under his yoke. Several of your father's former knights are not happy that he is here.' She waved her hand in an exaggerated gesture of dismissal. 'Ah, you do not want to know. If you did, you'd have come to Kilkenny long ago.'

Isabelle sat up, stung by her mother's words, which had a ring of truth. 'We had more than Leinster to consider,' she said defensively. 'In the first days of our marriage, William was helping to govern England with the King away on crusade, and then he was acting as one of his commanders in Normandy.'

Aoife gave a scornful sniff. 'Hah,' she said. 'Your husband has a Norman heart, not an Irish one.'

'My husband was prepared to risk crossing the Irish

Sea on the edge of winter to come to Ireland,' Isabelle retorted. 'You do not know his heart.'

'I may not "know" it but I still have eyes to see,' Aoife said irascibly. 'Your father made his life here, but William Marshal is in Leinster as a matter of duty and marking time, not because he loves the land or wants to dwell here.'

'And he will do that duty, Mother,' Isabelle replied, 'by Ireland and by you to the utmost of his ability. He is an honourable man.'

Unable to get the better of the argument, Aoife gave a small shrug and a pout. 'So you say, and I suppose I will believe you for now.'

Isabelle wondered at her mother's disposition. Had she been sour and scratchy like this before? It was so long ago and she had been a child then, with a child's thoughts and perceptions. 'You say we do not want to know about the troubles we face, but you are wrong; we do and that is part of why we are here. You cannot hint at such matters and then wave them away. Tell me.'

Aoife smiled thinly. 'There speaks my Irish daughter within the fine Norman lady. So you have no qualms about walking into the lion's jaws?'

Isabelle reached for the mead jug. 'Oh, I have qualms, Mother, but knowing will prevent them from running amok.'

Aoife plumped the cushion at her back and settled herself in the chair. 'You must know of a man called Meilyr FitzHenry?'

Isabelle nodded. 'He's John's justiciar for Ireland.' She half closed her eyes. 'I think I remember him at Kilkenny when I was small.' Her mind filled with the hazy image of a muscular dark-eyed man with pugnacious features and a black beard.

'He was a coffin-bearer at your father's funeral. Followed him here from Pembroke – beached at Bannow Bay with him and carved his standing in Leinster with the might of his sword.'

'Why do you ask if I know of him?'

'Because he considers your husband an interloper and a threat – a Norman courtier whose abilities have been exaggerated down the years.' She raised her hand, palm outwards like a shield. 'Do not frown at me, daughter, I am only telling you what I have heard. I know Meilyr FitzHenry well but not William Marshal.'

Anger swept over Isabelle on William's behalf. She suspected her mother had enjoyed using such words about William, but since she wanted to know the rest and preferred to avoid a quarrel with Aoife on their first moment together in seventeen years, she checked her temper. 'Meilyr FitzHenry owes us fealty for Dunamase and other Leinster lands,' she said frostily.

'Hah! Even if he does, it makes no difference; Meilyr considers himself lord in this land and he'll brook no outsider telling him his business.' Once again Aoife reached for the mead jug. 'Of course, the de Lacys in Meath have no time for the lord Meilyr. You may be able to buy or persuade support out of them.'

'Walter de Lacy is son by marriage to William de Braose,' Isabelle murmured, eyes still narrowed in consideration, 'and de Braose is our ally.'

'Just so. How else should a mill grind corn except by turning the wheels within wheels?' Aoife filled her cup to the brim again. 'The native Irish lords hate all Normans, but will follow the one they dislike the least and whom they think will give them the most.' Setting her full cup aside, Aoife went to the coffer at her bedside. 'I have something for you, daughter.' Her movements wallowed, suggesting the mead was taking its toll. She removed a bundle of fabric from the coffer and shook it out. As old sprigs of dried lavender and chips of cedar bark fell from its folds, Isabelle saw that it was a woollen gown, the cuffs, neckline and hem heavily embroidered. The colour was a deep saffron-gold, favourite of Irish royalty, and the style was somewhat outmoded, given the current fashion for tight lacing and extravagant sleeves.

'It belonged to your grandmother, Môr,' Aoife said. 'It is yours to wear now, as a daughter of Ireland.' Her breathing had grown swift again and her eyes were hungry.

Isabelle rose and accepted the gown, feeling a sudden prickle of tears. This was her heritage; this was part of her belonging. The colour would make her look deathly ill, and in England and Normandy the women of the court would view the outmoded cut of the garment with disdain, but none of that mattered. It had been her grand-mother's and her mother had saved it to remind her daughter of who she was. She spread her palm over the wool and found it to be surprisingly soft. A slightly musty smell clung to its folds, blending with the aromas of the lavender and cedar.

'Indeed,' Aoife said, taking Isabelle's hand to draw her attention, 'you should wear it especially when the Irish lords come to talk to your husband, because it will remind them you are a woman of this country. Keep your chil-dren at your side since they are King Dermot's great-grandchildren and proof too that Richard Strongbow's blood lives on – particularly the second boy with that red hair.' Aoife's features hardened, emphasising the harsh lines of advancing middle age. 'My father paid the Normans to come to Leinster and help him win back his lands from the Irish lords who had stolen them from him, and they came and in their greed, they too stole what they could. They are still helping themselves today. If we want to survive, we have to make alliances with the strongest of them. It is said you are married to a great man, by all accounts a champion. Well then, use it to your advantage, daughter, and stand your ground.'

The mead swirled in Isabelle's blood. In the light cast by fire and candle, her grandmother's gown in her hands, she felt the connection so strongly it raised the hairs on her nape and she could almost see her Irish ancestors gathered around the fire in their saffron robes, watching her, weighing her in the balance, asking if she was worthy. 'Yes,' she heard herself saying, with a strange, deep surge that came from her solar plexus. 'I will do everything in my power to hold these lands and make them great.'

Aoife smiled and looked satisfied. 'Ah,' she said. 'Men are children even when they are grown. They never realise how strong we women are.'

8

Kilkenny Castle, Leinster, Ireland,
November 1200

Isabelle studied Meilyr FitzHenry circumspectly through her lashes. He had arrived in the early afternoon as the household was sitting down to dine. Before the gathered company, which included Hugh le Rous, Bishop of Ossory, and several of William's senior Irish vassals, he had sworn fealty to herself and William for his lands. Now he sat at the high table with them. He was a strong, barrel-chested man, fighting too much belly and a hairline in rapid retreat. As a grandson of the first King Henry through a bastard branch of the family he was kin to King John, who had granted him the post of justiciar. His smile was nailed to his face and as stiff as boiled leather, but at least he was here. She and William had half expected him to ignore the summons to Kilkenny to pay homage for the lands he held of William. By attitude and gesture, although not in so many words, he had made it plain he would not tolerate the Marshal faction usurping the position he had striven to carve out for himself over the past thirty years.

Between mouthfuls of duck in pepper sauce he expressed surprise to see William in Ireland at all. 'Surely your seneschal is competent to tend to matters in Leinster,' he said. 'You must have more important concerns elsewhere?'

'Each is important in its own turn, my lord,' William answered smoothly.

'Leinster is my birthright and my dower,' Isabelle added to Meilyr, her own voice sharp with irritation.

He pursed his lips as if he had a mouthful of sour wine. 'Indeed, my lady, but you have been long away and times have changed.'

Isabelle gave him a hard look. 'That is strange, for I was under the impression they had not, nor did you wish them to do so, my lord.'

Aoife cackled with approval, but when Isabelle glanced at William, he gave an infinitesimal shake of his head and lifted a forefinger against the side of his goblet in warning. Isabelle pushed down her irritation. He was right to remind her that while FitzHenry was beholden to them as a vassal, he was also Ireland's justiciar and a servant of the King.

'Your impression is mistaken, my lady,' Meilyr said, 'but you are newly arrived and bound to be unfamiliar with the way matters stand.'

'You will find I learn swiftly,' Isabelle retorted. 'I know very well which way the wind blows.' She flicked a glance along the high table towards their vassal Philip of Prendergast, whose indifferent expression did nothing to conceal the fact he was monitoring the conversation intently. His wife was Isabelle's half-sister, born to her father's Welsh paramour thirteen years before Isabelle's birth. Her hair was de Clare red and she owned a feminine version of Richard Strongbow's thin, fine features. Her manner was pleasant but contained and she had made no attempt thus far to set her relationship with Isabelle on a familiar footing. For her part, Isabelle was prepared to be welcoming, but she was wary too. Matilda had wed Philip of Prendergast when Isabelle was still a swaddled infant and they had no bond in common beyond their father's seed.

'The wind blows from many directions in Ireland, and changes on a whim, my lady,' Meilyr said and, having dismissed her with a perfunctory toast of his cup, turned away to William. 'How long do you intend remaining in Ireland, my lord?'

Isabelle tightened her lips and marked the insult on a mental tally.

William leaned back in his chair and folded his arms. 'Eager as you are to be rid of us, my lord, I am afraid we are going to be in each other's company for the winter at least. I won't risk a sea crossing before the spring and in the meantime I intend making the acquaintance of my vassals and neighbours.'

FitzHenry gave a sour shrug. 'You will find the weather much wetter than that to which you are accustomed. Sometimes it rains for months on end and the sea mist covers the land in such a dense blanket that you cannot tell friend from foe. You will need warmer tunics than those you have brought with you.'

Isabelle ground her teeth at his insolence but William merely raised an eyebrow and replied with composure, 'Fortunate then that my coffers contain clothes to cope with most weathers.'

'Most, my lord?' FitzHenry said with a hint of scorn. 'I have all.'

'No man has all.' William waved his hand in a gesture that swatted aside veiled threat and ambiguities. 'I esteem your reputation, Lord Meilyr, and I hope you have a similar regard for mine and my wife's, since we are your overlords. I am as content as you for the relationship to be one of formality rather than friendship, but I tell you this . . . we will have your respect.'

Isabelle coloured with pride and vindication at his words.

Meilyr tried to outstare William but the latter was accustomed to such contests at court and returned Meilyr's gaze implacably until Meilyr took refuge in his wine cup. 'My homage you are entitled to,' he muttered after he had drunk. 'Respect is different. It has to be earned.'

William nodded. 'Just so,' he agreed. 'And it cuts both ways. A reputation is one thing. Living up to it is another.'

Once she had dismissed their attendants, Isabelle sat down on their bed. William was already in it and occupied with threading his prayer beads on to a new length of silk cord, the old one having broken. Although his eyes were slightly narrowed, he could still see well enough in the dim light of a single candle to perform the task without too much of a struggle.

'I don't trust Meilyr FitzHenry,' Isabelle said.

He didn't answer at first, and she was on the verge of repeating her statement when he looked up from his task. 'Yes, he will bear watching,' he said quietly. 'He is brim full of his own importance and appears to believe that being justiciar gives him the power to do as he pleases. I think we gave him pause for thought tonight – and Prendergast too. He strikes me as one who will play both sides of the castle wall.'

'I thought so, especially since his wife is my kin.' Isabelle gnawed her lip, considering. 'FitzHenry bears the bigger grudge though. Whatever you say to him, he still believes himself the true power in Leinster. I don't remember much about him from my childhood, but I know my mother had little time for him in our hall.'

William bent over his threading. 'Your mother has little time for most things Norman. Certainly she makes it plain she has none for me.'

'That is not true,' Isabelle was stung to reply. 'She can be difficult, but no worse than Queen Eleanor in one of her moods.' Even as she spoke, she mentally scolded herself. She hadn't meant to say that – didn't want Aoife to become a source of friction between them.

'No, but Queen Eleanor has known me since I was a young knight and our appreciation of each other has always been mutual, whereas your mother and I . . .' He let the sentence tail off.

'She complimented you in her chamber yesterday,' Isabelle said, attempting to recover her ground. 'She said to me that your love of music has an Irish soul.'

William cocked a sceptical eye. 'Did she indeed?'

'My father had no ear for music and it was one of his worst sins in her eyes. He said it all sounded like cats mating in a cauldron.'

Amusement twitched his lips. 'He had a fine sense of humour to compensate though – not that I knew him well, but on the few occasions we did meet, he was good company.' He made the final knot in the prayer beads and, setting them aside on the coffer, gave her his full attention. 'I suppose your mother and I have the pleasure of music in common. God knows, I've been a courtier for long enough. If I cannot weave my way through my own family concerns and keep my hide intact, then I deserve to be flayed.'

She laid her palm against his cheek. 'I know your tolerance has been tested,' she said in a conciliatory tone, 'but it is hard for her. When last she saw me I was a child and now I return to her a grown woman with a powerful husband. She once had that herself and now it has gone – she is fighting to find a new position that retains at least an echo of glory. I would ask you to bear with her out of kindness, if not affection.'

'I will bear with her out of love for my wife whom she bore and out of duty,' William replied. 'I doubt I could do it for kindness.' He kissed her fingertips and changed the subject. 'Now that we're alone, I want to talk to you about something else. I've been thinking. As well as the religious houses, what would you say about founding a new port on the River Barrow? From what I have seen, Leinster has potential but we need more trade, more settlement.'

Isabelle looked at him, a spark of interest kindling. 'Go on,' she said.

'There's a place I have in mind. The channel is deep enough to bring goods upriver and ship them out without having to dock in Waterford. It will cost silver in initial outlay, but it would bring profit in the long run. We would control the docking fees. All the rents and revenues would be ours and we could use them to develop other projects.'

Isabelle gazed at him in admiration. Founding a new town on Marshal-held lands would boost their revenues and their influence. It was inspired. Many people, her mother included, underestimated William. They thought him little more than a genial soldier, a man who had won his success with a ready smile, the brawn of his sword arm and more than his share of luck, but his nature was more complex than that and he had a fine mind. He was quietly ambitious and nobody's fool when it came to fiscal matters. If he was open-handed to his men and his personality generous, then such generosity was founded on an astute grasp of finance and a balanced hand on the earldom's purse strings.

'Won't the King object? We will be adding to our revenues by taking from his.'

He waved aside her caveat. 'He owes me for rallying

the English barons to his cause. I have no doubt that Meilyr will have something to say, but he'll object to anything I do as a matter of course. We need to arm ourselves to deal with him, and anything that strengthens our personal grip on Leinster and adds to our revenues is welcome.'

'Then I think it a fine notion,' she breathed. The fact that he was prepared to do this, to shoulder the burden and responsibility when for so long he had resisted coming to Leinster, sent a fierce pang through her, compounded of love, pride and desire. She leaned towards him, almost touching his lips with hers. 'Perfect,' she whispered. 'When were you thinking of beginning?'

'Why not now?' he said. 'On the morrow.' Threading his hands through her hair, he took up her invitation, kissing her again and again. Through the bedclothes, she could feel that he was as aroused as she was. The talk of expansion was a potent aphrodisiac. She pulled off her chemise, peeled back the sheet and straddled his thighs.

He groaned as she sheathed him. 'My love, we will have to confess this in the morning, you do know that.'

Isabelle settled on him. 'Father Roger will absolve us,' she said huskily. He closed his eyes and hissed softly through his teeth. Outside a bitter wind whistled against the castle walls and smacked rain against the shutters, but the hangings enclosed their bed in warmth and intimacy. Isabelle undulated languorously like a summer sea and enjoyed William's exploration of her skin, his fingertips performing a subtle spiral dance that wove from breasts to belly to the place where their bodies joined. It was a sin to take such slow, licentious enjoyment from inter-course, and a double sin to indulge in the lewd and unnat-ural practice of allowing a woman to place herself over a man, thus upsetting the whole order of nature – but the forbidden made it all the more piquant. She bit her lip with lust and pleasure, and heard the catch in William's breathing. Feeling the tension shuddering through him, she smiled seductively and tossed her hair in a wanton gesture.

His swallow was audible. 'Christ, Isabelle,' he said hoarsely.

She licked her lips. 'What?' she asked. 'Tell me.' She knew that he was on the brink and was so close herself that it couldn't last beyond a few more strokes.

He seized her hips and held her still. 'You might get with child,' he gasped. 'Unless you want to take that risk, let me at least spill outside you. It won't cost more than an extra paternoster to add to my confession.'

His words shivered through her, adding a recklessness she knew she might regret in the morning, but for the moment, it only served to enhance her desire. Besides, from the swollen tenderness of her breasts and the fact that she had felt mildly nauseous this morning, she suspected they might be bolting an empty stable door. 'What God wills will be.' She pushed down on him hard once and again and, through the lightning flickers of her own pleasure, felt him arch and break deep inside her.

On a hill, above the ground cleared for the new town, Isabelle drew rein beside William and patted her mare's neck. Although the horse was smooth-paced and docile, Aoife had clucked her disapproval that a woman burgeoning with child should be riding at all instead of staying in her chamber with her spinning and needlecraft. Defiance was half the reason Isabelle had chosen to come out and watch the ground being cleared and the plots laid out for the new port on the River Barrow. Not for all the gold in Baye would she admit how sick and faint she was feeling, especially as Aoife had insisted on accompanying her, declaring that if her daughter was foolish enough to go riding and her husband not disposed to prevent her, then someone sensible needed to be on hand to deal with the consequences.

In the four months since their arrival in Ireland, the relationship between William and Aoife had reached a grudging stalemate. They avoided each other when possible, and managed to be civil when not, but there was no affection in their private thoughts concerning each other. William said little enough to Isabelle, but she sensed his irritation and knew he considered Aoife to be manipulative and interfering. Aoife for her part was suspicious and resentful of her son-in-law, giving him little credit even when it was due. 'When your father was alive' and 'If my husband were here now' were constant refrains of comparison in the bower, and William invariably came off worse. Torn in both directions by guilt and duty, Isabelle strove to keep the peace but sometimes it exhausted her.

Aoife joined them now, determinedly pushing her dappled gelding between Isabelle's palfrey and William's powerful dark bay. Until that moment his stallion had been standing quietly on a slack rein as William ranged his gaze over the bustle of labourers and masons toiling on the project, but now it lashed out and snapped at the intruder. The grey skittered in panic. Uttering a curse, Aoife slashed her short leather whip across the sensitive end of the bay's nose. Startled, unaccustomed to such treatment, the stallion shied and tried to bolt, with William fighting to stay astride and in control. Isabelle's palfrey put back its ears and although normally a placid beast, its hooves danced a drumbeat of agitation. Isabelle tugged on the rein, intending to draw clear of the fracas, but the palfrey's hind leg skidded on the wet turf and it stumbled, pitching Isabelle from the saddle. She didn't land hard but it was enough to shock and bruise. She struggled to sit up, but her body refused to obey her will and a grey sea mist engulfed her vision.

The smell of burning feathers brought Isabelle to her senses. Coughing at the acrid stench, she stared around, disoriented. She was lying on a pelt-covered bed bench in a timber long hall, similar to the one at Kilkenny, but not as large or well appointed. New too, for the smell of sawn and shaped timber lingered in the air. A cauldron was suspended over a firepit and a woman in a plain woollen gown was stirring the contents with a long wooden ladle. The door was propped open to let in daylight and she could hear voices outside, including William's, and the stamp and snort of horses.

'Daughter.' Aoife leaned over her, lines of anxiety furrowing her brow.

Isabelle struggled into a sitting position and took the cup. 'Where am I?'

'You fell from your horse and fainted,' Aoife said, suddenly looking censorious. 'I said you shouldn't be riding in your state. That stallion of your husband's is a menace. We brought you down to the town and he has sent for a physician.' She sniffed. 'God knows why. This is women's business; we don't need a man poking his nose where it isn't wanted.'

'I am all right,' Isabelle started to push back the covers, but Aoife stopped her with a firm hand on her arm.

'You need to rest. Who knows what damage you might have done.'

Isabelle compressed her lips but did as her mother bade. It was true that she felt queasy and tears were not far away.

'Just lie still,' Aoife said in a gentler voice. 'I'm here to look after you.'

Moments later William arrived, accompanied by a man wearing the dark bonnet of a physician. Hastening to the bed, William took Isabelle's hand and kissed her cheek, then her lips.

'Thank Christ,' he said. 'You are all right?'

She nodded and swiped angrily at her eyes as they filled. 'It was nothing.'

'I do not call it nothing,' Aoife said, glaring at William and the physician. 'Tell my foolish daughter she should not be gadding about on horseback when she is with child. Tell her that if she had stayed in her chamber with her women this would never have happened.'

The physician looked taken aback.

'It would never have happened but for your determination to push yourself between us,' William snapped, his usual courtesy worn to the bone.

'She is my daughter. *Mine*,' Aoife retorted, baring her teeth. 'Someone has to have a care for her welfare because plainly you do not.'

William's chest expanded. 'My wife well knows the care I have for her.' His voice was husky with the effort of controlling his anger. 'And it doesn't involve treating her like a witless girl.'

Aoife puffed herself up, preparing for battle without quarter, but Isabelle reached out from the bed and caught her arm. 'Peace,' she said. 'Please, I would have peace between you. That is what would benefit me the most . . .'

William looked at her and then at Aoife. 'As you wish,' he said curtly. 'I have no more desire for strife in our household than do you.' He nodded to Aoife, touched Isabelle's cheek and, with clamped jaw, strode out.

Aoife shook herself like a hen ruffling indignant feathers. She stood reluctantly to one side to let the physician look at Isabelle. 'Your father was the same. They don't understand the affairs of women.'

Isabelle closed her eyes. 'William is my husband,' she said with weary patience. 'I will not have you causing discord between us.'

Aoife bristled. 'Is that what you think I am doing – causing discord?' Her lips made a chewing motion and her breathing was rapid.

'Yes, Mother, I do. You may have my wellbeing at heart, but so does he. I am a part of this; I wanted to come today. William would have had to lock me in my chamber to stop me.'

Her mother fell silent and went to stand before the hearth. The physician made a swift assessment of Isabelle and, satisfied that all was well, advised her to rest and – with a swift glance towards Aoife's rigid spine – not to go out riding.

Aoife turned back to her. 'You will be leaving Ireland soon,' she said abruptly. 'Your husband is like a swallow preparing to fly. He did not want to come in the first place and now that spring is in the air, the vassals spoken to and this new town under way, he is restless to be gone. By his lights he has fulfilled his obligations. There is nothing here to make him stay . . . to make you stay.' Aoife crossed to the bed and touched Isabelle's cheek. 'Daughter, I know there is friction between your lord and myself. It does not take a fool to see he would rather couch down with vipers than dwell with me, but I have a desire to see my other grandchildren, including the one you carry in your womb.' A wheedling note, filled with pathos, entered her voice. 'It is many years since I saw Striguil, and I would set eyes on it once more. Could your husband be persuaded to relent his opinion of me and bring me with you?'

Isabelle looked dubious, imagining William's response to such a suggestion.

'I worry so much for you in your condition.'

Isabelle shook her head and laid her hand over her belly. 'It is only the sickness of the early months.'

'Carrying and bearing children is a time when every woman needs the support of other women and if one of them is her mother, so much the better,' Aoife said, lips setting firmly.

Lacking the energy to argue, Isabelle closed her eyes. 'I will speak to William,' she said, 'but you must swear to me that you will hold your peace and not pick quarrels with him.'

Aoife's smile lit up her face, making her look almost winsome. She signed her breast. 'I promise on the holy bones of Saint Brendan,' she said with such sincerity that Isabelle almost believed her.

'What else could I say?' Isabelle asked as she and William strolled along the banks of the Barrow that evening. They had opted to stay in the new port overnight and sleep in the long hall. Behind them followed an entourage of his squires and her ladies, but to all intents they were alone. Aoife had – prudently for once – remained behind by the fire, although the look and the tilt of her head to Isabelle as she set out had been eloquent.

'You could have refused,' William said, looking resigned but irritated.

'Yes, and the guilt would have consumed me whole by compline.'

They paused to watch a couple of red-sailed barges mooring up in the dusk, with a cargo of timber poles that would be unloaded in the morning.

'She has sworn not to quarrel with you.'

He snorted. 'And you believed her?'

'Brendan has always been her favourite saint,' Isabelle said. 'I think she will at least try.'

He made a sceptical face. 'Do you want her to come with us?'

They walked in silence for a while. The grass was damp and she felt the hem of her gown growing heavy and cold against her ankles. 'I will not sleep easily if we leave her,' she said at length. 'I owe her my duty as a daughter even as much as I owe my love to you as a wife and to my children as a mother. In truth, I do not think she is well herself and she does not want to be left alone again. It is for her own sake not mine that she desires to accompany us – and I cannot refuse her.'

William heaved a resigned sigh. 'Then let it be so and I will pray to Saint Brendan myself for all the patience he can give.'

9

Tintern, Welsh Marches, May 1201

On a spring morning, fresh and green, alive with bird-song, Isabelle and Aoife travelled the five miles between Striguil and the Cistercian abbey of Tintern, nestling in a dip of the Angiddy Valley close to the meander of the River Wye. The covered wain ambled at a gentle pace for there was no hurry. Isabelle's advancing pregnancy was a barrier to haste and Aoife had been unwell for several weeks with swollen ankles and breathlessness when she exerted herself. Today, however, she felt sufficiently well for the excursion and had even found the energy to grumble that the cushions inside the wain weren't plump enough for comfort.

Will, Richard and Mahelt rode their ponies hither and yon, covering five times as much ground as the wain as they ranged into the trees on either side of the road with the dogs. Pigeons shot skywards in flusters of indignant wings and hares fled in lightning zigzags that left the children no chance of catching them, but served as something to pursue. William's knight Eustace de Bertremont kept a watchful eye on the doings of the youngsters, but forbore to intervene. The road to Tintern was peaceful and they were unlikely to come to harm. The smaller children, Gilbert, Walter and one-year-old Belle, travelled with Isabelle and Aoife in the wain with their nurses, and had been playing clapping games and singing simple songs most of the way.

Aoife pursed her lips at Isabelle as they approached the abbey. 'I cannot believe you are planning to go to Normandy as soon as the child is born,' she said sourly. 'Your husband will be in the King's service and likely in the field. He won't have time for you. I didn't follow your father there when he had to serve the King. I didn't drag you and your brother from pillar to post.'

They had already had several variations of this conversation since returning to Striguil. Isabelle had tried to let it wash over her head, and to an extent she had succeeded since she was always more placid and unflappable as she entered the later months of pregnancy. Nevertheless, her mother's persistence was beginning to wear holes in her defences.

'Longueville is my home in Normandy,' she said wearily. 'It is not as if myself and the children will be living in a campaign tent. We'll be in a keep larger than Striguil.' She clenched her teeth for she had promised herself she would not rise to the bait, yet here she was, doing precisely that. William was currently away at court where the King was making preparations to cross to Normandy and put down the unrest that King Philip of France and Prince Arthur were stirring up between them.

Aoife threw up her hands. 'Go then, if you must,' she said dramatically. 'I can see how much it means to you. What do I matter?'

'Mother . . .'

'No.' Aoife drew Belle into her lap and played with the golden curls escaping the infant's linen bonnet. 'You have

100

lived without me for most of your life, so why should you not push Ireland from your mind and look to Normandy and all things Norman? I notice you've put your saffron robe to the back of the garderobe.'

Isabelle clung to her tolerance while the guilt bit deeper. 'That is because it is too warm for the summer. As soon as I return to Leinster, I'll bring it out.'

'And when will that be? In ten more years? I'll long be bones by then.'

Feeling as if she was being chewed to pieces, Isabelle prayed for patience. Within her womb, the child kicked vigorously, as if sensing her tension. It didn't help that her mother was right. Although William had begun the task of making his mark on Leinster, he could not be in three places at once and out of Normandy, England and Ireland, the latter would always come last. Another visit was less than a speck on the horizon and both she and Aoife knew it.

At Tintern, Abbot Eudo greeted them warmly. Isabelle's grandsire had founded the abbey seventy years ago and the de Clares had always been generous patrons. William had asked for monks from Tintern to colonise his new Abbey of the Vow in Ireland and with such patronage, grants and donations had flowed into Tintern's coffers.

The older children, having ridden off their excitement during the journey and knowing what was expected, behaved themselves. Of the younger ones, Walter was stoical and quiet anyway, and Gilbert loved churches and was too absorbed in everything going on around him to be up to mischief. Only Belle ruined the proceedings by yelling her head off until her nurse prudently took her to feed bread to the tench in the fishpond.

Isabelle, Aoife and the children attended the sext service in the church and Isabelle made an offering of two marks of silver, one for the abbey and another for distribution to the poor.

'I would not mind resting here when my time comes,' Aoife said as she and Isabelle walked down the nave following their prayer. 'It is so peaceful.' She watched Mahelt make a game of hopping from one tile to another, a strand of rich brown hair bouncing against her cheek.

Isabelle gazed at her mother in surprise. Aoife was so often contrary, selfish and manipulative; when a different side of her personality shone through, it was like a sudden bar of sunshine illuminating beauty out of darkness. 'You would rather lie with your in-laws than your own kin?' she said incredulously.

Aoife smoothed her thumb over the prayer beads in her hand. 'Your grandparents lie at Fearns but I have never been fond of that place. I don't like the Bishop. Your father and your brother are in Dublin, but since I never slept in peace with the man when he was alive, I would rather not be his bedmate in death. Here it is tranquil, and I know I would not be alone. You come here often, as you will not come to Fearns or Dublin. It gives me comfort to think of my grandchildren's hands on my tomb and their children's after that.'

Isabelle opened her mouth and then closed it again. What her mother had had the delicacy not to say was that, in the fullness of time, Isabelle herself would be entombed at Tintern and certainly some of her offspring. Aoife was ensuring her place in the matriarchal burial plot. Isabelle suspected what her mother was thinking but not saying was that, one way or another, she would eventually have her daughter to herself.

A month later and, despite the encroachment of summer, the weather was not so clement. Rain pelted the Marches in unceasing grey sheets and the River Wye, churning the foot of the cliffs below Striguil's keep, was as choppy as the sea.

William hunched his shoulders against the driving rain and, with Jack Marshal, Jean D'Earley and Ralph Bloet at his heels, hurried down to the outer ward where a motley assortment of men were awaiting his inspection in the shelter of a timbered store house. William had returned from the court three days ago, but was due to set out for Portsmouth within the week and rejoin the King, who was about to cross to Normandy and deal with his nephew and Philip of France. William needed soldiers for the campaign and while he intended hiring men once across the sea, he wanted to season their ranks with Welsh and Irish mercenaries. The latter were fearsome axemen, and the Welsh bowmen of Gwent always earned their pay.

'You've weeded them already?' he asked, and Jack confirmed that this was so.

'I got rid of one who turned up more pickled than a piece of January salt beef, and another who's known to be light-fingered round the town. I thought you wouldn't want them, so I sent them packing. Plenty more to take their place.'

As William expected, the men awaiting his scrutiny were a rough lot, both the salt and the scum of the earth. Men who were surplus to their villages and settlements: younger sons who were an extra mouth too many to feed; older ones with wanderlust in their veins; former crusaders who had returned home and not settled back to the yoke. William sought the latter out first because they knew what to expect and had a harder edge than those who were coming soft from the village and plough, leaving family and familiarity for the first time. He kept the ones who cared for their weapons and declined those who did not. He accepted an elderly man who could read and spoke fluent French, and a small, light youth who had few fighting skills but could coax the speed of lightning out of a horse. There was always need for wisdom and fast messengers among the soldiers, and he sent the lad over to the stables to be put in the employ of Rhys, his senior groom.

Satisfied with his selection, William gave the men a succinct résumé of what he expected of them and what they could expect from him and left them in Ralph's charge. 'We'll recruit again in Normandy,' he said as he bent his head into the slanting rain and hastened towards the great hall. 'I don't doubt a quarter of them will change their minds as soon as they see the sea.'

Jean grinned. 'And you won't, my lord?'

William laughed grimly at the sally, although in truth his fear of crossing the Narrow Sea had diminished since his close escape from drowning in the Hibernian one. Had he been going to die on a ship, that would have been the occasion. Having faced his demons and lived to tell the tale, he could be more sanguine – if not less seasick.

There was no sign of Isabelle in the hall. He mounted the stairs to the upper chambers, the first of which was currently Aoife's domain, although usually it was his and Isabelle's solar, adjoining the main bedchamber. Frequently the women sat there at their sewing and he knew they would not venture far from the hearth today.

Isabelle was sitting at her mother's bedside, her embroidery frame drawn up. Aoife was fully clothed, but lying upon the bed, her back supported by an array of colourful cushions and bolsters. A rug of Irish plaid covered her legs. Her complexion was the hue of tallow. Grey shadows lay beneath her eyes and her lips were blue. 'Is the wind from the west?' she asked him, her breast heaving with the effort to talk and breathe.

'Indeed it is, madam.' William handed his cloak to one of his wife's women and came to the bed. 'Are you unwell today?' He glanced at Isabelle, who gave a tiny shake of her head. He knew Aoife was ailing but she had been well enough to attend mass this morning, and one never knew with her how much was artifice and how much was truth.

'Better for knowing it's an Irish wind. I thought I could smell the pastures of home when I woke at dawn.'

'What you can smell is the Welsh hills,' William said.

'Hah, and I knew you'd even argue with a sick woman,' Aoife said with a wave of her hand and a sour smile to show that she was almost in jest. 'I know the scent of Kilkenny and I won't have anyone telling me different.'

'Then I am sorry,' William said. 'I am mistaken.'

Her gaze hardened, although the amusement remained. 'You're a fine courtier – almost as fair a tongue as an Irish bard, but I'm used to men who have the gift of smooth words.' Her breath sucked and whistled in her lungs as if they were a pair of worn out bellows.

William raised his brows. 'Then I hope familiarity does not breed contempt, madam.'

She narrowed her eyes at him. 'My daughter will better talk of what it breeds,' she said with a glance at Isabelle's pregnant belly, and paused for a moment to muster her strength. 'You sail for Normandy soon, my lord.'

'What of it, my lady?'

'I want you to swear you will not forget Leinster even when your heart is drawn to other lands. Leinster is my daughter's heritage and I will not have you throw it to the wolves.' She had to stop again for breath and Isabelle laid a concerned hand on her arm.

'I will not forget,' William said. 'I swear on my oath as a knight that no wolves will tear it from my grasp, or your daughter's.'

Aoife gave a brief nod. 'I hold you to it, and may you be damned if you do not.' After a moment she pointed to the fastened shutters. 'Open them. I would hear the falling rain.'

Isabelle was dreaming about the sea crossing to Ireland. They were taking Aoife back to Leinster, but the ship had sprung a leak and although everyone was bailing frantically, using pitchers, bowls, jugs and even helmets in the case of the knights, the waters continued to rise. There was no sign of William but, looking down, Isabelle saw that she was holding his sword in one hand, bloody along its edge, and an empty skull in the other with which she had been bailing. Her mother, sitting above them on a throne, was shrieking like a banshee that the wolves were coming and were going to devour all of them.

She woke with a loud cry and jerked upright on the bed, her heart pounding and her body dewed in sweat. The vivid images lingered in her vision as if they were in the room with her. She had gone to lie down for a short while – had only meant to nap while her women kept an eye on her mother, but from the way the light had moved across the room she realised several hours had passed.

Pain ground through her loins and lower spine. Looking down, she saw with shock that her gown and the coverlet were saturated with fluid and more was leaking from between her thighs. The contraction of her womb had made her belly as tight as a drum. Her cry brought Jean D'Earley's wife Sybilla running from the other room. With a single swift glance at Isabelle, she shouted for help and sent one of the others to fetch the midwives.

'It is too soon!' Isabelle gasped as Sybilla reached her and grasped her hand. 'Holy Saint Margaret, it is too soon!'

The contractions surged one after the other swift and violent as an equinox tide. With brisk efficiency, the midwives presided over the labour whilst outside the rain continued to pour as if the days of the Flood had come again. Isabelle's body became an instrument of pain, stretched and plucked, the tune strung on notes higher and higher until she thought she would burst with the agony. Weeping, clutching the women, she pushed and grunted, pushed with clenched teeth and tendons straining in her throat, until the midwives told her not to push, that the head was cresting. There was a blossoming fullness at the juncture of her thighs, a hot slippery flood, and the midwife held up a wizened, blood-streaked little creature that was making faint squeaking noises and was, praise God, alive.

'A girl child,' the midwife said, cleaning the newborn's nose and mouth of mucus before wrapping her in a warm towel and, with the cord still attached, placing her in her mother's arms. 'Small, but she'll do.'

Isabelle looked into the baby's pointed, kitten-shaped face. By her reckoning, her new daughter was early by a little less than a month, probably conceived on William's return to England last autumn before they sailed for Leinster.

She murmured softly to the baby, who opened her eyes. A worried frown furrowed her already wrinkled forehead, making Isabelle smile, and then frown herself. Her dream and the baby's early birth had to be a sign from God, but she could make no sense of the portent, except to know it was a warning.

* * *

That night the rain stopped and Aoife died. Father Walter had heard her confession after vespers when it became plain that barring a miracle she would not see the morning. Aoife had lived long enough to hold her new grand-daughter Sybire in her arms, and Isabelle had come, pale and weak from childbed, to clasp her mother's hand and pray for her in her last moments. With a supreme effort, Aoife gathered her strength and whispered, 'Protect yourself from the wolves.'

The words had entered Isabelle's blood like melting ice and, as her mother ceased to breathe, she began to shiver, her teeth chattering uncontrollably. Murmuring in concern, her women took her back to her bed where they warmed the covers with a hot stone wrapped in a woollen cloth and made her drink scalding beef broth. Slowly her colour returned and warmth flowed into her limbs, but at her core she could still feel a frozen residue of terror, and mingled with it feelings of guilt, foreboding – and grieving loss.

It fell to William to escort Aoife's coffin to Tintern for burial and to preside over her funeral. The birth had not been long but Isabelle had lost much blood at the delivery of the afterbirth and was confined to her chamber on a diet of enriching foods to recover her strength, and it would have been unthinkable for a woman still bleeding from childbirth to enter a church.

Mahelt took her mother's place at the bier, and solemnly lit candles, her seven-year-old gravitas both amusing and throat-achingly poignant. William thrust the thought to the back of his mind that it was fine practice for the future. His older sons played their part too, acting as men of the family rather than small boys. Not so small, William amended as they distributed alms to the people who had followed the cortège in expectation of charity. Will was eleven, Richard nearly ten. A few more years and they'd be sent to train as squires in another household. Where did the time go?

Standing outside the abbey, he watched cloud shadows pass over the valley floor so that one moment the abbey was quenched and dark, and the next it was gilded in a benediction of deep sunlight.

Mahelt came to stand at his side and slipped her small hand into his. 'She will be happy here,' she said. It was a statement, not a question.

'Yes,' he replied, gently squeezing her fingers. 'Or at least as happy as anywhere else.'

10

Vicinity of Longueville, Normandy, July 1202

Bare sword in his hand, his destrier controlled on a tight rein, William circled the captured French supply train of ponies and carts. Several corpses littered the ground, blood glistening in dusty red veins and puddles on the road. Their more fortunate companions stood with their hands on their heads and fear in their eyes as they watched their Norman ambushers. William nodded tersely to his nephew Jack and sheathed his sword. 'Strip them of anything you consider valuable, then let them go,' he said. 'There has been enough blood spilled and none of them are worth holding for ransom.' He reined to face Jean D'Earley who was examining the baggage wains.

'Mostly timber, my lord,' Jean said. 'Some wine and salt pork too.'

William rode over to study the shaped lengths of wood piled in the carts. Among them were barrels of grease, stout ropes and heavy coils of iron chain. 'Dismantled trebuchets,' he said with a satisfied grin. They might not have struck a pay convoy of silver, but snatching a couple of King Philip's siege engines from under his nose was not a bad haul, not to mention rations for his troops. He knew how important food was to men who were seated outside castle walls, bored out of their skulls and waiting for something to happen. 'Bring them along. We can certainly make use of them.'

In a fine mood, the reconnaissance party gathered their spoils and turned back for the Norman camp. William felt sufficiently secure to remove his helm and push down his mail coif but still took the precaution of setting outriders and scouts to keep an eye open for trouble. Their closeness to the French lines meant there was always the danger of encountering an enemy raiding party such as their own.

Jean had been investigating one of the pack-pony panniers and produced two wheaten loaves and a wheel of sheep's milk cheese veined with blue.

'Dinner,' he said cheerfully.

William took one of the loaves, tore a chunk off, poked a hollow and stuffed it with cheese. Fighting was hungry work. Thirsty work too. 'Broach a cask of wine,' he said between rotations of his jaw. 'Let each man have a measure. There'll be plenty left for the rest of them in camp.'

'My lord.'

As he ate and drank, and the troop jingled along at a steady pace through the green summer countryside, William gradually relaxed, the agitation of battle sloughing off him, the tension leaching from his muscles.

William wasn't surprised that the Lusignan family had rebelled against John. The humiliation of having Hugh's bride stolen from under their noses would have riled less warlike men and the Lusignans were not peaceable at the best of times. John, flexing his kingly muscles, had dealt with their protests in so high-handed a manner that they had appealed to Philip of France. Unable to pass up such a God-given opportunity to make trouble, Philip had invaded Normandy with an alliance of Bretons led by Prince Arthur. The latter was opining loudly to all who would listen that his claim to the Angevin lands and the English throne was much stronger than John's.

John had appointed William commander of the baili-wicks of Arques and Caux. Eu on their borders was under Lusignan control, Ralph of Exodoun being another member of the family, and his hatred of John just as implacable as that of his siblings. He had seized Drincourt and Eu, and overrun all of the area between the Rivers Bresle and Béthune. William had soundly retaliated, taking Lillebonne and the lands of the Count of Boulogne.

John had vouchsafed William money to pay his garrisons, but it was still not enough. Baggage trains of silver arrived and baggage trains of silver departed. William had even had to resort to borrowing extra silver from the mayor of Rouen. Paid soldiers were far less likely to desert than men starved of their wages, but sometimes he felt like a small meadow pipit stuffing worms down the gullet of a ravenous young cuckoo. He had to find the wherewithal though, especially now that King Philip was camped before the walls of Arques and determined to take it.

William devoured the last morsel of bread and cheese and washed it down with a swig of wine from the horn his squire had filled for him. There was the matter of Ireland too. The work on the new town was developing apace and he had replaced de Quetteville with his knight Geoffrey FitzRobert, who had a more forceful personality, but it was a temporary measure and not ideal. Only yesterday, William had heard disquieting rumours that Meilyr FitzHenry had been encroaching on Marshal terri-tory to the north of Kilkenny. The situation required a

112

firm military presence and sustained effort on his part, neither of which he could give just now, despite his promise to Aoife.

Their return to camp was greeted with whoops of delight. William deposited the cart containing the siege machines outside his own pavilion and told Jean to see the salt pork and the wine divided equally between the men who had taken part in the ambush. It was a relief to shed his hauberk and gambeson. Stripping off tunic and shirt he was engulfed in the pungent odour of battle sweat. The French had fought hard for their siege engines and field rations.

An attendant fetched a latten bowl of tepid water and a piece of white Spanish soap. William lathered his face and upper torso, discovering the odd bruise and strained muscle but nothing worse. He had been lucky this time. Neither he nor any of the men had suffered more than superficial injuries. He was drying himself on a square of coarse linen when his chamberlain approached. Osbert had clearly been poring over his accounts in the sun without his hat, for his wide forehead, his cheeks and the bridge of his beaky nose were campion-pink.

'Supplies have arrived from the Countess at Longueville, my lord,' he reported. 'I sent the pigs and the geese to the butcher and had the baggage chests and silver put in your tent. The messenger's waiting at the serjeants' fire in case there's a reply . . . oh, and Earl de Warenne requests you to dine with him and the Earl of Salisbury as soon as you may.'

William thanked him and, pushing aside the canvas flaps, stepped inside his pavilion. Closed off during the day, the atmosphere was damp and hotly heavy with the musty smell of earth and grass. A dozen small barrels and a couple of stout leather travelling chests stood beside

113

his camp table, on which were spread several parchments, weighted down by stones, showing the positions of the French besiegers of Arques. William's spirits lightened. The silver would keep the troops in the field a while longer and he could indulge himself tonight by sending for the messenger and sifting the news from home. Longueville was not that far away – a day's ride in good weather, but given the current situation, God alone knew when he would see it.

He opened one of the chests. Neatly folded at the top was a tunic of soft, squirrel-coloured twill. A simple chain pattern of embroidery worked in blue and yellow thread decorated the sleeves and throat.

'The messenger says the Countess wants you to know the embroidery was worked by your eldest daughter,' Osbert said.

William smiled and felt the domestic warmth of his absent family reach out and touch him. The needlework was simple, but excellent for an eight-year-old. He suspected an adult's guiding hand, but all the same, it touched him deeply. He loved all of his children, but Mahelt, his firstborn daughter, held a special place within his heart.

Having pulled on a clean shirt, he donned the tunic and pinned it at the throat with a round brooch. The chest also contained a new embroidered belt and two pairs of hose. There was a box filled with rose petals and violets boiled in sugar, and at the bottom, a bolster that smelled of attar of roses and had a lock of Isabelle's hair neatly stitched into the corner. William laughed aloud and shook his head. His wife knew exactly what would bring him comfort away from home. He placed the bolster on his camp bed, combed his hair, and crunching a splintered piece of sugar-boiled violets, took the box outside to his squires who were tending to his equipment. 'Here, Matthew, Bartholomew,' he said, 'a gift from my wife to accompany your labours.'

The youths' delighted gratitude ringing in his ears, he collected Jean and Jack and walked through the camp to the pavilion of William, Earl de Warenne, who was cousin to King John.

The Earl had recently come into his inheritance and had invested some of it enhancing his dignity in the form of a new tent and sundry luxuries. The former was a large, circular affair of red and gold canvas, adorned with a finial in the shape of a snarling golden lion as a reminder to all of his royal connections. Elaborate crimson hangings screened his bed from sight. Salisbury and de Warenne were already eating at a trestle table covered with a white damask cloth, but as soon as de Warenne saw William, he beckoned him to join them and snapped his fingers to a squire.

William took his place at the table, washed his hands in the proffered fingerbowl and dried them on the towel presented to him by another squire. A platter of roast capon and a small loaf were set before him, together with assorted green leaves dressed with a sharp strawberry sauce.

'You have had a profitable day's work, so we hear,' said Salisbury as William set to.

'You might say that.' Cheerfully, William regaled his fellow Earls with the story of the day's raid. 'So that's two siege machines that Philip is short,' he concluded, 'and his mercenaries will go hungry, while ours are fed.'

Salisbury rubbed his hands. 'It will certainly help Arques. Your scouts are to be commended, Marshal.'

'I pay them well,' William said. 'When I was learning my trade, I was taught that it was the lord with the best

115

reconnaissance and the swiftest response who had the better chance. Also the best supplied, and my wife is very good at that.'

Salisbury chuckled agreement. 'I saw your pack train arrive.'

William grinned. 'She sends me scented bolsters and fresh linen and sweetmeats. She knows the things that matter.'

'I wish my Ela was so inclined,' Salisbury said a little enviously.

De Warenne was not interested in domestic comparisons and preferred to keep to the point. 'Let us hope King Philip and the Breton brat are not so well served,' he growled. Reaching to the wine jug, he swore when he found it empty, and thrust it at a squire to refill. As the lad left, de Warenne's usher, resplendent in chequered livery, appeared at the tent entrance, a travel-stained Benedictine monk in tow. 'My lords.' He bowed. 'Brother Geoffrey brings news from the King.'

De Warenne nodded, dismissed the usher and beckoned the monk forward. 'Speak,' he said.

The man knelt. 'My lords, the King has won a great victory. He sends you tidings that he has captured Prince Arthur and Hugh and Walter de Lusignan.'

'What?' William gave the monk a peremptory gesture to rise.

The monk stood up. 'At Mirebeau, my lord, whilst they were besieging Queen Eleanor.' Gratefully, he took the wine that William directed a squire to give him.

'I thought the King was at Le Mans.' De Warenne frowned. 'That's nowhere near Mirebeau.'

The monk surfaced from his cup. 'Eighty miles, but he covered it with his army in two days . . . riding day and night.' He blotted his lips on the sleeve of his habit.

Salisbury looked puzzled. 'What was Queen Eleanor doing there?'

'Start from the beginning,' William said. 'What happened?'

The man drank again and composed himself. 'Prince Arthur came to King Philip and did homage for Brittany, Aquitaine, Anjou and Maine, and then he set out immediately to take Aquitaine with the loan of two hundred of King Philip's knights.'

Salisbury swore and the three Earls exchanged glances.

'Queen Eleanor heard what he intended and left Fontevrault to go to Aquitaine and raise the barons against him, but these days she is not in good health, as you know, and had to stop for respite at Mirebeau. Prince Arthur and the Lusignans arrived and besieged her there.'

'Disgraceful,' William muttered, filled with protective rage that a woman almost eighty years old should be hounded and harassed by her own grandson and his vile Lusignan allies.

'The Queen sent to the King for aid, but with little hope since he was in Le Mans. Prince Arthur promised to let her go if she would agree to yield him Aquitaine. She pretended to think about it to play for time, but said to her own people she would rather crawl the length of Aquitaine on broken glass than yield an inch of ground. Arthur and the Lusignans took the town and the castle – all but the inner keep, where she barricaded herself in.'

Unable to sit still for his fury, William jerked to his feet and paced to the edge of the awning. He stared at the camp. He knew what he would do to the Lusignans – and Arthur – if his hands and their throats ever came into contact.

'They received their just deserts,' the monk said in a voice of grim satisfaction. 'As soon as my lord King received the Queen's cry for aid, he set out to bring it. He rode through the night and the day and the night again, and came upon Mirebeau at dawn. Prince Arthur and the Lusignans never knew what struck them. One minute they were breaking their fast and preparing for the final assault, the next they were at sword point. Three of the Lusignan brothers have been taken prisoner as well as Prince Arthur, and two hundred French knights. It's a disaster for Philip of France and the Bretons.'

'Hah!' Salisbury banged the trestle with fierce triumph. 'I knew John had greatness in him, I knew it! It's a feat worthy of anything Richard could have done! Let them all laugh on the other side of their faces for once!'

The refilled wine jug arrived and the three Earls toasted the victory with raised goblets while the monk was furnished with a platter of the capon and bread.

William was perturbed. What had been done to Eleanor lingered like a bad taste on the palate. He was doubly pleased to have persuaded Hubert Walter against supporting Arthur for King. 'When you have rested, perhaps you would bear another message,' he said softly to the monk.

'Gladly, my lord,' the man replied between mouthfuls.

William cupped his jaw. 'A priest has immunity and can tread where I would not send one of my own messengers. I ask you to go to Ralph of Exodoun in the French camp. He needs to know his brothers are in custody.'

The monk spluttered.

'I will make it worth your while,' William continued, before the shock could become refusal. 'If you do not feel you can accept a fee for yourself, then I will gladly give alms to your foundation.'

Backed into a corner, the monk reluctantly agreed, although the heavy pouch of silver William dropped into his hand went some way towards lightening his expression. 'I always pay my debts,' William said and allowed the monk to think that he was talking of the silver he had given him. But his remark was privately aimed at the Lusignans too.

11

Longueville, Normandy, April 1203

'Papa's home,' Mahelt said. She had been sitting in the window-seat overlooking the bailey, feeding her pet caged linnet seeds from a dish in her hand.

Isabelle, who had been discussing a letter with her clerk concerning a gift to the cathedral at Glendalough in Leinster, ceased speaking and went to look out of the window. What she saw caused her to issue brisk orders to her women and run down to the hall to greet him. William entered the room at full stride, as if either trying to keep up with a giant or running away from one. He was always brisk with energy, but Isabelle could tell that something was badly wrong. Usually his vigour was zestful and exuberant, but she could almost see the anger rising off his skin like vapour as he made for the stairs, with only the most perfunctory greeting to the retainers and hearth knights in the hall.

Isabelle dispensed with formal words of welcome, waved away the servants, and followed him back to the private chamber. She took his cloak, signalled her women to keep out of the way and had the nurses take charge of the children. Mahelt was desperate to show him her linnet but Isabelle prevailed over tears and tantrums and sent her out in the care of Sybilla D'Earley.

She organised the swift provision of a meal: thick slices of beef, bread, salat greens, marrow tart. She had a bowl of hot water brought and fresh linen towels, still smelling of the sunshine that had bleached them as they blew on the drying ground.

'How bad?' she asked as the door closed behind the last servant and she poured him wine.

He dug his fingers through his hair which was still deep brown through the crown and nape, but showing glints of silver at ears and brow. He had muttered more than once that until John came to the throne he had not had a single grey hair, and in essence it was true. Taking the wine from her hand, he drank, set it down, then, going to the hot water, he sluiced his face and hands. 'I don't know yet.'

'Is Longueville threatened?'

William dried his hands and face. 'Not so far, but John can probably manage its loss by midsummer if he's so inclined.' He hurled the towel across the coffer. 'He has only gone and released the Lusignan brothers and lost the support of William de Roches into the bargain.'

Isabelle bit her lip. That was certainly not good.

'If I hadn't seen it with my own eyes, I wouldn't have believed that Queen Eleanor's son could be so stupid. All he took from them was a promise to go in peace and not rebel against him again.' William picked up his wine again, drank it in several fierce swallows and slamming the cup down refilled it. 'Their cause was dead but John has just reattached the head to the torso. A Lusignan will keep his word the way a whore keeps an oath of chastity. They're all brigands and outlaws! Christ on the Cross!'

Isabelle had rarely seen him so riled. Usually he allowed

121

troubles to slide off him like rain off waxed leather. 'What of de Roches?' she asked. He was the seneschal of Anjou; a man who was scrupulous and principled. While acknowledging that Prince Arthur had certain rights and claims, he had been horrified at the youth's attack on Queen Eleanor at Mirebeau and had spearheaded John's rescue mission and the subsequent capture of Arthur and the Lusignans. 'What has John done to him?'

William picked up a marrow tart. 'De Roches gave his aid at Mirebeau with the proviso that he be allowed a say in what happened to Arthur afterwards.'

'Yes,' Isabelle murmured. 'I knew of that.'

'Well, John refuses to let him see Arthur at all, and won't negotiate with him over custody. De Roches says Arthur is the rightful heir to Touraine and Anjou – which is true. He says John should accept Arthur's surrender, make him grovel and let him go.' He gestured with the tart. 'He asks how hard it can be to keep down an adolescent youth. Now John's turned as stubborn as a constipated mule and transferred Arthur to the Tower of Rouen.'

'Have you seen him?'

'Yes, last week.' William's upper lip curled with distaste. 'He's a spotty, obnoxious brat, and so full of bile that I'm astonished he hasn't burst. Had he been one of ours, I'd have taken him by the ear and tanned him over a barrel.' He gave her a look alight with anger. 'Threatened to have Pembroke off me the moment he was King. I told him it would take more balls than he's got between his legs to break me and that since I don't care for blood sports, I wouldn't like to see him try.'

Isabelle shook her head. 'Perhaps it's all a boy's bravado.'

William devoured the tart and reached for another one. 'If so, it's bravado that has been carried too far and for too long. De Roches insists it is right to free the lad. I agree. Arthur might act like a young wolf, but underneath all the swagger and posturing he's a scared pup with his tail between his legs. He hates John, but that's not the point. Hatred comes as part of an Angevin king's birthright.' He sighed heavily and brushed crumbs from his tunic. 'If I was John I'd pen him in Brittany. The whelp wouldn't be able to do much damage and folk would soon tire of him and his attitude. As it is, de Roches has lost his patience with John and ridden off to join Philip of France.'

Isabelle looked at William in dismay. De Roches was like his name, a rock, and John could ill afford to lose him.

'So now we have lost one of our staunchest allies to the French and where he goes, others will follow,' William said.

'What's to be done?'

'God knows,' he said with exasperation. 'I pray that John sees at least some sense before it's too late. He can't put the Lusignans back in their cage, but if he would let Arthur out of his . . . if only into a larger enclosure. A month ago we had the upper hand; we were winning. Now we might lose it all.'

She eyed him closely. 'You mean lose Longueville and our lands in Normandy, don't you?'

William shrugged. 'It might happen. I'm not saying it will.'

A shiver ran down Isabelle's spine. She had never seen William in such a pessimistic mood before. Even when times were bad, he had a gritty determination to succeed – a relish for the challenge. 'Surely there must be something we can do to safeguard them for the future?'

William refilled his cup and sat down on the cushioned bench before the fire. 'It would help if John was prepared to negotiate with the French, but persuading him . . .' He sighed heavily and shook his head.

'You have friends and kin in both camps. You have to try.'

'And so I will, love, but leading a horse to water is not the same as making it drink. I used to think Richard was difficult, but at least he was straightforward, not devious. If he drank, he drank and moved on without planning to kick you in the groin in retribution. Ah God, enough of this. Where are the children? I'd rather distract myself with the pleasure of their company than swill myself into a wine-stupor.'

In the Tower of Rouen William de Braose did not have the comfort of his wife and children as an alternative to wine. His gut was roiling, his bladder full, his feet unsteady as he staggered outside to take a piss and breathe fresh air. He had left the King drinking steadily with his household knights and cronies, casting dice, arguing petulantly. His paymaster; the man whom he had set on the throne by his sworn oath that it was Richard's dying wish to make John his heir. The man who owed him everything. His wife said he should ask for everything too whilst John's need and gratitude was still as fresh as wet lime-wash. The more they had, the more power they would be able to wield.

The torches of the guards were tares of smoky flame as they patrolled along the battlements. One of the towers was known as Conan's leap. In his youth, King Henry the first of that name had pushed a man to his death from the parapet in a fit of rage. De Braose gazed at the parade of torches, then wished he hadn't as he lurched and had to grab the wall. After a moment he recovered sufficiently to fumble in his braies, find his member and, with a sigh of relief, begin pissing against the wall. His bladder was so full that his urine emerged as a trickle and his coordination was so impaired that he splashed his silk-embroidered shoes and the fur-edged hem of his tunic.

Two men emerged into the bailey from a darkened doorway. De Braose eyed them warily. Even half-inebriated, he was attuned to danger. Power came at a price and he had made many enemies along the way and very few friends. The men were moving furtively, but even so he recognised them as a couple of John's hired swords: Poitevan mercenaries with the status of knighthood but not welcomed amongst the habitual bachelors of the mesnie. John kept them because they would do anything for a fee. André, the taller of the two, had been given the daily task of feeding Arthur and emptying his slop pail, ever since the youth's transferral from Hubert de Burgh's safekeeping at Falaise to the deepest, darkest cell in the Tower of Rouen.

De Braose watched the men from his eye corner, but they appeared intent on their own business. Moving furtively, they crossed to the gate, bribed the porter on duty with a clink of silver and slipped out into the night. De Braose finished pissing and adjusted his clothing. He didn't recall John having ordered them to do any clandestine work, but then the King was so secretive that it was difficult to know his mind from one dark thought to the next. De Braose turned to go back to the hall, but something made him hesitate and sway over to the doorway leading down to the cells, from which the mercenaries had just emerged. He paused there, unsteady on his feet, his stomach sour and his bladder tender from its distension. Instinct told him to leave well alone, to walk away, but curiosity and a sense that something was wrong made him lurch across the ward to the porter's lodge. The porter, who was cooking himself eggs and bacon over a brazier, looked round incuriously.

The smell of the food brought saliva to de Braose's mouth and nausea to his belly. 'Give me your lantern,' he growled.

The man handed the item over without comment, as if it were usual for great lords to demand such things of him in the dead of night.

'Where were those two going?' de Braose asked.

'Brothel in the town, so they said, my lord. Appointment with a French whore.'

'Plenty of Norman ones around without resorting to the French.'

'Told 'em I'd not let 'em back before morning and that they were risking the curfew, but that sort don't listen. Futter their own mothers against a wall for a penny.'

De Braose grunted and walked unsteadily back across the ward to the entrance. He descended the stairs with exaggerated care, fearing to slip in his soft-soled shoes and break his neck. His breathing sawed in his throat and the bristles of hair at his nape stood on end like those of a hunting dog confronting a wild boar.

The dank chambers at the very base of the Tower housed the cells. De Braose had been here on numerous occasions; he had been witness to the methods employed in persuading prisoners to talk, had employed some of those methods himself, and knew the narrow passage and the trap door that gave access to the fast flow of the Seine – a convenient dumping ground for waste of all kinds.

Arriving at a particular cell, not far from the passage, de Braose set the lantern in a niche in the wall and, after a moment, heaved back the heavy draw bar and creaked

126

open the door. A foul stench hit him, compounded of rank straw, faeces, urine, mouldy damp – and blood. Inured as he was to the stink of such holes, he had to stifle a retch. He could hear the low moans of an animal in agony, the rustle of straw as it moved. The scuttering and squeak of rats. De Braose lifted the lantern in his left hand and, drawing his dagger with his right, ventured into Prince Arthur's cell.

The youth was curled on a pallet of fouled straw, his knees drawn up towards his belly. His hose, once gaily striped red and blue, were so smirched and stained that it was hard now to discern their colour. He was whimpering to himself and breathing shallowly through chattering teeth. André and his friend had obviously been having some fun before going out into the town, roughing him up for their entertainment. It wasn't something John minded, and de Braose had no feelings about it one way or the other. The youth needed the pride and belligerence drubbing out of him. No harm in that. He drew closer, raising the lantern for a look at the damage, expecting Arthur to raise his head, but he didn't. And then de Braose saw the blood webbing the boy's hand and saturating his tunic.

'Holy Mother of God,' he whispered. The sound of his voice caused Arthur to turn and begin shrieking like a rabbit in a snare. De Braose stared at the ruined face, the swollen sockets filled with a black jelly of clotted blood, the streaked red mask beneath, the screaming open mouth, and he lost his gorge, vomiting and vomiting again until his stomach and throat were raw. 'Christ, oh Christ in heaven!' he heard himself crowing.

'Please . . .' sobbed the creature that had so recently been a gawky, truculent youth of sixteen and was now a crawling thing, alive on the edge of death and wearing the visage of a crossroads corpse pecked by crows. 'Please . . .'

De Braose didn't remember the journey back to the great hall, but he must have made it, for suddenly he was treading across the dais to John who was sitting sideways on to the trestle, elbow leaning on the wine-stained cloth, a near empty flagon at his side. His eyes were bright, the pupils almost obliterating the tawny iris, and his cheeks were flushed. One of his bachelors, Johan Russell, was owlishly trying to tell him something, but was too drunk to do much more than slur and dribble.

John looked up and caught de Braose's eye. 'Faugh,' he said, with a curl of his lip. 'You stink of piss and puke. Get out. Go and clean yourself up.'

De Braose swallowed and swallowed again. He had thought himself done with retching, but he was very close to heaving bile into John's lap. 'Sire, there is something you need to see . . .'

John laughed coarsely. 'Unless it's got yellow hair and paps the size of udders, I don't think so, eh, Russell?'

'Papsh . . . udders . . .' slurred the latter, putting his head down on the board and closing his eyes.

De Braose gulped. He leaned closer to John and murmured the terrible knowledge in his ear. For a moment John's expression did not change. The cynical smile remained; the eyes glittered with malicious humour. And then the words began to sink in and his face changed. 'Blinded?' he said.

De Braose nodded and flicked a glance at Russell. 'Yes, sire. And André and Raimund of Poitou have left the Tower.'

John jerked to his feet and almost overbalanced. When attendants advanced on him, he gestured them away as if shooing flies. As Russell tried to stand he shoved him back down. 'Go to your bed,' he growled, 'or kennel here, I care not. You are dismissed. De Braose, come with me.

'Who else knows?' John asked as he and de Braose made their unsteady way through the night and down the precarious stairs to hell, both of them breathing a stertorous haze of wine fumes.

'No one, sire, as far as I am aware.' De Braose swallowed a belch. 'I felt that something was not right, so I went on my own to look . . .' He hoped against hope that by the time they returned, the boy would be dead. His mind's eye kept filling with the vision of those clotted, sightless sockets and blood-drenched features.

John paused before the cell door. Any hopes de Braose had nurtured about Arthur being dead were dispelled by the high-pitched continuous keening still coming from within. John shot the draw bar and entered, boots crackling softly on the straw. Turning his head aside, de Braose raised the lantern on high and watched the flame shadows lick against the glistening walls. He would be blind too. He would not see.

Fastidious as a cat even in his cups, John trod across the cell to the pile of red straw where his nephew lay. John was silent for a long time while he looked. 'God's bones, I will kill the sons of whores for this!' he hissed. De Braose sensed him crouch, saw the shadows on the green-slimed walls move and dart as John examined Arthur and Arthur writhed and screamed.

De Braose shuddered. 'What are you going to do, sire?'

'What can I do?' John asked in a blank voice. 'I cannot show him to the world like this. The blame's already at my door.'

De Braose had regularly seen John in a temper. Once or twice he had witnessed furious, foaming rage, but the quality of this was different. It was as jagged and sharp as broken ice; it possessed that same bitter, frozen burn. John was in full command of his faculties, but it was a John that de Braose had never seen before: one who had reached a precipice and was preparing to leap off the edge.

'Sire?' He was a strong man, but his voice quavered like a squire's.

'It's pointless keeping him alive. He's not going to recover from this. I'd put a dog out of its misery. I'll do no less for my nephew.' Reaching to his belt he drew the small, sharp knife he had been using to pare slices off an apple earlier in the evening, at the same time planting his foot across Arthur's neck to pin him down.

De Braose turned his back and squeezed his eyes tightly shut, seeing blood-red stars behind his lids. There was little sound to accompany the deed. A soft grunt of effort, the spurt and patter of blood, the rustle of the straw as Arthur kicked in his death throes, and then silence, except for de Braose and John's breathing, heavy as lead. De Braose half expected to feel the blade at his own throat next.

'There's work to be done,' John said in that same tone of winter ice. 'Put the lantern down and come and help me.'

De Braose shuddered as if he too had suffered a mortal blow. His teeth were chattering, as Arthur's had been a moment before the knife entered his throat.

'Pull yourself together, man,' John snarled. He had avoided the spray of Arthur's blood, but de Braose could still smell its salty sweetness in the air. 'You are a party to this and you stand in as much peril as me.'

'I . . . I did nothing . . .' De Braose stared at John, horrified.

'And who will believe you?' John scoffed. 'People know you for my guard dog. It's said in every corner of the

130

court that William de Braose will do anything for a grant of land or a gift of gold. You can't afford to let this see the light of day any more than I can. For better or worse you are in this up to your neck. To enable us to swim my nephew has to sink without a trace. Do you understand?' He moved close, breathing wine fumes into de Braose's face. 'Without a trace ... If one word of this comes to light, I will know where to seek and there will be no hiding place for you – or your family – for eternity.'

De Braose swallowed and nodded. He would go to hell when he died, but he probably wouldn't know the difference because he was already there.

12

Longueville, Normandy, Summer 1203

Isabelle rubbed the fabric between her forefinger and thumb, assessing the quality. It was good Flemish twill, woven from English wool and dyed a rich, deep blue with the best woad from Toulouse. The cloth merchant, who had made a special journey to Longueville to exhibit his wares, watched her as attentively as a trained hound awaiting a command.

The sound of children's shouts rising from the courtyard sent her to the open shutters to look out. Will, Richard and six-year-old Gilbert were practising their sword strokes at the pell under the supervision of one of the mesnie knights. They were growing so fast, she thought with sadness and pride. At thirteen, Will was shooting up faster than spring wheat and his voice, although still that of a child, was preparing to change. He was developing muscle too, beyond the sinewy strength of active boyhood. It didn't seem a moment since she had cradled him newborn in her arms. Now he ducked away from affectionate touches and eschewed the women's bower for the company of men whenever he could. And where he went, Richard would rapidly follow, for there was only eighteen months between the brothers.

Other youths were training with her sons, including a couple of the younger de Braoses. Lady Maude was visiting Isabelle at Longueville while their husbands were in the field with the King. Isabelle was not fond of the lady Maude, but could hardly refuse the wife of an ally and one of the most powerful men in John's entourage. William de Braose was riding so high in the royal favour, he was like a hawk soaring over partridges in the grass. Wardships, grants and castles had come his way in huge abundance, but for all her husband's success, the lady Maude seemed ill at ease. Usually brusque and confident, she had developed a nervous habit of constantly rubbing her hands together as if washing them. Isabelle wondered if the strain of maintaining that height was beginning to tell.

Returning to the bolts of cloth, Isabelle informed the merchant she would have the blue wool.

Maude de Braose, who had been examining a bolt of linen, snorted with derision. 'I would have thought you too busy packing for a retreat, Lady Marshal, to waste time adding cloth to your burdens.'

'The children have to be gowned, my lady, and Flemish twill is a better price here than in England. I think you will find me prepared for anything.'

'That is what I used to think, in the days when I was naive like you,' Maude said harshly.

Isabelle stiffened her spine. 'Do not mistake courtesy and good nature for naivety,' she retorted. 'I know the ways of the world.'

'Do you?' Maude gave a scornful shake of her head and one of her humourless yellow smiles. 'Like me you have fine, strong sons to be proud of. Your eldest are on the verge of becoming men – aye, I have seen you watching them; I know what goes through your mind. Two more years and the eldest will be a squire, chasing girls, bedding them if he gets the chance, going to war, even while his siblings are babes in the cradle – or still in the womb.'

Isabelle flushed and had to stop herself from placing her hand on her belly – which was ridiculous because she had had her flux last week and knew she wasn't with child, even if William had come to her from the field on several occasions, hurting, frustrated and in need of bodily comfort. 'Yes,' she said quietly, 'I am proud of my sons, and rightly so.'

Maude's gimlet expression softened. 'Like mine to me, they are the pinnacle of your achievement. All mothers love their sons, although I wonder about Queen Eleanor and what she thinks of John these days. He must be a grave disappointment.' She fingered the linen again. 'Have you nothing better?' she demanded of the merchant in a querulous voice. 'This looks like material for a peasant's shroud.'

Ears reddening, the man burrowed amongst his wares. Maude turned back towards Isabelle. 'I don't want to lose my boys. I have a care to them, and you should have a care to yours.'

Fear slithered through Isabelle's sense of security. 'I wish you would speak plainly, my lady.'

Maude shook her head. 'I will say nothing. God sees all. Sooner or later He will weigh us in the balance and some men's deeds will damn them to hell.' She gestured roughly at the merchant. 'I'll have two ells of that scarlet over there. It will do for my husband . . . God rest his purblind, foolish soul.'

Maude stayed to dine on the main meal of the day, but didn't linger over the candied fruits and flowers, insisting she had to be on her way to Dieppe to be ready to take ship for home. Isabelle saw her out of the keep and on to the road with a sigh of relief and considerable misgiving. She tried to put her unease behind her by playing a game of hoodman blind with the children, throwing herself into the romp with giddy abandon, but when the game was over, when she had finished with the breathless laughter and the children were otherwise occupied, her anxiety returned.

She summoned her chaplain Father Walter to the solar, and when he had bowed into her presence, she drew him to the bench set in the embrasure and bade him be seated. 'Lady de Braose was acting very strangely today.' She told him what Maude had said.

Father Walter tugged at his earlobe, a worried frown developing between his deep-set brown eyes, which studiously avoided hers.

'Don't you turn into a clam as well,' Isabelle threatened.

He looked affronted. 'My lady, I hope you know and trust me well enough by now to know I would not do such a thing. I had heard rumours about Prince Arthur, but it's no more than speculation and it might have nothing to do with Lady Maude's behaviour.'

Isabelle gave her chaplain an eloquent look. 'Whenever Arthur's name is mentioned, trouble follows. Has John freed him? My lord said he should do so.'

Walter's frown grew heavier and he shook his head. 'My lady, I am afraid not. The Prince has . . .' He folded his arms and stared over them at the toes of his boots. '. . . disappeared.'

'What do you mean: "disappeared"?'

Father Walter looked uneasy. 'Nothing has been heard from him since he entered the Tower of Rouen. King

Philip has demanded to see him several times, as have the Prince's own vassals, but to no avail.'

'You believe he is dead?' She began to wish she had not sat down to this conversation.

He shook his head. 'I do not know what to believe, my lady.'

Isabelle thought of Maude's restlessness, the veiled, ambiguous comments that could have meant all or nothing. Holy Mary. What if Arthur were dead – murdered? William de Braose would be in a position to know because he was always at John's side and he was constable of the Tower of Rouen. She looked towards her sons, who were absorbed in a game of knucklebones, and her blood turned to ice.

Father Walter leaned forward and clasped her hands between his own in an attitude of prayer. 'Peace, my lady,' he said. 'It is but gossip. The truth will out in the fullness of time, and God sees all.'

'Yes.' She tried to feel comforted by his words, but they did little to alleviate the chill in her soul. 'God sees all.' She closed her mouth before she finished the reply with the blasphemous comment: '*And does nothing.*'

13

Canterbury, Christmas 1203

Sipping sweetened spiced wine and nibbling on fried almonds, Isabelle sat at a trestle watching dancers step and turn to the music of a carole. The young Queen was leading them, her gown shimmering with jewels and her hair dressed with silver braid. At fifteen years old, she had the curves of a woman, but was still as slender as a young deer. John was watching her with lust-narrowed eyes, and she was plainly discomforted by his scrutiny.

'I know how she feels,' said Ida of Norfolk, joining Isabelle. 'I was once in the same position as her: very young, dancing in a beautiful dress and being eaten alive by the eyes of a king who wanted to do nothing more than strip it from me.'

'And were you as frightened as she is?'

'Of course I was, but flattered at the same time that the King of England should pay me such attention.'

'She doesn't look particularly flattered,' Isabelle murmured.

Ida shrugged. 'She is the Queen,' she said practically. 'She has her own apartments and she can do as she pleases – within reason – when he is not by. He gifts her with jewels and gowns and likes to show her off in public. Once she has borne him a couple of heirs and a daughter, he'll let her be.' She laid a hand on Isabelle's sleeve. 'Don't frown at me like that. Of course I feel for the poor girl. I wouldn't want to change places for all the silk in Damascus. What I am saying is that there are compensations. She'll have power too, one day, when she's old enough to realise it.'

Isabelle remained silent. From her own viewpoint nothing would have compensated for being at the mercy of a man like John. To imagine herself at fifteen years old spread under him in the marriage bed made her stomach heave.

Ida had turned her attention from the young Queen and was looking towards her husband, who was talking animatedly with William and Baldwin de Béthune. 'Look at them,' she said affectionately, 'gossiping like old women.'

Isabelle followed Ida's gaze and she too smiled at the group. William was at complete ease, his stance casual, shoulders relaxed. Roger of Norfolk was describing pictures in the air and William was nodding agreement and laughing. It was good to see him thus for he had laughed very little of late, the situation in Normandy being as desperate as it was.

The King had returned to England at the beginning of December, leaving a shambles behind him. Vaudreuil and Radepont had fallen to the French. Gaillard was under siege; Rouen threatened. Longueville and William's Norman lands remained safe, but for how long was a moot point. King Philip had already promised one of William's keeps to the Count of Boulogne once they fell. John had pledged to address the situation in the spring and this visit to England was mostly about raising funds to drive Philip out of Normandy.

Ida said nonchalantly, 'Your eldest children are attending court, I notice.'

The statement appeared at first to be a non sequitur, but Isabelle recognised how the sight of their menfolk in close conversation might bring the subject around to offspring. Gatherings such as this were always an opportunity for bargains and alliances to be explored. Will and Richard were amongst the dancers, as was their sister. Isabelle had noticed with amusement the way Mahelt had been eyeing up the gowns of the court ladies with a professional female eye. 'They are old enough to take part without disgracing themselves,' she said and turned to greet Baldwin's wife, Hawise, Countess of Aumale. The woman had once been a beauty, but time and dissatisfaction had rendered deep lines upon her delicate features until little of it remained. During the full flowering of her looks she had briefly occupied John's bed. Handed on from marriage to marriage since then, she was now a dried and faded flower, her lands of far greater value than her person. Her union with Baldwin appeared to be a lacklustre one, with a single daughter born during the first year of their relationship.

Isabelle and Ida exchanged the usual pleasantries with her. Hawise of Aumale smiled and nodded, but without connecting with either woman.

'I see your son is here,' Ida remarked. 'Is he to remain with you and Baldwin?'

Hawise shook her head. 'He returns to Poitou in the New Year,' she replied, her tone flat. 'To his father's lands.'

'Ah,' said Ida, with sympathy. Her own firstborn son, begotten of her liaison with King Henry, had grown up in the royal household rather than with her at Framlingham. 'You will miss him. I know I missed my William terribly.'

'He is better remaining where he is,' Hawise said in a brittle voice.

Ida exchanged a helpless glance with Isabelle, who gave a small shake of her head. It was widely known, but not spoken of, that Hawise's son was not the child of her second husband, William de Forz, but a cuckoo planted in the nest by John before she was sold off in marriage. Isabelle glanced at the boy, who had been born the same year as Mahelt. There was indeed a look of John about him and he appeared to possess some of John's traits too. Earlier she had seen him yanking the braid of a servant girl hard enough to make her cry . . . although perhaps it was caused by anger or unhappiness rather than a cruel whim. For the moment she reserved judgement. 'And your daughter?' she asked, changing the subject with polite diplomacy. 'How is Alais?'

Hawise gave a small shrug. 'Well enough, my lady,' she replied. 'She is too young to come to court and I am thankful. There is too much danger here – too many predators.'

'You are right,' Isabelle agreed. 'But perhaps you and Baldwin will visit us at Caversham. I can promise you safety there and a warm welcome.'

'That is kind of you, Countess.' Hawise looked as if she was about to cry. Abruptly she made her excuses and hurried off towards the privies.

'Poor woman.' Ida's soft hazel eyes filled with sympathy. 'There but for the grace of God and good husbands go all women.'

'Is Baldwin not a good husband to her?' Isabelle's gaze darted towards the three men. Baldwin was slapping William on the back and had obviously just said something very funny because they were laughing heartily.

Roger of Norfolk was doubled up. She concluded it must be a very rude joke – she would have to ask William later.

Ida gave a little sigh. 'I know your husband and Aumale have been close friends since their youth – and that in the fullness of time your eldest son will probably marry his daughter. Baldwin is a good man, of course he is, but that is among other men. It does not necessarily make him a good husband.'

Isabelle raised her brows. Ida of Norfolk was no intellectual, but she understood people well and with her contacts at court was often party to rumour and gossip. Not that she went about spreading what she heard. She was far too wise and compassionate, but her knowledge was bound to colour her judgement and sometimes she dropped heavy hints.

'The Holy Virgin knows,' Ida said, 'sometimes I want to sit my Roger on a barrel of pitch and light a fire under him, but when we retire at night, it is usually to the same chamber and we talk of things that have happened in our day. We face our difficulties together and he values my company as I enjoy his. I know from what I see that it must be the same for you and your lord. But Baldwin and Hawise . . .' She gave a small shrug. 'The fire in their hearth is cold, and I am sorry for them. I would hope that any match my children make is one to warm the heart.'

'Amen to that.' Isabelle turned as Mahelt skipped up to her, ruddy brown hair escaping from its blue ribbons, eyes as bright as stars. Having curtseyed politely to Ida, she tugged at Isabelle's sleeve.

'Mama, come and dance,' she implored. Laughing, Isabelle allowed herself to be pulled towards the turning circle of women.

'You too,' she said to Ida, who needed no urging to take Mahelt's other hand and join them.

141

Isabelle danced several times with her daughter, but then the steps changed and the carole became one involving men and women in two interlinking circles. Mahelt was thrilled to partner Hugh Bigod, Ida's eldest son, now a striking youth nineteen years old. Her face aglow, she let him wind her through the chain and back. Isabelle and Ida exchanged glances and said nothing, but both women smiled.

Isabelle was grasped by William de Braose and engulfed in the stench of his wine-sodden breath. His rich silk tunic was stained with drips of gravy and sticky crumbs of marchpane. The latter had congregated in his beard too. His breathing was harsh and his eyes bloodshot. He often sought William's company at court, calling him 'friend', 'neighbour', and slapping him on the back almost hard enough to drive William's shoulder blades through his sternum. He would want to share flagons too, which William tried to decline, saying to her in private that to serve King John one had to be either completely stupid or possess wits like a newly sharpened sword, preferably the latter. Befuddling them with wine was not recommended.

Isabelle forced herself to take de Braose's hand, turn and pass on. He stank of stale sweat as if he had not bathed in an age and his gaze was as shiny and blank as black glass. Relieved to be rid of him as the dance moved on, she realised she had gone from frying pan to fire as John took her hand.

'A long time since we danced together, Countess,' he said pleasantly. 'As I recall, you were a bride and still rosy from the pleasures of your marriage bed.'

'Indeed, sire, you have a good memory,' Isabelle replied demurely, as if the timbre of his voice did not raise the hair at her nape. He had been cat-light on his feet back then, and although he had put on flesh, he had lost none of his nimbleness, or his threatening sexual charisma. Isabelle knew how much he enjoyed discomforting the wives of his lords . . . and sometimes he did more than discomfort. Several men had bought royal favour by sending their wives or virgin daughters to John's bed. Isabelle did not believe he would dare with her these days, but even so, she was wary – and knowing his taste for innocent flesh, she had an eye to Mahelt too.

'Yes, and a long one,' he said with a vulpine flash of white teeth. 'Time passes quickly, does it not? Your eldest son was nought but a thought in your belly last time we danced, and now he's almost a man – and his brother too. You have most handsome sons, my lady.' If de Braose had hardly registered Isabelle as his partner, John's scrutiny was intense, probing to gauge reaction and internal response. She forced herself not to look in panic at her children and to maintain her smile.

'Thank you, sire, I am proud of them,' she murmured, 'as is my husband.'

'I am sure he is,' John said silkily. 'I hope that one day the sons I have of my own wife will be as robust.' He bowed and moved on.

The words had been spoken in a courtly fashion and Isabelle could not fault his behaviour; yet she felt disturbed, as if he had run his hands over her body, or kissed her with his tongue in her mouth.

Lying abed with William that night at their lodgings, she tried to make sense of all the disjointed snippets of infor-mation she had garnered at court. In some ways it was like being blindfold and putting one's hands into a midden pit, hoping to find a gold ring, yet knowing the more likely prize was a turd.

She glanced through a gap in the bed curtains towards their sons who were sleeping curled like puppies on a rope-framed truckle bed. Mahelt and her sisters were in the small antechamber with her nurse and two of Isabelle's women. William's squires slept on straw pallets by the door. Innocence. She wanted to wrap them in her arms and protect them from all the hurts the world was going to inflict on them, knowing that as they grew, she must do the opposite and let them go. Suddenly her eyes were hot and she was sniffing on tears.

Beside her William turned over and set his arm around her waist. 'What's wrong?'

'Nothing . . .' She gave a self-deprecatory shake of her head. 'They are growing up so fast, that is all. I see the murk of the court and I want to shield them from anything of that ilk, but I know I can't. In truth, the more they learn, the better protected they will be, but I do not want them to lose their joy in life.'

'They won't.' William nuzzled her throat. 'Have I lost mine, or you yours? You can still be aware and keep yourself intact.'

Isabelle wiped her face on the side of her hand. 'Aware of how much?' she asked. 'I saw William de Braose tonight.'

William said nothing, but leaned across her to snuff the candles and draw the hangings close around their bed. She would have preferred to see his expression and knew he had probably quenched the light so that she couldn't.

'Prince Arthur has been missing for eight months and John has said not a word as to his whereabouts. He's dead, isn't he?"

She felt him shrug. 'I would imagine so,' he said neutrally, 'otherwise John would have produced him by now.'

Isabelle laid her hand across his flat belly and played with the stripe of hair running from his navel into his groin. 'So if he is dead, and it happened in the Tower of Rouen . . .'

'It is pointless to speculate. Whatever has happened is in the past. You cannot change it.'

'No, but the fact of his disappearance is going to change our future, isn't it? It's happening already. The French have the excuse they need to overrun John's domains.'

'As long as Gaillard and Arques hold out, we have a foothold and we can negotiate with Philip.'

She tugged lightly on the crisp curls and her breath grew shallow. 'When you say "we" do you mean everyone in general, or just us?'

There was a long silence. She felt his hand on her arm and then her breast, his palm and fingers hard from wielding sword and gripping rein and shield strap, but infinitely gentle too. 'Therein lies the dilemma,' he murmured. 'What do we do? We have danced with John tonight, but if we are to keep our Norman lands intact, we must dance with King Philip too.'

'We need to be very careful.'

'I agree,' he said, 'very careful indeed. John might yet prevail and regain what he has lost. But if it comes to the crux, I would rather bargain with King Philip than lose Longueville, Orbec and Bienfait.'

'We have much to lose on this side of the Narrow Sea too,' she cautioned.

'Oh yes, it will be a fine balancing act and not one to undertake unless there is no other way.'

'Yes,' she said dubiously.

'Do you have faith in me to keep my balance?'

'I do . . . but the path has never been as narrow before and I'm not going to look down.'

145

'We won't fall.' He guided her hand lower and kissed her, and Isabelle lost herself in the pleasure of love-making because it was easier for the moment to feel than to think.

14

Caversham, Berkshire, March 1204

Isabelle was again with child and feeling decidedly peaky. Not even her rose-coloured gown could bring colour to her face. Spring water sweetened with honey and ginger was keeping the worst of the nausea at bay, but she was still lethargic, sleepy and sick.

Ida of Norfolk was full of sympathy. 'I know how it is,' she said. 'I am too old to quicken now, thank the saints. I haven't had a flux in two years.'

Isabelle grimaced. Her own child-bearing years were far from over, unless William failed, which, as matters in their bedchamber stood, seemed unlikely. The notion of producing sixteen offspring like Maude de Braose was not one she wished to contemplate, but this new pregnancy meant she was halfway there. There were supposed to be potions one could take to avoid conception and various preventative methods which could be employed, but they were unreliable and they all carried the burden of sin.

'When will the child be born?'

'The autumn,' she murmured, placing her hand on her belly.

'Ah,' said Ida with a knowing smile. 'Men fight all

campaigning season, then come home and beget children.' She glanced towards her husband, who was talking animatedly to William. An armourer had stopped by Caversham with some sword blades from Cologne and William, Roger and the knights of the mesnie were poring over them with much argument and discussion, as were their sons. Will and Richard wore hungry, wistful expressions on their faces, and Hugh was testing the blades with the skill of a young man well into his training. Ida laughed and shook her head. 'You wouldn't think that a hammered piece of iron could keep so many males in thrall for so long. Next thing they will be off to the tiltyard, practising and showing off.'

'Not with those,' Isabelle said. 'They need hilts fixing.'

'No, but you wait. They'll be sending for the weapons chests and reliving their days as young knights on the tourney circuit.'

Ida was proven right and before long there was a full-blown weapons practice being conducted on the sward between manor and river. The women donned their fur-lined cloaks and, armed with hot spiced wine, went down to watch. Roger and William were due to join the court at Kenilworth in three days' time. This leave of absence was by way of arranging a betrothal between Mahelt and Norfolk's heir, Hugh. The ceremony, conducted by William's chaplain Nicolas, had been touching and poignant. Even if it was a business matter, it was one cemented out of genuine friendship as well as the need for alliance. Mahelt was besotted with Hugh. At nineteen and almost grown, he was less enamoured of his nine-year-old wife-to-be, but time would likely remedy that.

'I hear you have made another betrothal too,' Ida murmured casually as she sipped her wine and stroked the squirrel-fur collar of her cloak. 'Your heir to the daughter of Baldwin de Béthune.'

Isabelle watched Will parry an attack from Richard. 'It has long been agreed,' she said, 'but now the King has given his consent and the contract has been drawn up.'

'John said nothing about his interests in the matter?' Ida asked curiously.

'His interests?'

'You must know that Hawise's son is reputed to be of his siring.'

'What has that got to do with betrothing Will to Alais?'

Ida shrugged. 'Probably nothing, given his agreement. Lay what you want at his door, John always does right by his bastards. I just wondered if he objected to the boy losing some of his inheritance because of his sister's marriage portion?'

'Not that I know of,' Isabelle said, 'but he could hardly declare his interest in the boy without losing him the de Forz estates, since de Forz is supposed to be his father.'

'It's worth keeping your eyes open . . . just in case.'

'Yes, I will,' Isabelle said thoughtfully and regarded Ida of Norfolk with strengthened respect. She was like a contented cat. Her paws were soft but only because her claws were sheathed.

Ida touched Isabelle's sleeve. 'A messenger.'

Isabelle turned and watched the man hastening across the grass towards them. He had but recently dismounted from his horse for he moved with a stiff, bow-legged gait and his cloak and boots were liberally mud-spattered.

Bowing to the women but not stopping, he hurried down to the men and sought out William and Roger, who were laughing as they sparred like a pair of squires. The man bowed, and whatever he said as he straightened up caused William's face to set into the blank mask that Isabelle knew and dreaded.

149

'Trouble,' said Ida, starting towards the men. Feeling queasy, Isabelle followed.

'Château Gaillard has fallen to King Philip,' William told them, shaking his head in frustration and disbelief. 'I'm summoned back to court immediately.'

'But Gaillard . . .' Isabelle bit the words off unspoken. Château Gaillard had been King Richard's pride. Built on an island in the Seine to guard his borders from the French, it had been both a strategic fortress and a symbol of Angevin virility. Richard had been wont to boast that Philip would never take Gaillard, even with twenty thousand men. He had called it his 'Saucy Castle' and reckoned it impregnable.

'Philip's commander sent his men up through the latrine shaft,' William said. 'I'd have done the same in his position if I'd thought of it. What's a smear of shit against the greatest castle on the Seine?'

'You know what this means,' Roger said gloomily. 'Now the French will strike at Rouen.'

William tossed his practice sword to his squire. 'Best fetch the real thing from the armoury, lad,' he said.

William tasted the wine that King Philip's attendant had poured for him. Smooth and rich with an almost peppery taste at its heart, it was better than anything his own cellars had to offer. John had sent him to the French court at Bec, together with the Earl of Leicester, the Bishops of Ely and Norwich and Hubert Walter, to try to negotiate an honourable peace – thus far with little success. They were staying in the Benedictine abbey and had taken over the guest house for the meeting.

Philip of France was close to forty years old, a plain-looking, slender man with the eyes and mind of a fox and the cautious air of one sniffing the air at a den entrance.

He had always been jealous and afraid of his vibrant Plantagenet neighbours and now he had John cornered, he was thoroughly enjoying himself.

William and Robert of Leicester had striven without success to bring him to agree to a treaty; Philip had listened courteously but had thus far declined. Hubert Walter, who did not have lands to safeguard in Normandy, was less disposed to be conciliatory than William and Leicester and was saying little, except to emphasise that, despite his losses, John was still strong enough to cause trouble.

Philip stroked his beard in contemplation of the arguments laid before him. 'Show me Prince Arthur and I will consider negotiating a treaty,' he said in a mild, reasonable voice. 'Without him, there can be no way forward except through war. I hear disquieting rumours about his disappearance, but no one has the courage to come forward and say what we all know. If I did have proof there would be no safe place on this earth for your King.' He made a lofty gesture. 'If not Arthur then give me his sister. Fetch the girl out of her nunnery and let her hold Anjou and Brittany. Let John do that and I might be willing to talk. Otherwise, by my faith, I will destroy him and take apart his towns stick by stick and stone by stone.' He curled one hand towards himself and studied his fingernails. 'Those are my final words on the matter, my lords. Let my cousin of England deal with them as he may.'

They were bowing from King Philip's presence when William noticed a knight waiting amongst the hangers-on outside. The last he had seen of this particular Poitevan was a year ago at the Tower of Rouen when he had disappeared about the same time as Prince Arthur. It was disturbing to find him now in the French camp. The knight met William's stare, then avoided it and, turning on his heel, walked rapidly away.

It was near midnight and the two Bishops and the Archbishop had retired to bed. However, King Philip was keeping late hours and William and the elderly Earl of Leicester were keeping them with him. The peppery wine had been replaced with one that was slightly effervescent and Philip's cook had provided strips of toasted bread with a sanglier terrine. Attendants moved unobtrusively around the royal bedchamber, trimming the lamps, replacing candles as they burned out, replenishing flagons and platters.

Philip was wearing a bedrobe of fur-trimmed embroidered silk over hose and shirt. Luxury abounded, but it existed to boost Philip's status rather than to please his senses, which he had never allowed to rule him in any form. 'I have no quarrel with you, my lords,' he said. He had an open look on his face that might or might not have been genuine: it was difficult to tell. 'You are men of honour and worth. Should you choose to give me your homage, I will not turn you away.'

'Sire, my oath of allegiance is to King John,' William replied.

'As is mine,' Leicester said in a rusty voice. Excusing himself, he coughed and spat phlegm into the floor rushes. His health was failing and the damp spring was playing havoc with his lungs.

'And I respect your loyalty, my lords,' Philip said, 'but think upon the kind of man you are sworn to follow.' He rubbed his palms together. 'At least none of my nephews has disappeared without trace.'

Leicester eyed him darkly. 'If you have proof involving John in Arthur's disappearance then show it to us.'

Philip snorted. 'John was at Rouen when Arthur vanished. If he is not the commander of his own castle and what goes on there, then tell me: who is?'

'Sire, sometimes men act of their own accord and for their own motives,' William said sharply.

Philip took several fastidious sips of the effervescent wine. A sleek gazehound that had been dozing by the hearth padded over to him to have its ears fondled. 'But a king has ultimate authority, my lord Marshal.' He paused for a moment to fuss over the dog, then looked at his visitors through calculating, half-closed lids. 'When Normandy falls, and make no mistake it will, any baron desiring to retain his lands there will do me liege homage for them.'

William exchanged glances with Leicester. Swearing liege homage would oblige them to fight for Philip should he summon them, and that might involve opposing John. It also meant changing allegiance for their Norman lands and holding them of Philip. 'Sire, that is impossible.' William shook his head at the enormity of what they were being asked to do. 'It would be an act of treason against our first-sworn lord.'

Philip opened his hands. 'I know you are both loyal to your King. You have served the Angevins to the best of your abilities, but we are men of the world. We have our own interests to serve too.' He lifted a delicately cynical brow. 'Indeed, neither of you would be standing here without that element of self-interest, would you? I say, why should you lose your lands because of your King's folly and sinfulness? It is not your fault Normandy is almost lost. You have fought well and done your best in difficult circumstances.'

William drew breath to speak, but Philip held up his index finger to forestall him. 'I am not unsympathetic to your dilemma and I will give you time to think on the matter, my lords. For a consideration – shall we say five hundred marks? – I will grant you a year's respite to make your decision. During that time you will hand over your castles to me and I will garrison them with my troops. Should you do me homage within the year, or should your King produce Arthur and come to terms with me, I will grant you leave to restore those castles to your authority. If not, then without your liege homage, your lands and castles are forfeit.'

'Those are harsh terms, sire,' Leicester said heavily.

'They are the only terms, my lord, and could be harsher still. I'm sure you'll find them acceptable if you think on them.'

The two Earls finished their wine and made to take their leave. On his way to the door, William paused to address Philip, speaking boldly because they had known each other for a long time. 'Sire, I wonder why traitors whom you would have executed at one time are now allowed to flourish under your protection.'

For a moment William thought Philip was going to play the aloof, dignified monarch and dismiss him out of hand, but then the King of France shrugged, and petted the dog. 'It is a natural thing, Marshal,' he said, a fastidious curl to his lip. 'Such men are like rags. One uses them as arse wipes and when one is finished, throws them down the latrine to be rid of them.'

William swallowed. Feeling unclean, his skin crawling, he bowed from the room. Leicester eyed him askance. 'What was all that about?'

William shook his head. 'Nothing,' he said, tight-lipped. After all, rumour and gut instinct were not proof. Philip's own mind might have been on Norman castellans such as Robert FitzWalter and Saher de Quincy, who had turned traitor to John and yielded up the towns they were

154

supposed to be guarding – half the reason for the fall of Gaillard. He was dancing very close to that line himself tonight and it made him feel unclean. 'Nothing you want to share, you mean,' Leicester growled. 'Half the business of the court is conducted under cover of darkness and in the shadows. Time was when honest men could meet in broad daylight and have their say.' He adjusted his fur-collared cloak like a cat grooming ruffled fur. 'Are you prepared to do liege homage to France for your Norman estates?'

William sighed and pinched the bridge of his nose. 'I don't know,' he said. 'We have a little leeway to think on it.'

'And by agreeing to think on it, we allow French garrisons into our castles and pay five hundred marks for the privilege.' Leicester's expression was grim.

'What's the alternative? Philip has us in a cleft stick and John on the tines of the Devil's pitchfork.'

Leicester heaved a weary sigh. 'I am near the end of my days and glad of it,' he said. 'At least I will not live to see the loss of Normandy. It's going to take a miracle, you know, and I doubt that God has any in his pocket for John.'

'I know,' William said with resignation.

Leicester looked obliquely at William. 'The Bishops will disapprove of our private negotiations.'

'It is for us to decide what happens to our lands, not them,' William said irritably.

When he entered his chamber, a visitor, who had been seated on a stool waiting, sprang to his feet and strode to greet him with arms open wide. After a startled moment, William's expression lit with joy and he opened his own and clasped them hard around his youngest brother, Ancel.

'Christ, how many years has it been? How many years!' Ancel thumped William's spine with a clenched fist, tears brimming in his eyes.

'Too many. God's bones, it's good to see you . . . even if you are a Frenchman these days!'

Ancel laughed and broke away, wiping his eyes. 'And whose fault is that, brother? You set my feet on that particular path.'

'I did, didn't I?' It was more than twenty years since Ancel had joined William's company of tourney knights: an eager youngster with few prospects. A summer spent jousting in France and Flanders had brought Ancel to the notice of their cousin, Rotrou, Count of Perche, who had offered him a position in his mesnie. Long ago, William thought wistfully, when the summers had stretched to the horizon and that horizon itself was a promise of pastures new.

'I thought you'd want to drink a measure of wine with your long-lost kin, so I had the squires purloin some from the King's table.' Ancel indicated the brimming flagon set on a coffer.

William nodded, resigning himself. To refuse would be churlish, and since he had been careful whilst drinking with Philip, he still had the capacity for a couple of measures.

The wine proved to be more of the peppery red from earlier, but still drinkable. William looked at his cup then raised it in a toast. 'To ships that pass in the night, may they pass more often,' he said to Ancel.

'Amen to that,' his brother responded in a heartfelt voice. 'And may they never meet on the battlefield.'

William fetched a campstool from the side of the room, unfolded it and sat down. 'We're getting older,' he sighed, 'but I doubt any wiser.'

'Hah, you said that years ago before you were wed. By your own lights, you must be ancient by now.'

William's laugh was wry. 'I feel it sometimes.'

Ancel grinned as if he didn't believe a word. 'From what your servants say, I'm soon to be an uncle again, so there's no failure in that area, is there?'

'That's Isabelle's doing.' William rubbed the back of his neck. 'She holds me to my duty. Apparently it's going to be another girl – something to do with her wanting to eat cheese all the time. I suppose it will make a balance – four of each.'

For the next hour, the brothers drank and exchanged news while the wine in the flagon diminished and the candles burned down to stubs. William sent a sleepy squire to fetch new ones.

'Will King Philip agree to a treaty, do you think?' Ancel asked.

'I doubt it,' William said. 'He has the whip in his hand and he's not going to put it down for the sake of pleading, not when the scent of victory is in his nostrils.'

Ancel looked sombre. 'You stand to lose a great deal. What are you going to do?'

'I . . .' William looked round as his squire returned with a bundle of wax candles tied with string. Jean D'Earley was with him, and his expression was sombre.

William's first thought was that Hubert Walter and the Bishops had learned about the clandestine meeting between King Philip, himself and Leicester and were already pursuing the matter as only churchmen could. 'What is it?' He rose to his feet.

Jean came to him and bowed. His gaze flickered to Ancel with surprise and then he bowed to him too. Ancel reciprocated. 'My lord, there is sad news.' He hesitated for a moment, obviously unsettled by what he was about

157

to say, then he took a deep breath. 'Queen Eleanor has died at Fontevrault. She passed away peacefully in her sleep last night . . .' He stopped speaking and looked anxiously at William.

Ancel crossed himself. 'God rest her soul,' he muttered.

William felt as if the words had formed a great frozen mass inside him and now pieces were breaking off and daggering through his veins. He'd known she was frail and of late had been ailing. It was not unexpected, but he was devastated.

He sat down heavily on the campstool and stared at the painted brickwork pattern on the wall. 'She took me into her household when I was a stripling hearth knight,' he said after a long pause, his throat aching. 'She stood by me; she raised me up. If I am Earl of Pembroke it is by her intervention. All that I have, I owe to her patronage.' One of the guttering candles went out in a wisp of black smoke. The squire made to replace it, but William stopped him. 'Let it be,' he said hoarsely. The grief was a physical pain at his core. 'I worshipped her when I was young,' he said in a cracking voice. 'And even when the glamour wore off, the shine remained and I loved her as a friend.' He watched another candle gutter and go out. Those that were left caught the glimmer of tears on his cheeks. 'The world will be a colder, darker place without her flame to light it.'

There were candles at Fontevrault, hundreds of them burning in the chapel for the soul of Eleanor, Duchess of Aquitaine, former Queen of England and France. William lit a single one of his own to her memory, and gave alms that it should be kept alight and replaced each time that it burned down to the wick. The frozen lump at his core had dissolved in the days since the news of her death had reached him, but it would be a long time before the melt-water ceased to chill his blood. Spring was here and, for the first time in his life, it was a spring that Eleanor's eyes would not also see.

Her effigy had yet to be carved, but the Abbess told him Eleanor had requested to be portrayed reading a book. The nun's eyes sparkled with humour. 'She told us she needed something to do to pass the waiting time until Judgement Day. She said, "Let people decide for themselves the kind of book it is. Those who knew me well will not need to be told."'

Through his grief, William found a smile. The words brought Eleanor vividly to life before his eyes and he felt a healing touch of comfort, as if she had reached out to him and gently pressed his arm in greeting and farewell.

On the ship back to England, with the news for John that Philip was not prepared to make peace unless John produced Arthur or his sister Eleanor, William watched the sea hiss against the galley's side and tried to ignore the slow churning of his stomach. He had made an agree-ment with Philip, had promised him five hundred marks and yielded him custody of Longueville and Orbec, on the understanding that he had a year's grace to choose what to do. A year's grace in which, if he was fortunate, a treaty might be agreed between the two Kings, and if he wasn't, he would have time to ponder his decision.

His nephew Jack joined him near the prow to watch the sun climb the sky. He had recently grown a beard and in profile so resembled his father, William's older brother, that William found it disquietingly like standing beside a ghost.

'You wanted to talk to me?' Jack said.

'Yes.' William folded his arms. 'About Ireland. I want

you to go there with authority as my seneschal and take command until I am able to return.'

Jack stared at him. 'You want me to go to Ireland?' he said on a rising note.

William nodded. 'You're my nephew – a Marshal by blood. You're experienced in battle and capable of bearing the responsibility. FitzRobert is doing his best, but I need someone there with more authority than he has. I wish I could afford the time, but with the situation in Normandy as it is, I cannot give Ireland the attention it requires.'

Jack looked nonplussed. 'I knew you were considering the matter but I thought . . . I thought you would ask Jean. I know he is . . .' He changed his mind about whatever he had been going to say, his expression turned studiedly bland. 'He is your nephew too, through marriage to my sister, and his children share your blood.'

William eyed the young man and wondered at the words beneath the words. 'I did consider asking Jean,' he said, 'but I decided you were better suited to the task. If you do not want to go . . .'

Jack cut him off, shaking his head, smiling – albeit a touch bleakly and thus looking even more like his father. 'No,' he said. 'I will be honoured to be your seneschal . . . and I won't let you down, I swear.'

15

Cilgerran, South Wales, November 1204

The weather was mild for mid-November, but it was wet. Fine drizzle off the Irish Sea had misted the coastline, moved inland and beaded everything in a hoar of droplets. Isabelle's Spanish mare was mizzle-grey and against her dappled neck the bridle bells gleamed like raindrops turned to silver, and chimed softly with an eerie, otherworldly sound.

Isabelle wore a heavy cloak of double-layered wool, and a hood of the same, pulled up over her wimple. Thus far, she was managing to remain moderately dry. She could have repaired to the baggage cart and travelled under cover, but from girlhood she had preferred to ride when possible. Will and Richard escorted her either side, attired beneath their cloaks in quilted gambesons of the kind worn by the serjeants, and useful protection against weather like this. She had left the other children at Pembroke, for they would have added too much to the size of the baggage train and she did not know what conditions to expect at the end of their journey. The baby, Eve, was almost three months old and Isabelle had handed her over to a wet nurse, thus leaving herself free to travel.

Glancing at her eldest son, she felt a twinge of poignant amusement as she saw his posture and the way his gaze sought ahead through the rain. She could tell he was pretending to be a knight, one hand at his hip, the other guiding the horse. He was testing his wings, preparing to leave the nest. His father had been considering various kin and allies with a view to fostering Will to knighthood once he reached fifteen years old. William of Salisbury had offered, although Isabelle was not certain that she wanted the King's half-brother caring for her eldest son, even if her husband thought it a good idea. Baldwin de Béthune was another candidate, and the one that Isabelle preferred, especially as Will was to marry his daughter. It would be useful for him to train to knighthood in Baldwin's entourage and become familiar with his future bride. Richard was only eighteen months behind Will. They would have to find somewhere to place him as well. She thought tuition at Framlingham might suit, under Roger of Norfolk.

Suddenly Will sat erect in the saddle and pointed, his voice rising in pitch. 'There it is,' he cried. 'There's Cilgerran!'

Squinting hard, Isabelle made out a ditch and ring-works through the misty rain. She could see neither tents nor pavilions outside the fortifications so assumed the men were inside the protection of the palisade. Outriders were cantering out to meet them, dark ghostly shapes at first, becoming more distinct as they drew closer.

William's herald, Henry Norreis, greeted Isabelle with his customary ebullience and escorted her and the boys up the steep slope of the earthwork defences and through the castle gates. Guards paced the palisade wall walk, spears at the ready and attitude alert. As she had suspected, the bailey was full of pitched tents. Cooking fires steamed in the soft

162

drizzle, giving off a pungent aroma of woodsmoke and onion pottage and soldiers were busy around them, mending equipment, eating, arming or disarming, depending on their state of duty. Her gaze went beyond a blacksmith in a covered forge busily turning out horseshoes and settled on William as he hurried down from one of the palisade walks to greet her. He was wearing his old padded tunic, but not his hauberk. His hood was down, his hair was wet and wind-blown and he looked eager and refreshed. A pang went through her, compounded of strong affection, a glimmer of lust and more than a touch of exasperation. Her husband was always invigorated by practical military projects. She sometimes worried that he was growing too old for such pursuits, but he had just run down the stairs as easily as any of his young knights and his eyes were alight with pleasure as he strode to greet her.

He helped her down from the horse himself and kissed her with enthusiasm. His lips were cold, but the creases of pleasure around his eyes made her glow. 'Welcome to Cilgerran, my lady!' He swept her a playful bow, making her laugh. 'I am afraid there is not much to offer in the way of comfort at the moment, but that can soon be remedied.' He turned to his sons, rested his hand on the hilt of his sword and took a backstep. 'Holy God, I thought you were both men-at-arms!'

Will flushed with pleasure and Richard gave a bright grin.

'You protected your mother well on the journey, hmm?'

'Yes, sir,' they said in unison, and William tousled their heads.

'Come,' he said. 'Come and look at what we've gained.'

Gathering her skirts, Isabelle followed him up to the gate-house tower and stood beside him and their sons as he pointed out the pertinent defensive features and landmarks.

Both boys nodded seriously as they absorbed the lesson and occasionally joined in. Isabelle could see them imagining themselves as commanders in years to come.

'You had no trouble from the Welsh?' she murmured.

William gave a wolfish smile. 'We came upon them so fast that the garrison hadn't even time to arm up before we were through the gate. The only victim was an old packhorse that foundered under its load.' He turned to address his sons. 'Cilgerran was once part of the de Clare lands belonging to your mother's kin, but it has been more than seventy years in Welsh hands. Now it belongs to de Clare again . . . and to Marshal.'

Will's eyes were agleam as he folded his hands around his belt. William chuckled. 'I do believe he has inherited your sense of possession, my love.'

'*My* sense of possession?' Isabelle said indignantly. 'What about yours?'

William laughed buoyantly and squeezed her waist.

In the lord's chamber on the upper floor of the guard tower, Isabelle drew an antlerwork comb through her hair. She had dismissed her maid; the hour was late, but she and William were using the lees of the day to snatch some privacy before slumber.

'So,' she murmured as she worked. 'Now that the King has given you Cilgerran, do you think he hopes you will forget Longueville and Orbec?'

William shrugged. 'It might be part of his reasoning, but we were in agreement that with Rhys ap Gruffydd dead and his kinsmen occupied with feuding over who gets what, it was the perfect opportunity to tackle them for Cilgerran.' He gave her a perceptive look. 'We'll keep Longueville for our sons, I promise you that – even if I have to do homage to King Philip for them.'

'It will be dangerous.'

He came to her, took the comb, and began to draw it through her hair. 'Yes, it will, but the alternative is losing them. I hope I know John's nature well enough to deal with it.' His tone was easy and the movement of his hands measured and gentle. She didn't think it was artifice aimed at placating her, or that he was comforting himself, but rather that he had made his decision and was prepared to deal with whatever consequences arose.

'Speaking of our sons,' she said, 'we need to find good foster homes to send them for squiring. Will is more than ready, and Richard not far behind.'

He combed and smoothed with the flat of his palm. 'So often I have seen women striving to hold on to their children and refusing to cut the cord that binds them to the womb, but you have the foresight to let them go.'

Isabelle drew away and faced him. 'You dress me in false robes,' she said. 'I want to hold on to mine too – desperately. My heart is in my mouth every time there is fever or sickness in the castle. I fear for my sons when they go to train with the men or ride their ponies at the tilt, or venture out hunting with three serjeants and a tent. I don't show that fear to them because it would fetter their growth into manhood, but I feel it all the same. While I have the little ones to nurture in my arms, it is not so bad . . . and perhaps when I am the mother of grown men, it will ease a little too, but to be the mother of boys growing into manhood . . . Ah' – she threw up her hands – 'pay me no heed. This season of the year makes me maudlin with all its grey.'

William gently turned her round and continued his combing. 'You have the wisdom to let them go,' he said, 'and that is worth its weight in gold. I fear for them too, but even less can a man show it . . . and my daughters.

165

It will be the hardest thing I have ever had to do, to see Mahelt go in marriage, even though I have done my best for her.' He worked in silence for a moment, and then added quietly, 'I confess though, that I have ever loved this season.'

'You have?' Isabelle gave a small, incredulous laugh.

'Not for the cold and the chilblains and riding abroad in the wet, I can do without those, but it is a fine time to coddle oneself by the hearth with one's family – or linger abed.'

'So you say, but at the slightest opportunity you're off on campaign like a hound on a fresh scent.'

'Well, this one was short,' he said defensively. 'The Welsh were expecting me to be sitting by my hearth in November, so how else should I take them by surprise?'

'Eminently sensible,' she agreed, looking wry. 'And Leinster?'

'Jack will do what he can for now. I'll deal with the situation regarding Longueville, and then we'll go to Ireland – providing it's not in the winter season,' he added quickly.

'No,' she said, 'I wouldn't do that to you again . . . or myself come to that.' Taking the comb from him, she laid it on the coffer. 'Come to bed,' she said. 'It's late. Let all else wait until morning.'

He gave her a slumberous look. 'And being as it's November, we can linger there awhile.'

She smiled knowingly. 'If you want.'

16

Nottingham Castle, March 1205

The goldsmith knew his client and he knew how to sell. The rings he had brought for King John's delectation shone against a backcloth of padded dark-red silk. Inside an artful border consisting of rings of incised gold were cushioned others of more intricate detail: gimmels in the form of two clasped hands; circlets formed from numerous twists of gold wire; flowers of pearl and opal. At the centre of the display lay the most enticing examples of the goldsmith's skill: the rings set with gemstones that had travelled across distant empires, deserts and wide salt oceans to reach this destination. Indian rubies and sapphires, diamonds from the mines at Kulur, lapis and turquoise from the Persian interior: all scintillated like coloured raindrops upon their silken couch.

John lifted a particularly large and brilliant sapphire ring from the middle of the display and slipped it over the knuckle of his left middle finger. He held out his hand, studying the effect for a moment, before looking at William.

'You want my permission to do Philip homage for Longueville?' he said impassively.

William had steeled himself for this meeting and was prepared to receive short shrift. He was also prepared to persevere. 'Sire, if I do not, I will lose my lands in Normandy. I had a year's grace to decide what to do, and it is almost at an end. I have to act. Perhaps if I was able to secure King Philip's willingness to consider a truce between you and him . . . ?'

'Pigs will fly before that happens, Marshal,' John said brusquely. He showed the ring to his young Queen and asked her opinion. Ysabel made an admiring sound and slanted John a look compounded of desire for the rings and apprehension at what she would have to do before he would add one to her jewel casket. 'Is there one for me?'

'Greedy wench,' John retorted playfully and ran his hand over her buttocks. She suppressed a shiver, turning it into a laugh. She was learning, William thought, but not the right things.

'Even so, I am requesting your permission to go to France and at least speak with King Philip,' he said.

John narrowed his eyes. 'I have created you Earl of Pembroke, I have given you Cilgerran, and more grants and gifts than my scribes have parchment to list. Yet still you want more. I may begin to think you have more avarice than my wife . . . and she at least is pretty to look upon. When she kneels before me to ask my indulgence, I know I am going to receive something to my liking in return.'

Ysabel flushed and moved away from John, although her gaze flickered with telling trepidation towards his crotch.

William pretended not to see. 'Sire, I am grateful for all that you have given me, but it would be a great pity for my children not to retain their full patrimony for want of a few words.' He made sure to emphasise the end of the sentence, knowing John would understand the inflection. A 'few words' were what had given him his kingdom.

The young Queen had been offered a box of brooches by the goldsmith and was picking amongst them like a glutton trying to decide which sweetmeat to try first. With eyes fastened on her, John heaved an impatient sigh and waved his hand in brusque dismissal. 'Oh, go, do what you can to salvage your estates – within reason.'

William bowed, and silently thanked the young Queen's desire for gee-gaws and John's desire for his wife. 'I will need a letter of authority to show to King Philip.'

'Yes, yes,' John said irritably. 'I'll see to it.'

As William bowed from the room, John approached Ysabel. 'They are all as insatiable as starving wolves ringing a stag,' he said, 'even the sainted William Marshal, who tries to pretend he is above all that.' He ran his hand over the taut curve of her buttocks again, imagining his fingerprints standing out as red brands upon her firm, white flesh.

Ysabel tried to pull away, but he drew her tight against him and leaned to bite her earlobe. 'He was one of my brother Richard's most trusted knights and companions. My mother loved him, God rest her soul. He is of the same ilk as Richard was, you see, a *prudhomme*, a man of high courage and heroic deeds. Such men are . . .' His mouth contorted as if filled with verjuice. 'Let us say that while he is useful to me, I keep him, but his self-righteousness makes me sick.' He dismissed the hovering goldsmith with a flick of his fingers. Taking a large brooch set with amethysts and pearls, he pinned it at her bosom, then set his hands to her shoulders and pushed her to her knees.

* * *

169

Isabelle watched her youngest daughter, Eve, crawl across to the bench and with determination reach up, grasp the edge and pull herself to a standing position. The infant showed every sign of having inherited her father's agility and coordination. The instant the swaddling bands had been removed at three months old, she had commenced exercising her limbs like a soldier warming up on the practice field. Within days she had been rolling over; by five months she was sitting up, and now at eight months, could crawl on all fours almost as fast as a cat could walk. Eve looked round at her mother and laughed at her own cleverness, showing four small white teeth. She bounced up and down, flexing and straightening her little knees, and Isabelle laughed too at her antics.

A squire put his head round the solar door. 'My lady, the Earl's barge is mooring up at the wharf,' he announced.

The words shot through Isabelle like a lightning bolt. The waiting had been fraught and interminable. She had tried not to think, because that way lay worry and sleepless nights, the latter uncomforted by the emptiness on the other side of the bed. Caversham had been swept from top to bottom, the servants chivvied to within an inch of their lives. She had completed an altar cloth that had been waiting her needle for months, and dictated so many letters, writs and charters that her clerk had had to send to London for more parchment.

Scooping Eve into her arms, Isabelle sped from the manor down to the riverside. A cool April breeze ruffled the water. On the far bank a pair of swans and four new cygnets paddled and dabbled amid the reeds. William was stepping from their barge on to the jetty. He was wearing his heavy, fur-lined cloak as a protection against the cold wind off the river and talking to Jean D'Earley and Jordan de Saqueville as they too left the barge. Isabelle searched

170

her husband's face, but could read nothing particular into it. His expression was quiescent. He was thinner though, and lacking the vigour and ebullience he had possessed at Cilgerran.

Seeing her waiting, he strode to her side, kissed her in greeting and, taking the baby in his arms, pressed his lips to her cheek, making her squeal with laughter. She saw him drink in the sight of Caversham as if he was dying of thirst, and her trepidation increased. Forcing herself not to start pestering him, sensing his current need, she gave him space to greet the other children and involve himself in their chatter whilst servants brought washing water and food.

Mahelt wanted to show him her new acquisition. Her pet linnet had died shortly before William left for France, instigating a week of deep grief. She had buried it in the herb bed, scattered the tiny grave with rose petals and said prayers for its soul even though the priests said that birds didn't have them. Secretly she thought they might. In the linnet's stead she now had a three-legged dog. Father Walter had discovered him wandering the outbuildings, starving and flea-ridden. Having a soft spot for animals and made curious by the dog's missing limb, he had brought him to the bower. The sight of the emaciated, scabby brown and white mongrel had hit Mahelt straight in the raw, aching space left by the death of her linnet and that was that. 'Tripes' as Father Walter had named him, saying that it was the Latin for 'three-legged', had rapidly become a staunch member of the household. Since his name was also associated with offal, everyone felt it was entirely suited.

Once bathed and rid of the worst of his fleas, Tripes slept on Mahelt's bed and followed her everywhere, adoration shining out of his limpid brown eyes. Fed on the choicest tid-bits and scraps, his ribs no longer stared through his coat, which was developing a sheen like sun on snow.

William eyed the dog dubiously while it wagged its tail at him like a branch in a high wind, then licked his fingers. 'How does it piss?' he asked with a straight face.

Mahelt reddened. 'He squats,' she said primly.

William's lips twitched.

'He killed a rat yesterday. He's better than the kennel-keeper's terriers.' Her voice filled with protective challenge.

'Sweetheart, I am sure he is, in the same way that I could always defeat certain knights on the tourney field with one hand tied behind my back.'

Mahelt gave him a severe look and he laughed and tugged one of her ruddy brown braids. 'Ah,' he said, 'it's good to be home.'

'So,' said Isabelle when she could contain her impatience no longer, 'are you going to tell me what happened, or is it so bad that you have buried it beyond recall?'

Sybire, now nearly four, sat on his knee, her head resting in the crook of his arm. Eve was using his other knee to cling to and stand up. The rest of their offspring were gathered in close proximity, waiting their opportunity for his attention. Tripes was lying across his feet.

'Why are you smiling?' Isabelle asked as he responded to her with a tired but eloquent grin.

'I was thinking that the Queen's first question to John in this situation would be: "What have you brought for me?" You are the same, but instead of rifling my baggage for silks and jewels, you demand information.'

She folded her arms. 'You tread dangerous ground saying that,' she warned. 'I might take offence, and then you would have to placate me with a rope of pearls worth at least fifty marks.'

'Point taken. Next time I will bring you information *and* jewels.' His expression sobered. 'King Philip is still refusing to treat with John unless John produces Arthur, and that is never going to happen.' He gave her a reflective look. 'He was willing to accept my homage for our Norman lands though, so at least some good has come of it.'

Knowing him well, Isabelle sensed the tension beneath the deceptively calm surface. 'Yes,' she said, 'but there is more, isn't there?'

A squire presented a platter of hot, crisp wafers dusted with cinnamon and grated loaf sugar. 'It makes less appetising hearing than this food.' He took a wafer and broke it to give half to Sybire. 'I had to do liege homage to Philip for the lands, and John is not best pleased . . . Careful, sweeting, it's hot.'

Isabelle looked at him in dismay. 'You had his written permission though.' She was not reassured by William's hearty appetite as he demolished his half of the wafer and reached for another. Personal troubles seldom put him off his food. Her stomach would be stuck to her spine with anxiety and he would be devouring a piled trencher with relish.

'Yes, but he chooses to believe he did not give it and there are always enemies at court willing to shake the tree in the hopes of seeing us fall.'

'Then what does he say he gave you?' Isabelle demanded. 'You have his written permission as proof!'

William swallowed and reached for a third wafer. 'John seems to think it was permission to do Philip homage for Longueville and give him the required military service owed by the Norman lands.'

'But liege homage is different?'

'It means that if John takes an army across the sea to war against Philip, I cannot be a part of it because I am Philip's vassal – I owe him my absolute loyalty on that side of the sea.'

Isabelle exclaimed in dismay.

'What was I supposed to do?' he snapped. 'Let it all go? It's like dancing on swords. You stay nimble and you pray.' He lifted Sybire off his lap, detached Eve from his leg and went to gaze out of the open shutters on the late spring afternoon. 'I haven't sullied my honour with regard to either Philip or John, no matter what John says.'

The rise and fall of his shoulders and his defensive tone of voice told Isabelle that despite his words, he felt he had pruned his honour close to the bone. John was one to hold grudges. It worried her that sometimes prayer and nimble feet were not enough.

17

Portsmouth, June 1205

The sky was bereft of cloud and the sun would have been unbearably hot without the refreshing breeze blowing off the sea. Coins of light dazzled away to the horizon and the deep blue water was festooned with galleys, nefs and cogs bobbing at anchor offshore. Other shallow-draughted vessels were drawn up on the shingle and soldiers toiled up and down laden with weapons and military supplies. Sailmakers laboured over swathes of canvas with their needles and shipwrights were manufacturing and mending industriously. The smell of hot pitch from newly caulked seams wafted across the shore and the tapping of hammers and the chunk-chunk of adzes on wood were constant points of sound against the roar and wash of the sea.

John was preparing an expedition to Poitou from which he intended to launch an offensive against Philip of France and had summoned his vassals to assemble at Portsmouth. Reclining on a pile of furs at the top of the beach with his young household knights, he dined on cold roast capon and watched the work go forward, a restless, petulant expression on his face, which was turned frequently in William's direction. The latter was sitting nearby with

Baldwin de Béthune, not directly with the royal party but close enough to be an offshoot. William's stomach was sour but the feeling was not caused by the notion of impending seasickness. Although he had obeyed the summons to Portsmouth, he knew he couldn't set foot on any ship heading to make war on Philip of France.

Halfway down his fourth cup, John rose to his feet and plodded across the shingle to William, his hearth knights in tow like hunting dogs following the lead hound.

William stood up and bowed.

John took up a belligerent stance. 'Marshal,' he said, 'I am still wondering why you allied with Philip of France behind my back. It seems to me entirely dishonourable, yet you always make a show of how honourable you are.' His tone was light, sarcastic and dangerous.

William felt the hungry stares of the hearth knights as they scented blood. John's malice was tangible. 'Sire, I have made no alliances behind your back. You gave me permission to treat with King Philip. What I did was by your leave.'

'By Christ, it was not!' The great vein at the side of John's neck bulged with his fury. 'I did not give you permission to swear liege homage to him. You will accompany me to Poitou, Marshal, and when I order you to take up arms against the King of France, you will do so.'

In the heat of the day, William felt the sweat in the creases of his palms and the hard pulse of blood in his wrists. 'Sire, I cannot do that. I would be breaking my oath to King Philip if I took up arms against him.'

John flung round to his bachelors. 'I call on all of you to witness that here, before us all, William Marshal condemns himself out of his own mouth,' he snarled. 'I call him traitor!'

Sensing the development of an interesting situation,

176

other lords gathered around the altercation. Several, like William, had no intention of going to Poitou – not because they had sworn oaths to King Philip, but because it was service abroad and they did not see why they should be called upon to fight in a war in which they had no vested interest.

Aware that they were his only chance, William drew breath and raised his voice. 'My lords, look at me! Today I am an example and mirror for all of you. What happens to me now will be your fate on the morrow. I had permission to seek an understanding with King Philip concerning my Norman lands. I have a fair copy in the King's own words, yet he chastises me and says that he did not give it.'

'God's sweet bleeding hands, I will not stand for this!' Turning his back on William, John withdrew a short distance to confer with his knights. A hothead named John de Bassingbourn detached himself from the group and marched up to William. 'It's a well-known fact that any man who fails his lord as you have done loses his right to hold land of him,' he hissed into William's face, the words spoken so close and with such contempt that he sprayed William with spittle.

Muttering under his breath, Baldwin de Béthune shouldered his way forward and seized de Bassingbourn by a fistful of his tunic. 'Hold your tongue!' he commanded. 'It is not for the likes of you to judge a knight of the Marshal's stature.' He spread his free arm to encompass the battle-camp where more soldiers had stopped work to stare at the squabble. 'Amongst all these men, there is no one capable of proving with his body that the Earl Marshal has failed his lord. Would you challenge a man twice your worth who is here because of his loyalty, not his treachery?' He released de Bassingbourn with a shove, his voice filled with revulsion. 'Do not presume to stand in judgement of a man whose peer you will never be.'

William grasped the top of his scabbard with his left hand and stared at de Bassingbourn without blinking, aware that half of the battle lay in attitude. Down the years, his reputation had become legendary, and if he had to trade on it, he would. He was the only man ever to have unhorsed King Richard and it was the kind of detail men remembered with respect and fear. De Bassingbourn dropped his stare and turned away, shamed and angry, but too much aware of the value of his own life to challenge William to a trial of arms. John said nothing, for there was nothing to say; the wind had been snatched from his sails and it was obvious he wasn't going to win the argument. Flinging round on his heel, he crunched from the beach, his knights following in his wake in small avalanches of shingle. From a safe distance, many cast threatening glares over their shoulders.

Baldwin wiped his brow and gave a shaken laugh in which there was no humour. 'My God, William, you like living dangerously, don't you?' he said and, stooping to the flagon they had been sharing, filled his cup with a trembling hand. 'I thought for a moment that de Bassingbourn was going to take you on.'

William lifted his hand off his sword hilt and breathed out hard. 'What else could I have done? John gave me permission. I have patent copies under his seal.'

Baldwin gave him a significant look. 'So you keep saying but I don't think he expected you to do full liege homage, and you knew that . . . Admit it to me at least.' He gulped a mouthful of wine and handed the cup across.

'Christ, Baldwin, I don't know what he expected,' William said. 'He was naive if he thought Philip would take less, or perhaps he didn't want to see at the time.'

Lowering the cup, he wiped his mouth on his cuff. 'I'm trapped in a dilemma, as is everyone who has lands in Normandy and England.' With sudden frustration he punched his arm towards the ships on the glittering swell and gave vent to his anger. 'Do you think this fleet is ever going to put to sea? You've heard the dissent in the tents and taverns. The only men who will go with the King are his hearth knights and mercenaries. The Archbishop doesn't want him to go: he's publicly admitted it; nor the justiciar. You know the trouble we suffered in England when Richard was on crusade. John has a stable full of bastards, but no legitimate heirs of his body. If he dies fighting in Poitou, we may yet see a French king on England's throne.' He cast Baldwin a challenging look. 'Will you take ship with him, my lord of Aumale? How many here will follow him when it comes to the crux?'

Baldwin sighed and rumpled his receding hair. 'I know and I agree with you, although I haven't confronted him like you have.' He grimaced at William. 'You've incurred serious disfavour. Best watch yourself.'

William forced a smile. 'Do you still want your daughter to marry my son?'

Baldwin made a derisive sound through pursed lips. 'Don't be an ass. You've weathered storms before; you'll survive this one. My daughter will marry the heir to Pembroke or no one.'

Isabelle loved picnicking outdoors on hot summer days. She hadn't discovered the delight until her marriage, and it was partly the memory of that first lazy July spent in dalliance with William that drew her to the pastime when a moment could be stolen from the cares of the world. Opportunities these days for idle recreation and privacy were rare. Even at sleepy Hamstead, William's birthplace and quietly rustic by the standards of their other holdings, the bustle of their household resembled a court. William had told her all those years ago they should enjoy their solitude while they could, that it would be like this, but she had been eighteen years old then, with no idea of the intensity to come.

Nevertheless, she refused to be defeated. Today she had overseen the packing of the baskets of food with stubborn determination. She had taken William by the arm and dragged him away from chamberlains, stewards and clerks, insisting that a few hours would make no difference to his burdens. He had acquiesced readily enough, indeed almost with relief, she thought. The children were accompanying them, and an entourage of knights, squires and nurses, but it was still pleasant to ride the horses along the meandering riverbank, and listen to the wind through the sedges and the plod of their horses' hooves on ground that had dried out after the rain of three days ago. Tripes scurried along the path fleet as a deer despite his three legs, nosing amongst dandelion and grass, being more circumspect of nettle.

As the sun beat down, William removed his cloak and she saw his shoulders relax. The set of his mouth softened. He began to look about and Isabelle watched him absorbing his surroundings as the tension within him uncoiled. The last month had been difficult. He was out of favour at court, but how far the King's displeasure would go and how long it would last remained to be seen. John had been livid to the point of white rage when most of his barons had followed William's lead at Portsmouth and refused to embark on the expedition to Poitou. The limited number who did agree to sail were scarcely enough to fill one ship and he had had to abandon his plans, almost weeping with rage and humiliation as he did so.

He had placed much of the blame at William's door and cold-shouldered him at court.

Ranulf of Chester had been out of favour recently too, for supposedly conspiring with the Welsh, although Ranulf swore he was innocent and had gladly given up property and hostages to prove his sincerity. The argument had blown over and Ranulf's credit had been restored, but John's mood towards his barons was volatile. It hadn't helped matters when Hubert Walter had died three weeks ago. His influence and authority had been both stabilising and far-reaching. He and William had not always seen eye to eye, but they had respected each other and been able to work together on most matters, compromising where necessary. Now a new archbishop would have to be chosen and a new working relationship established.

They stopped to eat where a stand of willows over-hung the river. The squires hobbled the horses a short distance away and then set about unpacking the cold roasted fowl, bread, cheese and smoked sausage. Tripes settled down by the food panniers, beads of moisture sparkling along his whiskers. Will, Richard and the sons of Jean D'Earley and Stephen D'Evereux took their bows and went off for a prowl in the woods.

'I doubt they'll catch anything,' William said with a smile.

'You don't know,' Isabelle defended her son. 'Will's a decent woodsman for all his youth. He can move as quietly as a deer when he chooses.'

William conceded the point with a wave of his hand. 'They still won't catch anything,' he said. 'Not with four of them.'

Isabelle looked at him sidelong. 'Will certainly caught one of the dairy maids the other day,' she said. 'My groom happened on them in the barn . . .'

181

William had been about to bite into a chunk of bread but her words stopped him. He lowered his food and began to grin.

'You won't be smiling so broadly if she gets with child,' Isabelle said irritably. 'Holy God, he has only just turned fifteen.'

He sobered. 'It had gone as far as that then?'

Isabelle shook her head. 'To be fair, no, but only because they were interrupted, I suspect. You need to speak to him, remind him about duty and responsibility.'

William absolved himself from a reply by eating the bread. When Isabelle continued to glare, he waved his hand. 'I know, all right. I'll have a word.'

'Sooner rather than later,' she said.

He nodded. 'Better have the girl spoken to as well. If she's inclined to go into barns with youths of fifteen she's asking for trouble.'

'Perhaps she thought to make a good exchange for what she was going to give,' Isabelle said shrewdly. 'He's your heir.'

William made a non-committal sound and resumed his eating, but there was a thoughtful look on his face.

They spent the rest of the afternoon in rare and pleasant dalliance. William removed his boots and hose and sat with his feet in the stream. Thus encouraged, Gilbert, Walter and his daughters did the same while Isabelle played with the baby. He taught Mahelt a new song he had heard at court: a rotrouenge celebrating the beauty of the summer season.

The youths returned from their 'hunt' with twigs and burrs in their tunics and a few bramble scratches. Will had bagged a rabbit: a descendant of some escapees from Hamstead's coney-garth where they were bred for meat and fur. William was impressed and murmured to his wife as he was putting his hose back on that their eldest son seemed thoroughly adept at coney-catching, thereby earning himself a sharp dig in the ribs.

As William prepared to boost Isabelle into the saddle for their journey home, he paused to pull her close and kiss her. The sunlight was honey-coloured, the shadows lengthening and populated by dances of midges. 'You knew I needed this,' he said. 'Thank you.'

Smiling, Isabelle reached up to tidy his hair. It was long over his ears and in need of cutting. 'I confess it was purely selfish,' she said. 'I wanted you to myself for a while.'

'Hardly that.' He gave an amused glance around.

'You know what I mean.'

He kissed her again. 'Yes,' he said. 'I do, and I promise not to be so neglectful in future.'

Isabelle set her foot in his cupped hand. 'Then you had better begin with your eldest son,' she said.

On the ride home, William dropped back from her side to ride with Will, gesturing a curious Richard to go and accompany his mother. Then he looked attentively at his heir as he had not done in a while. Will's skin had the sheen of adolescence, with a few blemishes here and there and the dark down of an embryo moustache feathering his upper lip. He was a handsome lad, fine-featured and lithe. William could understand what a dairy maid might see in him, and from the indications of his son's incipient manhood, the delights that Will might well find in a dairy maid.

The youth lifted his chin and looked at his father with wariness and a touch of defiance. William forced himself not to smile. The lad obviously knew what was coming and was prepared to receive a dressing down.

'I'm not going to lecture you – or not much,' William

183

said. 'If I did, it would go in one ear and straight out of the other. I could whip you, but I've never noticed that whipping a horse or beating a dog improves the beast in question. Besides, you're growing to manhood, and straying into barns with willing girls is part of that process.'

The youth's eyes widened and a look of surprise crossed his face. William controlled his amusement at Will's expression, knowing how tender pride could be at that age. Besides, what he had to say was serious. 'But growing to manhood means you're not there yet. When you are, you'll know that while straying into barns might be the most tempting thing in the world, it's not advisable. You'll learn to resist and to . . . keep your hands to yourself, shall we say. Sometimes a girl is only willing because you are the lord's son and she fears retribution if she doesn't agree.'

'She wasn't a virgin . . . she was willing,' Will protested.

'Then ask yourself what she wanted. The risk is not only to the girl.'

Will's complexion was fiery. 'Before you married, you must have . . . ?'

William chuckled. 'On numerous occasions, but not with a dairy maid, and not under the family roof. My own mother would have killed me. Of course on the tourney circuit and at court, it's a different matter, but you still have to be careful.'

Having cautioned Will and given him food for thought, he changed the subject and praised his son's hunting skills – skills that he himself did not have. It was a pleasant interlude and made William realise how little time of late he had spent with his heir. They were in danger of not knowing each other – a danger that ought to be rectified.

They arrived at Hamstead as the last rays of evening sunshine were dazzling on the Kennet like enormous golden bezants. William was dismounting in the courtyard, when his clerk Michael came out to them, carrying a packet in his hand, his usually bright expression sombre.

'From the King,' he said, which William knew already by the sight of the familiar seal dangling from a length of braid attached to the vellum. 'The messenger had elsewhere to go; he didn't stay.'

William slapped his palfrey's rump and saw the groom lead it off towards the stables. 'Read it,' he said tersely.

Michael broke the seal and unfolded the letter in a crackle of new vellum. The language was Latin and Michael translated it into French.

The King to his beloved and faithful William, Earl Marshal, greeting.

We command and summon you to deliver your eldest son to us that he may be raised to knighthood at our pleasure, and stand as surety for your good faith.

Witness ourself at Lambeth on the third day of August in the sixth year of our reign.

William compressed his lips. The endearment in the greeting meant nothing. He knew exactly how 'beloved' he was at the moment and the content of the letter only confirmed it.

Isabelle's eyes had widened in horror as Michael read the words. Her hand went to Will's shoulder and gripped. The youth had not been slow to grasp the meaning of the letter either, and his own gaze had grown round with surprise. He glanced from one parent to the other.

'The King wants me to squire for him,' he said with twin notes of excitement and fear in his voice.

'So it would seem,' William answered tonelessly. He exchanged glances with Isabelle and gave a tiny shake of his head, then started towards the keep. 'But not quite yet. Such matters need thought and preparation . . .'

The door closed behind the last maid, leaving Isabelle and William alone in their bedchamber. The atmosphere was as heavy with tension as the air before an August thunderstorm.

'I will not yield our son to John,' Isabelle said. Her stomach felt as if it was weighted with stones.

'We have no choice. The King already suspects me of treachery against him. Refusal to comply will only worsen the situation.'

She tossed her head. 'You are lord of Striguil, Earl of Pembroke and lord of Leinster. There are few men to match your power and none to match your reputation. John needs you more than you need him.'

'Even so, I am sworn to him,' William said. 'He is within his rights to ask for Will as surety for my good faith.'

Isabelle's upper lip curled with contempt. 'You are prepared to trust him even though he doesn't trust you? He took his own nephew prisoner and no one has heard of him since. Do you think I am deaf to the rumours?'

William rubbed his temples. 'John will not harm Will. As you say, I am Earl of Pembroke and my reputation will keep him from harm.'

Isabelle shook her head. 'That is not a gamble I am prepared to take. Arthur's kinship didn't save him, whatever you say.' She clenched her fists. 'Sweet Christ! Your father sent you as a hostage to King Stephen when you were a small boy and you were almost hanged. I don't understand how you can do the same to your own son!' Emotion strangled her voice and she turned abruptly from him, striving to compose herself.

He went to pour himself a cup of wine. His movements were so measured and calm that their effect on Isabelle was the opposite and made her want to scream. 'The circumstances are different. Will is the heir to Pembroke, not a younger son. He's fifteen years old and ready for squirehood. I'm an earl of the realm, not the castellan of a few scattered holdings as my father was.'

She flung round. 'And that makes it all right, does it? What sort of things is Will going to learn at the court of a debauched lecher like John!'

He looked at her and said patiently, 'John may not be the best mentor for a boy to have, but others at court will see him on the right path. One day Will is going to be Earl of Pembroke and he must acquire the skills. He has to be a courtier, a soldier and man of the world. He can only do that by experience. Either we have taught him decency, or we have wasted our time.' He took a gulp of wine, the swiftness of the gesture revealing that he was not as relaxed as he was trying to seem.

She dug her fingernails into the palms of her hands. 'I don't want him to go to John.' Her voice cracked again despite her best efforts to control it.

'Neither do I, but every young hawk must fly the nest. I was going to ask Baldwin to take him, but the court offers more opportunities. We can have people watch over him. He won't be without support.'

Isabelle shook her head and turned away, her hands to her mouth, pain raking her from chest to belly as if her heart was being torn out on long red strings.

'Isabelle . . .' He put the cup down and came to fold his arms around her. 'You have to see this as an opportunity for him, not an obstacle.'

She shuddered in his arms, then pushed away and looked up at him. 'Why can't we go as far away from

John as possible? Why can't we take all of our family to Ireland? We can raise our children as we see fit, without him putting his mark on them.'

William's grip tightened and now there was an edge of exasperation in his tone. 'Have you not been listening?' He gave her a gentle shake. 'Do you not understand? Our children are already marked. Will is the future Earl of Pembroke and Richard will be lord of Longueville. They have to know the world of the court as well as they know this household. I had experience at court in royal service for twenty years before I became lord of Striguil and even now I struggle. How do you think Will is going to cope with naught to grasp but apron strings?' Releasing her, he returned to his wine. 'Christ,' he said through his teeth, 'this argument is going round in circles.'

Isabelle's rage and grief boiled over. 'When you were a hostage, your father told King Stephen he still had the hammers and anvil to get more and better sons if he lost you,' she said, her shoulders heaving. 'Well, do not expect me to be your anvil. I will not bear sons for you to throw to the wolves!'

For the second time William put down the cup, his action quietly precise. 'If that is how you interpret matters, I am sorry. Will is going to court; let that be an end to it.' Turning on his heel, he left the room, lifting and dropping the latch with a soft click.

Isabelle stared at the door. How dare he . . . how dare he! She grabbed the cup he had used, thought about hurling it at the door, but found the will to tip the dregs into the rushes and pour a fresh cup of her own. Shaking like an old woman, she drank it down. She had just been given a glimpse of the implacable Earl of Pembroke, the man of the justice bench, council chamber and battle-field. The adversary.

She wiped her wet face on the heel of her hand. 'Where does it go from here?' she asked the empty room in a desolate voice. They had been each other's support for sixteen years. She had walked at his side every step of the way, in partnership, but suddenly they had reached an obstacle and they were choosing to go their separate ways around it. They had often quarrelled over small things – marital spats that were healed with good humour, apology and grace on both sides. But this wasn't a small thing. It was fundamental and the wound was deep. She still couldn't believe that he had turned his back on her and walked away.

Going to their bed she lay down, her head aching and tears still seeping from behind her lids. There was a lump of leaden misery in her stomach. She had very seldom cried because of William, but she was crying now. 'I won't give him up to John,' she said, but knew her words were as empty as she felt.

'They've been fighting,' Richard said. He was sitting on his rope-framed bed, stroking Tripes who had come to him for a fuss.

Will was whittling a piece of wood with a dagger his father's Welsh groom Rhys had given him. It had a handle of polished antler and a blade of pattern-hammered steel so that it looked as if waves were breaking in spume all over the surface. He felt nervous; his parents rarely quarrelled and when they did, it was quickly mended. Sometimes, after an argument, they would close the bedchamber door – not to sleep, but to take each other to bed; tonight, however, he had seen his father emerge from that particular room minus his smile and the air of heavy satisfaction that usually accompanied such encounters. His expression had been blank – frozen on to his face. He had been terse with a lingering servant and had ordered a groom to saddle his courser.

'Mama doesn't want me to go to court.' He flicked wood shavings off his coverlet. 'She wants to keep me with our household.'

Tripes rolled over, flopping his paws, and Richard rubbed his belly. 'Do you want to go?' he asked with curiosity and interest. He rather liked the idea of travelling to court himself, but it frightened him too.

Will shrugged. 'Our father was my age when he left his home to become a squire and then a great knight. Of course I want to go. He knows I do – that I'm ready, but Mama doesn't like the idea of the court.'

Richard gave him a keen glance. 'They don't have a choice anyway because the King wants you for a hostage as well as a squire.'

'I don't mind. It's not as if I'm going to be thrown in a dungeon, is it?' Will said with bravado. Although he did want to go to court and begin his full military training, he was also nervous, but would never admit as much to a brother only eighteen months his junior. He had occasionally seen prisoners awaiting trial in the dungeons when the family stayed at Gloucester Castle over which their father had jurisdiction. He would hate to be locked up in one and there had been some dark rumours about King John and his treatment of prisoners – rumours that he wasn't supposed to know about. 'Our father says the court will be good training. I've learned all I can at home.'

Mischief lit in Richard's eyes. 'Mama's worried you're going to learn all about whores and dice and drinking. I wish I was going with you.'

Will found a grin. 'You're too young,' he said.

* * *

Isabelle watched Will mount his horse in a single lithe motion without need of a block. He had a new, dappled palfrey for his ride to court. The saddle cloth had a border of green and gold braid woven with the red Marshal lion. The breast-band was tasselled in green and gold too. A new scarlet cloak with squirrel lining was pinned at his shoulder and his boots had garnet fastenings. His hands grasping the reins as he turned the horse were William's, competent and strong. He had a groom to attend him, and a body servant. William himself was escorting him to court and handing him over to John.

Isabelle steeled herself. She had said her farewells earlier, in private; she had embraced him and kissed him on either smooth-skinned cheek and had felt the return of that embrace dutifully given. William was right. He was ready to leave the nest for the wider world, but her heart bled at the thought of giving him to John for the finishing. She was bidding farewell to her firstborn. The boy still dwelt in his eyes, but she could see the man waiting to take over, and knew that when she set eyes on him again, he would be irrevocably changed.

She watched them ride away and felt as grey as rain. Will didn't turn, but his father did, giving her a look over his shoulder that made her ache to the bone. They still hadn't resolved their differences. They had talked and they had lain together, but the spaces between the words had been chasms, and she had been too numb and resentful to think about leaping across them. They had wounded each other and, despite a semblance of unity, nothing had healed.

18

Portchester, Hampshire, May 1206

Wearing her court gown of blue samite and the brooch set with sapphires that Queen Eleanor had given to her as wedding gift, Isabelle curtseyed formally before King John. She had prepared for this moment, rehearsing it in her head, practising her control until her shield was complete and nothing showed on her face but bland placidity. She would rather die than give John the satisfaction of knowing how deeply he had struck at the heart of her family.

He and the Queen sat on thrones draped with matching silk embroideries. Two painted stone leopards crouched either side of the chairs and behind their heads a magnificent banner embroidered with the royal Angevin lions sparkled with light. The knights of John's household guard stood close to their sovereign, swords at the ready; the other men in the room – bishops, barons and magnates – went unarmed except for their finery.

John was again preparing to embark for Poitou, but this time had not tried to force his barons to accompany him. Instead he had asked for their aid. William had tactfully provided him with a number of knights and serjeants.

While he refused to go in person, he was prepared to make a delicate compromise and at least give John a conroi of fighting men.

'Countess, it is a pleasure to see you at court. You should visit more often,' John addressed Isabelle pleasantly.

She murmured an appropriate response and kept her gaze lowered. Let John think her a dutiful and submissive wife if it saved her from having to interact with him.

William glanced at her. He had already made his obeisance to John and for the moment an uneasy peace existed between them, rather like the truce in his marriage. Patched up, holding, but unlikely to last.

John smiled benevolently at Isabelle. 'It is fortunate you are here, Lady Marshal. Your son will want to see you, I am sure, and make his farewells.'

Isabelle's head came up and her eyes widened. William made a surreptitious gesture of warning. 'His farewells, sire?' he asked, stepping into the breach.

John feigned surprise. 'I assumed you knew he was travelling to Poitou in my entourage?'

'No, sire, I did not,' William answered. 'I thought you would be leaving him behind.'

'You underestimate your son's talents, Marshal. He's a fast learner.'

Isabelle fought not to show the fury and fear John's words had ignited within her. She knew the more agitation a victim revealed, the more pleasure John derived.

'I am his father; I know how swiftly he learns, sire,' William answered calmly. 'I am pleased you find him so invaluable that he is a necessary part of your entourage.'

John's smile was mocking. 'Don't worry, Marshal, I won't let anything happen to him – even if you do have three more sons to carry your line and the means to beget more.'

Isabelle made an involuntary sound and sent John an eviscerating look through her lashes.

John smirked at her, his own stare bright with lust.

'Sire, I am reassured to hear that you will keep him safe,' William said. 'I wonder if you might extend the same trust that I yield to you and grant me leave to visit my Irish lands.'

John regarded the clean white borders of his finger-nails. 'You should know better than to ask, Marshal. I need you in England while I am gone – I need your gover-nance.' He looked once more at Isabelle. 'I'll arrange for that son of yours to dine with you and your lady tonight. Perhaps he will be able to convince her that I am not about to use his guts for girth straps.'

William bowed and fixed a smile on his face because as a courtier he was an adept. 'And perhaps I can convince her not to do the same to yours,' he replied. His timing and delivery were flawless and John laughed, appreciating the barb, but his eyes were calculating, and William's, despite his relaxed stance, were wary.

Isabelle's fears for Will were making her sick with worry, but she tried not to show it when he came to their pavilion later that day. She could not believe how much he had changed in nine months. He was never going to have William's height and breadth; he took after his slighter grandsire, her father, but he was strong and supple. The muscles beneath his linen tunic and shirt were hard and adult and he was going to need new garments to accom-modate the extra girth.

'Oh, it's so good to see you!' she cried, embracing him. 'We've missed you!'

He gave an embarrassed smile and a shrug. 'It was strange at first,' he admitted, 'but I've become used to it.' His voice was deeper, the masculine apple in his throat more pronounced and his stubble more than fluff. Isabelle felt unbearably proud and unbearably sad. As Will and his father embraced, again she saw the closeness and the distance and knew that the latter was bound, for a while at least, to grow.

While they were eating, she broached the delicate subject of Poitou and discovered to her chagrin that John was right. Will was eager to go, like a young warhorse champing at the bit. She had to bite her tongue on caveats and nay-sayings, knowing they were born of her anxieties, not her son's. Gilbert was fascinated by the detail that the King had books to read for pleasure and had even had chests made especially to transport them. Richard listened with rapt attention and envy as Will spoke of Gibbun, John's great white Norway hawk and how he had been allowed to handle him in the mews and fly him at the lure on the practice ground.

William observed and listened with his arms folded and a knowing half-smile on his lips. 'You shouldn't forget to mention the length of time you have to be on duty and all the fetching and carrying you have to do. You never eat when everyone else does because you're serving the meal, carving the meat, carrying the wine and finger-bowls. You have to sleep with your ears open lest your lord should call you in the night and you have to come to his presence fully dressed and with your senses alert. Then there's all the polishing and caring for armour and being courteous whatever the provocation.'

Will shrugged. 'At least I'm not bored,' he said, and then looked guiltily at his mother.

Isabelle sighed and shook her head. 'Knowing your ancestry, I suppose I should expect no less.' She smiled. 'But as a mother I would rather have you bored than endangered.'

'At least he won't be endangered by dairy maids where he is now,' Richard said impishly and received a good-natured cuff from his father.

'Well,' William said to Isabelle when Will had returned to his duties and they were preparing to retire for the night, 'have your fears been allayed?'

Still clad in her chemise, Isabelle got into bed. 'I am glad to have seen him and to know that he is content,' she murmured. The latter was true, but she also suspected John was deliberately trying to wean Will away from them, although she didn't say so to William. She had enough self-knowledge to realise that some of her misgiving was caused by protectiveness and resentment.

William yawned. 'Good.' He thumped the bolster into a comfortable shape.

'Do you think John will give us permission to go to Ireland?'

'It'll be like pushing a cart full of boulders uphill with our hands tied behind our backs, but yes, he'll give it . . . eventually. I loaned him a hundred marks today, and he borrowed two tuns of wine for his table. He's affable enough for the moment.'

'Well, that's because he thinks he has the better of us. You might not be accompanying him to Poitou, but he's got our heir, which is the next best thing – and he'll play it for all he's worth.'

'Of course he will,' William answered with laboured patience. 'Don't worry. Will's in good hands. Salisbury is going too. He's promised to look out for him.'

Isabelle sighed. 'I know.' She closed her eyes and tried to blank thought from her mind so that she could sleep.

Beside her, William did the same but with little success. Outside he could hear the voices of some of the mesnie knights, gathered round the fire near their pavilions. Conversation; muted laughter. The scrape of Richard's breaking adolescent voice as he joined them. William was tempted to go and lose his troubled thoughts in wine, jest and camaraderie, but knew his presence would change the atmosphere and deny him the very thing he sought.

The sight of Will closing fast on manhood and the husky sound of Richard's voice had suddenly made him realise how late it was. When he had married Isabelle, there had seemed acres of time to plant seed and harvest, but suddenly there was only a small corner remaining and too much to accomplish. He had once asked God for the grace to see his children grow up and now the eldest were almost there. He could still do most things he had done at thirty: wear his mail shirt without going short of breath; go blade to blade with any man and win. His reflexes might have slowed a little, but since they had been faster than lightning in his youth, they still served him well. Experience and reputation made up for the rest.

There remained much to accomplish in Ireland. He knew he had neglected it for far too long. The foundations had been laid but he needed to go there himself and oversee the building – while his faculties were entire. Normandy was lost to them for the time being. Even if he had secured the lands for his heirs, it would be stupid to go there and risk John's ire so badly that he forfeited his English estates. Best for now to leave Longueville in the hands of a steward until Richard was old enough to take up the reins.

Normandy was the landscape of his young manhood and it was in the past; there was no point wallowing in nostalgia. Eleanor and Henry, Richard and the Young King were in their graves. Restlessly he turned over. Isabelle's back was turned and all he could see was the heavy mass of her hair gilding the coverlet and the pale shape of her linen-clad arm. She was twenty years younger than him. Queen Eleanor had lived four-score years and he had no delusions that, barring a miracle, he would be here should Isabelle have such a span. He had a duty to ensure while he lived that the lands she held in dower were secure for her future – her widowhood. Since Leinster was the richest part of that dower it behoved him to do something about it.

She turned over in a rustle of bedclothes and opened her eyes. In the dim candlelight their changeable flecked blue was as dark as midnight. 'You are not sleeping,' she said.

'Neither are you.' He put his arm around her and she moved into his embrace. It was one that held comfort and familiarity. Sensing the boundaries, he did not over-step them. Despite his recent personal examination of his faculties and the awareness that all were still intact, tonight was not an occasion for hammers, anvils and the forge.

19

Framlingham Castle, Suffolk, January 1207

Mahelt's wedding gown was of silk of Damascus, shot with hues of silver and green and sparkling with crystals and pearls. The peacock tones suited her complexion and ruddy brown hair. A silver belt at her waist emphasised its narrowness and the lithe curves of recent womanhood.

Pride glowing in her eyes, Isabelle watched Mahelt dance a bridal carole with her new husband. At three and twenty, Hugh Bigod towered over his still-growing bride of rising thirteen. He showed no discomfort in the disparity of age or size, but then he had younger sisters of his own and was accustomed to their ways. He was treating Mahelt like a queen and she was blossoming under his attention. Isabelle felt tearily happy for the pair, but her heart was also filled with trepidation.

Beside her William watched the dance with a closed expression on his face, although when Mahelt looked his way and smiled, he did too and raised his hand in a gesture of reassurance. In honour of the marriage he had donned the full regalia of an earl, something he seldom did, and his hair was banded with a gem-set coronet. Isabelle knew he was finding it hard to see his daughter go in marriage and so soon – perhaps harder than giving his son as a hostage. Mahelt was his firstborn daughter and had always held a special corner of his heart. No longer would she run to him in greeting when he returned from campaign, nor show him things, nor have him teach her songs in the chamber of an evening. All of that was now reserved to her husband and his family.

'The marriage had to be now,' he said regretfully. 'I wish we could have brought her to Ireland with us, but there is no knowing how long we will be gone. It's probably safer for her to be here at Framlingham as a Bigod wife anyway.'

Isabelle forbore to say that now he must know the wrench she felt when giving their son to John. It would be a blow beneath the belt and the circumstances were not the same. William had felt the loss of his son too, and she was going to miss Mahelt dreadfully herself. At least their daughter would be growing to maturity in a welcoming household with a strong moral code. Suffolk was far enough removed from the court that Mahelt wasn't obliged to attend unless she wished, but the castle at Framlingham was new, strong and comfortable. Ida was an excellent mother-in-law too. Her nature was maternal, but not smotheringly so, and she was happy to share her bower and her duties with her eldest son's wife.

Isabelle placed her hand upon William's sleeve. He was wearing cloth of silver and it shimmered as she touched it. 'She has the leisure now to acquaint herself with her new family before she takes on all the responsibilities of being a wife,' she said practically.

His eyelids tensed at the words 'all the responsibilities'.

Isabelle firmly squeezed his arm. 'She has your courage and determination to do all things well, and Hugh has a kind nature.'

'I was there when John married his Queen,' William muttered. 'She was about the same age as Mahelt and at a similar stage of growth.' A look of revulsion crossed his face. 'I know what John did to her and if I thought—'

'Then it is a good thing you do not think,' Isabelle interrupted. Again she was tempted to mention their son, but unless William was blind he must see the parallels for himself. 'This is a decent household like our own and they will look to her welfare. Ida and Roger will protect Mahelt. Hugh is a fine young man, you have said so yourself, and it was one of the reasons this marriage was agreed upon. You insult him by such notions . . . and you insult your own judgement.'

William grimaced. 'You are right and the rational part of me knows you are, but even so . . .' With a shake of his head, he excused himself to visit the privy.

Isabelle was immediately joined by Ida of Norfolk, resplendent in blue wool and sapphires. 'Is the Earl Marshal all right?' she asked, looking concerned.

Isabelle smiled to reassure her hostess. 'He worries about leaving Mahelt because she is so young. I suppose I worry too, although I know she could not be better placed.'

Ida took Isabelle's hand. 'Of course you do. You are her mother, and she is still of tender years for marriage. I'll care for her as I would one of my own daughters. My son is under sworn oath not to lay a finger on her until she is grown enough for the marriage bed and he will hold to it. Mahelt will be given all the time she needs.'

'I know that, and we could not wish for a better match, or son-by-marriage,' Isabelle said, being tactful, but meaning what she said. She was glad that William was absent at the privy. Men were always accused of being

201

rough and crude, but in some situations their sensibilities were tissue-thin. He probably would not have coped well with this discussion about his daughter.

'Has John actually agreed to let you go to Ireland?' Ida enquired to change the subject as William returned to the room.

Isabelle shook her head. 'He's still procrastinating but William will have agreement out of him in the end. He cannot keep refusing and in the meantime we make our preparations.' She looked again towards the dancers. Mahelt was laughing at Hugh, her face flushed and her eyes alight. It was going to be easy for her, Isabelle thought. She had tumbled into love with him and, providing he wasn't a fool, which she knew he wasn't, she would tumble as easily into his bed when the time was right.

Spotting her father, Mahelt excused herself from her new husband's arm, and running to William with the fleetness of the child she still half was, tugged him into the circle of dancers. He went reluctantly at first, but then Isabelle saw him laugh and give Mahelt a hug.

Ida patted Isabelle's shoulder. 'Shall we join them?' she asked. 'I adore dancing and what's more fitting than to do so at my son's wedding to the best bride we could have chosen for him.'

Isabelle smiled. 'You are right,' she said, loving Ida for her kindness and tact. 'What could be more fitting?'

John studied the piece of parchment in his hand. It was water-stained by its journey from the Welsh Marches; it had been very wet this last week and although the messenger's satchel tucked beneath his cloak had protected it from the worst and saved the ink, it was still dimpled and hinted at damp.

'This is the fourth time William Marshal has written

202

requesting permission to go to Ireland,' John said to his friend and familiar, Peter des Roches, Bishop of Winchester. 'Do I give him licence to go?' The words were couched in the flowery language of William's clerk, Michael – John recognised the man's style. The effusive flourishes and greetings were certainly not the Marshal's. He gnawed at a painful strip of skin at the side of his thumbnail. 'He's been to court once since I returned from Poitou and that was only to make sure his boy was still in one piece and to ask about Ireland again.'

Des Roches absently stroked the embroidery on his bejewelled dalmatic, the way other men might stroke a pet animal. The garment had belonged to Hubert Walter and was almost priceless. 'He's certainly making enough preparations, sire. I have heard he is assembling men and victuals at Striguil and Pembroke. He married his eldest daughter to Bigod's son in January, now she's of age. It looks to me as if he's tying up loose threads and preparing to be gone for a while – otherwise why marry off the girl now?'

John looked thoughtful. Marshal and Norfolk. The combination made him uneasy. 'I won't miss him if he does go to ground in a bog, self-righteous old fool,' he growled, 'but I'm not certain I want him out of my sight being self-righteous in Ireland too. His wife's grandsire called himself King of Leinster, and I'll not have William Marshal setting himself up in that capacity.'

Des Roches smiled as if at an absurdity. 'I could imagine no man less likely to do that than William Marshal.'

'And so I thought until he knelt in liege homage to the King of France and refused to sail to Poitou. I have trusted men only to have them go behind my back. Ranulf of Chester, Saher de Quincy, William de Braose . . . and de Braose is a Marshal ally.'

A telling silence fell between the men. Des Roches was far too ambitious and sensible of his own hide to comment on the matter of why de Braose was out of favour, and John would not speak of it because he was striving to prevent the past from bobbing to the surface like a rotten corpse and destroying him.

The tension was broken by the arrival of the young Queen. Ysabel entered her husband's chamber accompanied by two of her ladies, her walk stately and graceful, stomach slightly thrust out. The palm of her right hand was deliberately pressed against her belly. It was only five weeks since she had missed her flux, but she was making sure everyone knew of her probable condition, especially John.

He looked at her. He had been beginning to wonder if God was having a jest with him – allowing him to make bastards with other women while keeping his wife barren. Finally, however, the seed appeared to have taken root. As yet she hadn't started puking and she looked as radiant as a jewelled Madonna. He toasted her with his cup. 'Let the Queen decide,' he said with a humouring smile. 'Do I give the Earl of Pembroke leave to go to Ireland, or do I leash him here at court where I can see him?'

Ysabel shrugged indifferently. 'Does it matter whether he goes or stays?'

'That's what I'm trying to decide.'

She walked slowly to the chest where the flagon stood and beckoned to a servant to pour for her. She was learning the uses of power and how much the seed growing within her womb had enhanced her standing at all levels of royal life. 'I like the Countess,' she said. 'She's nice to me when she comes to court and clever at choosing clothes and furnishings.'

John snorted. 'I'm not sure I'd agree with you. I consider

Lady Marshal a prize bitch with more than a touch of the wild Irish about her.'

'Then Ireland is probably the best place for her.' Ysabel gave a languid wave of her hand, the gesture intimating that she did not know what the fuss was about. 'Let her and her husband go. You have their son, don't you? If they are out of your way, they won't be able to annoy you so much.'

'Don't be so sure,' he muttered sourly, but his expression relaxed. 'So be it. I can recall him at need, and as you point out, I have his son.' Going to her, he set his arm around her waist and cupped her belly. 'As you have mine.'

Des Roches prudently dismissed himself.

Ten days later, Will was playing dice-chess outside the royal chamber at Marlborough with one of John's knights, Thomas Sandford, and Robert Flemyng, a young messenger. The King having retired early, Will, despite being on duty, had a moment's leisure.

'My father grew up here,' he said, rattling the dice in their horn cup. 'The Marshals used to be its constables.'

Sandford grunted. 'They don't own it now though,' he said with a half-smile, to show that no offence was intended. He was a stolid, tow-haired knight. His younger brother was a retainer in the Marshal household.

Will shrugged and cast the dice. 'My uncle John lost it because he rebelled against King Richard and it was never restored to our family.'

'I don't suppose you mind,' Flemyng said, leaning his elbows on the board. 'Your family's been well enough compensated over the years, haven't they? Are you sure those dice aren't loaded? That's the third set of sixes you've thrown.'

Will flushed. 'I'm not cheating. You've been using the same ones.' He moved his piece on the chessboard. 'I think my father would still like Marlborough back. He says he and his brothers used to sleep in these chambers when they were children.'

Flemyng gave a salacious chuckle. 'You mean the Queen's lying in your father's bed? Now there's a cause for scandal!'

'Pay him no heed, Will,' said Sandford easily. 'He's drunk and he never knows when to shut his mouth.'

'I can keep silent if I have to,' Robert retorted. 'And I could drink both of you under the table.'

Will ignored the challenge in the young messenger's voice and handed him the dice.

'There you have it, drunk and boastful,' Sandford said with good humour.

Flemyng made a sarcastic face. He shook the cup and rolled the dice. One bounced off the table and disappeared amid the floor rushes. 'Bastard!' Dropping to his hands and knees, he began groping around in the candle-pooled darkness.

'You'll never find it,' Will said, then looked up as the stairway curtain parted to admit two of the household knights and another messenger to the antechamber. The former were carrying a heavy chest between them and the latter was mud-spattered, wind-blown and decidedly sober. Will eyed the bulging satchel sticking out from beneath the man's riding cloak and the weighty sword at his hip. The fact that he had shown up so late at night came as no surprise. Messengers often kept odd hours; it was the nature of their trade and he was accustomed to the same in his father's house. However, many of the comings and goings from John's chamber were covert and clandestine. Orders were frequently given verbally or in coded fashion with secret signals and handshakes.

'What's this?' Thomas Sandford rose to his feet.

'News from Ireland,' the messenger said. Will's ears pricked up. He knew his father was about to go there, and wondered what messages the Irish lords were sending to John. The King's justiciar there, Meilyr FitzHenry, was not a Marshal ally. The chest looked interesting too. He doubted it was yet more books.

Thomas went to the door and banged three times, craving admittance and stating his purpose. As Flemyng swayed to his feet, minus the elusive die, Thomas addressed him over his shoulder. 'Best sober up,' he said. 'You may be riding tonight if there are messages to take.'

The King called a reply and Thomas opened the door to usher the knights and messenger inside. Will seized the night flagon and cups from the trestle and slipped through in their wake. Thomas flicked him an amused look that said he knew what Will was about, but he didn't make him leave.

John was sitting before the fire, wearing a loose robe and reading a copy of Wace's *Roman de Rou*.

The messenger knelt and handed over his packet of letters. John took them, examined the dangling seals, and broke open the first one. Will stood by the door, breathing shallowly, making himself inconspicuous lest he was noticed and dismissed.

Rubbing his chin, John read rapidly and began to frown. He looked at the messenger and the knights. 'The money?' he said.

One of them produced a key, unfastened the padlocks and pushed back the lid to show John numerous leather moncy bags. The King hefted one, tossed it up and down in a harsh jingle of sound, then dropped it back in the chest. He studied the letter again, raised his head and stared directly at Will, thus letting him know he was here because John wished it so, not because he had escaped notice.

'Your father.' John's upper lip curled. 'Your sainted, chivalrous father, that *prudhomme* . . . and your haughty bitch of a mother too . . .'

Will's stomach turned over at the expression in John's eyes.

'Well,' John said softly, 'all great men can be brought to heel, and ground under it if necessary . . . and their haughty wives too.'

Will swallowed. 'I do not understand, sire.'

'No, but I will make your father do so on his knees. Tell me, boy, why does he want so desperately to go to Ireland?'

Will's palms were moist with cold sweat. 'The lands are my mother's dower estates and they need attention, sire.'

'Do they indeed?' John tossed the letter on the trestle. 'And why can't he stay in England and let his deputies administer them, hmm?'

Will mutely shook his head.

'Marshal will challenge my justiciar and therefore my authority on every point of law, and take matters into his own hands; I know him. My lord FitzHenry writes that he is most concerned on this matter.'

Gazing at the chest of silver, Will began to understand. He had been only ten years old on their first visit to Ireland, but he remembered how angry Meilyr FitzHenry had been at what he saw as their invasion of his territory. His attitude had obviously not mellowed and Will knew his father was going to Ireland with the intention of getting to grips with the situation. No surprise then that Meilyr had written to John and sent a chest of silver to add lustre to his argument.

He became uncomfortably aware that John was looking

208

at him with the speculative manner of a wolf considering a raid on a sheep pen. 'You're a fine lad and doing well,' the King said. 'Your father gave you up willingly enough, but I should have asked for more.' For a moment he mused upon the chest of silver, then he raised his head. 'I sold my goodwill far too cheaply. Time, I think, to increase the price.'

Spring sunlight washed the walls of Tintern Abbey in primrose gold and flooded the nave with a warm benediction of rays. Isabelle knelt at her mother's tomb in the choir and prayed. The effigy, carved from Purbeck marble and painted in rich colours, had been completed the year after her death. There was perhaps a hint of Aoife in the short nose and set of the mouth, but then again, it might be a trick of wishful thinking. Isabelle thought that her mother would have been pleased by the elegant drapes of the gown the stone carver had designed for her. Her vanity had always been a large part of her personality.

'Mahelt isn't here today,' Isabelle informed the effigy, setting her own hand over its praying ones. 'She was married at the feast of Saint Agnes to Hugh Bigod, Roger of Norfolk's heir. I think you would like him – even if he is a Norman.' She gave a tremulous smile. 'She's a Bigod now and I will miss her sorely, but I know they will care for her as their own. William didn't want to let her go. He's always had a tender spot for her. She is so much like him.' The cold stone warmed under her hand and Aoife's face gazed serenely heavenwards, yet Isabelle gained the sense that somehow she was listening.

She voiced her concerns about Will's continuing absence at court, a worry she kept to herself given the differences between herself and William on the matter. It was curative to speak her troubles aloud and know she was not being indiscreet. Finally, drawing a deep breath, she told the effigy her other news, the bit she reserved until last. 'We're returning to Ireland,' she said. 'As soon as the weather is right. William has the King's permission. He says he intends to prepare the ground so that my dower will be my sustenance should he not . . . should he not survive me. You were the Countess of Hibernia. Now I go to be the same. I swear I will do the best I can, and my children after me.' A sudden swim of tears filled her eyes, but they were of healing and good sorrow, rather than mourning grief.

Feeling more at peace than she had done in a while, Isabelle crossed herself and left the abbey, emerging into the spring sunshine and a world cladding itself in tender green. Belle, Sybire and little Eve were crouched in the grass, picking the first daisies of the year, heads close together, shoes and gown hems dark with dew. Arms folded, sons beside him, William was talking to Abbot Eudo as he waited for her. He glanced up as she came out to him, and as always, Isabelle's heart leaped. Even now; even when there were gaps between them where no gaps had existed before, that look of his still stopped her breath. She went forward to speak with Abbot Eudo and murmur pleasantries. She saw alms distributed in her mother's name to the poor waiting at the gate, and she gave more to the Abbot for later use as well as two chests of cloaks and shoes to be shared amongst the crippled and needy. William stood by her as she did all this, quietly escorting, but taking no part, for Tintern was particularly hers, having been founded by her great-grandfather.

When she was ready to leave, William took her horse from her groom and boosted her into the saddle himself, his hand lingering briefly at her ankle. 'Ireland,' he murmured. 'I never thought I would say this, but I'll be glad to see its shores. I need . . .' He looked at her and made a rueful gesture. '. . . I need time, of which I never seem to have enough.'

'Time away from King John is always worth twice that of any other,' she said, thereby earning a tight smile in response.

'I was going to say the same about time spent with my wife,' he answered gracefully and rubbed his thumb over her ankle bone before turning to his own palfrey. Isabelle watched him and felt her lids prickle. She blinked hard, shook her head and turned a gracious smile of farewell to Abbot Eudo.

At Striguil, the banners of Marshal and Clare flew from the battlements and decorated the freshly whitened walls. Shields bearing the arms of kin and allies had been fastened to the crenels: the gold background and red cross of Bigod, the blue and silver of Salisbury, the silver scallop shells on red of D'Earley. It was a sight to gladden the eye and fill the heart. The keep bulged at the rafters with soldiers and retainers, with supplies and equipment for transportation to Ireland. Baggage carts and sumpter horses thronged the bailey, ready for the morrow's leave-taking. From here, they would go to Pembroke and then embark for Ireland. Today was to be one of feasting and farewell.

William's knights had organised a small tournament as a surprise. A wooden balcony had been decorated with evergreen and banners, and padded benches brought so that William and Isabelle could sit and watch the contests of arms. A blushing young knight craved a favour from Isabelle, and she gave it with a radiant smile and a kiss on the cheek.

'A good thing I am not a jealous man,' William murmured.

'You should be,' Isabelle retorted. 'He's very handsome.' She touched her lips. 'And grown for his years, to judge by his stubble.'

'Never judge a man by his stubble,' William said playfully. 'It's what he keeps on the inside that counts.'

'I should hope he does in the presence of ladies,' Isabelle retorted and drew Eve into her lap. Belle and Sybire presented favours too, both of them flushed with pride and full of giggles.

'That's not a promise of betrothal!' William warned Stephen's son, young Thomas D'Evereux, as Belle tied a scarf to his sleeve, her small pink tongue protruding between her teeth in concentration.

'Shame,' japed D'Evereux. 'We'll just have to elope.'

William snorted. 'In that case you had better go practise your swordplay.'

D'Evereux bowed. 'My lord,' he said incorrigibly, kissed Belle's hand and departed.

At ease for the first time in an age, William settled down to enjoy the day and watch the men perform for his benefit. 'I was one of them once,' he said nostalgically, 'putting on a display for Queen Eleanor, or wearing the favour of the Young Queen Marguerite.' He observed Richard sparring with one of his squires and was pleased to note his son's swift coordination of hand and eye. The lad was carrying puppy flesh, but he wasn't soft. 'It was long ago,' he said and felt a sudden pang of nostalgia.

Isabelle laid her hand to his sleeve. 'Not that long ago, my lord. If it weren't for the fact that they are doing this for you, I know you'd be down amongst them showing off too.'

William's eye corners crinkled with humour. 'Would you have me join them?'

She was seeking a diplomatic reply when Osbert, one

212

of the chamberlains, came out on to the gallery. The tension emanating from him took the amusement out of William's gaze. 'What is it?'

Osbert rubbed his hands together. 'My lord, my lady, Sir Thomas Sandford is here bearing a message from the King.'

Isabelle's stomach dived. Face expressionless, William thanked him. 'Bring him here,' he said quietly.

'Holy Virgin,' she muttered as Osbert left. 'Can't he leave us alone? What trickery is he planning now? If he has done anything to Will . . .'

William gripped her hand in a calming gesture. 'I do not know what he wants, but there is no point in speculating. Whatever it is, you must not react; John thrives on the wounds he inflicts. Thomas Sandford is a good man and his brother serves us, but the King will still expect him to report back word for word and gesture for gesture. Be on your guard.'

Isabelle nodded and managed to compose herself. Swiftly but without fuss she summoned her women and had them remove the younger children to a different vantage point to watch the sport. Moments later, Thomas Sandford was ushered on to the gallery.

'Welcome, Thomas,' William said pleasantly as the knight bowed to him and to Isabelle. He gestured him to be seated on the bench.

'My lord.'

'It is good to see you, but I hazard you have not ridden all this way to say farewell to your brother or take part in our tourney?'

Sandford shook his head. 'I wish with all my heart that I had, my lord. I will not lie and say that I am the bearer of glad tidings.'

William watched a couple of knights fight forward

213

and back using sword and shield. He studied the foot-work. It was all about speed and balance; a deadly dance. 'I didn't think you were, Thomas,' he said without taking his eyes off the men. 'I hardly think the King would send a man all the way to wish me Godspeed. You might as well tell me. You know me well enough by now. Even if the news is the worst in the world, I won't take it out on you.'

Sandford didn't look relieved; if anything his anxiety deepened. 'My lord, the King desires you to hand over your son Richard to him as surety for your good conduct in Ireland. If you do not, he will revoke his permission for you to go.'

'I see,' William said without emotion.

All the colour drained from Isabelle's face. 'No.' Her voice rang with passion and she slammed her hand on the gallery rail. 'I will burn in hell before I give Richard to him as well!'

William shot her a cautioning look.

'I am sorry, my lady,' Thomas said woodenly. 'The King insists upon it as a condition of your going to Ireland.'

Isabelle made a mewing sound and, hand clapped to her mouth, excused herself.

'Why should he insist on such a thing when I have sworn him my loyalty?' William asked, managing to keep his voice level. After a single look after his wife, he had ignored her precipitous exit.

Thomas gave an uncomfortable shrug. 'Because he has changed his mind, my lord. He does not want you to go. To be blunt, Meilyr FitzHenry has written to him saying that if he lets you loose in Ireland, he will never be its master again. He sent a chest of silver with his letter in proof of his own sincerity.'

William raised one eyebrow.

214

'I am sorry,' Thomas said unhappily. 'I tell you this as a friend and because you are my brother's lord.'

'And indeed I am grateful for that friendship.' William rubbed his chin reflectively. 'Meilyr FitzHenry thinks that Leinster is his pie and he doesn't want to share it with the likes of an English soft-sword. I know from my nephew he has taken Ui Chennselaig for himself and is making other encroachments on my territory.' He looked at Thomas. 'If there's a thorn in your side what do you do: let it fester, or pluck it out?'

'Do you desire me to answer that, my lord?'

William shook his head. 'No, I don't. Go, wash and eat – talk with your brother if you wish. There's a bed for you tonight in the hall. You will appreciate I need to discuss matters with my advisers . . . and my wife.'

'Yes, of course, my lord.'

He watched Thomas Sandford leave and when he had gone, covered his eyes with one hand and and muttered an oath.

Isabelle sat on the bench in their private chamber with several of the senior knights, summoned from their sport. Jean D'Earley still wore his gambeson. There was a grass stain on the knee of his chausses and a streak of mud across his cheek. Jordan de Saqueville and Stephen D'Evereux had removed their quilted tunics, but wore their swords. Ralph Musard was dabbing at a trickling cut on his cheek. She had told them the news and after the exclamations of negation and horror they had fallen silent, waiting.

William entered the chamber, quietly shut the door behind him and walked to his chair, the one where he sat to take his ease, to be comfortable after a long day, to let the cares slip from him. Only now it was one from which he must give a hard decision and take burdens upon himself. Hitching his hose at the knees, he seated himself with deliberation.

'I have told them the news,' Isabelle said in a voice brittle with control and holding a trace of earlier tears. 'The whoreson is bent on destroying us.'

Absently William rubbed his thigh where the ghost of an old wound sometimes pained him. 'His mood is certainly fickle,' he said.

'Why this sudden increase in his suspicion?' Jean D'Earley looked puzzled. 'You have done nothing to warrant it.'

'Going to Ireland is warrant enough,' William said. 'Meilyr FitzHenry has warned John that his authority will diminish if I set foot in Leinster and he has sent the King a large bribe in silver to keep me away. Now John says I must send him Richard if I want to go to Ireland.'

Jean's mobile mouth curled with disgust. 'You shouldn't do it, my lord. One son is more than enough. It's like bandaging a finger that isn't wounded.'

Isabelle could no longer contain her emotion and catapulted to her feet. 'I say let us load the carts and the sumpter horses and be on our way. We can be safe in Ireland within the week – all of us, including Richard.'

De Saqueville and Musard looked at the ground and then covertly at William. Jean opened his mouth as if to agree with her, but no words emerged. As often as he took her part, he was more cautious than she was.

William shook his head. 'How far do you think we will get if we choose open defiance? John was lord of Ireland long before he had anything else to his name. If we flaunt our banners too close to his face, he will do no more than bring his army to Dublin. He desires us to leave our deputies to cope as best they can but it is no good to us. You will have no dower lands to speak of very soon if the lord Meilyr continues to have his way. The lands have to be secured, especially the new port and the abbeys.' He folded his arms. 'John has demanded Richard. So be it. I say we hand him over, thus obeying the King's word, and then we leave.'

'No!' Isabelle bared her teeth. 'I will not do it. God save me, William, I will not!'

He opened his hand. 'You have no choice unless you are prepared to stay here and allow Meilyr FitzHenry to swallow Leinster whole and decimate the lands your father – and mother – left in trust to you.'

'I will yield him neither Richard, nor Leinster.' Isabelle's voice was raw with emotion. 'They are both mine. I'd rather walk from here to Jerusalem upon sharpened knives than give up either of them to hellspawn like John!'

'You are speaking from the spleen, and that is of no use to anyone,' William said impatiently. 'The situation has to be reasoned through. If we stay here and keep Richard, the King will have achieved his purpose. If we go to Ireland taking Richard with us, it gives John the excuse he needs to turn us into fugitives for disobeying his will. I won't give him either satisfaction. Richard must go to court.'

'No!' Isabelle stared at him, appalled.

'The answer has to be yes,' he said grim-faced, 'for all our sakes.'

'He is our son! How can you sit there and speak as if you're discussing the sacrifice of a sheep?' she demanded incredulously.

William's men stared at the floor, at the rafters, anywhere but at him and Isabelle. The emotions were too raw, too intimate for a council chamber.

He pinched the bridge of his nose between forefinger and thumb. 'Christ's bones, Isabelle, do you think this is easy for me? My heart bleeds at the decision I have to make, but it is the only one.'

'No, it isn't and you know it!' She made a flinging gesture at him. 'You are the Earl of Pembroke. In God's name, use that title for what it means!'

He spread his fingers and drew his palm down across his face as if donning a mask. 'And who gave me that title?' he asked and the look in his eyes was bleak. 'Either put on a brave face to our son, or stay here if you cannot. Richard is going with Thomas Sandford and you will not send him on his journey with wailing and tears.'

'So help me,' Isabelle said, quivering with passion, 'If anything happens to him, I will hold you responsible and . . . and hell will seem cold in comparison to my wrath!' She stalked from the room, her head carried high, her eyes brimming with unshed tears.

An uncomfortable silence fell in her wake.

Jean cleared his throat. 'The Countess will come round,' he said much too heartily.

'That remains to be seen,' William replied in a tired voice. 'She is right. The responsibility is mine, and while I am prepared to shoulder it, that doesn't mean it isn't one of the heaviest burdens I have ever had to carry.'

William studied Richard, trying to gauge his reaction. They were in the chamber where the boys slept and he had just told him that he was to go with Thomas Sandford on the morrow and join his brother at court. 'It'll be a chance to polish up your own skills, hmm?' He was aware of the false bonhomie in his voice and knew that Richard had sensed that all was not well.

'You mean I'm not going to Ireland?' Richard raised wide grey eyes.

William picked up the practice sword that his son had been using earlier to such good effect. So much promise, but all precariously balanced on the whim of a King who had shown himself capable of great misjudgement and cruelty. 'Your grandsire, your mother's father for whom you are named, went to Ireland and carved himself an inheritance out of nothing,' he said. 'He was a fine soldier and an honourable man of high courage who would always look you in the eye. I met him several times when I was a young knight – he even asked me to come to Ireland with him, but I was already in the service of King Henry's eldest son by then – otherwise I would have accepted his offer, and who knows where my life would have gone from there.'

'You would have known Mama when she was little,' Richard said.

The comment drew a surprised smile from William. 'Yes,' he said ruefully, and put down the sword. 'I need you to be like your grandsire now.'

Richard nodded. 'I'm going to be a hostage,' he said, stating the obvious with a practical forthrightness that tugged at William's heart and conscience.

'You can see it like that, but it is also an opportunity to learn the ways of the court and see your brother again. When you come of age, your life will be in Normandy, at Longueville and Orbec, hopefully out of the reach of King John, but it is still necessary for you to learn the way of the court. I know it is daunting, but I need you to have wisdom beyond your years in this matter.'

Richard frowned and rumpled his coppery hair. 'I can do it,' he said. 'I . . . want to go.' His voice was nervous, but tinged with anticipation.

William considered him thoughtfully. 'You have been something of a fish out of water since Will and your sister left,' he murmured. 'Walter and Gilbert are not the same company for you, are they?'

Richard mutely shook his head.

William suspected that Richard had also been a little jealous of his older brother riding off into the world and leaving him behind. Now, for better or worse, he had the opportunity to join him.

Isabelle stood beside William to watch Thomas Sandford ride away with their second son. Her smile and her stance were as rigid as if she were practising to become her own effigy. Within that shell she felt as if she had been shattered into a thousand pieces. The King was set on destroying her family for daring to try to protect what was theirs, and perhaps out of vindictive jealousy that they had managed to keep their lands intact whilst he had lost great tracts of his patrimony across the Narrow Sea.

She had always known that William had a steely, pragmatic side. One did not rise to the heights he had achieved without that element, but until recently and despite eighteen years of marriage, she had not realised its true extent because he had never exposed its full measure at home with his family.

'Now both of our eldest sons have gone to couch with wolves,' she said desolately. She loved all of her children, but the two eldest boys were particularly precious. They had been born during her first flush of adoration for their father at a time when she was tasting the joy of freedom and the exercising of power after many years mured up in the Tower of London as a royal ward.

'They will return,' he answered, his gaze centred on Richard's back.

'Yes, but changed, and how do we know for the better? John will take them and turn them into what he wants. They should be here with us, or placed with men we trust to look after them. When we have gone, they will be our heirs for Striguil and Normandy and Leinster. What happens to them now will determine the kind of men they become. You are missing the point.'

William's eyelids tensed. 'I miss nothing,' he replied curtly. 'I know what we have lost, and what we would have stood to lose without yielding our sons. Do you have so little trust in the way we have brought them up? Do you think so little of them and us?'

She shook her head. 'No,' she said before her throat closed with anguish. 'It is what I think of John that gives me cause for grief.'

John raised his head from the illuminated copy of *Historia Regum, Brittaniae*, his forefinger halting upon an illuminated capital bearing the image of a crowned king. 'Well?' he demanded of Thomas Sandford and gestured him to rise from his kneeling position.

Sandford did so and ran his fingers nervously around the brim of the felt riding cap between his hands. He had ridden hard to reach Winchester before curfew and he was hungry and tired – not that those were considerations when it came to reporting to the King. It was late dusk now, the dinner hour over and he would have to make do with leftovers from the kitchens. 'Sire, the Earl of Pembroke has sent you his son Richard as you requested.'

'Has he, by God?' John removed his finger from the image and closed the book. His gaze was as sharp as amber glass.

'He . . . he said that since you had given him permission

to cross the sea, he was still of a mind to do so – that for good or ill he had to tend to his affairs in Leinster, and in token of his good faith, he sends his boy to you.'

'And did you make it clear to him that I did not wish him to go?' The King's voice was a soft snarl.

Sandford cleared his throat. 'Very much, sire, but he would not be swayed. He said he was sorry you did not trust him but he gladly trusted you with the welfare of his heirs.' He increased the rate at which he drew the brim of the cap through his hands. 'Even as I set out to bring the boy to you, the Earl's servants and grooms were loading up the carts and packhorses to leave for Pembroke.'

'Hah, he trusts me, does he?' John asked savagely. 'What did his Countess say? The virtuous Lady Isabelle?' He could not have spoken with more contempt had he been talking of a common prostitute, and Sandford inwardly flinched.

'The Countess agreed to be bound by her husband's will. She had a mother's reluctance to let the boy go, but she was dutiful in the end.'

John sprang to his feet, took three paces towards the hearth, swung round and turned back. 'Christ on the Cross, William sainted son-of-a-whore-and-a-thief Marshal. All my life I've had to swallow people telling me what a paragon he is, a *preux chevalier*, the greatest, most chivalrous knight in Christendom. My mother thought the sun shone out of his shit, and Richard laboured under the same delusion. But not me, I can see his shit for what it is.' Spittle flecked John's mouth corners.

Thomas said nothing. He supposed that if he were John, he'd be irritated too. William Marshal had cut the meat of honour to the bone to retain his lands in Normandy. He was so popular with his peers and so powerful that John was bound to be disturbed. William

222

could choose to ally with the French monarch or build himself a nice little kingdom in Ireland since his wife's grandfather was Irish royalty. Thomas doubted William would ever do such a thing: the honour that John so scorned would rein him back; but the King's suspicious mind and his own way of conducting business might make that hard for him to believe.

'Where's the boy?'

'Waiting outside, sire. If it's too late I can take him—'

'You make a fine nanny, Sandford,' John said scornfully, 'but don't overstep your bounds. The hour is not that late, and you won't slip him past my attention that easily. Bring him in.'

'Sire.' Feeling anxious, Thomas left the chamber, returning moments later with his young charge.

Richard knew what was expected of him. He had been well taught by his parents and Thomas had given him additional schooling on their ride to Winchester. Keeping his gaze firmly on the floor, he knelt at John's feet. The latter grabbed a fistful of Richard's tunic and hauled him upright.

'So, you are my beloved Marshal's second pup, eh?' John said. 'Well, barring the red hair and freckles, you've a look of him, but that's not necessarily to the good. Do you know why your father sent you to me, boy?'

'Because you asked it of him, sire,' Richard answered calmly, although his heart was thundering in his throat.

'And do you know why I asked it? Did he tell you that?'

Richard flushed. 'No, sire.' He had overheard some of the discussion between his parents and the senior knights of the mesnie, but no one had told him in detail, except that he was to be brave and remember what he had been taught at home. 'He said it would be an opportunity to polish my skills and that I was to make the most of it.'

John's laugh was unpleasant. 'Well, your father certainly seems to have a knack for making the most of anything, whether it's sanctioned or not. Welcome to my household, boy, and let us hope for your sake that you polish up fast. As for your father . . .' He half closed his eyes. 'Perhaps he needs a reminder that if you bite the hand that feeds, you don't get fed, eh, boy?'

'Sire.' Richard glanced swiftly at John, then down. The look on the King's face made him feel afraid. Something terrible was going to happen, either to him and Will – or to their parents.

20

Kilkenny, Leinster, April 1207

Resplendent in the full dignity of a new saffron-coloured gown, gem-encrusted, embroidered with gold and made especially for her return to Ireland, Isabelle presided over the feast in Kilkenny Castle's great hall. As the Countess of Leinster, she sat in state at the centre of the table on the high dais, with William, her consort, beside her, garbed in the tunic of cloth of silver from their daughter's marriage, coronet at his brow. More prosaically, he wore his sword as a symbol of his ability and willingness to uphold her authority.

The meal was a formal celebration of their arrival in Leinster. All the important lords had been invited and the vassals summoned, notably Hugh and Walter de Lacy from Meath, and Philip of Prendergast, who was married to Isabelle's half-sister, Matilda. The latter had been effusive in her greetings and full of feminine compliments about Isabelle's gown, but Isabelle was not taken in. While the envy in Matilda's eyes was natural and understandable with reference to the gown, Isabelle had also noted the way she and her husband had studied the great hall, as if making a minute inventory of what they hoped to own.

Hugh de Lacy and William had seen eye to eye immediately: a boon since de Lacy was one of the most important lords in Ireland – almost a prince in his own domain. Should he have proved hostile, he could have made life difficult for his Marshal neighbours. Isabelle was delighted to see him and William laughing together, and genuinely so, their entire faces involved rather than a tactful parting of the lips. Further along the board, William's nephew Jack was not laughing so much. He had been seneschal of Leinster on his own for three years and Isabelle suspected that his nose had been put out of joint by their arrival and the way William had immediately taken over the reins of government. Isabelle made a mental note to devote some time to smoothing ruffled feathers. Jack was a hard worker, tireless and solid, but he was ambitious too and enjoyed having authority and prestige. Had he not been born out of wedlock, he would have been heir to the Marshal lands in England. He never said it rankled with him that the lands had gone to William, but she had a suspicion that at times it did.

Meilyr FitzHenry had not put in an appearance, but it came as no surprise. Had he done so, he would have had to discuss his seizure of lands to the north-west of Kilkenny that belonged in William's authority. Demands to have the estates restored had been pointedly ignored. FitzHenry had been harassing William's tenants, disrupting merchant trade and whipping up as many Norman barons and native lords as he could to support him against what he contemptuously called the invasion of the 'English softswords'. His campaign was one of the reasons that Isabelle was sitting in state at the centre of the feast table, robed as befitted the granddaughter of Dermot MacMurrough, High King of Leinster, and the daughter of Richard Strongbow, legendary conqueror of the same. Her sons and daughters were seated at the dais table too, boosted on cushions where necessary. They were proof of the virility of the bloodline – that William literally had the balls to deal with Leinster, and that not only was she a great lady, but her womb was fruitful. Walter was fidgeting as always, but doing well by his lights and hadn't said anything too loudly or out of turn – yet. Her daughters were under the watchful eye of their nurses, but thus far even little Eve was behaving beautifully.

The Bishop of Ossory was particularly taken by Gilbert's fluent grasp of Latin and his ability to recite the creed and the paternoster, and not just by rote, but with a deeper understanding. He was also amused by the number of saints' tales that Gilbert knew, from the pious suffering of Saint Edmund, to the more dubious recounting of the legend of Saint Nannan's fleas, which had been banished from the saint's bedding but now so badly afflicted a particular field in Connacht that no one could walk through it for fear of their bites. 'A truly Christian household,' remarked the Bishop to Isabelle with a smile, 'but one that knows how to laugh too.'

'I hope so, my lord,' Isabelle murmured, 'although in truth there has not been much laughter of late and I sometimes think that our troubles rival Saint Nannan's fleas in number.'

The Bishop wiped his lips on a napkin. 'I am sure you and your lord, with God's help, have the strength to deal with them. It certainly seems the case from what I have witnessed thus far.' He lowered his voice so that it would not carry further along the board and he flicked a brief but telling glance at Philip of Prendergast and the knight at his side, David de la Roche, who was slouched in his seat drinking wine and looking bored. 'You must impose your will on these Norman lords who call Leinster their own. They see themselves as a tougher breed than newcomers. Why should they support an interloper such as your husband? What is there to gain in following him and not Meilyr FitzHenry?'

Isabelle drew an indignant breath to answer, but the Bishop raised a swift forefinger. 'Peace, my lady, I am reporting what I have been told. For myself I believe allegiance will come with time, and you have made a good start. Men are here today to look at you and assess your chances. They owe a debt of loyalty to Richard Strongbow and his line. You are the glue. Without you, I believe it would all come apart very fast indeed.'

'I am sorry, you are right to be forthright and I value your honesty,' Isabelle said, with a gesture of apology. 'My husband may be good-humoured and approachable, but men should not mistake such traits for weakness. He has a will of steel and as much if not more experience of battlefield and council chamber than those who malign him. His men would spend their last drop of blood for him. I do not think Meilyr FitzHenry will ever command that kind of loyalty.'

The Bishop reached to his goblet. 'You may be correct, my lady, but you should still be cautious. Meilyr FitzHenry's advantage is that he was a young adventurer in your father's entourage and with him when he laid the foundations for what exists now. FitzHenry's a hard man in battle – he's carved his reputation with a sword and he's respected for it. Of course,' he added thoughtfully, 'not all are pleased by his arrogance and high-handed attitude. He'll only take orders from the King and he uses that authority to feather his own nest.' He bent her an earnest look. 'Your husband will need to be as good at winning men round as his reputation suggests if he is to gain control here, and you must play the part of Strongbow's daughter to the hilt.'

Isabelle dipped her head to show she was taking heed of his advice. 'It is not a part,' she said quietly, sending a glance around the great hall. 'It is who I am.'

William's mood was ebullient when they retired to their chamber. He dismissed the squires and Isabelle's women, and sat on the bed to remove his shoes. They were of softest kidskin, stamped with the Marshal lion, covered with gilding, and the toggle fastenings were of ivory, secured with lacings of braided thread of gold. He looked at them, grinned, shook his head and put them down beside his old, tough, unembellished calf-hide boots that were worn to the shape of his feet and ten times more comfortable.

He turned to look over his shoulder at Isabelle. 'Hugh de Lacy is willing to write to King John to complain about Meilyr's government of Ireland, and to stand with me on the matter of the lands that have been seized.'

'That is excellent news,' Isabelle said. 'Having Hugh de Lacy for an ally will make matters much easier.'

William nodded. 'De Lacy resents King John and Meilyr far more than he does my intrusion. We're natural allies. And then of course there is you . . . Strongbow's daughter.'

Isabelle removed the jewelled band from her head and the gold tippets from the ends of her braids and put them away in their enamelled caskets. 'Will your name be on this letter to the King?' she asked dubiously.

'That would be an open challenge and I don't want to do that. Diplomacy is all. John will take the meaning well enough. He'll see we have the backing of the most important Irish barons without us having to throw it in his face personally. It's more subtle . . .'

Isabelle sat down and, taking up her antler comb, began working it through her loosened hair. 'Let us hope for our sons' sake that John sees it as diplomatic and subtle,' she said a trifle waspishly. Relations between herself and William were still unsettled following his decision at Striguil to send Richard to court. Their differences of attitude and opinion continued to be a source of friction. Neither had sought forgiveness and none had been given. He didn't answer her now, but she sensed his irritation and felt a moment of barren triumph.

He stripped the gold rings from his fingers, unpinned the ornate brooch at his throat and removed the silver tunic. He was untying his shirt when there came a pounding on their chamber door.

'My lord, my lady, there's a messenger from England,' Osbert's voice announced through the wood.

Going to the door, William opened it on his chamberlain and Hywel ap Rhys, a son of William's chief groom and one of his most trusted messengers. It had started to rain and Hywel's woollen cloak glistened with fine droplets in the torchlight. William ushered them into the room. Hywel made his obeisance to William, then delved into his battered leather satchel and withdrew a vellum packet. Dangling beneath it from a plaited silk cord was the sickeningly familiar royal seal.

'Do you know what this contains?' William asked.

Hywel shook his head. 'No, my lord. The royal messenger brought it to Caversham, and I set out from there a week ago.'

'No point keeping you then. Go and find yourself some food and a bed.'

Hywel bowed and departed. Isabelle stared at the letter as if it were poisonous. She felt ill with dread lest something

230

had happened to their sons. William sat down on their bed, cut the tags and opened up the letter. 'If it were about Richard or Will, then Hywel would have known,' he said, as if he had seen into her mind.

She was not reassured. 'You cannot be certain of that.'

William handed the letter across to Osbert. 'Read it,' he said.

Osbert's eyesight was not good in candlelight. He squinted, bringing the letter closer to his face, holding it away, before finally beginning to read in a voice that was still slightly slurred from the wine he had imbibed at the night's feast. Isabelle and William listened in growing dismay as one by one John's letter stripped them of all the awards and privileges they had taken for granted down the prosperous years of royal favour. The custodianship of Gloucester Castle; William's position as sheriff of Gloucester; Cardigan Castle; the keeping of the Forest of Dean and the castle at Saint Briavel's. Sundry wardships and toll rights . . .

The chamberlain's voice died into numb silence. He looked apologetically at William. 'I am sorry, my lord.' He stifled a wine-sour belch. 'Is there anything I can do?'

'Yes,' William answered with phlegmatic composure. 'Go to bed. I'll need you in the morning and with a clear head. Go on, get you gone,' he added as Osbert hesitated.

After the chamberlain had bowed from the room, William tossed the letter on the coffer. Sitting down on the bed, he put his head in his hands. 'Christ's holy blood,' he muttered.

Isabelle had stood rooted to the spot throughout the dreadful recitation. She had felt an initial swoop of relief when the document had made no mention of Will and Richard, but the contents had left her shocked and enraged. If he could do this to their holdings, what might he do to their sons?

'He's punishing us for coming to Ireland.' She felt as if winter had rushed into her blood and frozen it to ice.

'It's more than that,' he said bleakly. 'He's punishing me for daring to do homage to Philip for our Norman lands and for refusing to accompany him to Poitou. He is venting his spleen and making an example at the same time.'

'We cannot let him get away with this.' She folded her arms across her breasts. 'It's . . . it's like rape.'

'Look at what happened to Ranulf of Chester – at what's happening to William de Braose. It could be much worse.' He removed his shirt. 'John doesn't want me in Ireland. He will do everything in his power to prise me away from it. He's angry too, so if he can lay some stripes on my back while he's at it, so much the better as far as he's concerned.' He flexed his torso in an unconscious gesture, showing a musculature that was still honed and taut. 'It's strong enough. I'm gambling that he needs me and has enough sense not to take it too far.'

'That is a terrible gamble to take, especially with Will and Richard in his grasp,' Isabelle said, shivering.

'What would you have me do? Whichever way we turn the channel is sharp with rocks.' He continued to undress, his actions methodically grim.

'Holy God, I do not know how you can be so calm about it all!' she cried. 'As if it's no more of a problem than . . . than weevils in the cheese!'

He raised his head to her. 'Because how else do you steer a ship through a storm – especially a ship that's already battered and leaking, with no certainty of safe harbour? If I abandon the helm and wring my hands in panic with the rest of the crew, then we go down . . . and fast.'

Isabelle inhaled sharply. The expression in his eyes brought an ache to her throat that made it impossible to swallow. He had called her his 'safe harbour' from the moment of their marriage. Returning to her from war and the political battles of the court, she had always been his haven – his fixed peace in a turbulent world – until too great a storm had left her sea defences in broken disorder.

Half turning towards the candlelight, she fumbled with the lacing at the side of her gown, but the silk cord was knotted tight and she couldn't see to pick it apart for the tears in her eyes. She gave a small gasp of effort and frustration, the sound almost a sob.

Without a word, William turned her to face him, gently pushed her hands away from the knot and bent over it himself. His eyesight was still keen while Isabelle knew hers was not as good as it had been for close work these days. Unpicking the knot, he was as dextrous and delicate as an embroideress and it fascinated her to watch the movement of sinew and tendon as he worked, the tracework of veins on the back of his hands, the fine hair that on his wrists and arms was still the brown-gold of his youth. Her breathing shortened and an unexpected spark of lust jolted through her. It had been a long time since they had lain together. Even before the chasm had opened between them, their lovemaking had become a thing of routine and comfort – safe, taken for granted. Now, suddenly, her loins felt heavy and exquisitely sensitive.

'Done,' he said, freeing the lace and gently pulling the ends loose.

She looked at him through her lashes, captured his

right hand, his sword hand, and meshed his fingers through hers. 'And the other one?'

'It isn't knotted.'

'No.' She gazed directly into his eyes and moistened her lips. He deftly unplucked the other lace then slipped his hand inside the gown, against her chemise. Isabelle gave a small, luxurious shiver as she felt the warmth of his palm through the fabric. He moved his hand up her body, between the layers, grazing the tip of her breast in passing, making her gasp. Reaching the strings of her chemise, he gently tugged until they came untied. 'How many more knots must I unravel to reach you?' he asked with a slow smile.

'I am already unravelled.' Isabelle gave a tremulous laugh. His touch was slow and unhurried. Isabelle reached to the drawstring of his braies. 'You have some of your own though.'

'Then I trust you to do the same for me,' he said in a slumberous voice and, setting his hands in her hair, kissed her. Drawing her to the bed, he pulled off the saffron gown of the Countess of Leinster and the whisper-thin linen chemise beneath it.

'More knots.' He grinned breathlessly as he unfastened the garters securing her hose, and peeled the latter slowly down her legs. Then he shed his loosened braies and covered her. Isabelle closed her eyes and wrapped herself around him, drugged with desire, savouring the moment, wanting it to last and last, but driven by the ravenous starvation of abstinence. When so much had been taken away from them, she needed to plant her banner and stand her ground. If not here in their own bedchamber at the heart of their own castle, where else were they as strong?

Her climax took her breath away with its force and she

clenched her hands upon his hipbones as her inner flesh swallowed and swallowed again. He groaned against her throat and she felt him flex and let go within her. It was a good sign, she thought, the mutual release of seed.

'God grant us another child,' she gasped as she recovered. 'One to bind the Irish lords to us and be a symbol of Strongbow's blood.'

'Are our others not that?' William panted when he could speak, his body still locked tight within hers.

'Yes, but they have all been birthed elsewhere.' Even while she stroked his face with tenderness, her voice was fierce. 'This one will be born on Irish soil.'

21

Tower of London, July 1207

Under the watchful gaze of Thomas Sandford, Will grasped the practice shield by the straps and launched himself at his brother. Richard parried with the speed of a viper and Will had to work hard to prevent the younger boy from breaking through his guard. Richard still carried the puppy flesh of boyhood. That, coupled with his red hair, made people underestimate his supple ability and his imagination with a blade.

Sandford intervened to correct Richard's footwork and positioning, but at the same time offered words of praise. 'Your father, or your father's knights have taught you well,' he said. 'Both of you.'

Richard gave him a broad, enthusiastic smile. Will's expression was a lot more wary and his lips barely curved. He had learned to be anonymous at court; to tread softly, listen, and say nothing, to avoid being in the wrong place at the wrong time and not to excel too brightly at anything. To fit in and fade into the background. Richard hadn't caught on yet. He thought that if he was pleasant to people, they would be pleasant to him in return, but that wasn't necessarily so. With their father out of favour at court, Will and Richard were natural targets for the spiteful, especially Richard who did not know how to make himself small. He was jeered at for his red hair, for his size, for having native Irish blood. He had been raised to see the latter as a source of pride, that his great-grandfather had been a high king of Ireland, but at court it counted for nothing except to earn him the taunt of 'bog-trotter'. Sandford put a stop to it when he was around, but he couldn't protect Richard all of the time, and the King's bachelors went out of their way to mock and ridicule. Richard's nature was optimistic and resilient, but Will knew from the way he felt himself that Richard must be hurting somewhere inside that he didn't show to the world.

'Again,' said Sandford, and Will raised his shield and turned his wrist to parry and throw off Richard's fierce, fast assault.

As they continued to spar, William Longespée, Earl of Salisbury, came striding over the sward towards them, fine scarlet cloak flowing from his shoulders like a banner. The youths lowered their blades and bowed. Salisbury was twice over their kin by marriage. Although he also happened to be King John's half-brother, he was affable, and treated Will and Richard as relatives rather than dirt under his shoes. Just now he appeared to be thoroughly agitated.

'Is there something wrong, my lord?' Sandford asked, looking up from his own deferential bow.

Salisbury glanced briefly at Will and Richard and lowered his voice. 'A messenger's just arrived from Ireland. He's with the King at the moment.'

'And the King desires to see the boys?'

Salisbury shook his head and looked alarmed. 'He hasn't asked for them yet, thank God, but he may well do so – and it would be better if they weren't here. Take them out riding, Thomas, or upriver on a barge. Go to Smithfield or Holy Well. Just get them out of here.'

Will pretended to be busy examining the leather binding on the hilt of his practice sword, but his ears were agog. He sent a swift look under his brows to Richard and slightly shook his head in a warning not to look at the adults.

'Ah.' Sandford scratched his head. 'Bad news then?'

Salisbury cleared his throat. 'Meilyr FitzHenry has written to say he's been commanded to return the Marshal lands in his custody or face reprisals.'

Sandford looked incredulous. 'William Marshal wrote that?'

'No. Hugh and Walter de Lacy wrote it, together with half a dozen other Irish barons opposed to FitzHenry's rule, but you could see the Marshal's hand behind it. He's dividing and conquering and there is going to be one almighty upheaval. In God's name, Tom, remove them now. There's no telling what John will do. I'll try and settle him, but it won't be easy, the mood he's in.' Heeling about, Salisbury strode back towards the King's apartments.

Sandford's sigh contained a curse as he turned to face his charges. 'I know you were listening,' he said tersely. 'You're not consummate courtiers yet, even if Will thinks he is.' He marched them to the stables and ordered the grooms to cease forking hay and saddle up their mounts.

'What did my cousin of Salisbury mean?' Will demanded. 'What has my father done?'

'Made a fool of the King,' Sandford growled. 'You know when you poke a stick in a nest of red ants? Well, your father's gone and done the same in Ireland and he's liable to get bitten.'

Richard bristled with indignation. 'Meilyr FitzHenry's my father's vassal. He's wrongly seized some of our land; I know because I heard my parents talking about it before I came to court. It's part of my mother's dower and he has no right to it.'

Sandford leaned against a stall post and shook his head. 'The King is lord of Ireland even if your father and the de Lacys have the privileges of princes over what they hold by the sword. He will not brook your sire stirring up other barons against his justiciar. Neither would I, if I were in his position.'

Will strove to control his breathing. 'Are we in danger?'

Sandford laid a reassuring hand on Will's shoulder. 'Not of your lives, but if the King is in an ugly temper and your father the cause of it, he won't want to see your faces on duty tonight.'

Not in the least fooled, Will went to help the grooms tack up their mounts, a prickling sensation between his shoulder blades.

Awake and restless despite the lateness of the hour, John paced his chamber, his night-robe dragging on the floor rushes. He had calmed from his initial rage on reading the letter from Ireland, but he was still bitterly angry. He would have to deal with William Marshal and deal with him hard. Wherever he looked there was treachery and defiance. The Church was in rebellion against him over the election of the Archbishop of Canterbury, and he was rapidly losing patience with both Canterbury and Rome. And now this on top of everything else.

'William Marshal is my vassal and he forgets it at his peril,' he growled to William of Salisbury who had been playing dice with him earlier and had stayed to keep him company and drink wine. 'I'll not have him and the de

Lacys setting up their own little kingdoms in defiance of my authority. I forbade him to go to Ireland and he ignored me.'

Salisbury shook the dice and flicked them across the wine-puddled table. 'You demanded his second son; you didn't tell him not to go.'

John's eyes flashed with irritation. 'He knew what I meant by it, but he still chose to disregard me. Now he's interfering in my affairs.' He flung his arms wide. 'Look at that port he's building. Look at the revenues it's going to generate for his coffers. He's clearing land for more settlements and making himself cosy with the Church. My brother should never have given him the de Clare bitch to wife. He should have made him make do with Heloise of Kendal like our father first intended. I won't let him rule the roost in Ireland!'

'What are you going to do then?' Salisbury asked in a casual voice.

John checked himself, remembering that Salisbury was kin to the Marshals both through his wife and his Bigod relations. 'I'm thinking about it,' he said vaguely. 'Go on, get to your bed. It's late and that fresh young wife of yours will be finding someone else to warm your space if you're not in it.'

'Not my Ela,' Salisbury said, but all the same he pushed to his feet. 'Still, as you say, it's late. Besides, you've won all my money.'

'It was mine to begin with,' John said scornfully.

Salisbury conceded the point with a shrug. At the door he hesitated and looked round as he adjusted the set of his cloak. 'Don't take out your anger at William Marshal on his sons, will you?'

John exhaled on an exasperated grunt of comprehension. 'I might have known you were responsible for putting them out of harm's way this afternoon. You're too soft, brother.'

'But you won't harm them . . .'

'No, of course not.' John's eyes brightened as if he had just been given a pleasing present. 'My displeasure is with their father, not them.'

When Salisbury had gone, John refreshed his goblet and paced the room in thought. A pity that the older Marshal boy was not on duty. He could have sent him out to fetch one of the court whores, but such sport would suffice for another occasion. There was plenty of entertainment to be had in the future. He wouldn't harm a single hair on their heads, but there were other subtle ways of doing damage, and opening up dark chasms in the fabric of the soul. Oh yes, he knew all about those.

As to Marshal himself . . . John took a drink of wine and rolled it around his mouth. Well, there were several ways of snaring a lion and drawing his teeth, even one as dangerous as Pembroke. The first ploy hadn't worked, but that didn't mean the pursuit was over. The plan just needed some tweaks and adjustments.

22

Kilkenny, Leinster, Autumn 1207

'My lord, I should go with you,' Jean D'Earley pleaded in agitation. He was close to tears. 'You cannot trust the men who are accompanying you.'

William leaned back in his chair and looked fondly at his former squire. 'Precisely. I would rather have them where I can see them, and know what they are doing. I know if I leave my trusted men to guard my wife and her interests, I need not worry about knives in the back.' He glanced in Isabelle's direction and she gave a tight-lipped nod of agreement. He had called a council in the private chamber to discuss the summons he had received from the King that morning. John had commanded William's presence at court, and Meilyr FitzHenry's too, so that the dispute between them could be laid to rest. There was no question of not obeying such a summons but it was imperative to protect Leinster during his absence.

'Jordan, you will take the land from the Ballygauran Pass and defend it as far as Dublin.'

Jordan de Saqueville gripped the hilt of his sword in a businesslike manner. 'Not a sparrow will fart that I don't know of it, my lord.'

William nodded brusquely. 'Jean, your responsibility will be the heartlands of Ui Chennselaig and Ossory.'

Jean was silent and William noticed that the knight's warm olive complexion had paled. 'What is it?'

Jean opened and closed his fists. 'My lord, I do not know if I am capable of doing such a thing. I . . . I am afraid to fail you. If it please you, give the charge to someone else and I will serve him to the best of my ability.'

William eyed him for a moment. Jean had been his ward and his squire and William had given him the best training possible. Jean was past thirty now and as ready as he was ever going to be for major responsibility. Being expected to lead and make decisions rather than competently follow those given by others, however, raised the stakes to a higher level. 'No,' William was adamant. 'It does not please me to give the charge elsewhere. You are capable of doing whatever is necessary. Stephen will be your deputy and your right-hand man. You will naturally consult him for advice – as you will the Countess in all things. You'll also have FitzPayn, FitzRobert, Mallard and others at need. I am not abandoning you to the wolves like a naked babe on a hillside.'

Jean bowed acceptance, but continued to look anxious.

'If I had the least doubt about your ability, I wouldn't have given you the position,' William gave him a searching look. 'There's something else, isn't there? You're looking at me as if you have a mouthful of pips you're longing to spit out, but think I might dismiss you from my presence for bad manners.'

Jean rotated his jaw as if William's comment was a fact rather than analogy. 'Forgive me, my lord, but you should safeguard yourself against treachery. Take hostages from those most likely to turn on you. Some of them will think twice if their sons are in your custody.'

'As John has taken my sons?' William asked scathingly.

Jean reddened but held his ground. 'Yes, my lord, just like that. I think it would be wise.'

'He's right,' Isabelle had been listening in silence, but now she rose to her feet. 'You should have some hold over them.'

William shook his head in refutation. 'I try to bind men to me by other means than making hostages of their children. I don't want to rely on vassals who are only serving me out of fear.'

'And perhaps respect,' Isabelle said in a hard voice. 'I know these men as you do not. They have admiration for harsh measures.'

'And if they renege when you have the hostages, what do you do? Kill their sons? Throw them in the dungeon to starve? No,' he said with quiet vehemence in which there was distaste, 'I will not take hostages when nothing is proven against anyone because that way lies dishonour for both parties. I trust you all to govern Leinster while I am gone. If Meilyr tries anything by proxy, then by all means do as you will to safeguard our interests and protect yourselves. Fight if you must, and fight to win, but don't be the first to draw swords.'

Isabelle staggered away from the latrine shaft where she had spent the last five minutes heaving. She felt drained and utterly wretched. 'It's going to be another boy,' she said weakly to William.

Humour glimmered through his concern. 'How do you know?'

'I'm always more sick when carrying the boys, and at all times of the day.' She took a napkin moistened with rose water from Sybilla D'Earley and patted her face and throat.

'Boys are always more trouble,' Sybilla said with a knowing woman-to-woman look.

Isabelle gave a heartfelt nod of agreement. She didn't add that pregnancy was only half the reason for her queasiness, the other half being worry. William was about to depart for the English court, leaving her in nominal command of Leinster. This baby, above all her others, was truly going to earn the heritage of his ancestry.

Maeve, the Irish midwife, made her rinse her mouth with an infusion of ginger and bog myrtle to ease the nausea. Her maids robed her in a silk chemise and the saffron-gold gown William had stripped from her on a rainy spring evening when they had begotten this child. With her first babies, tight young muscles had kept her figure from ripening until the sixth month, but these days, she began to show at three . . . and to her benefit.

William wore his court robe of silver silk but instead of adorning it with the ornate belt of gold bezants, he had donned his plain leather swordbelt and his scabbarded blade hung at his left hip.

Elizabeth Avenel fetched a small pot of red powder from the cosmetic coffer and Isabelle suffered a tinge to be rubbed into her cheeks. She didn't want to resemble one of the painted women of the court, but from the way she felt knew her complexion needed a boost – just enough to make her look robust and capable of governing Leinster while William was gone. Sybilla draped a wimple of cream-coloured silk over Isabelle's braids and pinned it at her throat with a circlet brooch of amber and gold.

William nodded his approval. 'Beautiful,' he said, 'and regal . . .' His gaze dropped to her belly and a smile curved his lips. 'And with child. Just the right note, I think. Are you ready to face them?'

She drew a deep breath and nodded. Somehow, she

would ignore the nausea; somehow she would hold her head up and smile.

At a formal pace, William escorted Isabelle into the hall. She laid her hand over his in courtly fashion and walked with the grace of a queen, her spine straight, her expression imperious. Behind them came their children, Isabelle's women, and the knights of the mesnie, the latter all wearing their swords.

Isabelle and William halted at the centre of the dais and faced the company in the well of the hall at the feasting benches. Their children and Isabelle's women assembled to the left and the knights stood on right with Jean, Jordan and Stephen taking up places close to their lord and lady.

Their gathered vassals had risen at William and Isabelle's entrance and all eyes had turned to the dais. Isabelle saw wariness, speculation, hostility and the occasional spark of warmth. She and William would have to depend on the loyalty of these lords in the months to come. Most had not brought their womenfolk, although there were a few in evidence – for the most part older women, sure of themselves, and the occasional young wife whose husband preferred to keep her in his sight rather than leave her to temptation at home.

William waited for the scrape of benches and the murmur of conversation to subside, letting the silence draw out for just long enough to further embed the focus, then he drew breath and made full use of his rich, strong voice.

'My lords, here you see the Countess, whom I have brought by the hand into your presence. She is your lady by right of birth, the daughter of Richard Strongbow who enfeoffed you all with lands once he had conquered them with his own sword.' He gazed at Isabelle to accentuate the connection between them before looking again

246

to his audience. 'She remains among you, pregnant with his grandchild. Until, God willing, I return, I pray you all to serve and protect her faithfully, as is her right. She is your liege lady as well you know and I have no claim to anything here except through her.' Turning to her, he knelt in homage, putting his hands between hers as would a vassal. Isabelle felt a sweeping surge of love and pride. Her eyes welled with emotion. Stooping, she bestowed on him the formal kiss of peace, and then kissed him again, as her husband, her gaze tender.

One by one, the barons came to the dais, knelt and swore their oaths of fealty to her while William stood a little to one side, now taking no part, emphasising the fact that the right was indeed Isabelle's and that he was only present to support her. Everyone in the room made obeisance and swore; not one man demurred; but both she and William knew it was still play-acting.

Once the oath-taking was complete, Hugh le Rous, Bishop of Ossory, blessed the food and the gathering sat to dine.

'I have done my best,' William said as he served Isabelle and himself from a steaming dish of mussels. 'I have appealed to their sense of identity and their loyalty to you, but it remains to be seen how many will abide by their word.'

Isabelle looked out over the gathering below them, watching their guests setting to with industry – very willing indeed to take their bread and salt and drink their wine. 'I know the value of the oaths I've been given and how they equate to the men who knelt in homage.' She gave him a warm look. 'Yours was made of gold.' Her expression hardened. 'But some I know offered dross. I have my eye on them.'

*　　*　　*

While William was feasting his vassals and allies at Kilkenny, Meilyr FitzHenry was in Dublin making his own final preparations to leave for England. He fastened his cloak with a large silver pin, stabbing it down through the thick red wool of his cloak. Smoothing his hair, donning a cap edged with gold braid, he turned to his nephew and the mercenary captain with whom he had been talking while he dressed. 'You are clear what to do?' he asked.

'Yes, my lord,' said his nephew, his dark eyes eager and bright. 'We are to wait until you have been gone for seven days and then begin our work.'

Meilyr nodded, then wagged a peremptory finger. 'But not for a seven-day, be certain of that, Robert. Give me time to be away and Marshal too. He mustn't have the opportunity to turn back. And be thorough. I want that pride of his cut down to the size it should truly have, not the grand cockstand he flaunts at the world.'

Meilyr's analogy met with appreciative grins from both men and their good humour was further increased by the pouch of silver he gave to each of them. 'Go now,' he said, 'and I want to hear well of your endeavour.'

'And good fortune go with yours, my lord,' said his nephew as he headed to the door with a young man's swagger.

Meilyr smiled thinly. 'I intend it to.'

23

Newtown, Leinster, Autumn 1207

The harvest had been good and the barns at Newtown were full of grain and hay that would take people and livestock through the winter months. The town itself had passed from the embryo stage of raw earth and a few crude buildings to become a thriving infant. Houses abounded now, from modest abodes of timber and thatch to fine stone buildings of two storeys, owned by the merchants who had been encouraged to settle. The jetties and moorings along the riverbank had been improved and were being further developed. Cranes were busy on the wharfside unloading building materials for more dwellings and supplies for the hinterland and anchored trading vessels thronged the quay.

Hywel and Dai, the sons of William's senior groom, had travelled into the town to pick up two mares and a stallion that William had sent over from Pembroke. Hywel was usually employed as a messenger to his lord but, being between missions, had a couple of days to socialise with his older brother. Having collected the animals, the young men repaired to the small hostelry near the town wall to share a jug of bog-myrtle ale before setting out for

Kilkenny. A pair of off-duty soldiers lounged at another trestle, playing a desultory game of dice and the hosteller's dog was lying amid the rushes, grinding a bone against his back teeth.

Hywel stretched out his legs and contemplated his ale. He was glad to see the soldiers; they gave him a sense of security. For most of the week he had been feeling the same uncomfortable prickling sensation between his shoulder blades that came over him when travelling dangerous stretches of road on business for his lord. Thus far nothing had happened to sanction the feeling but it hadn't gone away either. The Countess had doubled the guard at Kilkenny and Jean D'Earley had sent out extra patrols . . . but Hywel still slept with his sword at his bedside.

The hosteller's daughter stooped at the hearth to check on some oatcakes as they browned. A twirl of hair had escaped her cap and dangled against her cheek in a glossy hazel curl. She glanced up, met Hywel's gaze, and smiled before looking down.

'You've no time for dalliance.' Dai kicked him under the table. 'We've to sup up and get the beasts on the road.'

Hywel made a face. 'There's always time for dalliance.' Ignoring Dai's scowl, he went to make small talk with the girl. Shaking his head, Dai drained his mug and went back out to the horses.

Hywel had got as far as asking her name, one eye cocked to the looming bulk of her father, when Dai burst back into the tavern, his eyes wide with alarm. 'Raiders!' he yelled. 'FitzHenry's men are firing the barns!'

The two soldiers shoved away from their trestle and charged outside, drawing their swords as they ran. The hosteller grabbed his wife and daughter and bundled them out of the back of the hostel, through the door leading to the outbuildings and pigsty.

250

Hooves thundered in the street. Outlined against the door, Hywel watched a mounted knight stand in the saddle and hurl a flaming torch at the roof. An instant later another brand flew through the entrance and landed in the rushes near the hearth. Hywel ran to stamp it out, his arm across his eyes, acrid smoke catching his lungs. Above his head, he heard the crackle of blazing thatch. Dai shouted, the sound rising to a shriek and then abruptly cutting off. He fell at Hywel's feet, a spear embedded in his spine. His mouth opened and closed but no sound came. Instead there was blood, pulsing dark, like vomited wine. Hywel stared in horrified shock. 'Dai? God's holy face, Dai!'

His brother's eyes were already black with death and they didn't know him. A soldier clad in a short mail hauberk strode through the door, round shield in his left hand. Grasping the spear embedded in Dai's body, he wrenched it loose and hefted it. Hywel did the only thing he could. Head down, he charged the man and in attacking, rather than fleeing, took him by surprise. For a moment they grappled back and forth. Hywel had had some training and was a strong, brawny lad fighting for his life. While the hauberk protected his opponent, it also slowed his movements and put more strain on his muscles. Breath sobbing in his throat, Hywel succeeded in tearing the spear out of the soldier's hands and then, because it was kill or be killed, he reversed the haft and rammed the blunt end hard against the other's throat, crushing his windpipe. The man fell, writhing, dying, making sounds that Hywel never wanted to hear again. Above his head the roof was as red as the vault of hell and the room was wreathed in choking tentacles of smoke. Functioning on the instinct of a hunted animal, Hywel ran out of the back entrance, the spear still gripped in his hand.

The hosteller lay amongst his leeks with his throat cut; his wife was sprawled nearby and she too was dead, a great red stain over her heart. Down at the sty, beside the slain sow and piglets, two men had caught the daughter. One had mounted her and the other had his boot on her neck, pinning her down while his comrade committed rape.

Rage engulfed Hywel in a massive red tide that took away all reason. One moment he was shaking his head, gasping denial, wanting to run, the next he was upon the men. The one standing had time to raise his axe but he was too slow and Hywel speared him in the belly, dragged the weapon free and turned to plunge it into the second one who was striving to lift himself off the girl. Hywel heaved him off her and seizing the axe from the dying first man, used it to finish the other with a shattering blow to the skull.

The girl rolled to one side and staggered to her feet. Blood-freckles stood out against the pallor of her face and her pupils were enormous with shock. The red wave in Hywel's brain diminished and he stared at the dead men in surprise and revulsion. The exposed buttocks mooning the air; the great wound in the head of one; the dark hole in the other's belly. He swallowed and swallowed again. From the street came the sound of cries and screams, the clash of weapons, the roar of flame. He looked frantically round the enclosure, saw the withy brake screening the latrine pit from the view of the tavern, and grabbing the girl's arm, pulled her across to it.

'They won't come looking in this place. To make a run now would be too dangerous – we're safer going to ground.' He dropped to his knees behind the wattle fencing, his legs suddenly feeling as if the marrow had run out of them. He could no more have run and fought now than a newborn child. The girl flopped beside him, teeth chattering with shock. After a moment, Hywel pulled her into his arms and she clung to him, her fingers digging so hard into his flesh that he would have a memento of purple bruises for weeks to come, but they would be as nothing compared to the horror engulfing his mind. The world was on fire, his brother was dead, and nothing would be ever be the same again.

Isabelle laid her hand on Hywel's shoulder as he knelt at her feet. He had staggered into Kilkenny with a straggle of refugees from the sacked town. All of the storage barns had gone up in flames; so had most of the houses. Meilyr FitzHenry's men had descended like wolves, looting, raping and slaughtering. Twenty of William's soldiers and serjeants were dead and as many townspeople, including the parents of the girl on her knees at Hywel's side.

'They struck out of nowhere, my lady,' Hywel said. 'One minute I was drinking with Dai in the tavern, the next we were in the midst of a raid and Dai was . . . Dai was . . .' He gulped, unable to go on.

'He will be buried with all ceremony and masses said for his soul,' Isabelle said gently, and then her voice hardened. 'Those who undertook this vile slaughter will be brought to justice, I promise you that. I will not let this pass.'

'My lady.' He gave a surreptitious sniff and wiped his cuff under his nose.

Rage filled Isabelle like a burning stone. Had she been able to lay hold of the perpetrators at this instant, she would have torn them limb from limb with her bare hands.

She watched Hywel solicitously escort the young woman down the hall to where her stewards and almoner were supplying food, blankets and clothing to those in need, then she turned to Jean D'Earley and Jordan de Saqueville, who had been in the hall all morning, talking to survivors.

'Go to Newtown, or what remains of it,' she said to Jean. 'I want you to take messages of support and tell the people that they will be protected. Nothing like this will happen again. Say that the Countess, their lady, swears it on her soul and may she be damned if Meilyr FitzHenry's men harm so much as a single hair on the smallest child's head ever again. Arm yourselves. Get your patrols out and bring those responsible to me.' Her eyes blazed. 'Do what your lord would have done.'

'You do not need to urge me to my duty, my lady,' Jean said grimly. 'We will bring those who did this to justice.'

Isabelle gave a curt nod. 'As my lord wished, we did not start hostilities, but you have my leave to finish them.'

'My lady.' He bowed over her hand and strode from her presence with a vigour that spoke of distress and determination. Isabelle went among the wounded and the homeless who had fled here to Kilkenny rather than continuing to take their chance at Newtown. Listening to their tales fuelled her anger. She was accustomed to the vagaries of warfare and *chevauchée*, was married to a man who had carved his living and his rise to power out of the tourney and battlefield, but this was different because it was personal. The war was on her lands, harming her people and her reputation. She had been challenged and found wanting and it left her feeling sick, vulnerable and so angry that she was afire. She vowed that Meilyr FitzHenry would pay, and that the cost would beggar him.

'I have let her down,' Jean said bitterly as he rode out of Kilkenny at the head of a patrol. 'And my lord. What will he say when I tell him that twenty of his men are dead?' He tugged fitfully at the nasal bar of his helm.

Jordan de Saqueville grunted. He was five years older than Jean and although not more experienced, his easier nature sometimes allowed him to see more clearly. 'My lord was expecting something of the kind to happen. He won't blame us or think less of us – unless we fail now. We must think about the task in hand, not whip ourselves bloody over what has passed.' He glanced across. 'If we can catch the bastards and bring them before the Countess, it will make up for much.'

The words served to steady Jean and bolster his courage. It wasn't that he was unable to lead, more that he was accustomed to having a higher authority in the background – someone who would grasp his hand should he slip. Now he was treading the edge of a precipice without that prop and the fear of failure was acute, especially as in his own eyes he had already been found wanting.

Shortly before midday the Irish trackers and lightly armed scouts returned to the main party with the information that they had discovered the raiders' camp set up in a wood to the north-east of the road with tents pitched and booty deposited from the sack of Newtown.

'I'd say, my lord, that they're going to attempt some more mischief before they ride home, or they would be long gone by now,' said one of the scouts. His name was Hakon and he was of Dublin Viking ancestry with fierce blond whiskers and ice-blue eyes. A vicious-looking axe was stuffed through his belt and his tunic was almost indecently short, threatening to expose his buttocks. 'They've got guards posted all round and scouts of their own out, but they didn't see us – too busy sorting their gains and making sure of their own portions.'

'They are still in camp now?' Jordan asked.

'Aye, but preparing the horses. There's mischief afoot.'

Jean forced himself to think beyond his anxiety. What

were they after? What was left? 'The grange upriver,' he said aloud. 'And the cattle pens. They'll go for them.'

'You think they'd dare those?' Jordan asked.

For a moment Jean was assailed by doubt, but he forced it down. He had to be decisive. 'What else can it be? Yesterday's raid will have emboldened them. They've been told that we're easy meat and after their success at Newtown they believe it. Yes, I'm certain. They'll try for the granges.'

They came not shyly or in stealth, but boldly in full daylight with torches kindled ready to burn all to the ground, and weapons drawn to deal with any guards they encountered. Axe-wielding Irish warriors, bare-legged and long-bearded, the wealthier ones marked out by their shirts of saffron yellow. Some rode ponies bare-backed and bridled with rope in the native fashion. Their paymasters and overlords wore Norman mail and rode with stirrups and curb bits on their stallions, and their footsoldiers carried spears and shields.

Jean watched them come, his heart hammering at his chest wall, his stomach a sick hollow. His men were ranged behind him, blocking the road to the barn, and he had archers covering him as he waited for Meilyr's men, his destrier held in tight and his sword bare in his fist.

Their leader signalled a halt and then paced his stallion forward until he faced Jean. His glance flickered over the red shield with its blazon of silver scallop shells. 'Marshal's lap dog,' he sneered. 'Come to get his tail singed.'

Jean drew himself up. 'You will yield yourself and your men to me and you will make reparation for the burning and looting of the property of the Countess of Leinster,' he said icily. 'Otherwise, suffer the consequences.'

The knight let out a belly laugh. 'You even whimper like a cur too. You English couldn't fight your way out of a rotten flour sack. How many did your dead number yesterday?'

'Too many to let you go further down this road,' Jean replied. 'Yesterday will not happen again.'

'There speaks a fool,' scoffed the knight. 'You won't stop me, nor will any man who serves a Marshal. Stand aside, turn tail and flee, or die like your comrades did. It's all the same to me. I've killed better men than you.'

'Then it's time you joined them,' Jean retorted and signalled the attack.

The fighting was swift and brutal, but as Jean wielded his sword and controlled his destrier, he lost all fear and apprehension. He was accustomed to the fray; he had been trained by a master of this art; and his equipment was of the best. His men too had been trained to the rigorous standards set by the Earl of Pembroke and they were fired up and eager to avenge their comrades. FitzHenry's men could not deal with such concentrated skill and aggression. The chance-come mercenaries scattered like feathers from a torn bolster; the lightly armed Irish skirmishers fell beneath the onslaught of mailed men and destriers; the Norman-clad core could not hold. Some on the outskirts succeeded in escaping, but many more were brought down or cried surrender.

Breathing hard, the edge of his sword slick with blood, Jean lowered his aching arm until the edge of the blade nudged the windpipe of the knight at his feet. Corpses of men and beasts littered the road. Weapons strewed the dust. A few of the downed men were twitching and groaning. 'I should finish you here and now,' he said between heaves for breath.

'Do that and there'll be no ransom.' The knight's wrist

was twisted at an odd angle, plainly broken. Blood was dribbling from a leg wound.

'You think your piddling ransom money matters more to me than the lives of my comrades?' Jean was sorely tempted to lean on the blade. He could see the beginnings of terror in the man's eyes beneath the bravado. It would be good to hear him scream for mercy as he choked and bled. Too good. Jean drew a deeper breath and shuddered. His lord would never countenance such a deed. 'Think yourself fortunate for the moment that the Countess wants prisoners, not corpses,' he said, withdrawing his sword. 'And unfortunate that she is going to be the one to deal with you.'

Seated in the lord's chair on the dais, Isabelle stared frigidly at the battered and bloodied men who had been flung on their knees before her: murderers, mercenaries, rebels, traitors; all at her mercy to do with as she chose. She knew what she wanted to do: build a scaffold outside the hall and string them up to dance in full view of all. Perhaps for good measure emasculate them all too as they kicked and died. However, she curbed the bloody demands of her rage. While it would give her great pleasure to deal with them thus, it would create complications from which there would be no way back. Done was always done. She had others to think about and she did not want to jeopardise William or her sons at John's court because of any impetuous act on her part.

Their leader was kin to Meilyr FitzHenry – the son of his sister and a prize captive. Currently his neck was pinned under the sole of Jean D'Earley's boot. Aware that all eyes in the hall were upon her, that she was the lady of Leinster, dealing judgement in her own hall, Isabelle motioned Jean to step back and rose to her feet.

Jean lifted his foot off the knight's neck and, drawing his sword, positioned the blade to strike at a moment's provocation.

'Look at me,' Isabelle commanded. She pitched her voice low, the way Queen Eleanor had been wont to do when dealing with men.

White-faced with pain, blood-streaked and grimy, FitzHenry's nephew raised his head. Isabelle met the hatred, misery and fear in his eyes without flinching. 'Tell me why I should not hang you and your men forthwith for what you have done to me and mine,' she said.

He lifted his chin and said with a spark of defiance, 'I am nephew to Lord Meilyr and worth your while to keep alive.'

'You are nothing and worth less than nothing,' Isabelle retorted, eyes flashing. 'Does a vassal's oath mean naught to you or your lord? Your ransom will not pay for the sack of Newtown and the death of my loyal men . . . but a blood price might go some way towards assuaging the damage.'

He bared his teeth. 'You will need us to exchange for your own life when King John comes to lay siege to your walls, and come he will, my lady: make no mistake about that. You and your lord will fall.'

The words struck Isabelle like a blow to her soft and vulnerable core, but she managed to look indifferent. Jean's foot came down again, hard, and Meilyr's nephew choked against the floor. 'Why bother with the expense of a scaffold?' Jean demanded. 'I could finish him here, my lady.'

Isabelle dug her nails into the palms of her clenched fists. Against the wall of her womb she felt the child kick. 'No,' she said. 'It would be my dearest wish to see you do that, but I will not yield to the heat of anger. While these men are captive they can do us no more harm. Let them stand hostage for my lord Meilyr's behaviour when he returns from court. None are to be ransomed until I deem fit. As to King John?' – she gave the knight a derogatory look – 'I have met him. I know him as you do not, so do not presume to tell me, the Countess of Leinster, what he will and will not do.' She gestured to Jean and the prisoners were yanked out of her presence with a certain amount of gratuitous brutality. The cells beneath the hall were dank and cold. Perhaps some would die of their wounds tonight. Let them. On the morrow, those who survived would be given minimum provisions to keep body and soul alive until William's return. And if William and her sons did not return, then the prisoners would never see the light of day again.

Isabelle summoned her women and rapidly left the hall. Reaching her chamber, she staggered over to the privy and was wretchedly sick down the waste shaft, her body riven by tremors of revulsion. Her concerned ladies wanted to send for her physician, but she refused and made them summon her chaplain instead.

'I have letters to dictate to my husband. He has to know what has happened.' As she spoke, her voice steadied. She took the cup of potent Norwegian ice-wine that an anxious Sybilla D'Earley handed to her and waved away further protests. 'With the Earl gone, I must play both lord and lady,' she said with grim determination. 'I have no choice but to be strong; I have to do what is necessary.' She moved to the great bed which was made up with the day covers and the hangings tied back. 'Nevertheless, there is nothing to say that I cannot dictate to my husband from our marriage bed . . . indeed, perhaps that is the best place.'

As she had known they would, her words caused her

women to relax. She felt tired and shaken and it was good to slip off her shoes and rest against the bolsters and cushions, but her resolve remained iron hard and when Father Walter entered the chamber with his quills and inks, she bade him be seated at the bedside and without hesitation told him what she desired him to write.

24

Woodstock, Oxfordshire, November 1207

William had never been fond of the chase the way that other men were. When they gathered in enthusiastic huddles to discuss every twist and turn of the pursuit, every thrust of spear and flight of arrow, his attention would wander and his eyes glaze over. He enjoyed eating the fruits of the kill – he was extremely fond of roast boar with cammeline sauce and the cook at Striguil had a particular way with venison that made it worth a fifty-mile detour just for the pleasure of dining on the dish. However, he had a small army of huntsmen and foresters to bring such delicacies to his table. Chasing some poor dumb beast in order to put a blade through its heart was not a pastime he enjoyed.

King John had desired to hunt and William had had no option but to join him and the rest of the court in the extensive deer park surrounding the palace. William did not have to be at the forefront of the chase though, and had dropped back off the pace. The halloo of the hunting horn sounded through the woods, made plaintive by distance. King John and his immediate party, which included several of William's Irish vassals, Meilyr

FitzHenry amongst them, and William's own eldest son in his capacity of squire, had raced off in pursuit of a ten-pointed hart. William had let them go, retaining only his nephew and his knight Henry Hose as escort.

'Not joining the fray, Marshal?' William de Braose joined him. His horse, a powerful grey, was sweated up and nervously sidling. De Braose was out of favour with John too. Ostensibly it was about the vast sums of money de Braose owed to the Crown for land grants, but there were undercurrents, some of them so murky that no sane man would dip his hand into them.

'No,' William answered wryly. 'They are intent on their prey for the moment and I wouldn't want to distract them from their victim.'

De Braose grunted with caustic humour. 'Me neither, but you're a brave man not to listen to what they're plotting behind your back.'

'They won't have time to plot anything in the thick of the chase. It's all about building patronage and alliances while making me know that I am as welcome as a leper at a marriage feast. The plotting will come later.'

'And it does not bother you?'

'Of course it does, but I will not waste my energy at this stage on what cannot be changed.'

De Braose's mouth twisted as if he had bitten into a piece of bread and discovered it full of weevils. 'Philip of Prendergast is wed to your wife's half-sister, is he not? These men are your vassals, and your kin by marriage. How can you let them plot treachery under your nose?'

'Better that than leaving them to their own devices in Ireland. Besides,' William added drily, 'they haven't committed any treachery yet.' He ducked as he rode beneath a low oak branch, then reined his courser in the direction of the far-away sound of the horn.

'Perhaps not,' de Braose growled, 'but the stench of it would still outdo a fox den in the mating season.' He clapped spurs to the grey and rode on.

'What was all that about?' Jack Marshal asked.

William glanced at his nephew. 'The King desires to curb de Braose's power and influence the same as he desires to curb mine.' He looked thoughtful. 'De Braose is in debt beyond any means of getting out of it, and John is hounding him.'

'But de Braose is . . .' Jack began, then glanced at Henry Hose and changed what he had been about to say. '. . . is one of the King's staunchest allies.'

'An ally who has demanded far too much for services rendered,' William said with a pointed look at his nephew. He knew Jack had been about to speak of de Braose's claim to have heard King Richard's deathbed statement naming John his heir. De Braose had also been in Rouen at the time of Arthur's disappearance and that was a subject no one mentioned.

Far away, he heard the mort being blown. William did not have to add that he too was endangered by the wolf pack; the more so because he had brought his with him.

'See Marshal, a fine ten-point hart!' John boasted as William rejoined the hunt. 'A pity you couldn't keep up with us for the kill, but at least your son knows his part.'

William glanced at his heir. Will was carrying a spear. A hunting knife hung at his left hip, a finger smear of blood daubed his right cheek and his eyes shone with exhilaration. He was surrounded by several of William's Irish vassals. Meilyr FitzHenry was openly smirking. The dead deer had been gutted and was being borne between poles carried by four huntsmen.

'Your Irish lords are doughty huntsmen,' John added

with malice. 'They don't hang back like finicky old women. What kind of leader shirks the fray?'

'The kind whom men do not respect, sire?' Meilyr FitzHenry responded as if giving a civil answer to a genuine question. 'In Ireland such a one would not last for long.'

John looked amused. 'What do you say to that, Marshal?'

'Nothing, sire,' William replied evenly.

John looked disdainfully surprised. 'Nothing?'

'There is no point. Lord Meilyr is entitled to his opinion concerning leadership, but he knows that the hunt is not the same as the battlefield – or I hope he does, for his sake.'

An irritated expression crossed Meilyr's face. 'You will not find me lacking in either skill,' he said haughtily. 'I remind you that I have dwelt in Ireland for more than thirty years, and you have not.'

William inclined his head. 'Indeed, my lord, and I have dwelt at court for the same and you have not, so which one of us is a fish out of water?'

Meilyr opened his mouth to retort, but John pre-empted him with a look and calming gesture. 'This is neither the time nor the place for such debate and the dinner hour waits at the lodge. Let every man who took part in the hunting of this fine beast have a place at my table. Let those who stayed back find their hospitality elsewhere.' As he spoke, John leaned to place an avuncular hand on Will's shoulder. The meaning, aimed at William, was explicit. *I have your son and under your nose I am making of him what I choose.*

There was a flurry of laughter at William's expense, some of it good-natured, but much of it tinged with malice. William absorbed the snub impassively, telling himself that at least he didn't have to sit at a table and be pleasant to Meilyr for the rest of the day, but nevertheless, he felt the cut, and he was filled with apprehension on Will's behalf.

On returning to the palace, William sought out Thomas Sandford, who had day-to-day custody of his second son. Richard was cheerfully polishing harness and talking to another squire as he worked. A soft fuzz of moustache and beard framed his developing features. William was both amused and envious. Growing a beard of any kind had been beyond him at sixteen.

'You're doing a fine job,' he remarked with a nod at the shine on the harness.

Richard flashed a grin. 'I don't want to be whipped for bad work.' His voice had deepened several notches since the spring and was still going down.

Thomas Sandford made a rude sound between pursed lips. 'The reason you are polishing harness in the first place instead of riding with the hunt is in lieu of a whipping, and well you know it, lad.' He cast an exasperated glance at William. 'He put a dead rat in a lady's travelling satchel on the road here, and he skipped mass to attend a cockfight when I had given explicit orders that he be in church.'

Richard studied his shoes, his expression as modest as a demoiselle's. William tried to look severe, but couldn't prevent a smile tugging at his mouth corners. Thomas relented and, with a laugh, tousled Richard's bright hair. 'Ah, it's the usual squire's mischief, and no real harm done,' he said. 'He has a good heart and he works well. As long as his head doesn't swell out of proportion to the rest of him with all the thoughts it contains, he'll prove a fine knight.'

Sandford's praise gave William a much-needed boost of pleasure. 'When I was his age I was known as "Guzzleguts" and "Slugabed",' he said. 'And I had to endure a deal of jealousy and taunting from men who resented me.'

Sandford cleared his throat. 'Well, life doesn't change much. I watch him as much as I can.'

'For which I'm grateful, if an accursed man's gratitude means anything.'

Sandford rubbed the back of his neck and looked embarrassed. He was a King's man, a royal servant and a healthy sense of self-preservation kept him circumspect.

'My other son . . . he is with the King much of the time?'

'Of late, my lord, yes, but he is well into his training now. He's an expert carver at the table and the King often employs him for that.'

Richard set the harness to one side. 'He's taken up with one of the court ladies, the one whose satchel I gifted with a rat,' he volunteered.

William raised an eyebrow. 'Has he indeed?'

'It's nothing,' Sandford said. 'All lads of that age have an itch in their braies.'

William eyed the knight. 'True, but who is she and how is he affording her price? I certainly couldn't have paid for the services of such women when I was his age – assuming that we are speaking of a courtesan and not someone's wife or daughter?' He knew all about the court whores. They followed in the royal train: bright, gaudy butterflies whose task it was to entertain men who were absent from home for long stretches of time, or who had the financial means and the appetites but not the wives to relieve their lusts. Most of the women had expensive tastes in one form or another and would not be inclined to waste time on a boy of seventeen whose father might be a magnate, but one who was dangerously outside the royal favour.

Sandford looked uneasy. 'That I don't know. I assumed that perhaps he had some income from you. Also, the woman seems to find him engaging. I was under the impression it amused her to take an inexperienced but enthusiastic lad under her wing and teach him things. No harm in that.'

William remembered Isabelle's fears that their sons would be morally corrupted by life at court and their young lives twisted in directions that neither she nor William would have chosen for them. No court whore would take a squire between her legs out of charity. Whim was probably not the motive either. The court prostitutes were established courtesans of the shrewdest order and were only kind for money or power.

'You'll only make things worse if you throw down a challenge to his manhood,' Sandford warned.

'You think so?' William gave an arid smile. 'The way matters stand, I doubt it.'

Lying on the camp bed in his pavilion, William abandoned the idea of sleep. He pillowed his hands behind his head and breathed slowly and deeply, relaxing his body even while his thoughts continued to dart and turn like shoals of small fish. Nights like this were more usual to him on battle campaign and he knew that providing he rested, he could do without the sleep. Knowing that he had Isabelle and their children waiting to welcome him home usually sustained him but now the security of his family was one of his darting thoughts. He feared for them. Meilyr FitzHenry had been casting him malicious smirks as if he knew something William didn't. William knew how vulnerable the Irish lands were. Jean was experienced but untried at the level William was demanding of him. Meilyr's capabilities were an unknown quantity. John's, however, were all too obvious. William shied from that line of thought because it led to anxiety beyond bearing. What he needed to do was concentrate on his own responses to the threats and therefore be prepared.

He turned to considering his eldest son. What to do about Will? Let matters run their course? Pretend that as a father he did not see what was happening? Thomas Sandford said that every youth sowed wild oats, which was true, but not every youth did it at court in the company of whores and unsavoury hangers-on ... and in the company of John himself, whose twisted soul had the capacity to bend others out of true. He thought of himself at that age. What would his father have done? Probably laughed and joined him in waywardness, purloining the woman along the way. On the other hand, he might have hauled him out by the scruff of his neck and thrashed him to within an inch of his life. The only predictable thing about William's father had been his unpredictability.

'What do I do?' he asked the canvas roof of his pavilion. The response was a soft spatter of rain and a flurry of chill November breeze.

'My lord, did you speak?' His squire poked his head around the flaps.

'Only to myself. Hand me my cloak, lad.'

'You're going out, my lord?' The youth's gaze widened with surprise.

'Yes,' William said. 'Put up another bed while I'm gone. I may be returning with company.'

William found his eldest son playing dice in a corner of the hall with a group of the King's mercenaries. A trestle from the earlier feast had been left in situ as their gaming board and their play was illuminated by half a dozen candle stubs rammed on wrought-iron spikes. A woman with cider-coloured braids and a figure-skimming gown of green samite was sitting in Will's lap. His tunic and shirt gaped at the throat and the woman's hand was very busy inside his braies. Will's face was drink-flushed and his eyes as glassy as those of a dead herring.

William hesitated briefly, then squared his shoulders and strode forward to the company. 'God's greeting,' he said pleasantly enough, and gave a separate, businesslike nod to the whore whom he knew from long acquaintance if not by personal commerce. 'Marie.'

She gave him a sultry look from eyes the deep brown of oak-gall ink and shamelessly continued to work her hand inside Will's braies. William considered her optimistic. The condition the boy was in, she had more chance of raising the dead than a cockstand.

'Marshal,' saluted the mercenary Gerard D'Athée, an unsettling combination of mockery and wariness adorning his blunt features. 'Have you come to play dice with the dregs of the earth?'

'Another time perhaps,' William said with icy good manners. 'I desire a word with my son in private – a family matter.'

Will lifted his head with a sudden jerk and attempted with only partial success to focus on his father. 'Tell it to me here . . . These're all my friends . . . won't mind listening . . .' He wafted a hand vaguely round the trestle to encompass his companions.

'I am sure they won't mind, but this is for your ears alone. Marie, go and find another suitor to play your games of catch the coney. This particular one's finished.'

She thrust out her lower lip in a red pout, but under

William's unyielding stare removed her hand from Will's crotch, lifted herself out of his lap and went to sit beside Gerard D'Athée.

'If he's leaving the game, then he needs to pay what's owed.' D'Athée gently shook the dice in his cupped hand. All his movements were measured and understated. The man himself was lethal.

'My chamberlain will pay you,' William snapped. 'See him.'

Will lurched to his feet and sat down again abruptly. William had to seize his arm and drag him upright. Supporting most of his son's weight, he drew him staggering into the raw November air.

'What'sh the news?' Will slurred owlishly. 'What family matter?'

'This,' William said and fisted him in the gut. Will collapsed and hung on all fours, vomiting. 'Get it out of yourself, boy, all of it.' When Will had ceased retching William seized him again, dragged him to the horse trough in the yard and dunked his head. Will took a wild swipe and missed, collapsing in a sodden heap on the hoof-patterned ground. William hauled him upright, lifted him over his shoulder like a huntsman with a roe buck, and bore him to his pavilion where he threw him down on the pallet his squire had prepared.

'Sleep it off,' he said as he drew a blanket and sheep-skin rug over his son's lean frame. 'In the morning, we'll talk.'

Lying down on his own bed, William pulled the feather quilt to his ears and within minutes was asleep.

Dawn arrived in a grey cloak that misted the tops of the trees and clad the white-washed walls of the palace of Woodstock in mizzle as fine as cobwebs. Standing outside

271

his pavilion, William inhaled the dank air and sipped steaming liquid from the cup in his hand. A few folk were up and about, and the thick smell of damp woodsmoke from cooking fires was pervasive. His cook was busy at a trestle, preparing the bread that another attendant had just fetched from the palace bakehouse. Muttering about the shortcomings of apprentice bakers, the man sliced the blackened bottom off one loaf and dusted ash from the side of another. A flitch of bacon and a wheel of cheese sat on the trestle beside the bread, ready to feed William and his knights.

From within the tent, William heard a groan and a tentative rustle of movement followed by the noise of a waterfall from the direction of the chamberpot. He started to smile and bit the inside of his mouth. A few moments later, Will parted the tent flaps and tottered outside, eyes squinting at the light, one hand clutching his midriff. His brown hair stood up in unruly clumps and his complexion was grey.

'You look more like a corpse tipped off a bier than a young man fresh out of bed,' William commented as he handed him the cup he had been holding.

Will took it, sniffed, and gagged.

'Honey and spring water,' William said. 'Your mother swears by it when she's breeding.'

'My lady mother can keep it,' Will retorted, thrusting the cup back at William and huddling inside his cloak, his expression one of abject suffering.

'I don't suppose you remember much about last night,' William said.

'I do. You hit me.' Resentment flared in the young man's voice.

'To make you sick so that you did not die in your own vomit. I'm not going to lecture you. Your malaise can do it for me.'

'You said something about a family matter. Was that a lie?'

William looked out through the misty haze. 'Depends what you mean by a lie. What I have to say to you is a private matter between father and son. Last night, I was more concerned with getting you out of the company you were keeping. If you must gamble, whore and drink, then at least have control of your purse, your cock and your capacity.'

Will said nothing, but his jaw took on a mutinous set that was becoming familiar to his father by now.

William stood in silence for a while, watching Woodstock come to life. Old King Henry had housed his mistress Rosamund de Clifford here. There were extensive pleasure gardens that in summer drugged the air with the sensuous perfumes of lily, honeysuckle and gillyflower. The three-tiered pond was threaded by a silver cascade of water from the spring, and at the heart of the garden, amid trellises of dog roses, stood an elaborate fountain of pink-flecked marble quarried from the Purbeck hills. A beautiful, tainted paradise, dormant now in the late autumn chill. Those for whose joy it had been built were dead.

'How long have you been bedding Marie de Falaise?' he asked Will.

There was a long silence during which William avoided the temptation to glance round.

Eventually: 'A month or two,' came the sullen reply. 'How do you know her name?'

'Because the court whores belong to the Marshal's department and because I've attended at courts of one kind or another for most of my life. I can remember Marie joining the royal train when Richard was king and you were still in swaddling.' He drew a deep, irritated breath. 'And no, I haven't sampled her wares. What I do know, though, is that skills like hers do not come cheaply and her heart dwells in her purse, not between her legs. What's more, it only beats for money.'

'She . . . I . . .'

'You are being used and abused,' William said brutally. 'There are those at court who want nothing more than to see the sons of William Marshal wallow in the gutter, and in your case, they appear to be succeeding.' He watched a twist of smoke rise from the chimney in the great hall block and forced himself to silence. He had trained squires to knighthood; he was used to the challenges posed in raising young males, so why was it so difficult with his heir?

Without a word, Will went to swill his face in the water pail by the tent flap, then plonked himself down before the cook's fire, his expression brooding. Sighing, William joined him on the crude wooden bench and, leaning forward, clasped his hands between his knees.

'There's no need to be perfect,' he said. 'God knows, I never was as a youngster – and I'm not now. Just be careful, that's all I'm asking.'

Will looked at the ground. 'It won't happen again,' he muttered.

William gestured to the cook's griddle where slices from the bacon flitch were sizzling in bubbles of melted fat. 'You should eat. It'll settle your gut.'

Will's nostrils flared and he swallowed hard. 'No,' he said.

'Did you enjoy the venison last night?' Without waiting to be served, William helped himself to a chunk of the rescued half-burned bread and a thick slice of bacon.

A trace of humour glimmered in Will's eyes. 'It was tough,' he said.

'Ah, pity.' William bit into the bread and bacon with

relish. Will clamped his jaw and looked green. Then his gaze travelled beyond his father and fixed on the messenger who was striding towards their fire. 'Hywel,' he said, and suddenly, despite his malaise, he was as alert as a hound.

William turned and his heart kicked in his chest. He had left Hywel in Ireland with Isabelle with the instruction that he was to be sent at once should anything happen. Choking down his mouthful, abandoning the rest of his breakfast, he rose to his feet and faced the young man, gesturing him to remain standing when he would have knelt. 'What news?' he demanded, and snapped his fingers at his squire. 'Ale,' he said.

Grey fatigue smudged Hywel's features and his eyes held shadows. A fading bruise dirtied one cheekbone. 'My lord, Meilyr FitzHenry's knights attacked your lands seven days after you sailed. They burned your barns at Newtown, sacked the houses, slaughtered the people and carried off booty. Twenty of your men were killed in the fighting . . . and my brother Dai . . . He . . . he was killed too.' Hywel's voice quivered. He took the cup from the squire and gulped down the contents.

William felt the hair rise at his nape and gooseflesh start along his arms. He set his hand to Hywel's shoulder. 'Ah lad, I am sorry,' he said. 'For both your loss and the news you bring.'

Hywel's throat worked. With a visible effort he gathered himself to continue reporting. 'Lord Jean caught the ringleaders attempting a grange closer to Kilkenny and brought them before the Countess. She . . . she has secured them in the dungeon. For herself, she says that she would rather see them hang, but she awaits your pleasure on the matter.'

That sounded like Isabelle, and in fighting spirit. 'Secured' William was certain was diplomatic language.

'Flung' was probably closer to what she had done. 'Go on,' he said.

'Your men have kept their grip on your Irish lands and Lord Jean says that it will not be dislodged. Rebuilding has already started at Newtown and the Countess has acquired fresh stores for the granges from the Pembroke lands and has borrowed and bought from the de Lacy and de Braose estates.'

William gave a terse nod and silently thanked God for the steadfastness of his wife and deputies. With less courageous personalities, he could have been listening to an entire catalogue of disasters rather than a single setback, already recovered.

'The Countess seeks assurances that you are unharmed and says that if you are well, then she is also well indeed.'

William thanked Hywel and, having offered more condolences, let him go and find his father. The young man had the unenviable task of telling Rhys that Dai was dead, that while one son had come to him, he would never see the other again. William clenched his fists. His need to be with Isabelle in Ireland was as fierce as a wound. He hated being stuck here in the midst of enemies and rivals, having to divide himself, having to fight a dirty political battle of wits rather than a clean one with sword and lance.

'Bastards,' Will said softly.

'I knew Meilyr would have his men attack our lands the moment I was gone,' William said, his eyes full of anger. 'His sneer has been telling me that ever since I arrived at court.'

'I suppose it'll be on the other side of his face now,' Will said with grim satisfaction.

'I do not doubt it, but battles aren't won by a single

276

skirmish. This is only the beginning ... and I pray God to help me because only He knows where it will end.'

'Your plans to curtail the Marshal appear to have suffered a setback, if the news from Leinster is true,' King John remarked acidly to Meilyr. Having dined in the great hall, he had retired to his private apartments with his favourites and advisers, among them the Irish lords who had accompanied William Marshal across the sea. It pleased John to fête them. In keeping them by his side and barring William from his private domain, it also ensured that the Marshal had but slender access to his vassals.

Meilyr scowled. 'It is only a minor check, sire, and it wouldn't have happened if I had been there to lead the operation.'

'But the Marshal wasn't there either,' drawled Gerard D'Athée who was sitting on a painted coffer, arms folded and thin features clad with a contemptuous expression.

Meilyr bared his teeth at him. 'No, but he brought his dissenting vassals with him and left behind the strength of his mesnie. He deliberately left his English knights in Ireland, and I know for certain that he has given authority to Stephen D'Evereux because he's wed to a de Lacy woman.' He turned to John, his manner as pugnacious and fierce as a terrier with the scent of a fox in its nostrils. 'Sire, if you give me permission to return to Ireland, I swear I will visit the Marshal lands with a rod of iron and personally see his ambition curbed. The same goes for de Braose.'

D'Athée gave a cynical snort. 'If you can manage that, then not just your rod but your balls are made of iron.'

Meilyr FitzHenry glared at the mercenary. 'They are,' he snapped. 'No man who followed Richard de Clare had anything else. My grandsire was King of England when the Marshals were no more than glorified stable boys with dung on their hands.'

D'Athée raised an eyebrow, but made no comment.

John knew it had been a deliberate ploy on Meilyr's part to mention their kinship, albeit that the line was a bastard one and Welsh on the distaff side. He could well do without the Welsh. 'I do not doubt the state of your manhood,' he said with a sardonic smile. 'You have my permission to return to Ireland and use it to beat down some walls.'

Meilyr thanked him, then leaned forward, his expression filled with cunning. 'Sire, I would have an even greater chance of success if you were to arrange to recall the men the Marshal has left in Ireland who owe you service.'

John eyed him with interest. Here was a notion worth playing with.

'Order them back to England under threat of confiscating their lands if they refuse,' Meilyr elaborated. 'Jean D'Earley is your tenant-in-chief and he has much to lose if he declines your summons. It will leave me a free hand to act in your interests – as your justiciar.'

John toyed with the sapphires and rubies hanging around his neck on a gold chain. Despite himself he was rather impressed. Meilyr was a man after his own heart. If the direct route was barred, then digging a tunnel and undermining the enemy was the next resort. In fact, sometimes digging tunnels was preferable. He couldn't lose. If William's knights abandoned Leinster to answer his summons, then it left the Marshal's Irish lands exposed and vulnerable. If they stayed, then John got to seize their English estates. Meilyr FitzHenry was expendable, whatever the belligerent little man's high opinion of himself, and if he fell in his attempt to unseat Marshal and de Braose from their positions of power in Ireland, then John had several excellent candidates to replace him.

'Your notion has possibilities,' he said. 'I will have letters written and sent to the Marshal's men. My messenger can travel with you, since I am sure, as my justiciar, you will want to see them delivered.'

A vindictive light kindled in Meilyr's eyes. 'It will be my pleasure, sire.'

Having dismissed Meilyr, John sat down to drink with Philip of Prendergast and Jack Marshal – men of high estate in the Marshal's entourage. When he chose to don the gown of affable, charming host, it fitted him very well and he enjoyed the wearing. He spoke of matters inconsequential: the weather, the fine buildings at Woodstock, yesterday's hunt, but all the time, like a cat in a garden, he was soft-padding after his vulnerable prey. Towards the end of the second cup of wine, he pounced.

'You are men of standing and dignity and it has been in my mind for some time to bestow you grants and privileges in Ireland to hold of me as tenants-in-chief – if you are willing to be accommodating.' With a smile and an enquiring look in his eye, he gestured the attendant to refill the cups. It was one of the best wines: mulberry enhanced with spices.

Prendergast's gaze darted to see who else was listening. A muscle ticked under one of his eyes and John saw his breathing quicken and knew his fish was hooked. Jack Marshal's expression, however, was one of surprise threatening to develop into unease.

'I remember your father very well,' John said to him smoothly. 'He died defending Marlborough as my castellan and he always served me loyally and well. But for a twist of birth, you could have had all of your father's lands.

He was the heir, after all. Instead they are held by your uncle and will pass in time to his son, not yours.'

Jack Marshal shrugged. 'It is the way of things, sire. I am not the only eldest son who has missed his inheritance due to being bastard born.'

John spread his hands. 'Indeed not, but a soldier of your standing has the potential to go much further than the modest lands you have gained through marriage. I would be willing to bestow enough on you to enhance your dignity. The same goes for you, my lord,' he said to Philip Prendergast. 'Your wife is the eldest daughter of Richard Strongbow. Like my kinsman Meilyr, you were settled in Leinster long before the Earl of Pembroke planted his feet on its shores. As lord of Ireland, I am in a position to reward you for your services . . . what do you say?'

'Jack, come here. What do you think?' William walked around the horse that the coper was offering for sale, studying it from various angles. It was a handsome blue-roan with the arched neck and powerful quarters of Spanish breeding. In the summer its hide would have the lustre of sword steel but just now the sheen was covered by a thick winter fell of hoar white. The coper, however, knew how to turn out a beast for the inspection of noble clients. Not a speck of mud or dung marred the plush coat. Its hooves had been oiled and polished, its mane and tail combed until they glittered like waterfalls in frosty light.

'For war?' Jack's tone was dubious.

'No, for breeding and hacking. My palfrey's getting long in the tooth. If I put him to a Flanders mare, he might produce destrier stock.'

'Ah, good then.' Jack moved in to perform the obligatory examinations, looking in the stallion's mouth, checking his legs, picking up his feet. Watching his nephew, William wondered what was wrong. Jack was hesitant and ill at ease and he wouldn't look him in the eyes.

'I think he's worth considering,' William said conversationally. 'He has excellent conformation and his temperament seems balanced – although as with all things, one can be surprised.'

The words sent a red flush creeping up Jack's throat into his face. He straightened from examining the stallion's forelegs and turned to William. 'Sir, I have a confession to make.'

William nodded at a suspicion confirmed. 'Since it is to me and not to God, I assume it concerns me and I am not going to approve.'

Jack bit the inside of his cheek. 'The King has offered me lands in Ireland and the position of his marshal there in return for the service of five knights.'

The news dismayed William but hardly came as a surprise. He folded his arms. 'So what are you confessing? That you've accepted them?'

Jack looked affronted. 'No, sir. I said I needed time to think. I thought it only honourable to speak with you first.'

'Do you want the lands?' William asked, then laughed at himself. 'Hah, of course you want them; you'd be a lackwit not to, but what else does the King desire of you besides the service of five knights, hmm?' A bitter smile twisted his lips. 'I should not be surprised. John is exacting his revenge for my homage to King Philip for Longueville.' He looked hard at his nephew. 'How far are your loyalties going to be split, Jack? What will you give to me and what will you give to John?'

Jack tried to return William's stare, but could not and

had to look at the ground. 'I do not deny he offers me something I cannot afford to refuse, but I will still serve you to the best of my ability.'

William gave a caustic laugh. 'You'll find that serving two masters is a double-edged sword.' He waved his hand. 'Go, take his bribe. I won't disown you.'

'But you will think less of me,' Jack said miserably.

'I think well of you for coming to tell me. That takes courage and I do not blame you for accepting his offer. You choose your path and you walk it without looking back. I doubt the others will come to me to justify themselves. I'll have to find out for myself who's been offered what – probably from public jibes and sneers in the hall.'

Jack's flush deepened to scarlet. 'You know about the others?'

'It's obvious, is it not?' William growled. 'The King is not going to bribe my nephew and leave them out of it. It's as much about diminishing my dignity as taking away my power.'

Jack looked morose. 'You should have done as Jean D'Earley said and taken their sons hostages before you left.'

'It wouldn't have made any difference since the King has my sons.' He sighed and felt a grey tide of weariness settle over him. 'So, whom has he been inveigling and who has succumbed?'

'Most of them.' Jack looked embarrassed and apologetic. 'Prendergast, de Barri, Latimer, both de la Roches, Adam of Hereford, Richard de Cogan, D'Angle, FitzMartin and de Haverford . . .'

William was braced but it was still unpleasant to hear the names. John had done a thorough job and all of the Irish vassals had shown their true colours. 'I will not say that you are in good company,' he said with a dour smile.

282

'What are you going to do?'

William grimaced. 'What can I do? I am besieged. I have to hope the walls I have built are strong enough to survive. You have done your duty in coming to me. From now on you had better stay clear of my company unless you want to find yourself trapped behind the wrong walls.'

'My lord, I—'

'Begone,' William said with a wave of his hand. 'I have the patience of a soldier, not a saint.'

Jack bowed deeply, with reverence, and then hesitantly walked away. William briefly closed his eyes, swallowed and turned back to examining the horse. The coper's expression was empty but it didn't mean his mind was too. William knew full well the news would be the main source of entertainment at the dinner hour. He told himself it didn't matter; it was one brief manoeuvre in a long and complex game. 'Saddle him up,' he commanded the man. 'I want to see how he rides.'

25

Marlborough, Wiltshire, December 1207

Breath misting in the icy air, William gazed around the chamber where he and his siblings had played as small children. He could still vividly remember the red wall hangings, the gold fringing on the bolster cushions, the broad bed with its winter coverlet of wolfskins where he and his brothers had slept. All still clear, but only in memory now except for the painted scrollwork designs on the white plastered walls. They were still the same. The chamber was currently the domain of the King's scribes and clerks who were huddled over piles of parchment, nibs scratching away, hands and noses red with cold despite the charcoal braziers that provided localised patches of heat.

There was glass in the window embrasure now. In his childhood, the apertures had been open to the sky, or screened off by shutters in the coldest weather. If he half closed his eyes, he could almost see his mother sitting on the window-bench at her embroidery with her women, one eye cocked to her full nursery of four boys, two girls and two older stepsons from her husband's first marriage. All scattered now: married in far distant parts of the country, dwelling in France . . . dead. His father had been castellan here, but had lost Marlborough with King Henry's favour when William was a youth. Years later, the keep had been restored to the family. His brother John had been given custody and, in his turn, he had lost it while rebelling against King Richard – had died in the great hall, defending the place, his heart and his hope giving out. Now King John held it in royal custody and came here often like a dog marking its territory. But although old scents and colours faded, the memory of their original intensity lingered. If the room was cold, it was because Marlborough had more than its share of ghosts, the living and the dead.

The curtain covering the doorway suddenly flurried as if blown upon and Meilyr FitzHenry strode into the room. He was booted and cloaked for hard travelling, and was accompanied by Thomas Bloet, a knight of the King's mesnie, who was similarly attired.

Meilyr stopped abruptly when he saw William and his hand flashed to his sword hilt. Remaining composed and still, William eyed his treacherous vassal with loathing. Meilyr's sallow complexion darkened. He took his right hand off his hilt, replacing it with his left and swaggered over to the scribes.

'What are you doing here, Marshal?' he sneered. 'Hoping that one of them will take pity on you and tell you what they've written?'

'What I am doing here is my own business,' William said impassively. He nodded greeting to Thomas Bloet who looked ill at ease but was courteous enough to return the gesture.

Meilyr held out an imperious hand to one of the busy scribes. 'You have writs for myself and Sir Thomas.'

John de Grey, Bishop of Norwich and the King's senior

administrator, gave him several documents tagged with the royal seal. His expression was neutral – eloquently so, and William was glad. He and de Grey saw eye to eye on a number of issues.

'A pity you are not returning to Ireland with me, Marshal,' Meilyr said, his tone and his smile implying the delighted opposite. 'But do not worry. I will deal with all outstanding matters.' He waved the documents under William's nose. 'You know these are summons to your men, don't you? If they do not come to the King, all their lands will be forfeit?'

'I know full well what is written, Meilyr,' William said in an impassive voice.

Meilyr's smile was gloating. 'I will be sure to wish your wife well when I come to Kilkenny.'

William dug deep and managed to hold himself together. 'You do that,' he said huskily, 'although do not expect my wife to do the same for you. Her notions of propriety may not be as well developed as mine, but you will find that her notions of possession are. I will also remind you that you are my vassal and I have the right to deal with you as I see fit within the writ of the law – whether you are the King's justiciar or not.'

Meilyr handed the sealed letters to Thomas Bloet to bear as official messenger. 'You are fuller of hot air than an empty pie, Marshal,' he sneered. 'Pray continue; the scribes will be glad of the warmth. I cannot stay to take advantage; I've work to do in Ireland and there's a ship waiting.' He left the room as he had entered, brisk with energy, his stride brimming with confidence. William half expected to hear him whistling with pleasure. Thomas Bloet followed him, but hesitated on the threshold and gave William a swift, apologetic look. 'I go where I am sent,' he said.

'I know,' William replied. 'No one in my household will abuse a messenger for the news he bears . . . You are the King's man, not my enemy . . . unlike some.'

Bloet gave a knowing hand gesture and went out after Meilyr.

William hesitated. De Grey had returned to overseeing his scribes and was obviously not inclined to comment. Letting out a hard breath, William left the room in the wake of Bloet and FitzHenry. While they mounted fast coursers and took the road to Bristol, William headed for the chapel to pray for God's help in the weeks to come.

'Not long now, my lady,' said Maeve the midwife, who had been gently examining Isabelle's belly. 'The head has descended into the pelvis and he's curled up neat and ready, so he is.'

Isabelle struggled upright on the bed. There was so much baby there didn't seem as if there was room for anything else. Her back ached constantly and she was at the stage where no position was comfortable, no matter how many cushions she placed at her back. A trading galley had brought the news that John's Queen had been safely delivered of a son at Winchester, named Henry for his grandsire. Isabelle hated John, but she wished the young Queen and her baby well and intended sending a christening gift when she was able. The sister-bond of childbirth and motherhood was a powerful one.

'How long is "not long"?' she asked as she took the loose blue gown handed to her by Lady Avenel. The panels in the sides were fitted above the waistline to give space to her girth.

'Could be today, could be a fortnight and more,' Maeve said. 'No telling.' A look of disapproval crossed her face.

287

'What I do know is that you should have retired to your confinement a long time since.'

'Oh, tush.' Isabelle waved impatiently at the woman. 'I do no harm by dining in the hall and talking in the council chamber. I cannot afford to retire for a month and sit on my bed waiting for the child to be born.' She gazed ruefully at her belly. 'I may resemble a great milch cow, but I have neither the patience nor the inclination to placidly chew cud and think of nothing.' She raised her hand to forestall Maeve, who had drawn breath to do battle. 'And do not say I should rest for the child's sake. If everything is progressing as it should, which you say it is, then providing I do not take one of my husband's destriers from the stable and go riding out at the gallop, clad in mail, I think you can assume my common sense hasn't deserted me.'

Maeve rolled her eyes in horror at such a notion, then sighed and shook her head. 'As you wish, Countess,' she said, but the tight purse of her lips continued to mark her disapproval.

Her ladies and the children in tow, Isabelle descended from her chamber to the great hall to eat – something she made a point of doing every day. Her sons and daughters had to learn to dine in a formal atmosphere and observe the manners and courtesies that would serve them in later life. They had to learn duty and obligation and Isabelle was making sure that they were well prepared.

Jean arrived shortly after the horn had sounded. He was wearing his gambeson, the wool heavily streaked with oil and iron from his hauberk. His sword was girded casually at his left hip and a dagger at his right. These days he wore the mantle of command with assurance. Organising the defence of Kilkenny and the heartlands, not to mention his success in pinning down the raiders sent by Meilyr FitzHenry, had kindled his confidence from uncertain spark to full flame. He had been supervising the training of the serjeants this morning, and talking to some merchants and settlers from Newtown concerning defence of the burgh where the rebuilding was going forward apace and the charred spaces rapidly being covered with new warehouses and dwellings. Her other overseers followed him in. Jordan and Stephen were in the keep today, although Jordan was planning to ride out on the morrow to patrol their border with Dublin with a full contingent of knights. Flexing muscle in public was part of the preventative battle.

Once the food had been blessed, everyone set to with a will. The men were ravenous; their new responsibilities and energies having gone straight to their stomachs. Besides, the gusting winds and raw cold of January required plenty of stoking to keep the weather at bay. Not that the fare was scintillating at this time of year. The main dish was a somewhat chewy beef stew supplemented with dried beans and plenty of cumin and pepper. Side dishes of roast leeks and parsnips added some interest, but the sin of gluttony was hardly a threat.

Isabelle was washing her hands in the fingerbowl before the second course of marrow tarts and sundry fried pastries and wafers when her usher approached the dais and, bending, murmured in her ear.

She paused in mid-swill. Then she took the linen towel from the youth attending on her and briskly dried her hands. 'Let them enter,' she said in a calm voice devoid of inflection. The usher bowed and departed and she turned to Jean. She had given the command with aplomb but her heart was galloping and she felt sick. 'Meilyr FitzHenry is here with a messenger from the King,' she said.

289

Jean recoiled with surprise and his gaze widened.

A wave of panic swept over her and she had to fight it down, trying to breathe deeply instead of yielding to shallow gasps of fear. 'He would not walk into the lion's den – even knowing the lion is absent – unless he believed he had the upper hand. Why is he here and not William?'

'Perhaps he has come to ransom his men.' Jean laid a reassuring hand over hers. 'We'll know better in a moment. I am sure my lord is safe.'

'Yes,' Isabelle said. Outwardly she had won her battle for composure, but her heart was still thundering frantically against her ribs. 'I would know if he were not; I would feel it in here.'

Jean squeezed her hand and she took strength from him with a grateful if preoccupied half-smile.

By the time Meilyr and his companion were escorted into the hall, she had shored up her defences and was able to watch his approach with an air of cold authority. Meilyr was wearing a richly embroidered tunic decorated with garnets and he moved with a bounce in his step that served to compound Isabelle's trepidation. Thomas Bloet walked two steps behind him, his expression taut and his own gait stiff with unease. On reaching the dais, Meilyr bowed with sarcastic gallantry. Bloet made his own salute with decorum.

'If you are here concerning your men, Lord Meilyr, then I must tell you that their freedom awaits the safe return of the Earl, and they are' – Isabelle raised a delicate eyebrow – 'perforce dining elsewhere.'

A look of sly malice settled on Meilyr's face. 'I believe you will give up my men long before you see your husband again, my lady,' he said. 'I have travelled from King John's court with Messire Bloet, who has summons for the Earl's knights which they will ignore at their peril.'

Looking distinctly uncomfortable, Thomas Bloet produced the sealed documents and delivered them to Jean D'Earley, who took them as if he had been given a nest of snakes. He cleaned his eating knife on a napkin, slit the tags and opened the vellum sheet. A glance at the letters for Jordan and Stephen confirmed that, apart from the salutation, the wording on each one was the same. He looked at Isabelle with dismay in his eyes. 'My lady, we are summoned to the King's side to answer to him. He says that barring ill weather, he expects us to join him within two weeks of receiving these letters.' He fixed Meilyr with a baleful glare. 'You arranged this, didn't you, you whoreson?'

Meilyr's response was a smug curl of the lips. 'The King arrived at his own decision. He is no fool and is displeased that the Earl has played him for one. The King chooses to keep him at court under surveillance and requires the men summoned to join him there and answer for their conduct. If they do not, their lands will be declared forfeit.'

The words hit Isabelle like a sharp slap. This was pure vindictiveness. John was trying to strip her and William of everything, she knew he was. Their sons, their lands, their dignity.

'Then they are forfeit,' Jean said to Meilyr, as if matter-of-factly passing the time of day. 'I would count it a disgrace to abandon lands which my lord has committed me to guard. Shame lasts longer than destitution.'

'That is your choice, my lord,' Meilyr replied with a shrug. 'But if you and your fellow barons refuse to take ship, you will face the consequences. I am here to enforce the King's rule in Ireland, and anyone who opposes me will be ruined.'

Isabelle laid one hand upon her gravid belly and easing

to her feet, facing Meilyr like a queen. 'Your message is delivered,' she said icily. 'Perhaps you had better not outstay your welcome.'

'Would you threaten me, madam?' Meilyr responded, his tone equally glacial.

'No more than you have ever threatened me, my lord.'

If Meilyr had bowed on arriving, he did not do so as he took his leave. 'I will see your men on the battlefield,' he said.

Thomas Bloet made to follow him, but Isabelle bade him stay a moment. 'Of your mercy, Thomas,' she said. 'I have known you since you were a boy at Striguil. At least tell me that in all this morass my husband and sons are well.'

He met her gaze without flinching. 'Yes, my lady, very well indeed, although the Earl is frustrated that he cannot be here.' He flushed and looked over his shoulder, then turned back to her and lowered his voice. 'You should know the King has been pleased to give land and privileges to many of those who accompanied the Earl.'

'Bribes, you mean?' Her nostrils flared. 'You do not need to name names; I can guess.'

'And you would be right, my lady . . . but even then perhaps your guessing would not go far enough.'

'Would it not? Prendergast, I suppose? I saw him and his wife taking stock of my keep.'

'Yes my lady . . . and your husband's nephew.'

'Jack?' She stared at him in dismay. Holy Virgin, that was cutting close to home indeed.

'The King offered to make him marshal of Ireland and to give him land worth five knight's fees.'

'He did what?'

Bloet shook his head. 'Jack came to the Earl for advice, and the Earl told him to take the land . . . He is a great man, my lady. A truly great man.' His voice was so vehement with admiration that it almost shook. 'Unlike some I could name.' Bowing, he strode rapidly after Meilyr FitzHenry.

Isabelle watched him leave, speechless, unsure what to think or feel but knowing she had to take control before she was sucked down by the quagmire of emotions threatening to engulf her from within. Retiring to her chamber, she summoned Jean, Jordan and Stephen to join her there. Within her womb, the baby swarmed and kicked as if already practising to be a knight. 'Hush,' Isabelle said, softly stroking her distended belly. 'Hush, little one, not now. Wait a while, just a while longer.'

Once the men were assembled, Isabelle faced them and drew a deep, painful breath. 'What are we going to do? If you stay here, you will forfeit your lands. I will understand if you choose to obey the summons.' It took all her courage to say those words, to give them the option of leaving her. In truth, she was not sure that she would understand, but she had to offer them a choice.

Jean shook his head. 'I suspect we would forfeit our lands whether we went or not,' he said. 'John would just find a different excuse. I will not abandon the Earl's trust, or yours. My wife is his niece, my children share his blood. I could not look any of you in the eyes again if I obeyed this summons.'

'It is about honour,' said Stephen D'Evereux gruffly. 'And loyalty. I speak for all when I say we would rather perish than fail the Earl.' His words received vigorous agreement from his companions.

Isabelle's shoulders sagged with relief and gratitude. 'Then thank you from the deepest fathom of my heart. When all this is over, you will not go unrewarded, even though I know reward is not in your minds.'

'We should appeal to the Earl of Ulster for aid,' said Jordan de Saqueville. 'De Lacy has no love for the lord Meilyr, but he and my lord see eye to eye on many subjects. If you add the plea of your condition, he may be persuaded to aid us. Draft a letter to him, my lady; I will willingly bear it.'

Isabelle nodded. 'I will do so immediately. Certainly, we will lose nothing by asking. We have a few days' grace, I think, because Meilyr will wait to see if you obey the King's summons.' She leaned back to ease her aching spine. 'He won't strike at Kilkenny first either. The walls are strong and stuffed for siege. He might want the return of his kinsmen, but he will aim for easier targets to start with. We need to do some reconnaissance.'

Jean's lips parted in a savage smile. 'I'll set it in motion straight away. The lord Meilyr may have fought against the Irish with your father and grandfather, my lady, but he has never fought against men trained by the Earl of Pembroke. He's going to receive the shock of his life.'

26

Guildford, Surrey, January 1208

The court was at Guildford and the weather was wild with gales blustering from the north and persistent freezing rain that chapped the hands and face within minutes of venturing out. It was a fortnight since the ship bearing Meilyr FitzHenry and Thomas Bloet had sailed ahead of the atrocious conditions. Since then the seas had been too rough for even the coastline-hugging fishing vessels to put to sea and no ships had ventured the crossing to Ireland. Two weeks of silence, of purgatory on the edge of hell. Each day that passed, William steeled himself to endure. He prayed with might and main that Jean and the other deputies did not obey the malicious royal summons, yet knew that, in so doing, he was condemning them to lose their lands.

Currently he was trying to take his mind off the situation by playing a protracted game of merels with the marcher baron Fulke FitzWarin, who held lands of him in two counties as well as in Ireland, and who, in the past, had had his own serious brushes with the King, resulting in his being declared outlaw for several years. Possessing such a background, FitzWarin was extremely sympathetic to William's dilemma.

He had brought his dog to court with him: a sword-grey Irish gazehound the size of a pony with a bare-fanged grin that caused the less courageous courtiers to back against the wall as it passed with its master. The beast had taken a fancy to William and kept trying to sleep on his feet, thereby threatening to crush all feeling from them. Now and again its front end snored and its rear end produced quieter contributions that were nevertheless impossible to ignore.

'It's the food at court,' FitzWarin apologised after the most recent eye-watering incident. 'It doesn't agree with her. You don't keep dogs yourself?' He made his move, his fingers poetic, slender and well tended. Their sensitivity was deceptive. FitzWarin was a skilled swordsman and expert jouster.

'My wife has a hound – a courser,' William said, 'her women have lap dogs and my children adopt creatures here and there, but on current form I prefer to remain unattached.'

FitzWarin chuckled. 'Irish dogs are like their chieftains,' he said. 'They stink, they have no manners, they'll do anything for a reward, but if you can win their love, they'll follow you through the gates of hell and face down the very Devil in your defence. Useful to have someone prepared to rip out your enemy's throat at a single command.' He raised a sardonic eyebrow.

William's lips twitched. 'I had not thought of it that way.'

'You should.' FitzWarin glanced behind William and made a covert gesture of warning. A moment later the King arrived and paused to observe the men at their game. His current mistress Suzanna was hanging on to his arm, her gown of silk brocade shimmering over her breasts and clinging so tightly at waist and hip that the dimple of her navel could be seen through the fabric at the front; she wore a foxtail under the gown at the back to cover her buttocks. The pair were accompanied by several young bachelors of the mesnie. William willed the dog to fart again, but there was an olfactory silence from the weight across his toes.

'Marshal, I do not suppose you have heard any news from Ireland?' John enquired with a smile that was almost a smirk.

'No, sire, I have not,' William said. He spoke warily since John had been snubbing him for a fortnight. This sudden approach and its manner was an alarming change.

'Well then, it will please you to know that I have.'

William was so astonished he was unable to prevent the startled widening of his eyes. The weather had been so vile that to his knowledge no ships had been able to make the crossing. Nor had he seen any hard-travelled, salt-stained messengers making their way to John's chamber, just the usual suspects. 'Sire?'

'I have been informed of a pitched battle outside your castle at Kilkenny. Your men took up arms against my justiciar. Stephen D'Evereux and Jean D'Earley are both dead, D'Evereux on the field and D'Earley from a spear in the gut. He died in agony, so I am told. Your Countess is now besieged with no one to protect her but common serjeants.'

He looked into John's face where the spite glittered like broken glass. William thought of the numerous occasions he had parried blows on the battlefield and in training bouts. Heft the shield, stay low, hold in tight. Give nothing away. 'I am deeply grieved to hear such news, my lord,' he said without emotion. 'The death of these fine men is a great loss; they were your vassals as well as mine and

297

have fought well for you in the past. Such a waste makes it an even sorrier affair – if it is true.'

John glowered at him. The fur edging of his robe rose and fell as he breathed heavily. Finally he turned on his heel and stalked off, Suzanna wiggling sinuously in his wake.

William gazed at the merels board but didn't see it. He moved a counter without the slightest notion of strategy.

FitzWarin's flint-grey eyes were full of pity and shock.

'If you have any touch of mercy in your soul, keep playing,' William said hoarsely.

FitzWarin pushed a counter, taking no advantage of William's blind move. 'Can it be true?'

William shook his head. Knowing he was being watched for his reaction, he kept his face straight, but inside he could feel John's words twisting in his heart and entrails like a knife. 'How could it be?' he said. 'There has scarcely been time for Meilyr FitzHenry to arrive in Ireland, let alone conduct a battle campaign. He is trying to unsettle me and I'll be damned if I'll give him that satisfaction.' He looked at the other baron. 'You know how it is, Fulke, you've ridden the tourneys; you've been on the receiving end of John's displeasure – more so than me, because he made you an outlaw and hunted you through forest and field for three years.'

'He didn't win, though,' Fulke said with a wolfish smile.

'Because you're a good commander. You know how to play the game and keep yourself intact.'

FitzWarin shook his head. 'Because I know how to make it up as I go along,' he said.

William laughed and, to those watching, it seemed as if he didn't have a care in the world and that the King's barbs had slid off a polished shield. 'Ah,' he said, 'then we are men of similar experience, but that doesn't mean it is the way I like things to be. At my age, I want peace and order . . . and no surprises.'

FitzWarin raised a sceptical eyebrow. 'There is always hope,' he said.

William slumped on to the bed in his lodging house. He had dismissed his men and his servants. A violent headache crashed from one side of his skull to the other. The sheer iron control that had carried him through the rest of the day after John's taunting news was now a constriction upon him. He had retreated, rammed down the portcullis, yanked up the drawbridge and locked himself up so tightly he felt as if he was being crushed. He couldn't put this pressure on anyone else: not his men; certainly not his sons. It was his to endure and to withstand without cracking. The pain intensified, shooting up from the rigid muscles in his shoulders and neck and into his head until his eyes watered with the pressure. There was no Isabelle to cajole him, ease his tension, put everything in perspective, lie with him and give him comfort. She was engaged in her own battles, physically more dangerous than his and demanding the same strength of will. Groaning, William put his head in his hands and sought the detachment to cope, aware that in so doing, he was piling up a debt that might beggar him when the time came to pay.

Jean sat before the turf fire in the cowherd's lodging on the road to Drakeland Castle. The turves gave off a soft red glow on the underside and the fragrant smell of burning peat filled the long room. Adjacent to the living quarters, under the same roof, the cattle pens were empty, the cows having been driven into the keep for safety. Not that Drakeland was impregnable; indeed, compared to the great Norman castles where Jean had cut his teeth, it was an easy target, almost a hovel, but that didn't matter. Meilyr FitzHenry wasn't going to receive the easy kill he was expecting.

Outside the weather was grim, cold and misty. A day to believe in crones conjuring over their cauldrons, and to wonder if the sleek dark heads bobbing in the coastal inlets were in fact selkies: enchanted young women wearing the sinuous garb of seals. He warmed his hands around his cup of hot mead, blew and sipped. His knights and serjeants were doing the same, hunkered down near the fire, waiting in silence. The trap had been baited. Meilyr's raiders had been led to expect that Drakeland would not resist an attack and that Jean and his men were dealing with another assault away to the north. What Meilyr did not know was that the bulk of the Marshal knights were here, waiting for him, and that the northern situation was being mopped up by Hugh de Lacy, who had sixty-five knights under arms and more than two hundred soldiers behind his banner.

As Jean drank, an Irish scout slipped into the hut and, stooping to him, murmured that Meilyr's troops had been sighted approaching Drakeland. 'His son is with him too,' the scout said. 'And Philip of Prendergast.'

The information lit a gleam in Jean's eyes. 'Three birds for the price of one slingstone, then,' he said and, rising to his feet, summoned his squires and captains to his side. Some of the younger men who had lost comrades in the raids on Newtown were eager to mount up and charge out to meet the enemy, but Jean cautioned them with raised hands. 'Your chance will come,' he said, 'but not if your zeal overwhelms you. It's like bedding your bride on your wedding night. Too eager and you will spill on her thighs and not in her womb.'

His words induced a ripple of ribald laughter, particularly when he drew his sword and polished it up and down on a soft leather cloth, but the warning had been made clear in terms that were well understood. Jean's heartbeat quickened and he forced himself to take measured breaths, as his lord would have done. Each man knew his part and everyone had confessed and been shriven ready for battle. All that remained was for Meilyr to close in and take the bait.

As Jean mounted his horse and donned his helm, Jordan joined him, his fox-brown eyes aglow. 'If we can capture Meilyr, then we've won,' he said. 'No one's coming to prise him out of the dungeon. He'll be finished.'

Meilyr had brought carts laden with siege machinery to Drakeland, including two stone-throwers and a dozen ladders. His troops were a motley assortment of Welsh, Irish and Norman, some of them drawn from his vassals, many more of them hirelings. Philip of Prendergast and David de la Roche, who had returned on the same ship as Meilyr, had supplied men too, from the estates recently bestowed on them by the King. They were none too happy that William's deputies had chosen to stay and fight and voiced their unease to Meilyr as they drew nearer to the castle.

'No matter.' Meilyr shrugged. 'They have forfeited their lands in so doing and who do you think will benefit? They cannot be everywhere at once. Drakeland's a simple enough nut to crack.' He scowled at Prendergast. 'You were content enough to do homage to John for your grants here.'

Prendergast stiffened haughtily. 'And I hold to that oath. Don't tangle with me on the matter of loyalty.'

Meilyr began to retort but the hot words turned to ashes in his mouth as he saw the troop advancing down the road to meet them and recognised the silver scallops of D'Earley, the D'Evereux blue and silver, the de Saqueville chevrons. 'God's holy feet,' Prendergast croaked. 'They're not in the north, are they? Your scouts must have their eyes in their arses.'

Meilyr tugged his hand axe out of his belt and twisted the loop around his wrist. 'We'd have had to meet them sooner or later,' he growled. 'They're English; they know nothing about fighting the Irreis.'

'They knew in the autumn,' de la Roche said grimly as he drew his own sword. 'We've been lured here; this is a trap.'

The Marshal array broke into a gallop, stirrup to stirrup, shields close, lances forested in horizontal symmetry. There was no time. Meilyr swung his shield on to his left arm and bellowed at his men to stand firm.

The shock of the impact was like a fist punching into a face. Meilyr had ridden against the Irish with Richard Strongbow and knew all about making a stand, but in those days his stands had been against Irish chieftains who rode barelegged with rope bridles and no stirrups. This time he was up against heavy cavalry, mailed to the teeth; men blooded on the tourney and battlefields of Flanders and Normandy and whose issues with Meilyr and Philip of Prendergast were bitter and personal.

Meilyr dug spurs into his stallion's flanks and, howling, rode at Jean D'Earley. He chopped down a footsoldier, struck aside a serjeant, then found himself close enough to launch his axe at D'Earley's horse. It took the beast in the neck, above the protection of the wide leather breast-band. The destrier pitched and went down, legs threshing. Meilyr had hoped that D'Earley would be pinned under his dying horse, but he was thrown clear and scrambled to his feet. A mercenary swung his axe at the knight, but D'Earley parried with his shield, kicked the man's legs from under him and made a swift killing thrust with his sword. Meilyr spurred in to take him, but the knight hurled his shield into the destrier's face. The stallion reared and shied and Meilyr in his turn was thrown. The impact dazed him and before he could gather his wits and launch to his feet, Jean D'Earley's sword was planted at his throat.

'It's over!' D'Earley gasped. 'I will have your unconditional surrender, or I will spill your life on this soil. It won't take much for me to do it, I swear. And your son's too.'

Meilyr glared at him with narrow-eyed malevolence. 'I yield.' He spat the words like a curse. 'But you and your kind will never prosper in this land.'

Through the red freckles of blood dappling his face, the knight gave a derisive grin. 'I would be afraid,' he said, 'except all your other schemes and predictions seem to have gone disastrously awry.'

Isabelle looked with revulsion at the fettered man who had been flung at her feet in Kilkenny's great hall. She had ignored the stabbing pains in her back and the threatening contractions of her womb to come from her chamber and greet the victory. Meilyr was bruised and bloodied – apparently caused by a fall from his horse in the thick of battle, although Isabelle wondered. With a flick of her fingers, she commanded the iron shackles on wrists and ankles to be removed. They were as much about humiliation as keeping Meilyr from escaping and they had served their purpose. Isabelle knew that no matter how much she desired to do so, it wasn't wise to keep the King's justiciar in chains.

He lurched to his feet, rubbing his chafed red wrists. 'This is an outrage,' he spluttered.

'Indeed it is, and you are paying the price for the perpe- trating,' Isabelle retorted. 'What you have done to me and mine, I will not forgive.' She drew breath through her teeth as a band of pain gripped across her mid-section. 'Take your life and be glad that I choose to spare it, but I will have your son as surety for your behaviour, and I will have the sons of your kin and the same from all your allies. Set so much as one foot outside of my tolerance, and their lives are forfeit.'

Meilyr looked at her with disgust in his eyes. 'I never thought when I followed your father that it would come to this. His own daughter . . .'

Her eyes flashed. 'Yes,' she retorted, 'his own daughter. Strongbow's heir – a fact you conveniently forgot in your rush to be lord of all Ireland. If you had cooperated with my husband instead of raiding and damaging and burning, you wouldn't be standing before me now in defeat.' Her voice was excoriating. 'How do you think the King will react to a justiciar who finds it impossible to keep order?'

A sheen of sweat dewed Meilyr's skin. 'He will come himself, and then you will smile on the other side of your face . . . Countess.' The last word was not a courtesy.

'I am not smiling,' Isabelle said with loathing. 'Ah, enough, take him away and lock him up where I do not have to see him. Jean, I trust you to see the letters written demanding hostages . . . and to send word to my lord as well. He should know as soon as he may . . . I . . .' She bit her lip as another contraction, stronger than the last, dug through her loins.

'My lady?' Stephen D'Evereux held out his hand in concern.

Isabelle made a gesture of negation. 'You will have to celebrate this victory without me,' she said, breathless with pain. 'I . . . I must retire. I am . . . I am in travail.'

Her women, who had been waiting at the back of the dais, hurried to attend her and between them bore her to her chamber while the knights dragged Meilyr FitzHenry to a locked room, there, under house arrest, to await the arrival of hostages as surety.

Within the hour Isabelle was delivered of a baby boy who slid from her body in a slippery rush that caught everyone by surprise, not least Maeve who almost dropped him. The cord was tangled around his feet and the bag that had encased him in the womb was wrapped around his body.

'Ah,' said Maeve with satisfaction. 'That's lucky – very lucky. Means he cannot drown.' She unwound the cord and, parting the baby from his caul, lifted him up. Smeared with blood and fluid, he roared his indignation to the world. He had a thatch of thick, dark hair, black brows and eyelashes, and long, sturdy limbs. Still gasping, stunned by the swiftness of the birth, Isabelle found herself laughing almost hysterically with relief and overwhelming emotion as she held out her arms for her new son. 'Ancel,' she sobbed. 'His name is to be Ancel as my husband wished.'

Maeve bundled him in a warm towel and gave him to Isabelle while the women prepared a warm bath for him and laid out swaddling bands by the fire. 'You should suckle him awhile, my lady,' the midwife said. 'It will help compress your womb.'

Isabelle knew the lore already, Ancel being her ninth child, but she made no comment and, lowering her chemise, put him to her breast. He was going to resemble his father, this one, she could see it already, and the thought brought a sudden rush of tears to her eyes. William should be here to greet his newborn son, not trapped miles away at the hostile English court. Will and Richard should be here as well to welcome their baby brother. Instead, their family was fractured, striving to hold together in the face of the storm. With a determined sniff, she wiped her eyes on the back of her free hand and felt her womb contract as the baby took strong suck. There was no point in thinking of what should be and wasn't. Here in Ireland they had won a victory. Meilyr was vanquished; and even if there were more battles to fight, they would not happen today. Let now be for rejoicing, even if it was for a brief, imperfect moment.

A vigorous wind blew William's cloak against his body and whipped white crests on to the choppy waves striking Bristol's harbour wall. The smell of the estuary was a weedy tang in his nostrils and his eyes were stinging from staring into the harsh salt wind. He was ravenously hungry too – to the point where his legs felt hollow and weak. It was Lent, a time of fasting and privation, and he had been observing it vigorously this year. God was often taken for granted in the good seasons, but the harsh ones made men remember Him.

There had been no news from Ireland throughout the late winter as the weather continued to thwart the passage between the two countries. John had carried out his threat and revoked the English lands belonging to William's deputies, although William wondered how the King expected them to have obeyed the summons when the dreadful weather of the past six weeks had meant that not a single ship had put into port from Ireland. A short while ago, however, his chaplain had interrupted William's morning cup of ale and break-fast of plain bread to tell him that a large ship had been sighted furrowing her way up the estuary. William had abandoned his meal and hastened straight to the harbour.

His gaze was now fixed on a trading galley with a red sail and red round shields lining her top strake. She was gusting into port at speed, furrowing through the choppy seas like a greased plough. The men standing on deck were so bundled up against the weather that it was impossible to recognise any of them.

'Certainly from Ireland,' said Baldwin de Béthune, joining him. 'Often as not they have the red shields.'

'Danish ones do too,' William said, without taking his eyes off the ship.

'But they'd come in up the Humber, not into Bristol. It's Irish all right.'

The crew clewed up the sail and the oars were broken out to guide her alongside the quay. Warps snaked out, were caught and made fast to bollards. Sailors lifted the gangplanks off the deck and slid them out on to shore. First on to dry land was Thomas Bloet, his legs as wobbly as a newborn calf's and his complexion a delicate shade of green.

'My lord.' He greeted William with a swallow and a stiff nod. 'Your own man is behind . . . been sick in the deck shelter most of the journey. Is the King here?'

'Yes.'

'Thank God. I'm not up to riding to find him . . .' Bloet made to walk on, but William caught his arm.

'Yours is the first ship out of Ireland since the end of January. By your mercy, at least tell me if you bring good news or bad.'

Bloet shrugged. 'Depends on who you are. For you it is good . . . at least for the moment.' He tottered away in the direction of the castle.

Several other passengers followed Bloet ashore, none

of them known to William. Then came Hywel, his complexion making Bloet's look positively healthy in comparison. Normally William would have been sympathetic, but for the moment his anxieties overrode all consideration. Hywel wobbled on to dry land, saluted William and dropped to his knees. 'Safer than falling down, my lord,' he said apologetically and leaned over to retch.

William gave an impatient wave of his hand. 'Never mind that. What news?' Searching the ship, he was relieved to see no sign of Jean, Jordan or Stephen. He had harboured an enormous dread that the very honour and uprightness he valued in them would cause them to obey the royal summons rather than read between the lines and ignore it.

'Two lots, my lord, both good,' Hywel croaked weakly. 'Your Countess sends you greetings and desires you to know that your men defeated Meilyr FitzHenry and Philip of Prendergast in battle at Drakeland. They have surrendered themselves to her and delivered up their sons as hostages for their word. She also desires you to know that on the day FitzHenry and Prendergast were captured, she was safely delivered of a son. He thrives and she has named him Ancel as you desired.'

William exhaled, feeling as if someone had punched the remaining strength from his body. He staggered as if he too had just stepped from a ship and Baldwin had to grab and steady him with an exclamation of alarm.

'I am all right,' William said, although patently he was not. 'It was the news I hoped for but it has been a long time coming. I need . . . I want . . . Christ . . .' He put his hands over his face.

Baldwin was sensible and pragmatic. He gave Hywel enough coin for food and lodging and told him to report to the Earl as soon as he was able. Then he escorted

William back to his house and, seating him before the fire, pushed a cup of hot spiced wine into his shaking hands.

'It is the best news,' Baldwin said. 'You've won and you have a fifth son to add to your quiver.'

William's teeth chattered against the rim of the cup. 'I haven't won,' he contradicted his friend. 'John won't allow it. All I have done is stand my ground in the hopes that he'll tire of breaking his teeth on a nut that's too difficult to crack.'

Baldwin wrapped his hands around his belt. 'Best to lie low for a while. The news is going to make him look foolish after what he said to you at Guildford.'

William drank again and felt the hot red wine surge through his veins. 'What did he say?'

'You know . . .'

William shook his head, his expression as blank as uncut quarry stone. 'No, I don't,' he said. 'I don't remember a thing.'

Baldwin looked baffled for a moment, then comprehension dawned. 'No,' he said flatly. 'Neither do I.'

Seated in the main room of their father's lodging house, Will and Richard absorbed their father's news. For Will, the fact that he had a new baby brother was neither here nor there, although he had given the obligatory pleased response. As the eldest Marshal child, he was accustomed to siblings arriving at regular intervals. The detail that Meilyr FitzHenry had been taken in battle by the Marshal knights was more interesting and brought a light to his eyes. His antipathy towards John had been growing steadily since the hunt in October, although this last month had really put an edge on it. How his father bore with the provocation and did not retaliate, he did not know, and was unsure whether to feel humiliated by the stoic refusal to react, or be proud.

'Now you can rub John's nose in it,' he said with satisfaction.

His father shook his head. 'No, son, that's the last thing to do. John is the anointed King and we owe him our allegiance.'

'There're the French,' Will contradicted eagerly. 'We owe Philip allegiance for Longueville.'

'Yes,' said William, 'but the French are not the rightful heirs to England and John now has an infant son. John will have heard the Irish news by now and he'll be smarting with humiliation. The last thing I am going to do is gloat at him.'

'But after all he has done—'

William raised his hand to silence his son. 'One day you will be the Earl of Pembroke and you will need every iota of wisdom and cunning to survive. I will not bow and scrape to John, but neither will I throw his defeat in his face. It isn't over yet by far; he could still destroy us.'

Will eyed him with incomprehension. 'I still do not know how you stomach it,' he said with the passion of adolescence.

William's nostrils flared with curbed temper. 'Because I must if we are to stay alive. Because in the end it is like an irritating scratch. Pick at it and it will get worse. Leave it alone and it has a chance to heal. Don't you understand?'

Will mumbled assent, but his body remained stiff with disagreement.

Richard looked quietly thoughtful. 'What will the King do now?'

William spread his hands. 'Only he knows that. I hope

he will give up his grudge against us and I intend to make it easy for him to do so.'

'You will lick his backside, you mean?' Will spat.

William gave him an icy stare. 'If you don't start learning soon, boy, it will be too late. God knows I could whip the lesson into your hide, but you'd probably be too stubborn to heed it.'

Will flushed red to the ears as if he truly had been struck. He felt angry, ashamed and resentful. He was almost eighteen years old, on the cusp of manhood, yet his father still treated him like an infant whilst preparing to sell the family pride to the King. 'I am listening and learning, sir,' he said in a voice gritty with controlled anger. 'Indeed I am.'

Once their father had gone, Richard made a face at his brother. 'You shouldn't have pushed him,' he said. 'He's been at court all his life. He knows what he's doing.'

'Don't you start,' Will snapped. 'You'd take his part whatever happened. You've always clung to his shirt tails and curried favour.'

Richard flushed with indignation. 'That's not true, you know it isn't. I won't be a scapegoat for your anger at him.'

The brothers glowered at each other. Then Will heaved a deep sigh. 'I'm sorry, I didn't mean it . . . but it sticks in my craw that we should still have to humour John after all he has done to us. Where does it end?'

Richard shrugged. 'I don't know.'

'You mean you don't want to.'

'No, I don't, except to know that I trust our father whatever happens.' Abruptly Richard picked up the flagon and poured wine for them both. 'To Ancel,' he said and drank. 'To our new brother.'

Will lifted his cup. 'To Ancel,' he said with a flourish. 'At least he's too far down the line to be taken as hostage.'

William came at John's summons and made his obeisance. 'Sire?'

John waved him towards a cushioned window embrasure, the gesture catching the light on the several rings adorning his fingers. 'You must have heard that a trader has arrived from Ireland?'

William took his time about sitting down, hitching the knees of his hose, manoeuvring his cloak so that it was not trapped beneath him. 'No, sire,' he replied. 'I've been asleep at my lodging. I'm afraid the days of a young man's vigour are far behind me.'

'I don't believe that for a moment, Marshal. If you've been napping, it's with one eye open, like a cat.'

'Even so, sire, I have heard nothing,' William said obtusely. 'What news is there?' He forbore to mention the last occasion when John had fabricated details in an attempt to break his composure.

John took several paces, rubbed his jaw, turned on his heel. 'Doubtless you will hear it from your own messengers very soon, but the gist of the tale is that my justiciar FitzHenry has unfortunately proven false and incompetent on all counts. It seems that he has been fomenting rebellion and unrest among the Irish barons. Your deputies, aided by Hugh de Lacy, defeated him in battle when he threatened your lands.'

William contrived to look interested and surprised. 'Indeed, sire, I never thought when I came to your summons that my lands would face such jeopardy.' He met John's gaze with a level stare. Each knew they were playing a game, but this was a time for diplomacy, not plain speaking.

John picked up a book from the coffer, examined the bejewelled cover and clasp, then set it back down. 'Since FitzHenry has proved unequal to the task of justiciar, I intend replacing him with someone more able and of clearer purpose.'

'I am pleased to hear it, sire,' William said, hoping that a man 'more able' would be one with whom he could work. One could not deny, for example, that a mercenary such as Gerard D'Athée was an eminently capable royal servant, but he was so steeped in moral corruption that dealing with him was like wading in sewage. He also knew that some tough negotiating lay ahead. He was going to have to make some concessions if he wanted to be left in peace and although the storm appeared to have broken, he was not yet clear of the outer edges.

'My man also informed me that your Countess had been delivered of a son and that both are well.'

'That is indeed good news, sire. The bearing of children is as great a danger to a woman as the battlefield is to a man.'

'Five sons,' John mused, eyeing William. 'You may have need of them all, Marshal. I was a fifth son, born late in the day, and look at me, the only one remaining.'

'As God wills it, sire.'

John gave a dark laugh. 'Then whatever the Church says of me, I must be in His favour, for He willed me to be King.' His upper lip developed a disparaging curl. 'My brother Richard rode all the way to the gates of Jerusalem for God – and for what? To die childless in the Limousin of a stinking wound. Geoffrey trampled by a horse, Henry dead of the bloody flux and William gone in infancy before I saw the world. It is no wonder that God's plan passes all human understanding. Have I shocked you,

Marshal? Do you think I'm a blasphemous danger to all of Christendom?'

'Only to the peril of your own soul, sire,' William answered impassively.

John snorted. 'My soul. You know that the Pope is threatening to lay the country under interdict because of our dispute over the Archbishop of Canterbury?'

'Yes, sire.' Most men were waiting to see which way the wind blew. There was sympathy for John, but some barons were seeing it as a cause célèbre which would help them foment rebellion, and many people were in true fear for their souls, or worried about what would happen if they died and could not be buried in consecrated ground. John had wanted the Bishop of Norwich for Archbishop, the monks of Canterbury had selected their own prior Reginald as candidate. The Pope had declined both men in favour of a protégé of his own, Cardinal Stephen Langton, a former teacher of theology. John, quite rightly in most men's minds, was annoyed at such blatant papal interference, but as the situation had escalated and tempers frayed, people were becoming increasingly uneasy.

'I will give him interdict.' John smiled at William, but it was not a pleasant expression. 'If the Church refuses to cooperate with me, then the Church will find that it cuts both ways. I will make them bleed silver until they squeal.'

William said nothing. Under interdict and with several bishoprics empty, John would be at liberty to milk the churches of their revenues. It was a somewhat useful but dangerous way to fill the royal coffers. Morally disquieting too, but that would not bother John.

Distantly a horn sounded to announce the dinner hour and an usher arrived to inform John of the same. The King clapped William across the shoulders as if they were bosom friends. 'You've kept yourself absent too long from my table. Come and share a cup and a trencher with a damned man and we'll drink a toast to sons and the pleasure of their begetting, eh?'

27

Glascarrick, Ireland, Spring 1208

William landed in Ireland at Glascarrick, a wild place with a few low-roofed fisherman's huts near the shore. There was a priory – a daughter house of Saint Dogmell's in Pembrokeshire – and William was pleased to rest there in the small guest house whilst word of his landing travelled to Kilkenny and his churning stomach had a chance to settle down. The crossing had been reasonable for the Irish Sea, which meant he was still capable of standing and able to keep down the spring water and bread and honey the monks served to him and his men.

The late spring dusk was streaking the sky with amber and turquoise and the sun was a melting ellipse on the horizon when Jean and Jordan arrived with a troop from Kilkenny. William had been sitting on a bench outside admiring the sunset, but now he rose to his feet and strode to greet his men, his chest suddenly tight with emotion.

Jean dismounted and clasped him fervently, his shoulders shaking. 'My lord, welcome back,' he said in a breaking voice. 'We feared for you . . .'

'How now, enough of that or you will have me weeping too,' William said gruffly and turned to embrace the more phlegmatic Jordan. Then he stepped back and frowned at Jean's attire. 'Why are you wearing your mail? Is the trouble not finished?' He glanced at Jordan, who was clad in a padded tunic and belted with his sword.

Jean made a face. 'My lord, not all keep the peace. You always taught me it was better to be safe than sorry.'

'Yes, I did, didn't I? Should I have mine unpacked from my baggage?'

'It wouldn't harm,' Jean said ominously.

William studied him. New lines seamed Jean's eye corners, and the raven hair held glints of silver. He wore his responsibility like a glimmer of polished steel, and he wore its price too. 'No, I do not suppose it would, Jean.' Retiring into the guest house he sat before the slow-burning turf fire. 'My wife and new son are well?'

Jordan nodded. 'The Countess was desirous of riding to greet you herself but Jean said she should wait. He had a hard time persuading her though. It was almost like the battles that you and she sometimes—' he broke off, looking embarrassed. 'She is eager to see you, my lord,' he amended.

William smiled. 'As I am eager to see her too, and my son.'

'Should I have brought her?' Jean said anxiously.

William looked him up and down. 'Not if you saw fit to wear a hauberk on the journey.'

The men gathered to talk over everything that had happened since the autumn. Listening, William was unsurprised by the detail. He was angry too, but he held that down because it created nothing but fire across the path leading to a solution. He needed to be dispassionate in order to manoeuvre, take advantage and compromise. Concerning his own experiences at the English court he was reticent. He had no doubt that others would gladly

317

fill in the detail over wine in the guardroom once they were settled at Kilkenny.

Jean was on the point of removing his hauberk – indeed, had unfastened his swordbelt to begin doing so – when they heard the clatter of shod hooves on the road and the sound of voices at the priory gate. Jean's breath caught. Drawing the blade from the scabbard gripped in his hand, he went to the door. William reached for his own sword and the room became filled with the soft rustle and clink of men taking up weapons and preparing to fight.

'Surely can't be travellers this late,' Jordan said. 'No one will have casual business here.'

'How many?' William demanded.

Jean cracked open the door and slipped outside with a lantern. Almost instantly he returned, his expression one of angry distaste. 'It's Philip of Prendergast and David de la Roche,' he growled, keeping his sword bared. 'Prendergast's son is at Kilkenny as hostage for his father's good behaviour.'

William considered this and, sheathing his own blade, gestured Jean to do the same. 'I doubt they've come to attempt murder on holy ground,' he said. 'Let them come. I am well enough guarded.'

Reluctantly Jean did as he was bid, but he buckled the belt back around his waist and laid his hand to his weapon hilt in a businesslike manner.

Prendergast and de la Roche left their mounts and their small retinue at the gate and approached the guest house on foot. A soft rain had begun to whisper down and when they arrived at the door, their cloaks were dewed in silver hoar and their hair tightening into curls.

On entering beyond Jean's pose of narrow-eyed guard dog, both lords bowed deeply to William and greeted him effusively, as if his return were the most welcome thing on earth.

'May God save you, my lords, if I have the right to wish you that,' William said sardonically.

De la Roche studied the floor as if it were of great interest, but Prendergast was bolder. 'My lord, you do have that right. We have sought you out in token of our loyalty to you.'

'Indeed?' William arched one eyebrow. 'How strange, because apparently you did not show it during my absence. The harm you did to my interests is known far and wide.'

'My lord, they are proven traitors,' Jean spluttered, unable to contain his indignation.

'We are here to give our oaths of allegiance,' Prendergast repeated, his jaw thrust out in the manner of a man steeled to take his punishment and get it over with. *See, I am no coward*, his attitude declared.

Jean choked and had to be restrained by Jordan. 'Which on past performance is worth less than a pot of piss!' he raged.

De la Roche flickered a single upward glance then returned to staring at his shoes. Prendergast ignored Jean and, red-faced, addressed himself to William. 'If we have wronged you, my lord, then we humbly crave your forgiveness.'

'"*If*" you have wronged him?' Jean's voice rose with incredulity.

'Be quiet, Jean.' William held up his hand. 'No man's oath is ever damaged beyond repair. Even if I am not disposed to forget, I may find it in me to grant that forgiveness – providing it is craved hard enough. I will give you the kiss of peace because you ask it of me, but do not seek more than that.'

Relieved, chagrined, smarting with humiliation, Prendergast and de la Roche knelt to renew their oaths to William and receive the kiss of peace from him, but they did not stay, for despite their oaths and the words of conciliation, there was no welcome for them at the guest-house hearth.

'I hope they pitch their tent in a bog and it swallows them,' Jean growled after they had departed. 'I am sorry, my lord, but I do not have the same nobility as you.'

William snorted. 'It wasn't out of nobility that I granted them their request. It cost me nothing. They know they are on probation and that the knights of my mesnie will rebuff them. Sometimes forgiveness is worse than being whipped. I have their measure.'

'And their sons,' Jordan said with grim relish.

William looked bleak. 'Yes, and their sons,' he said.

The heralds at the gate raised their horns and blew a fanfare.

'Mama, they're coming.' Six-year-old Sybire raised hazel eyes to her mother, her face rosy with excitement. She hopped from foot to foot. Her warm brown hair was bound back from her brow by a chaplet of silver wire.

Belle, eighteen months older and possessed of a big sister's dignity, told her in a superior tone to stand still. 'People will think you're still a baby like Eve,' she said scornfully.

'I'm not a baby,' Eve piped up, stamping her foot. 'I'm not a baby, am I, Mama?'

'No, you're not,' Isabelle said in a distracted voice and automatically moved to smooth her youngest daughter's amber curls. 'All of you be good now. Your father doesn't want to come home to find you squabbling among yourselves.'

'Yes, he's had too many squabbles at court,' said Belle, who was something of a know-all.

'Your father never squabbles at court,' Isabelle contradicted her. 'But he is home for a rest, not to be bedevilled by you.'

Belle assessed her mother, then gave her a sweet smile. 'I promise I won't,' she said.

Isabelle was not taken in by the innocence in her daughter's gaze, but allowed it to pass. Only let the girls behave for as long as it took their father to arrive and dismount. Walter and Gilbert she could trust. Her sons were level-headed boys, very much the men of the family and not given to giggles and exuberance at inappropriate occasions like their sisters. The boys stood side by side, Gilbert dark-haired like William, Walter sandy and freckled, showing his de Clare heritage.

Isabelle's breathing quickened as William's standard-bearers rode into the bailey, green and gold banners flying, the scarlet Marshal lion snarling across the field of silks. She was caught on emotional tenterhooks. In the public domain she had to play her role as Countess and chatelaine – be dignified, stately and calm. But she was also the wife of a husband six months absent in fraught circumstances for both. She was not the same person he had left, and she knew that he must be changed too. You couldn't go through the fire they had experienced and emerge unscathed. She was hoping against hope he would have Will and Richard with him; she knew it was probably in vain, but was still unsettled by that tiny glimmer of optimism.

And then William was riding through the gateway on the dappled stallion that Jean had brought to him at Glascarrick. As always, he controlled his mount with the consummate ease of a born horseman, but for the first time in almost nineteen years of marriage she saw his age before she saw the man, and it was a shock. He had lost weight; there were grey shadows of exhaustion beneath his eyes and the skin that usually sat so tightly against the strong bones of his face was slack and dull. He had chosen to wear his hauberk, which she supposed was Jean's doing, but he looked burdened by the weight of it. A swift search amongst his men told her that her hope to see her sons had indeed been in vain and she had to swallow the painful lump in her throat.

She watched William dismount. His movements were easy enough; there was no sign of injury, but then perhaps the damage wasn't physical. Forcing down her apprehension, she went forward to meet him, her steps slow and measured so that no one would guess how much she was trembling inside. She wanted to run to him; she wanted to run away. He stood looking at her and, for a fleeting, unguarded moment, she saw the same emotions cross his own face. It was unbearable, all this formality. 'William . . .' She spoke his name on a tight-throated whisper. 'Jesu, William!' She hesitated, reached a brink, and suddenly she was clutching her skirts above her ankles, running to him as if pushed by a giant hand, and he was taking her in his arms, binding them around her, kissing her as if they were alone in their bedchamber. The rivets of his hauberk were a hard shock against her body, as were his lips, and she trembled with the impact.

'Enough,' he muttered against her ear as he broke the kiss. 'Enough, love, or I swear you will undo me here, in my own keep, when I have held myself together for six long months.'

. She laughed brokenly. 'My keep,' she said. The words were like astringent balm on a wound and, with the tension broken, she was able to resume her role as Countess while William set about greeting the grinning audience in the courtyard. Belle was less than impressed by the kissing, Sybire insisted on holding his hand, and Eve was shy and not quite certain that she remembered him. Walter and Gilbert were serious and on their best behaviour, already trying on the coats of the men they would one day become.

'And this is Ancel,' Isabelle said, placing a swaddled bundle in William's arms. 'Born on the same day that I received the surrender of Meilyr FitzHenry here in the great hall.'

He had been gazing, absorbed, at his new son, but now he looked across at her, his eyes filled with a mingling of admiration and censure. 'Yes, Hywel told me.'

'It was a close-run thing,' Isabelle admitted, 'but I would not have missed it for all the cloth in Flanders, travail or no travail. It meant too much to me.'

'Christ, Isabelle.'

'We have a son born and bred in Ireland,' she said proudly. 'And born in the caul, so his sea journeys should be easier than yours.'

Her words drew a wry, heartfelt laugh from him, as she had known that they would.

When William and Isabelle retired it was late into the night, but in the great hall the carousing continued, his men not being ready to relinquish the joy of celebrating their lord's return from England and their own part in saving the Leinster lands from the depredations of Meilyr FitzHenry and his allies. William and Isabelle had played their part to the hilt, smiling, toasting, praising, even dancing a few measures like a bridal couple. And like a bridal couple they had retired, pursued by grins and knowing looks.

William dismissed his attendants, Isabelle her women. When the door had clicked gently shut behind the last one, William sat heavily down on the bed and pushed his hands through his hair. 'God, Isabelle, I need to rest. If we are intact, it is by a miracle.'

She gnawed her lip, torn between wanting to give him the tranquillity he needed, and her own desires. 'You have said nothing about what happened at court,' she said after a moment, 'or about our sons. Was it as bad as that?'

'Yes,' he answered after a long pause. 'It was bad, and in the hall I didn't deem it the time to speak of such things.' He lowered his hands and raised his head, visibly summoning the strength to answer her. 'Will and Richard are doing well enough there.'

'But they did not come home with you. I am their mother; I need to know more than that they "are doing well enough".' She sat down on a bench, removed her veil and unpinned her hair, her movements jerky with agitation.

He sighed. 'The King chooses to keep them for the moment, as he is keeping the sons of other men. What can I do? Open rebellion would not restore them to us – in fact the opposite.' He knitted his brow, seeking to assuage her hunger for news. 'Both of them have grown.' He suddenly looked amused. 'Richard is very proud of his beard but it looks more like dandelion fluff. His weapons skills are coming on apace and I'm pleased at his accomplishment. When the time comes, he will do well for our Norman lands.'

'And Will?'

He hesitated, then said neutrally, 'Will has been learning the usual young man's lessons about drink, gambling and women who bare their hair in public.'

Isabelle clucked her tongue in disapproval and took up her comb.

William looked wryly amused. 'I mean that he has learned by his mistakes, which has to be the best way where such vices are concerned. If he was ever bedazzled by the glamour of the court, he now sees its underbelly too, which is all to the good. Now he has to learn patience, and that will only come with age.' He gave her a long, aching look. 'I've missed watching you comb your hair.'

His expression and the tone of his voice made her bones gelatinous. She put the comb aside and came to the bed. 'I think of Will and Richard each time I look at the sons and the brothers that I have taken as surety from the men who burned Newtown,' she said. Kneeling at his feet, she began slowly unwinding his leg bindings. 'I told Jean that if you did not return to me whole, I would cut out their hearts with a spoon.' She looked up at him. Her hair was rippled from its earlier braiding. Smoothed by the comb, it shone like cloth of gold. 'But what I said was only the bravery of words. When I see them, I think of their mothers, and then I think of my sons. Do you know, if I could, I would keep their fathers hostage and let the sons go.'

'So, would you barter me for Will and Richard?' he asked quietly.

Isabelle rolled up the length of woven binding. 'That is an unfair question.'

'Perhaps, but I asked it. Would you?'

She started on his other leg and worked in silence for a moment, considering. 'As a mother, yes I would,' she said. 'They have their lives before them and they are of my flesh. I have carried them in my body, sustained them at my breast, watched over their first steps and comforted their scrapes and grazes. No matter the love and honour that I hold for you, their father, I would have to choose them out of my maternal heart.' She gnawed her lip. 'But as a countess and a wife it would break me to give you up. Six months has shown me what I can do and what is impossible. Yes, I have had able deputies, but that is all they have been: temporary helmsmen. Our boys are not yet ready to steer the ship and you still have an infant son to see grow up. I won't let you shirk that responsibility.' Her voice quivered and her gaze was suddenly liquid.

William's laugh had a hollow ring. 'Ah, Isabelle, I am of an age when other men have grandchildren at their feet, or effigies on their tombs. I am growing old.'

The words sent a jolt through her because they had been her first thought on seeing him in the courtyard. She could not lose him; the thought was unbearable. 'You are not other men,' she said fiercely. 'After all that has happened you are bound to be tired, and sea crossings always disagree with you.' Kneeling between his thighs, she reached to the ties attaching his hose to his braies and after a moment's nimble work, slanted him a look through her lashes. 'Shame on you for lying to me,' she said in a slumberous voice. 'There's certainly no old age here.'

This time William's laughter – somewhat breathless – was filled with genuine humour. 'I suppose that even in ancient oaks the sap still rises in springtime,' he said.

Gasping, William gazed at the green and gold canopy above his head and waited for his heart to cease its drumbeat racing and settle to a steadier rhythm. Although carrying no surplus flesh, he knew that he was slack and out of condition. He had been kicking his heels at court for far too long and he was stale.

Taking stock of himself, he knew, despite Isabelle's fierce

326

denial, that he was sixty-one years old and his remaining years were dwindling. His eyesight was still sharp, his teeth mostly sound and he hadn't yet started to shake with palsy. With a twisted smile at the canopy, he acknowledged that he was certainly not impotent. But in cold weather his knees ached, and although he could mount a horse without difficulty, no longer could he leap across a saddle in full mail. The intensity of the bout of lovemaking with Isabelle had left him shaking and drained. He had heard enough jests about old husbands dying on their wedding nights at the moment of supreme pleasure, and seen the knowing smirks of the young knights when old barons brought their toothsome young wives to court. He dreaded suffering a seizure that paralysed but did not immediately kill, or being rendered helpless by the incapacities of old age. The thought of being tied to life as a dribbling wreck appalled him, not just for himself, but for Isabelle. She was more than twenty years younger than he was. The notion of being useless to her and of seeing pity in her eyes or, God forbid, disgust was unbearable.

Ancel stirred in the cradle and whimpered. Isabelle quietly rose from the bed to tend him, drawing a loose bedrobe over her naked body. Time had changed her too. The once lithe flanks and high breasts had been replaced by the rounded soft curves of a woman who had birthed many children. Watching her through half-closed lids, William decided that it was probably not a good idea to voice his fears to her for it would make them more real and perhaps cause her to think in directions she had avoided before. If God was good then perhaps He would let him live to see this baby at least become a strapping youth.

As he drifted off to sleep, William made a decision to enjoy the years he had left, however many . . . or few they might be. He would make a good fist of governing Leinster, would leave a legacy of peaceful prosperity for Isabelle and their heirs. He was done with the hurly burly of John's court . . . forever.

Feeling nervous, Isabelle watched the servants unroll a magnificent length of tapis along the floor before the lord and lady's chair. The colours, scarlet, blue and gold, were richer and brighter than any flowers on God's earth. Light shone down on the carpet from the high arched windows above and illuminated the beauty of the pattern. She was not averse to spending silver when she had to, and neither was William, but she didn't want to tell him how much the piece had cost. She had obtained it from their Flemish broker and it had travelled the spice road from Persia, or so the man said in the letter that had accompanied it across the Irish Sea.

'What's this?' William asked her with sharp curiosity.

'I thought that we could hang it on the far wall in the solar,' she said, 'but today I want to make an impression on our vassals when they kneel before us to renew their oaths. None will have anything like this in their own homes, and the fact they must walk upon such luxury to reach us will emphasise our wealth and power.' Their Irish vassals had arrived to renew their allegiance and were waiting to be summoned.

'Our wealth?' He arched his brow.

Isabelle flushed. 'Worth it,' she said.

He looked her up and down. She knew he was taking in her new gown of dark-rose silk, stitched with pearls from the Indian Ocean, and the belt of brocaded silver thread. 'You are probably right,' he agreed. 'And perhaps this is one of those occasions when it is tactful for a husband not to ask his wife for an accounting.'

'Oh,' Isabelle said softly as he escorted her across the bright rug to her chair and took his place beside her, 'there will be an accounting today, indeed there will. I have been waiting for this moment.'

Those who had reneged and rebelled were to receive their just deserts. Isabelle wanted them to kneel on the tapis, feel the soft wool under their knees, see the rich jewel colours and know that they could not match the magnificence and power of their overlords. It would be sweet balm on the wounds caused by all the humiliation and uncertainty of the past months. She had never thought of herself as a vindictive person, but she would have restitution today.

William said nothing, but made himself comfortable, one hand resting on the chair arm, the other cupping his jaw in a deliberating manner. Then he sent his ushers to bring his vassals to him, and had the hostages assembled in an upper chamber away from the gathering.

The first man to cross the tapis was Philip of Prendergast. He moved gingerly, almost on tiptoe, and his gaze refused to settle on anything. When he looked up it was to shafts of light from the window and they brought his eyes down to the glorious rich colours of the tapis, symbol of wealth and status unharmed. Focusing straight ahead brought him the glacial blue stare of the Countess and William's impartial dark one. And so his focus vacillated, confirming to Isabelle that he was weak and not to be trusted.

Kneeling before Isabelle and William, he bowed his head and offered up his clasped palms to perform homage. Isabelle was taken aback when William accepted Prendergast's oath of loyalty without demur, giving him the kiss of peace and speaking to him formally but with warmth, as if there had never been a breach between them.

'Go and find your sons,' William said. 'They are in the chamber above the hall with the others who have been guesting here awhile. Take your wife – she will want to see them too, I warrant.'

Prendergast stared at William with astonishment. 'You want no more of me than that? You are willing to release them?'

'I want your loyalty, and I will have it,' William said. 'But rather given of your own volition than forced out of you. Go now, and think on this moment – what you have sworn and how I have acted.' He waved his hand in dismissal.

Expression dazed, unable to believe that it had been so easy, Prendergast staggered his way back across the tapis to find his wife and then go to his sons.

Isabelle's expression was dazed too. 'Why didn't you bring him to task?' she hissed. 'I cannot believe you let him off so leniently!'

William turned to her. 'I will not exact retribution unless it is going to be more effective than diplomatic persuasion. I have no need to smash every cup in the pottery to make my point; just the one that men thought at one time to have lustre.'

'You are taking generosity too far.' Isabelle's gaze was bright with anger.

'Better than the other way around.'

Biting back an acerbic retort, she gripped the arms of her chair hard as the next vassal came forward to make his obeisance, renew his vows and be given the kiss of peace.

William dealt with all the rebels in the same fashion that he had dealt with Philip of Prendergast. He spoke magnanimously, saying all men made errors of judgement, himself included. There was no edge to his voice and he returned the hostages with open generosity and kisses of peace all round. Isabelle continued to fume and was on the point of bursting when it finally came Meilyr FitzHenry's turn to walk the tapis and bow before them.

And now William sat up, leaned forward, and everything changed.

In the next few moments, as she watched him destroy Meilyr FitzHenry, Isabelle felt the hair rise on her nape and at her forearms. William didn't raise his voice; he didn't have to. The timbre was enough and the imposing language of his body that before had been so relaxed. Now he clad himself in the full power of the great magnate he was.

'I intend to keep your son Henry with me,' William announced. 'He will learn more about honour in my household than in yours. Be assured I will treat him better than you have treated me and mine.'

A look of dismay crossed Meilyr's face. William's expression remained neutral as he played indifferent, treating Meilyr with the courtesy due to a vassal, but one of small consequence.

'I have also looked into your marriage with your son's mother. Since it seems you were handfasted but never wed and have no formal contract lodged with any church, your boy does not have the hereditary right to the keep at Dunamase. It reverts to your overlord, who happens to be me. On those terms I am content to have you as my vassal and give you the kiss of peace.'

Isabelle managed not to gape at William but she was astonished. Meilyr and his wife not married? From where had he dredged that up? No matter. If it was true, and knowing William he would not have said so unless he was positive, it was the hammer with which to smash this particular cup.

Meilyr had turned the colour of parchment. 'You cannot do that!' he gasped.

William's stare was icy. 'I can, and I will. A man who rebels against his lord forfeits all. I do not expect your gratitude for not taking everything from you – it would be asking too much of your character – but I do expect your compliance. You have no choice but to accept my judgement. Who will support you? And do not say the King, because I have it on good authority that you are to be replaced by someone less incompetent.'

Meilyr deflated like a leaky pig's bladder balloon. Shaking like a man of ninety, pupils dilated with shock, he knelt to offer his hands to William, who clasped them tightly between his own. 'I hold you to this oath,' William said quietly. 'And may you be damned if you break your word.'

Once Meilyr had staggered away, escorted by two knights of William's mesnie, Isabelle turned to him. He had briefly closed his eyes and now she saw the strain in his face.

'How did you know about his marriage? Is it true?'

William opened his eyes and gave her a weary look. 'Meilyr has plenty of enemies waiting their chance to see him take a fall off fortune's wheel. Loyalty is cheaply bought and sold if you know the right places to haggle and you don't mind wading through the mire.' He eased to his feet and gestured a servant to roll up the length of tapis. 'Yes, it's true. He handfasted in the Welsh fashion and never married the woman at the church door . . . an oversight he's regretting now, but too late since she's dead.'

'Where are you going?' she asked as he turned away from the gathered folk waiting for them in the hall.

'To wash my hands,' he said. 'I've soiled them enough for one morning.'

28

Kilkenny, Leinster, September 1208

The autumn weather was wild and Isabelle was content
to spend a day in her chamber, teaching her daughters
to sew while she embroidered the hem of a new tunic
for William. Rain slammed against the tightly closed
shutters, making everyone shiver. Isabelle was wearing
her warmest undergown and a dress of thick salmon-
pink wool.

'Any more o' this and sure we'll be growing flippers
like the seals out in Bannow Bay,' grumbled Sorcha,
Ancel's wet nurse, as she tapped the cradle with her foot
to rock him to sleep.

Sybire giggled at the thought and Belle demanded to
be told yet again the story of the women who turned into
seals at the full of the moon and could be seen off the
prows of boats, diving and sporting in the ghostly silver
light. Isabelle gave the wet nurse a conspiratorial smile.
Sorcha was a born storyteller with an endless supply of
myths, legends and history. On days like this her tales
were a godsend, and since frequent rain was a standard
part of Leinster's weather pattern, she had more than
earned her keep. Isabelle selected some thread and plied

her needle through the fine blue cloth, half listening to the story and half allowing her thoughts to wander.

William had been home for five months. At first, after the initial business of the oath-taking, he had done little but eat, sleep and recuperate. He had exercised his horses, played with his children, taken her frequently to bed and listened to the harp player and bard in the hall of an evening, cup of wine to hand. Sometimes he had taken part in the singing himself, for he had a fine voice, and took great pleasure in using it. The knots had slowly begun to unwind. Colour and vitality had seeped back and the shadow had gradually become the man. Isabelle had seen it happen before. He had come from the funeral of old King Henry to marry her, raised on high by Richard, who until recently had been his enemy. She hadn't known William on their wedding day, nor had he known her. He had been suffering from an injured leg and the mental strain of months of warfare between Henry and Richard. She had not realised it then because she was only eighteen years old and unfamiliar with him, but he had been at the end of his tether and in desperate need of respite. The day after their wedding in St Paul's Cathedral, he had taken her to a secluded manor belonging to a friend, there to spend time and quiet with her, shunning all company and enjoying the simplest of pleasures. Then it had only taken him a week to recuperate, this time it had taken six, but as the days had lengthened and the spring turned the world to green, he had begun to sniff the air with a new, restless optimism.

By midsummer he had thrown himself into governing Leinster. A flurry of writs and charters had issued from his chamber. He had commenced plans for more settlements, had been busy with the merchants and ship owners in Newtown, developing strategies for increasing trade

334

and bringing prosperity to the port. He took Gilbert and Walter everywhere with him, showing them the business of governance – as he had once shown Will and Richard. The sight of him with their third and fourth sons sent a pang through Isabelle – of anxiety, and of painful longing for her two eldest boys.

Meilyr FitzHenry had retired to dwell in seclusion at Dunamase under the watchful eye of William's deputies. King John had stripped him of the office of justiciar and given it instead to John de Grey, Bishop of Norwich, a man up to the task. Isabelle rather liked de Grey, even whilst acknowledging that he was one of John's creatures and would not swerve from his master's orders. But at least a man who was openly ruthless was better than one who used low cunning and sneaked about in the periphery of one's vision.

Sorcha's story was drawing to a close. The man had lost his bride and she had returned to the sea, swimming out on the waves, looking for all the world like a sleek, dark-headed seal.

Belle, having seen seals out in the bay when they were visiting her father's Abbey of the Vow, wanted to know if such creatures really existed.

'Ah,' said Sorcha with a smile. 'Everything exists if you believe in it.'

The door opened and William entered the chamber, his cloak glittering with crystals of rain for he had come across open ground from the stables where he had been inspecting a mare with a new foal. A letter was clutched in his fist and his squires were following hard on his heels.

Isabelle looked from the letter to her husband's face and set her sewing aside. 'What's wrong?' As always, she felt a quickening of fear lest it was bad news about their sons.

William grimaced as he removed his wet cloak. 'You know the King took against William de Braose around the same time that he took against me?'

'Yes . . .' Isabelle had never understood the friendship between de Braose and her husband. William might walk up to the line, even scuff his toe along it at times, but he never stepped over. De Braose ignored the detail that a line existed at all, especially when it came to the acquisition of power for his enormous brood of offspring. He was a loud, bombastic oaf – all the things that William wasn't. 'What has happened?'

Frowning heavily, William fetched his heavy outdoor cloak of double-lined wool from the garderobe. 'John demanded his eldest son as a hostage and Lady Maude refused to give him up.' He gave her an eloquent look and set about changing his shoes for tough, calf-hide riding boots, liberally waterproofed with beeswax.

Isabelle felt a twinge of admiration and envy. She had refused to give her sons up at first, but had caved in to William's insistence, something she still regretted. Say what you wanted about Maude de Braose, the woman was indomitable.

'De Braose has fled here to avoid John's wrath and has sent to ask if we will succour him. He's at Wicklow with his wife and family and I'm riding out to meet him. That's as much as I know. The letter is a request for our aid.'

Isabelle looked at him in sudden alarm.

'Yes, I know,' he said. 'It's a dilemma. We don't want to antagonise John so soon after the last incident, but we cannot deny refuge to the de Braoses. It is likely that they will travel on to their de Lacy kin in Meath, but they need somewhere to stay for now and I will not turn them away.'

Isabelle nodded reluctantly. It was far too dangerous, but they were honour-bound to offer help.

William sighed as he latched the toggles on his boots. 'The King seems determined to ruin de Braose, but while there's the slightest hope of patching things up between them, we can err on the side of friendship. That's the way to play this and survive. No one has declared in my hearing that de Braose is my enemy, nor have I received letters from the King or his justiciar telling me to turn my men against him.' He leaned over, kissed Isabelle's cheek, squeezed her shoulder and was gone.

'Maude de Braose,' muttered Lady Avenel. Because of the presence of the children in the room she said nothing else, but the purse of her lips was eloquent.

Isabelle cautioned her with a look and stood up. 'Come,' she said, 'there's work to be done if we're to have guests.'

Isabelle was shocked when she set eyes on Maude de Braose. Gone was the florid, overbearing woman she remembered from Normandy. In her place was a raddled hag, broken veins mapping her face, hair a grey tangle sticking out from beneath her wimple, her body a shapeless sack within her rumpled, salt-stained clothing. Her tongue was still as sharp as ever, but behind its edge and in her eyes, Isabelle could see the fear.

'Surely my lady, the King and your husband can still come to some arrangement,' Isabelle murmured as she plied her unwelcome guest with hot wine. De Braose was in the hall with William and the knights, discussing what was to be done, but Maude had come to the private chambers to see her younger children put to bed after their exhausting ordeal.

Maude laughed harshly. 'Indeed they can, providing we are prepared to surrender everything and live as paupers. It's not my husband he wants anyway, it's me.'

'You, my lady?' Isabelle frowned at her guest. 'William said something about you refusing to give up your son . . .'

Maude threw her a scornful look. 'You might bow down to your husband and agree to sacrifice your children to that murdering spawn of the Devil, but I won't. John doesn't want my son for a hostage, he wants him for a corpse . . . He'd have us all dead if he could.'

Isabelle blenched and glanced around. Several of her women were within hearing and they were giving Maude de Braose wall-eyed looks. 'My lady, you should be careful when you say such things. My women are loyal to their last breath, but in other circles it could be very different.'

Maude drank down the hot wine, her throat rippling like a man's. Then she lowered the cup with a gasp and caught a drip from her chin on the back of her hand. 'You don't know, do you?' Her eyes filled with stark pity. 'You haven't heard.'

'Heard what, my lady?' Isabelle replied, feeling like an animal walking knowingly into a trap.

'Why do you think we are here, seeking succour from anyone fool enough to take us in?' Maude snapped. 'You think my husband is being persecuted because he owes the King too much money? Because he has too many possessions and he's a threat to John's kingship?'

'I—'

'He is being destroyed because we know too much. Has your husband told you what really happened to Prince Arthur in the Tower of Rouen?' She curled her lip. 'I do not suppose he has. He is good at changing the subject and avoiding what he does not wish to say.'

Isabelle lifted her chin. 'I do not think—'

'Hah, I wish I did not either, but I am afraid I do, all the time, every bitter moment of every day. I'll tell you

338

what my husband did not keep from me. John murdered Arthur – put his foot on his neck and cut his throat with a paring knife. My William was there and John made him dispose of the body afterwards – weigh it down with a block of stone and drop it in the Seine. I refused to give my son to a man capable of doing that to his own flesh and blood. My crime was to say so to the knights who came to take him into custody, and now John will not rest until I am dead too. He is coming for me and for my family and that is why we have fled.'

Isabelle clapped her hand to her mouth, feeling sick. She had always suspected, but had preferred not to delve too deeply. Now she had been forced to see.

Maude de Braose looked round. 'You have made a fine home for yourself, Countess. You and your husband have weathered the storms well. You will not keep us for long. You have a better sense of survival than that . . . and John already has your sons.'

'You must have known about Arthur long ago,' Isabelle said to William when they retired for the night. 'And yet you did not tell me.'

William sat up in bed and punched the pillows and bolsters until they were comfortable. 'I knew he was dead when John could not produce him at King Philip's demand, but I did not know the circumstances until now.'

Isabelle shuddered. 'How can you serve such a man? We cannot leave our sons in his hands.'

William sighed. 'I do not know what version Maude de Braose has told you, but it is almost certain that a French spy gouged out the Prince's eyes. John knew he could never show Arthur to the world in such a state, and the boy was in agony and would have died anyway. John put him out of his misery the way you would do a maimed

339

animal. Whatever he is, whatever he has done, he will not touch Will and Richard.'

Isabelle rubbed her arms. 'And whatever John is, you will serve him,' she said with revulsion.

He gave her a pointed look. 'I hope you know me better than your voice suggests.'

'William, you cannot shovel dung and not soil your hands. I know that much.'

'You have seen the plight that de Braose is in. I'll shovel as much dung as I must to prevent that happening to us.'

'Even give up the de Braoses to John?'

William swore. 'God's bones, woman, your mood is as contrary tonight as this vile weather. No, of course I won't give him up to John – because I have received no summons to do so. I will let them recover from their sea crossing and then I will send them on to their de Lacy kin . . . unless you would rather keep them here and risk that summons arriving whilst they are our guests?'

Isabelle looked at him and then away. She felt smirched, ashamed and rightly put in her place. 'No,' she said in a low voice filled with chagrin.

'Ah, Isabelle.' He reached for her and pulled her into his arms. She resisted him for a moment, then sighed and rested her head on his chest.

'Why is nothing clean and simple?' she asked with frustration and sadness.

He set his hand beneath her hair to stroke the back of her neck. 'When I was a youngster,' he murmured, 'I only had to worry about my horse, my armour and the morrow's tourney. I used to dream of being a great and powerful lord, never guessing that when I became one, I would yearn in the same wise for those days of joyous simplicity.'

* * *

A chill northerly wind was making the winter's day bitterly cold, and it had started to rain – icy droplets, each one like a small, frozen slap where it struck the bare skin of the face and hands. William's knees were aching fiercely and, as he rode, he thought longingly on warm fires and cups of mulled wine spiced with ginger and pepper. He had spent much of his youth in the warmer, drier climes of Poitou and the Limousin and it was ironic that now, when he would have benefited from that more arid climate, he was enduring the cold and damp. For his sins, he was escorting William de Braose and his family to the borders of Meath where Walter de Lacy was to meet them and take his in-laws under his wing.

The meeting place was a particular ancient stone marking the boundary between William's jurisdiction and de Lacy's. Reputedly it was heard to talk on the night of All Hallows' Eve, although William suspected that the culprit was more likely to be drink and an overactive imagination. As they approached the stone, de Braose joined William. He was riding a fine black stallion that William had gifted to him, and wearing one of William's winter cloaks, lined with Norwegian sable.

'You have gone as far as you need, Marshal,' de Braose said gruffly. 'Go back to your wife and your safe haven in Kilkenny.'

William gave a damp, uncomfortable shrug. 'I would do more for you if I could.'

De Braose made a sound of macabre amusement. 'Said with diplomacy, Marshal, but we both know the truth. I don't expect you to jump into the abyss with me. You have already been to the brink once yourself but fortunately your wife doesn't have the mouth that mine does.' He glanced briefly over his shoulder towards the woman riding behind them, her lips set in a grim line that was like a fissure in granite.

'Lady Maude is an admirable woman,' William said diplomatically.

De Braose snorted with derision. 'Depends what you mean by the word.' He drew the reins through his fingers and looked at the leather, worn to a shine by much handling. 'Were we right to do as we did, Marshal?'

William lifted his brows. 'Right to do what?'

'It was my word that put John on the throne. Had my ears heard King Richard's whisper differently at Châlus, we could have had Arthur over us. You went to England and talked the dissenters round. Without our backing, John would not have a crown.'

'He was the best in terms of choices. I doubt Arthur would have rewarded us for our support.'

'Hah!' de Braose scoffed. 'And now you see my reward from John. Strange that it should concern Arthur, is it not? He was always going to be my downfall.'

William said nothing. In essence it was true, but de Braose had contributed to his own fall from favour by pushing too hard and too long. There but for the grace of God . . . Surreptitiously he crossed himself.

As they approached the standing stone, grey shapes of men and horses rose out of the mizzle, armour and harness clinking softly. Drawing rein, William saluted Walter de Lacy. The lord of Meath nudged his stallion forward to greet William and welcome his in-laws. De Braose clasped William arm to arm, one soldier and comrade to another. 'God keep you,' he said.

'And you, my lord.'

De Braose laughed but it was a soulless sound. 'I doubt it,' he said. 'He may see the meanest sparrow fall, but He's forsaken me.'

Maude de Braose rode past William with the briefest of nods, as if he were a servant, as if he had not kept her under his roof in warmth and safety for the past several weeks. He had expected no grace from her and thus was not disappointed. Watching her ride away, though, he felt an icy trickle run down his spine and it had nothing to do with the damp that was gradually saturating his cloak.

29

Pembroke Castle, South Wales, June 1210

Will had not seen Pembroke Castle since the Cilgerran campaign and the sight filled him with nostalgia and nervous uncertainty. Then it had been palisaded with ash stakes and the gatehouse had been built of timber. Now masonry walls rose as a bulwark against the Welsh and proclaimed the wealth, importance and pride of the Earl of Pembroke. A strong, circular limestone keep towered behind those walls, dwarfing the older Norman hall built by Will's grandfather Richard Strongbow before he went to Ireland. Work on the castle was still continuing and the broad outer bailey was filled with the huts of masons and craftsmen.

In front of him, guarded by his mercenaries, King John straddled a distinctive dappled palfrey and gazed around with thoughtful interest, his eyes lingering on the scarlet Marshal lion rippling from the battlements in the warm June wind, proclaiming the residence of its Earl. Will noticed there was no sign of the de Clare chevrons, therefore his mother had remained behind in Ireland. Knowing her antipathy for John and some of those around him, Will was not surprised. John had camped his army at

Cross on the Sea not far from Pembroke where he was mustering a force to embark for Ireland with the intention of bringing de Braose and his de Lacy kin to heel. However, he had brought his immediate retinue to the greater comfort of Pembroke Castle.

'Our father is not going to like the expense of keeping the King and all his household until we sail,' Richard muttered out of the side of his mouth.

'That's deliberate on John's part,' Will said with knowing cynicism. 'He's piling the cost of keeping the court on to our father to spite him for being an ally of de Braose and de Lacy. There'll be more expense when we arrive in Ireland too because John's bound to stay at Kilkenny.'

Their father had come from Ireland at John's summons because his only other choice was to turn rebel with de Braose and the de Lacys, and he wouldn't do it. The de Lacys couldn't win, and John de Grey, the new justiciar, had a grip on the Irish situation that Meilyr FitzHenry, for all his posturing, had lacked. Besides, Will knew their father would die before he violated his oath to John. It was a matter of personal honour.

As the grooms and stable boys came to take the horses, Will saw his father emerge from the great hall and descend the timber stairway steps to greet the royal party. The genial expression on his face seemed legitimate and his posture was relaxed, but then he was a master of the courtier's art. Remembering how he had held himself together during the difficult time involving Meilyr FitzHenry, Will was filled with awe, pride and trepidation. How was he ever going to match up to that performance?

A little stiffly but without undue awkwardness, his father knelt to the King and bowed his head. John wore a smile on his face, but Will knew it was superficial. The surface

345

might be smooth and sunlit, but the undercurrents were dark and turbulent.

'See, I have brought your sons,' John said with a magnanimous gesture towards Will and Richard. 'Almost grown men in their own right.' He stepped back to allow the youths to embrace their father. 'Are you not glad of the care I have lavished on them?'

Will felt his father's strong grip at his shoulder, saw the veiled warning in the winter-river eyes and acknowledged it before lowering his own. 'Indeed, sire,' his father said in an easy, humorous tone, 'I am sure that you have been as careful of them as your own flesh and blood.'

John gave a vinegary smile. 'Not quite,' he said. 'But near enough.'

In the top chamber of the keep, the royal bathtub steamed with hot, herb-scented water. John luxuriated, a cup of William's best French wine in one hand, the other resting languidly along the side of the tub. Suzanna, his favourite concubine, knelt behind him, kneading his shoulders. His belly resembled a small, flesh-coloured barrel. A stripe of dark fuzz ran from navel to groin. The hair at his nipples was salted grey.

Attendants were assembling John's travelling bed and emptying chests of embroidered linen sheets, colourful blankets and a coverlet of red and gold silk under which the King – and Suzanna – would sleep that night. John reached to a platter of hot fried pastries conveniently positioned at the side of the tub, bit into one and gave the other half to his mistress, who laughed as she opened her painted carmine lips and took it out of his hand with her teeth.

'I see you have been able to muster a sizeable number of your own men, Marshal,' John remarked.

'They have answered from my Welsh lands as summoned, sire,' William replied. 'There are more to be had in Leinster.' The sound of swearing came from the direction of the bed as someone malleted his thumb instead of the pieces of wood he was trying to assemble.

'Guarding the Countess and your brood?' John mocked. 'I notice you've left Jean D'Earley behind again. It's a good thing you are neither a jealous nor suspicious man, Marshal. He's about her age, isn't he, and he's always carried a torch for her.'

Will, who was sitting nearby, feeding a hound with scraps of toasted bread, gave the King a fulminating look. William remained unperturbed and responded with a smile. 'Sire, I trust both my wife and Jean D'Earley with my honour. Until the day she died, I carried a torch for your mother, but it never once lit my way to her bed.'

John's eyelids tensed. 'You always have a clever answer, don't you, Marshal, which is more than I can say for de Braose. His wife puts all the words in his mouth these days. I know what I'd put in hers to stopper it, the stupid bitch . . .' His tone developed a petulant edge. 'You shouldn't have given de Braose succour and escorted them to the de Lacys. You know full well that you should have handed them over to me.'

William regarded him impassively. 'Sire, when last I saw him, he was at court with you and you were not enemies.'

John took a belligerent gulp of wine. 'Even if you claim not to have known then, you must have realised he was a fugitive when you gave him succour at Kilkenny. Only an idiot would have thought otherwise, and you are too clever by half.'

William said stonily: 'Since I had received no orders telling me to detain him, sire, I sent him on to his son-in-law in good faith and conscience.'

John glowered. 'I suspect that if orders to detain him had arrived, my messenger would have been prevented from delivering them until you had de Braose safely out of the way. I am not too clever, Marshal, just clever enough.'

'I hope you do not doubt my loyalty, sire.'

'Oh no.' John waved an expansive hand. 'I know I'm not about to be murdered in my bathtub, but you cut the meat of loyalty so fine that it's see-through when it comes to your own interests.'

The words hit William like well-flung stones, but he pretended that they had had no impact. Be impassive, show nothing. 'As I understand, sire, you yourself have given de Braose safe conduct to come to Pembroke and answer your summons,' he said reasonably.

John made a scornful sound. 'What's the wager he won't bring that hell-bitch of a wife with him when he knows it's her I want? After all, you didn't bring yours.'

'But you did not summon her, my lord, and besides, she is not long out of childbed with our new daughter.'

'Christ, Marshal, another brat?' John's laugh was vindictive. 'Are you trying to follow de Braose in the breeding stakes too?'

William suppressed the retort that at least all of his children were born in wedlock to the same mother. 'We have named her Joanna,' he said pleasantly instead. 'Had she been a boy, she would have been John.'

'God's cock, Marshal, you're not telling me you're hoping to curry my favour? It's a vain hope if you are. No, you wouldn't be so unsubtle!'

'Take it as you will, sire.'

John looked disdainful. 'Then I will take it you've named the whelp for your father and brother. What do I care?' He drummed his fingers on the side of the tub. 'Your

348

profligate breeding habits aside, it seems to me, in the light of your behaviour with de Braose, it would be prudent to take more sureties from you.'

'Sureties such as, sire?'

'Such as the keep at Dunamase, and your men who defied me before – D'Earley and de Saqueville among them.'

William heard Will make a strangled sound and threw him a quelling look that made the young man bite his teeth together. 'You already have my English castles, sire, and my two eldest sons,' William said. 'If you think it is going to increase my trustworthiness then by all means I will hand over what you ask.' His attitude carried a fine balance of injured patience and reproach.

John picked up a sliver of white Castilian soap scented with attar of roses. 'I am glad to hear it. We'll talk more in good time. Here, girl, wash my back.' He passed the soap to his mistress.

Dismissed by John, William walked down the tower stairs and emerged into the warm summer air of the bailey. A knight came towards him, intending to ask a question, sensed the atmosphere and changed his mind and direction. Not possessing the same sensibility, Will emerged from the tower and strode up to his father.

'How can you bear it?' he demanded, his young voice rough with anger and indignation. 'How can you let him humiliate you like that?'

William felt unutterably weary. He needed solitude. With an effort, he faced his son. 'Because I know what's at stake. The King was in a sour and mischievous mood. He was deliberately trying to rile me and I refused to give him that pleasure.' He waved his hand in abrupt dismissal. 'Leave him to his whore and his bath. I have no doubt they will mellow his mood.'

349

'I suppose this means I'll still be a hostage,' Will said stormily. 'I don't know if I can stomach any more.'

William forced himself to make an effort. 'It may be that I can get you sent elsewhere. There are plenty of royal castles in England – you don't have to follow the court.'

'I'll still be a prisoner though, won't I!' Will bared his teeth and suddenly looked startlingly like Isabelle in a rage. 'Hostage to a tyrant because you won't stand up to him!' He stalked off, his spine as straight as a lance and his stride hard with temper.

William closed his eyes and rubbed his forehead. Only age and experience would breed wisdom in the lad. He could not expect Will to be a replica of himself and react in the same ways. When he thought of the hard life lessons he had had to learn to bring him to this stage, and those he was still learning, he realised what a difficult furrow Will was going to have to plough. At twenty years old, William had had no prospects other than those he carved joyously with sword and lance upon the tourney ground. His eldest son had no such leeway. He was the heir to one of the greatest earldoms in the kingdom and, when the time came, he had to be ready to assume the mantle.

'Will the King want me for a hostage too?'

Isabelle looked up from pinning a brooch at her shoulder and fixed her gaze upon her third son. Gilbert had been scrubbed and polished until she could almost hear his skin squeaking. The King and the mustered troops from England were on their way to Kilkenny. The message from William had arrived just after dawn and she had sent riders out to greet the royal party and escort it in.

Gilbert had been very quiet and pale since the news had come and Isabelle had wondered if he was sickening for something. Now she realised why. He was thirteen, not quite old enough to be a squire, but sufficiently close should the demand be made. He was being tutored for the priesthood, but had entered no order yet and his father had insisted that he keep up his swordplay and training for a couple more years at least.

'No, of course he won't ask for you,' Isabelle said with more conviction than she felt. She wouldn't put anything past John. In the message William had sent, he said that the King was demanding Dunamase and all their best knights as hostages.

Gilbert looked relieved for a moment, but then sighed almost regretfully.

'Why? Do you want to go?'

Gilbert wrinkled his nose. 'No,' he said, his eyes wistful, 'but the King has many books and probably a lot I haven't read.'

Isabelle's lips twitched with exasperated amusement. Gilbert had always been studious, almost as if he knew from birth that his family intended him for a career in the Church. Not that he couldn't romp with the others when he chose, but he was never more content than when his nose was buried in a book, or puzzling over a more serious form of chess than the sort his sisters liked to play with dice.

'My lady, the King is sighted,' Jean announced, standing in her chamber doorway. 'Are you ready to go down?' He was resplendent in his court robes of scarlet wool, decorated with his wife's exquisite embroidery. His slender fingers were adorned with rings and a cross studded with rubies gleamed around his neck.

Isabelle made a face. 'If I must be,' she said, and gently ushered Gilbert before her. A swift gesture brought together the rest of her household: the other children, their nurses, her women and attendants. Like barnyard poultry, she thought with a flash of humour rapidly subdued because the imagery of hens before a fox was too close to the bone. Reaching Jean, she laid her hand briefly on his sleeve. 'I am sorry. You have endured a great deal at our expense.'

Jean looked down at her hand and his complexion reddened a little. 'No, my lady. What I have endured has been at the King's will. I am glad to stand hostage for my lord's word, and so are the others who have been asked . . . except for David de la Roche,' he added with a curl of his lip, 'but everyone knows what he is and no man will sit with him at table or speak with him.'

Her household in tow, Isabelle descended to the bailey to greet the King. For once, the weather was fine; the sun beat down with the strength of a clenched fist and the sky was almost white around its glare.

First came the heralds and outriders, caparisoned in red and gold, then the knights of the mesnie in full panoply, their horses barded in the royal colours. William's knights in their parti-coloured green and yellow were led by Mallard, proudly carrying William's banner, silk streamers fluttering, and close beside them rippled the colours of Aumale, followed by the blazons of six more earls and their immediate retinues. The main army of seven thousand remained outside the walls, billeted in houses in the town, or camped on open ground nearby.

Resplendent in a robe of silk damask, John rode a high-stepping palfrey the colour of fresh cream, its harness and trappings of red leather. William's blue-roan paced a length behind, and William's manner was one of professional deference.

Isabelle knelt and bowed her head, making sure with a surreptitious glance that everyone else was doing the same. For William's sake and their children's, she would do it, but had she possessed a free rein and no constraints, she would have stood erect and spat in John's face for what he had done and all that he was.

A squire assisted John to dismount. Handing him the reins, he paced forward to his kneeling subjects and extended a jewelled hand to Isabelle, drawing her to her feet.

'Welcome to Kilkenny, sire,' she said and was pleased to hear the courteous modulation of her own voice.

John looked her slowly up and down before considering the children, his expression so benign that Isabelle had to suppress the urge to fling herself in front of them and protect them from his gaze. 'A fine brood you have given your lord,' he said pleasantly, 'and yet another one to add, I am told.' He nodded towards Joanna, who was wailing fractiously in the arms of the wet nurse.

'Indeed, sire, but I sadly miss my two eldest sons. They were boys when last I saw them, and by now they must surely be men.' Still she kept her voice on an even keel.

'Almost, but not quite. Do not take my word for it, Countess. See for yourself.' He turned, raising his arm, and beckoned to two tall young men at the back of the entourage. 'William, Richard, greet your lady mother.'

Shock tore through Isabelle so hard that she gasped. She swallowed and swallowed again, her eyes filling as Will came to make his obeisance to her. The gangling youth of her memory was gone and in his place stood a young adult, deep-brown hair curling at his nape, his jaw edged with closely shaven stubble. Although not yet a knight, he had been permitted the dignity of wearing a sword. Richard, being younger, wore no such accoutrement, but the sight of him, copper-bearded, broad and muscular, sent such a pang of pride and loss through her that she could not speak.

Will's once open, eager expression was closed and wary even as he smiled. Richard gave her the grin she remembered so well, but even his eyes held shadows that had not been there before. Dear Jesu, what had been done to them? Knowing that John was watching and absorbing, she managed to hold herself together as she stooped to kiss both sons in the formal manner and raise them up. Richard, perceptive of her need, released the tension by going to embrace his brothers and sisters, including the two infants born while he and Will had been hostages. 'Hair to match her face,' he said, looking at his bawling tiny sister and running his hand through his own ruddy mop.

Isabelle laughed tremulously. 'It's your grandsire's de Clare blood.'

'All the more reason to be proud. He never gave up, no matter the odds. With the same from our father, we're doubly blessed.'

Isabelle blinked hard. 'Oh, my sons,' she whispered. It was one of the hardest things she had ever had to do, but she straightened her spine, raised her chin, and set about being a good hostess to a man she hated.

'So, what do you truly think of life at court?' Isabelle asked Will that evening in the private chamber. John had retired to his apartments with his retinue. The feast in the hall had ended, apart from the presence of a few desultory gluttons still picking at the subtleties and candied fruits. William was deep in conversation with Jean D'Earley and the other men who had offered to be hostages for his loyalty. Richard was playing chess with Gilbert and being soundly beaten and Isabelle was measuring Will for

354

new garments. They were to be two days at Kilkenny and if she and her women were quick, the young men could have new shirts and hose to take with them.

Will glanced around to make sure that no one was within hearing, and the way he did it made Isabelle wince. Such suspicion, such carefulness had not been a part of his boyhood nature but was a learned response. 'I've taught myself to live with it,' he said with a shrug.

'And the King? What is he like from day to day?'

Will hesitated. Measuring him from neck to waist Isabelle felt the tension stiffen his body. 'He can be kind and generous,' he said carefully, 'and he has a sense of humour that makes you laugh even when you know you shouldn't. He loves his children . . .'

Isabelle rolled her eyes.

'Truly, Mother, he does, both those born to the Queen and his bastards. He loves his brother the Earl of Salisbury too. But his moods are fickle and he trusts no one. He wants others to love him and he tries to make them do it, but he's watching them all the time.'

She moved round to face him and caught the bleak misery in his expression that he hadn't been swift enough to conceal.

'He surrounds himself with mercenaries and paid men who will do what he commands and agree with him whatever he says or does,' Will said, dropping his gaze.

Anxiety entered her voice. 'He has not harmed you or Richard?'

Will shook his head. 'He would not dare. Our father's name and reputation protects us and the Earls of Salisbury and Norfolk have their eye on our welfare.' Will extended his arm at her gesture so that she could measure him from armpit to wrist. 'He's testing my father. He tries people until they break, and when they do, he says that he was right from the beginning – that people are false and untrustworthy.'

Isabelle wondered pensively what would happen if she put to the test the loyalty that William owed to her and that which he reserved for the King, then pushed the thought away as she would a trencher of unpalatable food.

'John will not stop until he has Maude de Braose at his mercy,' Will said as if he had caught a trace of her thoughts. 'I've served on night duty sometimes, so has Richard, and you see and hear things you'd rather not.' Grimacing, he glanced across the room to the quietly conversing men. 'I hope my father lives for a long time yet. God help me, Mother, I could not give my oath to such a man.'

His words filled Isabelle's marrow with ice. The notion of a world without William . . . the notion of a twenty-year-old carrying the responsibility of this earldom on his shoulders terrified her. Will might be on the cusp of knighthood, might almost be a grown man, but he had no real experience as an adult save along the slime trail of the court and from what she had seen, it had already warped him out of true. He didn't have William's grasp and vision . . . not yet.

'God help us all,' she snapped, then folded her lips together as, having lost his game of chess against Gilbert, a disgruntled but amused Richard sauntered over to be measured for his own new clothes.

30

Carrickfergus Castle, Antrim, July 1210

The great de Lacy stronghold of Carrickfergus, fierce symbol of Norman authority, stood on a promontory thrusting out into the Irish Sea, three of its sides protected by the deep waters of Belfast Lough.

The sunset was staining the sky in hues of blood and fire as John's vast army drew up on its landward side and began pitching camp. William dismounted from his palfrey and handed the reins to his groom. It had been a hot day and both he and the horse were perspiring heavily. William wiped his brow on his cuff and gratefully took the cup that his squire knelt to offer him. Nearby the carts bearing the siege machines were rumbling into camp, supervised by their crews. Tents were sprouting in all shapes and sizes like autumn fungi. William's lips twitched as he saw a Welsh archer plant his banner outside his own modest canvas cover in the form of a pair of braies on a broom pole. Pedants such as the Earl of Winchester would have blustered with fury at the sight of a common oaf mocking nobility, but William was highly amused. Or perhaps he was taking refuge in crude humour because it was a comfort. He didn't want to be here, but to keep his own family and lands intact, he had at least to go through the motions. At dawn those siege machines would be assembled. At dawn the heralds would ride to the keep and demand the surrender of all within, including Hugh de Lacy and his brother's de Braose in-laws. He didn't want to think about it.

The royal tent was going up in a flurry of crimson and gold. William hoped he wouldn't be summoned to dine there tonight but knew it was more than likely. He was a senior commander and John would require his insights into how they were going to set about taking Carrickfergus in the shortest possible time. Crack the nut; extract the meat. William swallowed the wine and turned abruptly to where the green and yellow canvas of his own tent was being thrown over its frame. He wasn't sure what banner he should fly outside the pavilion. Perhaps the Marshal lion facing the other way in blindness.

As he expected, John sent a lad through the red-streaked dusk to summon him to the royal table. William considered sending the lad back with the message that he was sick, but knew John would see straight through such an excuse. William would have to be on his deathbed not to answer a summons. Morosely, he donned a clean shirt and tunic, fastened the gilded belt of the Earl of Pembroke at his hips, and went to do his duty.

John was in belligerent high spirits, William noted. Thus far the Irish Norman lords had scattered before him or hastened to bow at his feet and as always, when given the upper hand, John liked to hold a whip in it. 'They'll be quaking in their boots tonight,' he said with pleasure in his eyes. 'But by the time I have finished with them, they will have no boots to call their own. I want the trebuchets in place before first light and the archers ready.'

'Sire, perhaps they will be willing to talk terms,' said Baldwin de Béthune, who was present at the head of a Flemish contingent and the knights of Aumale. 'De Lacy's brother surrendered to you after all.'

John shrugged. 'It's a possibility, but Hugh de Lacy is more stiff-necked than his brother and he is the one succouring that viper and her get.' He flicked a jaundiced glance towards William to show that he hadn't forgotten how William too had given his aid to the de Braoses. *There but for the grace of God go you!* his expression said. 'He won't crack that easily, but breaking him will be the sweeter for it.'

'Still,' William said, 'it will be a good thing if you can take the keep without inflicting too much damage on its fabric. If you and de Lacy can come to terms—'

'Do not tell me how to manage my affairs, Marshal,' John snapped, his eyes narrowing dangerously. 'Yes, you are here to advise me, but when I want your words of wisdom, I will ask for them. I have seen the way you "come to terms" with people, including Philip of France. Even if I have to take that keep apart stone by stone, I will have Hugh de Lacy and the de Braoses on their knees at my feet. You succoured them, Marshal. I could have had you on your knees too. Think on that.'

William took the words although they were like a blow to the face. He had received similar treatment on several occasions now and he was becoming inured. Even Will, who was serving at table tonight, had managed to fix a blank expression on his features.

'Ah, leave me,' John said with a wave of his hand in impatient dismissal. 'You've nothing to say that I want to hear and your presence raises my hackles. I will see you under the walls at first light.'

William rose and bowed and left, each part of his leave-taking imbued with deliberation and power, rather than retreat at having been dismissed. Once outside, William breathed out hard then drew a deep breath of clean, grass-scented air. It would pass, he told himself. All he had to do was live through it and continue to steer his ship through the ever-narrowing channel between the rocks. There was light on the other side; he had to believe there was.

In the morning there was no reply from the walls of Carrickfergus. No heralds emerged to treat or negotiate. The walls held their secrets and remained tight-closed and barren. John ordered up the trebuchet teams to begin their assault while other crews assembled the siege ladders and brought forward the wicker shield protection for the archers. William eyed the ladders and shifted his shoulders to ease the weight of his mail shirt.

'I won't be taking my chance on one of those again,' he said to Jean D'Earley, who was standing at his side. 'Those days are gone.'

Jean curved a dry smile. 'Far be it from me to call you a liar, my lord, but I do not believe you.'

William laughed and pressed his knight on the shoulder. 'A little flattery never goes amiss,' he said, 'but I spoke the truth.' He sobered and stared towards the walls of the castle. 'He means to have them, Jean, and my heart is heavy at what the outcome might be.'

'Mine too, my lord, but we have done what we can.'

'Have we?'

Jean nodded. 'And what we must.'

William's eyelids tightened. 'What we must.' His voice was bleak. 'Those are barren words these days, Jean.'

The sound of shouting and the drum of hooves caused him to turn and watch a band of native Irish warriors riding into the camp, bareback as was their wont, guiding their mounts with rope bridles.

A slender, innocuous-looking man joined William and Jean. His garments were serviceable but drab and his leather satchel was scuffed and had seen better days. Men would look at him and then through him. 'You should be bending the knee, my lord,' he said.

'And why should we be doing that, Feargal?' William asked with a glance at his most accomplished spy. The man cost a fortune to employ, but the information he provided was usually of more value than gold.

Feargal scrubbed a forefinger beneath his sharp nose. 'That's Cathal Crobderg O Conchobair, the King of Connacht, coming to pay homage and offer support.' He looked around, his face screwed up in assessment. 'A mighty gathering, for sure. Pointless though.'

William's gaze sharpened. 'What do you mean?'

Feargal hitched his belt. 'You're laying siege to a husk, my lord. Hugh de Lacy and his de Braose kin are gone. Three days now and across the sea to Man or Scotland.' He eyed up the siege weapons. 'You won't be needing those, or only for show. The garrison won't hold out beyond the first strike from a trebuchet. Their treasure's gone.'

William stared at the walls of the keep. John was going to foam at the mouth with rage at being thwarted yet again of his prey. Cracking a nut, no matter how easily, was pointless if there was no kernel. The next few hours were not going to be pleasant, but for himself he could only feel relief that the de Braoses had fled ahead of John's army. Whatever happened now, it wouldn't happen in Ireland on his doorstep and while his conscience wasn't entirely clear, he could at least hold his head above the mire.

Slumping on the window-seat in a turret chamber of Dublin Castle, William took the cup of wine from his squire and, with a hint of irony, toasted Baldwin de Béthune. 'To peace,' he said. 'May it last longer than a day.'

Baldwin saluted a response and leaned back with a sigh. 'Amen to that.'

Around them the room was busy with servants bearing the royal furnishings down to the bailey. The King's bed had been dismantled and attendants were lumping spars of wood out of the room on their shoulders as if prac- tising for some bizarre Easter Cross-bearing ritual. Florence, the royal laundry maid, puffed past with a basket full of linen, her cheeks shining like polished red apples, her haunches jouncing. John was preparing to return to England and the court was on tenterhooks. John himself had retired to another chamber to wait out the moment for embarkation with a firkin of wine and a selection of books.

'Been successful for him.' Baldwin eyed William thoughtfully. 'The de Lacys brought to heel, new char- ters for Ireland with better advantages for him. Maude de Braose and her son his prisoners . . .' He broke off to contemplate his wine.

William plucked at a loose thread on the window-seat cushion and gazed at the embroidered pattern of a snarling lion with red claws. In his mind's eye he was not seeing the beast, but John's face when his messenger brought the news that Maude de Braose and her son had been captured in Scotland and handed over to his deputies. Even now they were on their way south to Windsor. There had been gloating triumph in the tawny gaze. The fingers had curled in pleasure on the finials of his great chair the way that a cat might curl its claws in its prey.

'The only fly in his ointment is that he didn't capture William de Braose with them,' Baldwin added thoughtfully, 'but he can live in hope – which is more than can be said for de Braose.'

An attendant came to take the cushion and gave William a sidelong look of suspicion as if blaming him for the loose thread on the exquisitely worked embroidery. 'He won't give himself up to the King, I know that much.' William rose to his feet. Still at large, de Braose had pledged in messages to the King to find the money he owed, but everyone knew he wouldn't. His debts at the exchequer amounted to more than the entire annual revenues of England.

'Then what's he going to do?'

William shrugged. 'What would you do if you were de Braose?'

Baldwin turned his mouth down at the corners. 'Head for France, sell my sword, tell everything I know.'

'Precisely, and then we'll have the French down on us like the hammer of God, not to mention the Pope champing at the bit.'

Baldwin looked bleak. 'Small wonder you choose to stay in Ireland with your lady and raise your children. No interdict here, and the King's business finished so he won't be returning soon.'

William acknowledged Baldwin's comment with a sceptical grimace. 'I'll enjoy what peace I can and pray that it lasts. My chaplain tells me that miracles still happen.'

A corner of Marlborough's stable yard had been the arena for a cockfight between a serjeant's rust and iridescent rooster and the cook's scarred but undefeated black who was named Rollo after the first Duke of Normandy. Will, having a penny to spare, had wagered on the mangy Rollo, reasoning that cunning and the will to live were worth as much as the strutting, glossy arrogance of the challenger.

It had been a fierce battle, as witnessed by the clotted feathers blowing around the yard and the dirty jewels of blood spattering the dust. The cook had taken away the rust and iridescent rooster, plucked him, drawn him and dropped him in a stew pot to simmer. The black cockerel, torn, bloody but triumphant, was resting in a corner of the kitchen on a cushion made from the down of former victims, one cocked eye as bright as a jet droplet, the other a sightless milky opal.

Jingling his winnings, Will sought Richard and found him lying on his pallet in the chamber shared by the squires, his hands clasped behind his head and his gaze on the rafters. It was rare to see his cheerful, energetic brother so contemplative, although Will assumed he was just taking a brief rest from throwing himself at life.

'Here.' He tossed the pouch of money on to Richard's broad chest. 'Old Rollo won again; Chanticleer's for dinner. Take half for yourself.'

Richard hefted the pouch indifferently and made no attempt to investigate the contents.

'What's wrong?'

Richard rolled on to his stomach and put the money on the pillow. 'Maude de Braose and her son are dead,' he said.

Will stared at him. 'What? How do you know?'

'I heard the King talking to a messenger from Windsor . . . You know John threw them in the dungeons there . . .'

Will swallowed. 'Yes, I knew,' he said.

'Well, he left them to starve to death. The ... the messenger told the King that the son had died first and that ... that there were bite marks on his arm where she'd ... where she'd ...' Richard fought his gorge. 'I moved away from the curtain then. Even if I was on duty I didn't want to be caught listening to that for my own hide's sake.'

'Filth,' Will muttered, filled with sick disgust. 'John is filth. I hope the barons rise against him for this.'

'There's more. I haven't told you everything yet.'

'I thought you'd moved away from the door?' Fear widened Will's gaze. 'It's not about Jean or Jordan, is it? He hasn't starved them to death too? Holy Christ!'

Richard shook his head. 'No,' he said quickly. 'Not that. It's nothing to do with our men. I heard this from a laundry maid and she heard it when she was gathering up the King's soiled linens. William de Braose has taken refuge with the French and told them everything he knows about what happened to Prince Arthur. He said that John murdered Arthur while in a drunken rage.'

Will's taut expression relaxed. 'That's old gossip,' he said, scoffing because he was pretending he was manly and unafraid. 'It's been going round since before we were made hostages.' Taking the pouch from his brother's pillow, he poured out the money and set about dividing it up.

'Yes, but de Braose has never spoken openly before. If he's told Philip the full details as an eye witness, it gives Philip the excuse he needs to come and take England from John.'

Will raised his head from his counting, a spark of interest lighting in his eyes. 'You think that'll happen?'

'I don't know; it might.' Richard shrugged. 'Our father will be honour-bound to answer the King's summons if he does come. You know him; he'll hold to his oath of fealty whatever happens.'

Will made a face. 'Let's hope he has the good sense to hold to it by staying in Ireland.'

'More chance of cooking one of Saint Colman's teal,' Richard said, referring to the Irish legend about certain sacred birds that if killed and put in the pot would remain raw no matter how long they were boiled. He scooped up his share of the coins and, clenching his fist around them, left his bed and went to the door.

'Where are you going?' Will asked.

'To give this in alms for the soul of Maude and her son,' Richard said, his expression filled with pity and distaste. 'At least some beggar can have the food she was denied.'

31

Pembroke, South Wales, Spring 1213

William was preparing to exercise his new warhorse, a handsome four-year-old with a liver chestnut hide so dark that it shone like polished jet.

Isabelle watched him feed the stallion a crust of bread on the palm of his hand, then grasp the reins, set his foot to the stirrup and swing astride. The weather was fine and dry and he showed no sign of the limp from an old injury that had plagued him in the winter cold. As always, he looked as if he was part of the horse. She tried not to worry, or at least not to show it. He would not thank her for coddling him when he was hard and fit enough to control a mettlesome young stallion. Gilbert and Walter were playing squire to their father, Gilbert holding William's lance and Walter his helm and new shield, the paint pristine and gleaming without a scratch or dent.

It was Isabelle's first return to England in six years, although William had been back on sundry occasions without her to deal with matters pertaining to the earldom and the King. For herself, Isabelle would have been content to remain at Kilkenny, tending Leinster and her household. She thought William had seemed satisfied too. For the first time in his life, he had been able to stay at home and not miss the growth of his offspring from babies, to toddlers, to swift, sturdy children. But even in the midst of the idyll, even while building a prosperity of towns and commerce for Leinster, she had sensed a vestige of restlessness within him. The warrior was quiescent, but waiting.

A return to England meant though that she would be able to see Mahelt and her grandchildren, the latter for the first time. Mahelt and Hugh had a son Roger, three years old at the feast of the Nativity, and Mahelt had borne another son, named for his father, at Michaelmas. Isabelle was keen to see them both, and her daughter. It had been far too long a parting.

Currently the feudal host of Ireland was camped in Pembroke Castle's outer bailey and the surrounding fields, including five hundred knights and additional serjeants and foot under the command of John de Grey, Bishop of Norwich and Ireland's justiciar, all assembled in answer to the King's summons for aid.

William took the lance from Gilbert and, giving the horse the lightest nudge of spur, rode down the tilt towards the shield on the end of the quintain post. He struck the shield dead centre and the post whipped round at speed, the sack of sand on the other end wobbling heavily up and down, but William was gone and already turning to approach from the other side.

De Grey joined Isabelle to watch the display. 'Your husband, they say, was something to see in his tourney days, and I can well believe it, my lady.'

Isabelle's lips curved. 'He still is,' she said proudly. Despite occasional differences of interest and opinion, she liked de Grey. In contrast to many churchmen, he was at home in the company of women; indeed appeared to take pleasure in it. He was direct, urbane and intelligent – a man with whom she and William could work. Her smile faded. 'He will need all of his prowess and luck unless I have misunderstood the situation in England and Wales.' William was leaving Pembroke for Dover on the morrow and Isabelle did not know if or when she would see him again. The French had declared war on an excommunicate king, and their army was massed on the Normandy coast, only waiting the moment to strike.

De Grey clasped his hands behind his back. 'I hope we will need these troops only to provide a show of strength, Countess. If the King makes peace with the Pope, then the French will incur the wrath of Rome, not its support, if they do invade.'

'I pray you are right,' Isabelle said in a heartfelt voice. The dispute with Rome had been rumbling for as long as she and William had been in Ireland and like an approaching storm had continued to escalate until it seemed that deluge and destruction were inevitable.

William trotted the new stallion over to her, leaned down from the saddle and swept five-year-old Ancel on to the destrier's back. The child was fearless around horses and already an accomplished rider of his own piebald pony. As the fifth son he was going to inherit little if anything in terms of land, and it was already accepted within the family that he would follow in William's footsteps and carve his own career with horse and lance.

Isabelle watched father and son trot around the bailey and tried to set aside her misgivings. So much for a life of peace and quiet to enjoy the setting of the sun, she thought, and not for the first time silently damned John for what he was. Perhaps the only good thing to come out of this was that the hostages he held might finally be released.

* * *

'He's going to be one of the best destriers I've ever ridden,' William enthused later in their chamber. 'Turns on a penny and I hardly need to touch the reins or use the spur.' He latched his belt and settled it comfortably at his hips.

Isabelle laughed poignantly. 'You are like a young knight with his first warhorse,' she said.

He chuckled. 'There's nothing like a fresh stallion under a man to make him feel green and limber again . . . Well, not quite. I can think of one other thing . . .' He gave her a teasing look, to which she responded with a slanting glance through her lashes.

'Well then, my lord, you are fortunate to have both before you leave.' She set her arms around his neck and kissed him. The gesture was affectionate and only mildly lustful, although it held potential. Their physical relationship no longer burned with the avid heat of the early days but there were still moments of fire and the intimacy continued to warm and illuminate their marriage. As in all things, William was still eminently capable.

Sighing softly, she drew away. 'So, is this dispute with the Pope going to be resolved or will the French invade?'

He gave a cynical snort. 'Even if it is resolved, we may still face an invasion. Philip has had his eyes on England for a long time and he won't let a small thing like papal disapproval prevent him. I doubt that anything short of a pitched battle will stop him in the end.'

Isabelle shivered as he said 'pitched battle'. 'But if John submits to the Pope . . .'

'Which he will.' William cut across her musing. 'He cannot fight the Church, the French and his barons all at the same time. If he yields to Rome, he snatches the papal bludgeon out of Philip's hand and gains it for himself.'

'So one moment he's an excommunicate, the next he's

numbered amongst the righteous,' Isabelle said with a disparaging twist to her mouth.

'Precisely.' William went to the window and looked out. Gilbert and Walter were practising their swordplay on the sward with the sons of some of his knights. He was amused to see Ancel dancing around them with his toy wooden sword, shouting insults and being a nuisance.

Isabelle joined him, slipping one hand around his waist and hooking her fingers in his gilded belt. Watching the children at their play, she tried not to think of the Welsh hostages whom John had hanged in Nottingham last year, including one little boy almost as young as Ancel. The news had chilled her blood. Jean had been a hostage in Nottingham at the time and she wondered if he had been an appalled witness to the deed. It was true the Welsh had risen against John after peace had been sworn, and that he was within his rights to deal harshly with the hostages, but even so, to hang little children went against all decency. Small wonder that mothers were reluctant to hand over their sons to him. If he demanded Ancel from her and William, she would refuse. Enough was enough. Troubled by her thoughts, she rubbed her cheek against William's wool-clad shoulder. 'Since you have come at his summons and raised troops for him, perhaps he will let us have our hostages back,' she said.

'I hope so, although . . .' He broke off to laugh as Ancel whacked Walter's haunch with his toy sword. Walter justifiably knocked him over. Ancel got up, thought about crying, but changed his mind and charged in with renewed determination, only to be sent flying again.

'Although what?' Her tone sharpened.

He sobered. 'Although Richard is one and twenty now and old enough to take on the Normandy lands.'

'Old enough, yes,' she said. 'But is he ready?'

371

'For his own wellbeing he has to be. If he's in France and serving the King of France for Longueville then John cannot touch him. We haven't had a family presence there since we left Normandy.'

Isabelle could see the sense in his thinking, but it hurt. She wanted her son back, not pushed further from reach. 'Yes,' she said bravely, 'it is the best thing for him. I just wish . . .' She shook her head.

Ancel's nurse arrived and pulled the child out of the fray, scolding the older boys, whose faces wore expressions of long-suffering and indignation.

'It's not that far from Caversham and Hamstead,' William said quietly. 'It's not farewell for ever.'

'No,' Isabelle replied, her voice a little too flat as she recognised she had bidden farewell to her two eldest boys years ago when they went to court.

'When Will is free, there'll be a wedding to arrange too.' His expression became introspective. 'It'll be a great pity that Baldwin won't be here to celebrate it.'

Isabelle squeezed his arm and kissed him. The sudden death from a seizure of the friend of his young manhood and tourney days had affected William deeply. He had said little enough when the news came, but his long silences and the amount of time he spent alone schooling his horse were evidence of his grief. Isabelle had never been particularly fond of Baldwin, but she had understood the depth of his relationship with William and the camaraderie they had shared. They had been friends on the battlefield, in the camp and at court, each knowing that he could trust the other with his life . . . and now one of those lives was in the grave, survived in the flesh by a single daughter, sixteen years old and betrothed to their heir.

* * *

Standing on the palisade rampart at Dover, William inhaled the fresh morning breeze, glad to fill his lungs with clean air after the stuffiness of the council chamber from which he had emerged a short while ago, blinking like a day-dazzled owl.

He gazed at the blue glitter of the Narrow Sea and imagined it teeming with a host of French warships. The English levies were camped around the castle and billeted in the town, tents of every hue, shape and size pitched wherever there was room. Beacon pyres stacked the clifftops ready to warn of imminent invasion and the local populace had made preparations to flee should the French take the victory, unhooking hams from chimneys and sending their cattle and pigs into the weald.

Pandulf, the Papal Legate, had arrived late yesterday evening, having come straight across the sea from the French camp and talks with King Philip. Last night at the council table he had emphasised to John how close the French army was to embarking. The wind was right and the men were ready. John had one last chance to come to terms with the Pope over the matter of the Archbishop of Canterbury. Either he capitulated and accepted the papal choice, Stephen Langton, or the French army would unleash itself upon England with full papal support. The discussion had strung out late into the night, candles burning down to their stubs, men growing red-eyed and bleary. Then again this morning, but at last and at the final hour, agreement had been reached.

William glanced at the tents belonging to his Irish and Welsh levies: the axe-wielding common soldiers from Leinster; the longbowmen of South Wales; the serjeants; the tough garrison soldiers of the Marches; the knights who owed him military service. They were hard men who would have stood their ground, and he would have stood with them should it have come to battle. He felt a tinge of regret and gave a self-mocking smile. He was like an old stallion, fed a ration of oats and champing at the stable door because he heard the distant clash of arms.

'Well, are the French coming?' Will asked, joining him. John had released him from custody and he had been waiting with William's men. Richard remained for the moment in royal service, although not officially a hostage.

William shook his head. 'I hope not. John's agreed to welcome Stephen Langton as Archbishop of Canterbury, to pay the Pope a thousand marks a year, and to make reparations to the Church. England's about to become a papal state under Rome's protection. If the French invade, then the tables turn and they become the excommunicated ones, not us.'

Will gazed at his father. 'You mean he's managed to wriggle off the hook?'

'With the help of his counsellors, yes,' William answered, giving Will a stare that warned him to be careful where he trod. 'We all had a say in advising him: Warwick, Derby, Surrey . . . myself. We told him he could not fight the barons, the French *and* the Pope – that he had to remove one of them from the chessboard if he wanted to survive and that Rome was to the best advantage.'

Will looked discontented. 'It is a good thing that we won't have to fight the French but . . . but who is going to stop John now?' he asked. 'If he's got the Pope's support, he'll ride roughshod all over us. He's not fit to be King. He sells off widows to the highest bidder; he disparages heiresses; he forces people to pay for his goodwill . . . throws the wives and sons of his vassals into prison and starves them to death, he—'

'Lower your voice,' William snapped. 'Have you learned nothing at court?'

'Hah! More than enough!'

'We make him fit to be King. Deposing him would be against God's law and against our honour. He has to accept Langton into the archbishopric and that will put a curb on him for a start.'

Will set his jaw. 'The French might still come,' he said obstinately. 'Philip's not brought his army all the way to Normandy to disperse it now.'

William shrugged. 'If they do, they'll be damned men. As soon as the Legate has taken the King's oath, he will go and warn Philip of the peril in which he stands.' He glanced round as John emerged from the papal tent where he had been conversing with the Legate. Pandulf's smooth, rounded features wore a smug expression. His lips were slightly pursed as if his mouth were a pouch full of delightful secrets. John was wearing one of his crowns, a beautiful thing of pearls, rubies and trefoiled gold. His expression was feline and satisfied; the way he looked when he'd been bedding a favourite whore. He was all smiling deference towards the Legate, and the Legate, in his turn, was being gracious towards John, as well he might.

John turned and knelt at Pandulf's feet and put his hands between those of the Legate. Pandulf leaned down to John and gave him the kiss of peace in the manner of one vassal acknowledging another. A ripple went through the crowd of witnessing barons, almost like the relief of discomfort when an overtight belt was slackened. Yet there were looks of anger and restlessness too. Not everyone had sought this outcome.

Will shook his head, watched until he could watch no longer and, thrusting past his father, walked away.

A short while later, Will stood on the clifftops beyond the castle, gazing at the sea hissing to shore on the beach far below and brooding on what had happened. He knew he should be glad that the French were not going to invade, but the emotions dwelling in his heart were savage.

The wind buffeted him, making it difficult to keep his balance. He contemplated stepping closer to the edge. A figure was toiling along the path towards him from the direction of the castle and he grimaced to himself when he realised it was Jean D'Earley.

Panting hard, Jean joined him and stood for a moment to regain his breath, one hand pressed to his side.

'Did he send you?' Will demanded.

Jean shook his head. 'If he knew I was here, he'd be vexed with me. Perhaps he'd be right, but I want to say something to you and it won't take long.'

Will prodded a head of pink downland clover with the toe of his boot. 'Say it then and have done. It won't change my mind about anything.'

Jean looked out to sea. 'I have known your father since he took me into his service as a stripling and raised me to knighthood. He became my father too. I love him dearly, and because of that love, I accept that his oath is to John. While there is breath in his body, he will do all in his power to keep him on the throne. Nothing will stop him – and that includes his sons.'

'Do not be so certain of that,' Will said mutinously.

'I hope you love him too,' Jean replied with quiet severity.

A lump constricted Will's throat. 'Do you always hit below the belt?' he asked tightly.

'Never.' Jean shook his head. 'I always aim for the heart.'

32

Caversham, Berkshire, Spring 1214

'What do you think of her, Mama?' asked Mahelt in a low voice that did not carry beyond the embrasure where she and her mother were sitting, stitching an altar cloth for Caversham's chapel.

Isabelle placed two neat stitches and then looked out of the window to her future daughter-in-law who was feeding Will's palfrey small pieces of bread on the outstretched palm of her hand. Alais de Béthune had arrived two days ago at dusk in the midst of a thunderstorm. The girl had been jittery with fear and worn out from the long journey. Isabelle had offered comfort, sympathy and a warm bed. Alais had brushed off the former, accepted the latter, and slept for the best part of a day.

'It is too early to tell. You have travelled with her. You must have more notion than I.' She looked at her daughter. Mahelt and Hugh had undertaken the responsibility of bringing Alais from the eastern wilds of Holderness to her new home. Chaperone duty was a good excuse for Mahelt to visit her parents while they were closer than the dangers of the South Welsh Marches to which they would soon be returning.

'She gives very little away,' Mahelt said, also glancing out of the window and resting her eyes on Alais de Béthune.

'Shy perhaps?'

'I would have said guarded . . . and with a lot of growing up to do.'

Isabelle's lips twitched with humour. Mahelt was twenty years old, the mother of Roger, aged four, and Hugh, who would be two at Michaelmas. Mahelt had done a great deal of growing up herself – no longer the newly-wed child-woman they had left standing at the gates of Framlingham as they rode away to Ireland, but a competent chatelaine, wife and mother in her own right.

Mahelt looked thoughtful. 'She didn't say much on the journey, but probably because she didn't know us, and with her mother so recently dead . . .'

'And her father last year. She has had a difficult time of late.'

Mahelt rested her sewing in her lap. 'Alais told me she was glad her father was dead.'

'Well, that doesn't seem very guarded, and why would she say such a thing about her father?'

'I don't know. She mentioned it when I told her how sorry I was that she had lost both parents so soon after one another, but I couldn't wrest any more out of her than that.'

'There must be a reason.'

'You won't find it easy to wring from her. She didn't say anything about her mother. I don't think they were very close.'

In pensive silence, Isabelle continued to watch her future daughter-in-law. Will joined the girl, a goshawk gripping his gauntleted wrist. As Alais turned from the horse and towards him, it was like watching the sun come out over both of them.

Mahelt giggled. 'Perhaps you should bring the wedding forward, Mama. You don't want the next heir to Pembroke born out of wedlock.'

Isabelle gave her daughter a reprimanding tap on the knee. 'Shame on you for such thoughts. I am sure Alais will be a virgin at her wedding.'

'But probably not as innocent as she is now . . .'

'Which is all to the good. Do not tell me that you and Hugh came to your own marriage bed without a certain amount of dalliance.'

Mahelt flushed. 'We heeded your wishes to wait until my ripening,' she said, 'but it didn't stop Hugh from handling the fruit to find out if it was ready to be plucked.' She gave her mother a meaningful look from wide, dark eyes. 'In the end, I think the fruit plucked him.'

Isabelle had to laugh; Mahelt was incorrigible. 'I fear you overheard too much bawdy talk from Elizabeth Avenel when you were a child,' she said.

Mahelt vigorously shook her head. 'Not at all. I learned from watching you and my father. I remember how often the bed curtains were closed when he was home . . .' The twinkle in her eyes grew serious. 'It was a good thing to see, because I knew that given the right man, I could have that too.'

'And Hugh is the right man?'

Mahelt glanced at her youngest son, asleep on a quilt, his face flushed and his arms surrendered either side of his head. 'Yes,' she said with an intimate smile. 'My father could not have done better.' Her gaze warmed with amusement. 'Not long after we were wed, Tripes chewed Hugh's new court shoes to shreds.'

'Oh dear,' Isabelle smiled. Her son-in-law was a handsome man who liked to dress well. He wasn't preposterously vain, but he knew the value of show and enjoyed playing the peacock if the occasion demanded.

'I think it was then I truly fell in love with him,' Mahelt said. 'I realised what I had been given.' She began to giggle again. 'Oh, he cursed. I have never heard such words – even from Will and Richard when they were holding a swearing contest behind the Bishop of Ossory's back, but when he'd done, he found the grace to laugh about it, and he didn't whip Tripes or banish him from the solar . . . he knew how much he meant to me with all my family gone and everything being unfamiliar. He said it didn't matter and he put his second-best pair on a shelf out of reach.' She looked at the infant again. 'How many men would do that for a wife, Mama?'

'You are right,' Isabelle murmured, feeling a warm glow that her daughter was so pleased with her match. There was never any guarantee of lasting compatibility even when all the signs were auspicious.

Outside, the young couple were mounting up. Will had given his hawk to an attendant and was boosting Alais into the saddle of a dainty bay palfrey. She was flirting down at him as she took up the reins.

'She sits a horse well,' Isabelle said judiciously.

'She's very pretty too.'

'That must come from her mother. Baldwin didn't have the looks to accompany his prowess, God rest his soul.' Isabelle picked up her sewing again, feeling a moment of sadness. 'We cannot bring the marriage forward,' she said to Mahelt, her thoughts running on with her stitches. 'Not until the matter of her inheritance has been settled.'

Mahelt looked startled. 'I thought the contract was agreed years ago at the betrothal?'

'It was, and the King approved, but her dowry is being disputed by her half-brother. As his mother's heir, he's claiming some of the lands the contract vouchsafed to Alais.'

Mahelt looked disbelieving. 'But if the King approved it at the time, he has no grounds. It's William de Forz, isn't it?' She cudgelled her memory. 'I was only small at the time, but I remember him in London. He kicked me, so Richard kicked him back.'

'It doesn't matter whether or not he has grounds,' Isabelle replied. 'What does matter is how far the King allows him to take such a claim.'

'You mean overturn the contract . . . he wouldn't do that.' She eyed her mother askance. 'He needs my father more than he needs William de Forz.'

'Mayhap,' Isabelle said, 'but it's not that simple. He calls himself de Forz, but his real name should be FitzRoy . . .'

Mahelt's lips moved, silently repeating the last word, then she gasped and put her hand to her mouth. 'He's John's bastard. Holy God, Mama!'

'He's never been officially acknowledged, but then his mother was an heiress in her own right and able to provide for him and de Forz made a convenient "father" for the cuckoo.'

Mahelt's eyes were as huge as platters. 'Did Baldwin know when he married her?'

'Of course he did. You couldn't dwell at court and not be aware of the scandal and it was never a well-kept secret. You wouldn't have heard because you were too young and it was not the sort of matter your father and I would have discussed in front of you . . . but we knew. That was why your father and Baldwin set out to put such a seal on the contract between your brother and Alais that nothing could break it . . . but it won't stop de Forz from trying or John from lending a sympathetic ear.'

Mahelt leaned back on the seat, still winded with surprise. 'Baldwin's wife never struck me as being the kind that John would want to bed – from what I've heard of his preferences.'

Isabelle gave her an amused look. 'And what would they be?' She thought of her own narrow escapes where John's lust was concerned.

Mahelt shrugged. 'Golden hair, breasts like cushions and brains to match.'

Isabelle compressed her lips and took several stitches, although it was hard to prevent her shoulders from shaking. She had the hair, although time had somewhat faded its glory; she had the breasts . . . and perhaps John also thought she had feather for brains. 'Like a hen then,' she said without inflection.

'The King takes pleasure in bedding the wives and daughters of his lords,' Mahelt said, 'and then it doesn't matter what they look like . . . Yes, and that's like a dunghill cockerel treading a hen.'

'I think that is what John did with Hawise of Aumale. He got her with child then pushed the bastard on to de Forz for a consideration.'

Mahelt pursed her lips. 'He can't do anything to prevent Will and Alais from marrying though, can he?'

'I would not put anything past John,' Isabelle said ominously.

Will rode through sunlit glades with Alais; the green of spring was in full bud and leaf. The sap in the trees seemed as if it was running through his veins too, like heavy honey, languorous and sweet. He could not believe that the young woman riding at his side and smiling at him through her lashes was the same scrawny little thing on whose finger he had set an overlarge betrothal ring ten years ago. She

wore the ring now upon her heart finger, a sapphire
gimmel shanked in gold. Her skin was as pale as ivory,
almost translucent, her braids a shimmering golden-
brown, and her eyes undid him. Like agates, they changed
in the light, now green, now amber, now tawny-brown,
but while their hue fascinated him, it was the shy flirta-
tion and worship in them that unravelled his being. He
was not used to having someone hang on his every word
and it was a heady sensation. She was a good horsewoman
too, handling her mount competently without having to
think about it. Some of the ladies of the court looked
like millers' flour sacks in the saddle, but not Alais.

'You ride like a queen,' he told her.

Pink colour stained her cheeks and, slanting him a swift
glance, she thanked him for the compliment.

'Who taught you, your father?'

'Yes,' she said and looked down. He saw her lips
compress and wondered if he had trodden on tender
ground. He didn't want to upset her.

'You must mourn him deeply. I know my own father
does.'

She said nothing for a moment, but moved in tune with
her horse. Her braids were as lustrous as the finest silk.
'I hated him,' she said passionately.

Her words were so different from those he had expected
to hear that Will could only stare at her in shock. Baldwin
de Béthune had been his father's bosom companion, the
bon ami of tournament and battlefield. He could remember
Baldwin tousling his hair, teasing him, play-wrestling with
him and Richard, poring over a game of chess. 'Why?'
he asked.

Alais thrust out her lower lip in a pout and the moist-
ness of it provoked a lust that shocked him. 'Because he
used to thrash me and lock me in an empty store room

383

with naught but bread and water . . . He used to hit my mother too.'

Will's jaw dropped and his stare widened until his eyes were at full stretch. 'Baldwin did that?' He could not have been more astonished had she told him that Baldwin had two heads and a tail.

'You don't believe me?' Now there was hostility in her voice, sharpening the sweetness with an almost shrill edge.

Will tightened his hands on the reins and closed his mouth. 'Yes . . . yes, I do, if only because people are never what they seem . . . but I . . .' He shook his head, nonplussed.

'He said I was insolent when I stood up for myself. He said he would not have a daughter of his humiliating him or shaming her upbringing by speaking out of turn . . . and it seemed that every time I opened my mouth, I did that. My mother and I were expected to know our place and it was under his heel like . . . like well-trained dogs. If we behaved as he thought we should, he patted us. If we didn't, we were beaten.' There was a sudden liquid shimmer in her eyes and if Will had been unravelling before, now he was completely undone.

'Don't weep,' he said hoarsely. 'You will unman me.'

A smile sparkled through her tears. 'I wouldn't want to do that, my lord.'

Will flushed. Liquid fire had run through him when she called him 'my lord', a title usually reserved to his father. 'No one will ever beat or hurt you again, not while I am your husband,' he said vehemently.

The forced smile became a genuine one that dazzled Will and destroyed all chance of his reassembling his love-scattered wits, but then her expression clouded over again. 'But what if my brother succeeds in taking away part of my dowry. Will the agreement still stand?'

'Of course it will!' He was horrified to think of any other outcome. 'My father and yours were bosom friends, and for that bond alone, you would still be my wife. Your brother won't lay a finger on your lands,' he added, a steely note entering his voice. 'I promise you. No matter what he says or John does, the marriage contract is as tight as a sword in a new scabbard. You are mine and your lands will belong to our children.'

She blushed and the look she sent him made him wonder how he was going to bear the time until they were man and wife and able to share a bed.

John eyed the young man who had just risen from his knees. A handsome lad, very handsome indeed, even if not overly gifted with height. The dark hair, the narrow mouth and the shape of the beard-edged jaw found their older counterpart in John's own face. William de Forz, lord of Holderness, was at court to pay his mother's death duties to the Crown and give homage for his inheritance.

'Be welcome,' John said. 'I would have been pleased to see more of you had your mother chosen to raise you in England.'

'And I would have been pleased to attend, sire, but my stepfather had other notions.' The voice was pleasant, rich and modulated, similar to John's own. Fine gold rings adorned his fingers and his tunic was trimmed with a narrow band of silk – significantly of royal purple.

'Your stepfather perhaps had his reasons,' John said delicately, and commanded an attendant to pour wine. 'Do you read?' He gestured towards several books piled on a coffer, some of them covered in plain leather, others gilded and set with jewels.

De Forz's eyes lit up. 'Yes, sire. Like you, I collect books.'

John walked over to the pile, selected one of the plain

leather covers and handed it to his guest. 'It belonged to Hubert Walter. Matters of the exchequer. You might find it useful.'

'Thank you, sire, indeed I will, especially if I am to find the money to pay the fines and dues incurred by my mother's death and the drain on the estate caused by my sister's marriage to the Marshal heir.' He rubbed his thumb over the scuffed leather edges, and glanced covetously at the gem-encrusted books. John saw the look. The young man was going to go away disappointed if he expected to receive one of those.

John stroked his chin. 'Your half-sister's dowry hardly swallows up the lands left to you by your mother. However, in her memory and because I need good men to serve me in these times, I am willing to forgo much of that debt. If you are willing to help me, then in my turn I will help you as much as I can.'

De Forz looked down at the book in his hands. He turned the pages, read a little, looked up with eyes full of ambition. 'My half-sister's father took liberties when he agreed to her marriage portion.'

John shrugged. 'That is out of my hands. The contract was witnessed and ratified by too many people. It must stand.'

'So there is nothing you can do to prevent the marriage or the loss of the lands from my patrimony?'

John looked at his clean, trimmed fingernails. 'Short of one of them dying, no,' he replied in an offhand voice.

'Yes, that's what I thought,' de Forz answered, his own voice equally neutral. 'What a pity.'

33

Pembroke, South Wales, July 1214

Isabelle smiled at her smallest daughter who was asleep against her skirts, having fallen prey to the exhaustion of over-excitement caused by her eldest brother's marriage and the hectic pace of the preparations and celebrations of recent days. They had given Isabelle a splitting skull and she would be glad when she too could put her head down and sleep. She was seated with her other daughters on a long padded bench that had been erected for spectators so they could be comfortable while they watched the jousting contests and feats of arms being performed on the castle sward.

The bride sat next to Isabelle on her gilded cushions, her hands demurely folded in her lap, her new gold wedding ring shining on her heart finger. A chaplet of white roses crowned her loose golden-brown hair. She wore a gown of pale gold silk damask with a long train, the sleeves deep and lined with more silk in iridescent blue-green. The girdle was belted high, with surplus fabric drawn through it, so that rather than seeing the bride's taut, slender figure, the impression was one of fecundity. Indeed, Isabelle had half wondered, given the strong attraction between Will and Alais, whether the next heir to the earldom might put in an appearance earlier than nine months from the wedding day. However, there had been blood on the sheets this morning and Alais kept shifting on her cushion as if in a certain amount of discomfort. From the heavy-lidded looks Will had been casting at her all day, and Alais's demure cat-that-has-just-eaten-a-bird glances of response, Isabelle hazarded that they had abstained from the final act in the months before their marriage, but were by no means novices.

She had been unable to pierce her daughter-in-law's wall of reserve. Alais seemed to prefer not to speak to Isabelle or her ladies, but remained with the younger women of the bower. She was resentful when asked to perform tasks. Although a skilled needlewoman, she pouted at having to sew clothes as gifts for visitors or household knights. She had little interest in accounts and tallies, nor did she wish to put herself out to socialise with guests unless they were of a similar age to herself. Alais was not gauche or shy, Isabelle was certain of that, rather she did not want to be bothered, and that was disturbing. At Alais's age Isabelle had had to be bothered as the entire domestic responsibility of an earldom devolved on her shoulders. Nevertheless, the girl appeared to enjoy possessing the status of Countess-in-waiting. She was fond of her mirror too, always preening before her reflection. Isabelle attempted to remain sanguine but it wasn't easy. She told herself the girl was still very young; she would change as she matured. Alais obviously adored Will – as he did her. That in itself was a blessing, for many marriages were not so fortunate.

Towards her father-in-law, Alais behaved like a demure young lady. She afforded him such deference and was so subdued in his presence, that William was torn between mirth and indignation.

'She makes me feel as if I am a hundred and twenty!' he grumbled to Isabelle.

'A good thing you have me to rejuvenate you then,' Isabelle had replied, making him laugh. She had noticed he didn't treat Alais as he did his daughters. There was no teasing, no braid-tweaking, no intimacy. The relationship was a polite one, functioning at arm's length, and it made Isabelle a little sad to see it.

William was in a fine mood today. The strained relationship between himself and Will had eased as they concentrated together on controlling the South Welsh March, and stayed away from the court. John had restored William to favour and granted him the castle of Cardigan and authority in Gwent, giving him full remit to do what was necessary to curb the Welsh. With the end of the papal interdict, there was cautious optimism in some quarters that the storm might pass over. News of a great naval victory against the French at Damme had kept the barons sweet, whatever their misgivings about the King. The Earl of Salisbury had surprised the French fleet in port, burned the ships and taken a vast amount of plunder. On the back of such success, hoping to recover the lands he had lost, John was currently in Poitou, conducting a campaign against King Philip.

Shouts of approbation echoed from the tilting ground before the stands as Will trotted forth on a showy chestnut destrier, barded in the Marshal green and gold. His surcoat was the same with the scarlet lion stitched at his breast; his shield too. Even his helm, carried before him on the saddle, was painted in the Marshal colours and plaited at the crown with streamers of green, gold and red.

'Doesn't he look handsome?' Isabelle said to her daughter-in-law.

For once Alais responded to Isabelle's approach with a bright smile of connection. 'There is no one to match him,' she said fiercely.

'Not now, perhaps,' Isabelle replied. Watching her son, she wondered if this was how William had looked as an eager young man embarking on the first adventures of knighthood. If only she could have seen him then, she thought with a small pang of regret for something not known. He had been magnificent as a man of two score, but in his fierce and slender youth . . .

William had been adjudicating the matches between the combatants but turned as Ancel ran up to him with the arming cap and jousting helm he had been sent to fetch.

Isabelle clenched her fists in her gown and did not allow her apprehension to show on her face.

'Is Papa going to joust too?' Sybire craned her neck. Her eyes glowed with anticipation.

Isabelle sighed. 'Probably yes,' she said, knowing that it would be impossible to prevent him. Long ago she had replaced pleas to her husband with prayers to God. She watched Jean D'Earley take William's place as judge. Walter and Gilbert arrived, leading William's powerful liver chestnut destrier Aethel between them. The stallion was high-stepping at a rapid trot, his mouth open, his crest arched and silver mane flowing. Fresh, Isabelle thought, very fresh, and looked with renewed worry at William who was lacing up his arming cap.

William took Aethel from his excited sons, rubbed his white-blazed face, patted his neck, then set his foot to the stirrup and swung into the saddle. William's movements were smooth and he worked with the horse, controlling the kicks and sidesteps with a firm hand on the reins and the grip of his thighs. Isabelle's eyes stung with pride even while her stomach clenched with fear. She had agreed with her daughter-in-law that there was no one to match Will, but now she revoked it, even if he was her son. Few men could have looked so fine on a warhorse, forty years on from being belted a knight. William's spine was still spear-straight.

William leaned to take his painted lance from Gilbert, and again his actions were easy and limber. Resting the lance across his saddle, he nudged the stallion with his heels. With a high swish of tail, Aethel launched into a smooth canter and William approached the stands. Drawing rein he made the stallion side-step, crossing leg over leg in a scissoring action. 'For your honour, my ladies,' he said, hefting the lance and dipping it towards them. His daughters laughed and clapped their hands. Belle removed the chaplet of flowers crowning her fair hair and threw it to her father. He caught it deftly on the point of the lance and smiled at her. Not to be outdone, Will pounded up on his new chestnut, clods flying, and Alais rose to bestow her own chaplet upon him, her movements gracefully dramatic.

Father and son saluted each other and rode in opposite directions, each to his end of the tilt, and Isabelle's heart was suddenly in her mouth. She shivered, disturbing Joanna who murmured a soft protest in her sleep and snuggled closer. Isabelle did not for one moment believe either would deliberately set out to harm the other, but seeing them at opposing ends of a tilt, even in a spirit of play, knotted her stomach.

At Jean's signal, William nudged Aethel and he broke into a balanced, steady canter. Will pricked the chestnut, and it shot forward like a burst of steam from under a cauldron lid. Hooves pounded the turf, the horses' breath sawed in and out and the men levelled their lances at each other's shields. Isabelle would have shut her lids to the sight, except that William had once told her that one of the core lessons of becoming a champion jouster was never to close your eyes. William's lance hit true centre of Will's shield. Will's own blow went wild because he was struggling to control his unsettled horse and his father's accurate strike had unbalanced him. Alais made a soft sound of dismay and kneaded her hands together in her lap as the men turned at the end of the tilt and came in again. This time Will had his horse on a tighter rein and his aim was true. The rattle of lance on shield was as loud as a thunderclap and William was forced back against the cantle of his saddle: only experience and expert horsemanship kept him astride. On the third turn, each man signalled to the other and this time, although they made a full charge of the moment, the rap of lance on shield was a polite courtesy, an acknowledgement of prowess that sought no further confirmation. Spectacle performed, honour satisfied, they turned to the quintain and a contest of lifting the ladies' chaplets off the hook attached to one end of the cross bar, leaving the joust to other knights who wanted to prove their valour and impress the ladies. Isabelle wiped her damp palms on her skirts and breathed out, relieved that, at least for the moment, the danger had passed.

'You were holding back,' she murmured as they sat to dine in the Norman great hall. The tables were spread with napery of bleached linen and the best glass and silver goblets were in use at the high table. 'Both at the joust and the quintain.'

William smiled towards his heir who was helping Alais to slices of venison simmered in a sauce seasoned with grains of paradise. 'So was he.' He looked rueful. 'He didn't want to best me before my household and smirch my pride. I stayed my arm because I didn't want to embarrass him in front of his bride. If we'd both opened up . . .' He spread his hands. 'Well, who knows.'

'And God forbid,' she shuddered. 'It froze my marrow to see you riding at each other.'

He waved his hand. 'Ach, it was nothing, a piece of display. Are you going to shiver and cross yourself every time he and I play chess or merels together?'

'You know what I mean,' she said crossly. 'Charging each other on horseback is not the same as playing chess in the solar.'

'A little more dangerous I grant you' – amusement crinkled his eye corners – 'but we knew what we were about.'

Isabelle drew breath to tell him what she thought of his reasoning, but was distracted by the sight of their messenger Hywel being admitted to the hall by William's usher. 'News,' she said instead.

William lowered his cup, looked at her, then at the man making his way between the trestles towards them. The humour vanishing from his face, he beckoned Hywel to mount the dais.

Isabelle noted the dust on Hywel's garments and his red-rimmed eyes with increasing trepidation. He'd been riding hard and the message was deemed sufficiently important to interrupt the feasting.

Hywel knelt to William and fumbled inside his pouch for the letters he carried. 'My lord Earl, my lady, there has been a battle at Bouvines on the road to Tournai . . . King Philip and his allies have carried the victory. There are a thousand dead and thousands more prisoners, including the Earl of Salisbury.'

Isabelle gasped and put one hand to her mouth. 'And the King?'

'Safe, my lord; he was not in the thick of the press, but his Flemish and German allies were smashed beyond hope of rallying. It was a rout . . .'

Isabelle whitened. 'My son?' she said. 'Is there news of Richard?'

Hywel withdrew a letter sealed in green wax and turned to her, holding it out. 'He sends you this, my lady, as a token that he is safe and well. He told me to say that he was on his sick bed and took no part in the battle on either side.'

'On his sick bed . . . ?' Isabelle took the packet gingerly and after a quick glance at the seal tag, opened the letter and handed it to her eldest son who looked stunned. 'Read it to me, Will.'

He did so, hesitantly with much squinting and frowning. 'God's teeth, he writes as if he's using the legs of a dead fly, not a quill,' he said with disgust after he had deciphered the greeting. 'Why didn't he have a scribe do it for him? ". . . camp fever . . . well looked after by the King's personal physician . . . need not concern . . . in better health and improving daily . . . recovered enough to go to Longueville . . . The" – something, something – "permission. The battle has left the lord King in much upset and disarray" something, something – "Earl of Salisbury to be exchanged for the brother of Count Robert of Dreux . . ."'

There were more salutes and reassurances that Richard was safe, and he had signed the parchment by pressing down with the quill, for it had obviously broken, spattering his signature with a pox of ink blots.

Isabelle took the parchment from Will. It certainly did appear to have been written by someone who had paid no heed to his tutors but the sight of it made her smile and filled her eyes with tears, not least because she was imagining his wrist shaking with fever as he fought to form the words.

William looked thoughtful. 'I'd say that his illness was useful in rendering him *hors de combat*. He didn't have to refuse to fight for John, and he couldn't answer the French summons to lead the men of Longueville.'

'You mean it's deliberate?' she said.

'No . . . fortuitous, and Richard has ever had the knack of making the most of what fortune sends him. If he's free and clear at Longueville, then so much the better.' He snorted. 'The boy has the constitution of an ox. How likely is it that he'd be too sick to hold a quill? I'd say this was written late at night on a rickety camp table in the aftermath of the battle. And what better way of letting us know he is safe than by penning the letter himself?'

Isabelle nodded and ceased chewing her lip, although her frown remained.

William curled his fist around his cup and stared into his wine.

'So,' Will said on a hard breath, 'it's all been for nothing, hasn't it? All the money-gathering, all the cajoling and pleading to get his barons to cross the Narrow Sea. And for what – for men to fall beneath French swords because he couldn't organise an orgy in a Southwark stew. If he wasn't finished before, he is now.'

William gave his son a reproving stare. 'He is still the anointed King.'

Will pushed abruptly to his feet. 'Yes, but probably not for much longer.' Grasping his wife's hand, he left the hall without asking formal leave.

'Perhaps he is right,' Isabelle said softly. 'Perhaps John has reached the end of the road.'

'Then so have I,' William said. Rising to his feet, he

too left the hall. Benches scraped as folk hastily rose and bowed at his passing, but William did not acknowledge them. Isabelle left her own place, waving her women to stay where they were. A second gesture bade the other diners to be seated and continue with their meal.

Outside, a summer dusk was falling, the sky hazily bruised towards the sea. She could hear the wheel churning at the tidal mill below the castle, and the mournful cry of gulls over the estuary. For a moment she stood breathing deeply, summoning her courage, then she approached the great keep and began the long climb to the battlements. The newly-weds had the chamber at the top. She contemplated knocking on the closed door and having a talk with her son, but abandoned the notion. There would be time later and he was with his wife now . . . as she should be with William.

Her husband was standing on the battlements, looking out on the estuary, hands braced on the crenel stones. The evening breeze rippled the edge of her veil and blew William's hair like liquid silver and carried to her the scent of salt and seaweed. For a long time she stood at his side in silence, and after a while, laid her hand upon his – not by way of apology, but in solidarity.

'What will happen now?'

A deep sigh shuddered through him. 'John will have to answer the barons' complaints and put his rule to rights, or he won't have one. But it also means he'll be thrown back on England. There'll be nothing to divert his energies in other directions, and this defeat is going to unsettle his temper.' He moved his hand so that he was holding hers and turned to face her. 'Will thinks I am loyal to the point of stupidity, but stupidity has not gained us all this. I am doing my best to walk between two fires without getting burned but it is not easy.'

'And Will?' Isabelle asked. 'I don't want him to get burned either, but I can see how close to the fire he is.'

'The only way some people learn is by being burned,' he said with a twist of his lip. 'I always thought it would be Richard . . . he was the child with his fingers near the fire out of curiosity, but he's got the sense to know that before you pick up a smouldering brand, you don a gauntlet.' He gave a half-hearted smile. 'Don't worry. The Welsh are going to keep Will busy for a while – as is his wife. It's astonishing what an accommodating woman can do to smooth the sharp edges off a man's nature.'

'I hope you are right,' she said, still feeling anxious.

'It has always worked for me,' he teased, then sobered and raised her hand to kiss her knuckles. 'I'll do my best with Will and hope he has the sense to compromise. Perhaps if his wife could soften him . . .'

Isabelle shook her head. 'The only opinion she truly cares for is Will's. If he burns his fingers, then she is likely to plunge her entire arm into the fire to show her devotion.'

William pinched his upper lip in thought. 'Then we'll have to work on both of them. Alais could learn a lot from you, and she's clever . . .'

Isabelle raised her brows but forbore to say that first you had to want to learn. She didn't want to burden William with domestic frictions. Being accustomed to coping with the fickle humours of adolescent girls, she would deal with Alais accordingly. For the rest, all she and William could do was hold on fast and prepare to ride out the storms should they threaten nearer than the horizon.

34

Pembroke Castle, South Wales, April 1215

Isabelle swallowed her irritation as Alais complained that sitting sewing in the window-seat was making her back ache.

'Wherever you sit your back is bound to ache,' she said frostily. 'The child is due next month.' Personally, Isabelle thought that it might be an early birth for Alais was carrying the child low in her womb and had been experiencing painless contractions for the past few days.

Alais had conceived in the first month of her marriage and although petulant and not at all pleased at the changes wrought on her body, she was smug at having succeeded in her duty so swiftly, and was basking in the attention lavished on her.

Isabelle continued to stitch while Alais stared moodily out of the window. 'With good fortune, the men will be home for the birth,' Isabelle remarked, making an effort at conversation.

Alais twitched her shoulders, which was a standard response to anything Isabelle said to her, but the compression of her lips and the hint of a wobble to her chin redirected Isabelle's annoyance into compassion. 'It will be all right, I promise you. I was the same when I was carrying Will – nine months after my marriage and among people I did not know well.'

Alais clenched her slender hands upon the detested sewing, her expression pinched and closed. It was plain to Isabelle that Will's bride didn't want to hear child-bearing wisdom from her, shunning it as she shunned all other advice and help from the older women in the bower.

Isabelle tried again. 'It is good news that your brother wants to make peace,' she said, referring to the messenger who had arrived yesterday at Pembroke, bearing letters from William de Forz to his half-sister. The words had been conciliatory, offering an olive branch with regard to the bitter dispute over her dower lands. He said he wanted to put the quarrel behind them for the sake of their mother's soul, and come to an amicable agreement.

Alais turned her head. 'It makes no matter to me,' she said. 'I do not know him, nor am I ever likely to move in his company.'

'But still, if he is your kin—'

'I have no fond memories of any of my kin,' Alais said and, leaving the alcove, swayed ponderously towards the door. 'I am going to lie down awhile.' She placed her hand over her gravid belly. 'And I want to be by myself.'

Isabelle inhaled to protest that she should have at least one lady with her, but changed her mind. Alais had a predilection for her own company and would only sulk and pout if she thought Isabelle was hemming her around too closely and perhaps spying on her.

Saddened, frustrated, Isabelle bent over her needle-work. Sybilla D'Earley joined her in the window-seat where the light was better for stitching. 'She does not have the easiest of natures, does she?' Sybilla said.

'She will change after the child is born – and she is

never at her best when Will is absent,' Isabelle said, attempting to put a positive slant on her daughter-in-law's sulky behaviour.

'Perhaps,' Sybilla replied dubiously. Isabelle gave her a questioning look and Sybilla rested her work in her lap. 'Everyone knows I am the quiet one, but it means I have plenty of opportunity to watch others going about their business. If the baby is a boy, she will be insufferable. He'll be the next heir to Pembroke and what use are old branches on the tree when the new ones grow? She wants to be Countess, but she has no more notion than a goose what that entails and she certainly doesn't want to learn from you. That girl believes her time is coming fast and you must put a stop to it.'

Isabelle gave a sour smile. 'I have no intention of dropping off the tree just yet ... and neither, I hope, has William.' She spoke with conviction, but she could understand her daughter-in-law's way of thinking. Alais obviously considered William to be in his dotage and not long for the mortal world. When he died, the earldom would pass to Will, and Isabelle could be elbowed off to Ireland as a dowager. Not that it would matter, Isabelle thought. If William died, she would retire to Kilkenny, or take a corrody at Tintern and not care. 'I know what she is,' she said quietly, 'and I hope I have the good judgement to deal with her.'

For a while, the women stitched in silence. From thoughts of her daughter-in-law, Isabelle turned to wondering how her husband and eldest son were faring. 'We've heard nothing from Gloucester,' she said. That was where they had been last, negotiating with a coalition of rebellious barons who had risen up against the King.

'They probably have little time to write,' Sybilla said pacifically.

Isabelle frowned with frustration. 'When last I heard, William said the rebels had been passing around a coronation charter of old King Henry – not the King's father, but his great-grandfather – and demanding John confirm the liberties.'

'It seems reasonable. What was promised then should hold true for now.'

'That's what William says and I agree. A man should have a set fee for his inheritance instead of having to pay whatever sum the King demands. He shouldn't be arrested and condemned without fair trial. A widow shouldn't be forced to remarry or pay a massive fine to keep herself free.' A cold frisson ran down her spine as again she was confronted with the vision of a life without William at her side. The word 'widow' terrified her. 'John won't look at the charter,' she said with curl of her lip, the expression saying more than words what she thought of the King. 'All he sees is an infringement of his free will and an attempt to curb his power.'

'Well, it is.' Sybilla held her sewing to the light.

'Yes, but if he'd acted honourably, it would never have come to this.' William had also told her in his last letter that John had thought about using Poitevan mercenaries to put down the rebels. William had persuaded him to abandon such incendiary tactics. Loyal or not, no English baron worth his salt would allow such men to ride over his lands and outright civil war would have been the only outcome.

Isabelle remembered William saying to her before he set out for Gloucester that trying to get both sides to see reason was like banging two stones together with one's hand between. Isabelle had replied somewhat waspishly that he should take his hand out then, but knew it was her frustration speaking, for in truth he could not. Will

401

had shown forbearance thus far and remained with the royal party, but he was restless and discontented. It would take little leverage to tip him over the edge and set father against son. She didn't want to think about it, but the notion dwelt in her mind like an unwelcome guest at her table.

Isabelle came to the end of her thread and, after a moment's deliberation, decided that perhaps she ought to go and try to talk to Alais. With the birth imminent, the girl was going to have to rely on the midwife and the other women, and a functioning rapport at least was essential. Quietly folding away her sewing, bidding her women stay where they were, she went from the room and mounted the stairs to the chamber above.

Solitude was a luxury Alais craved but seldom found in the Marshal household. Wherever she went there were always companions of one kind or another: the women; Walter, Isabelle's fussy little chaplain; various attendants for this or that; and of course Isabelle herself with her knowing gaze. There was very little peace from that, added to which she was always wanting her to do things and trying to instruct her in her duties.

'I know my duties,' Alais muttered rebelliously. She had performed the first one on her wedding night by getting with child straight away. She knew in her heart she had conceived then ... the experience had been too overwhelming not to result in this infant growing in her womb. It would be a boy, she was certain of it. A dreaming smile on her lips, she stroked the curve of her belly. The pity was that Will was not here for much of the time to watch her grow round with the future heir to Pembroke. She always felt more certain of her ground when he was by, but this foolish war between the King and his barons had deprived her of his company for months on end. Going to the window, she looked out on the bright spring day and tried to visualise him walking across the sward towards the keep. If she gazed hard enough, perhaps it would come true.

Behind her she thought she heard a soft footfall, and the hair rose at her nape. 'Will . . .' she said, and turned . . . straight into the path of a knife.

It was difficult mounting the narrow stairs hampered by long skirts, but the treads were arranged for defence, not domestic comfort, even if the chambers on the various floors were well appointed. Isabelle much preferred the older Norman hall, built by her paternal grandfather, and now used for dining and housing guests. The new keep was imposing, but didn't have that feeling of domestic comfort. Nor was it well endowed with privies. Screens and slop bowls were the order of the day.

She paused for a moment outside the door to catch her breath, not wanting to appear before her daughter-in-law gasping like a freshly caught trout. Then she raised the latch and pushed.

Alais was lying on the floor by the window, her body shuddering and her clothes saturated in blood.

Isabelle gasped and ran to her, thinking at first that she was having a traumatic miscarriage, but as she knelt and turned her, she realised with horror that the wound in her belly had been caused by a blade. Her baby, slippery with his mother's blood, lay unmoving beside her, the cord still attached.

'Mary, Holy Mother . . . Alais!' With shaking hands Isabelle tried to staunch the bleeding but the wound was too savage, and even as she spoke, Alais gave a final spasm and ceased to breathe. Isabelle stared, unable to believe, unable to comprehend. Who would do this? There was no sign of a struggle, and it must have happened here and quickly for the blood was all around and beneath her, not spilled elsewhere. She gazed about wildly, fearing for her own life, but whoever had done the deed was gone.

Swallowing nausea, Isabelle stumbled to the bed, dragged off the cover and used it to throw over Alais and the baby . . . her grandson . . . No, she told herself, don't think on it. Such things can come later. Concentrate on what needs to be done now. On trembling legs she tottered back down the stairs to the room below to raise the alarm. The sight of her blood-stained hands and gown, the pallor of her face caused consternation among her women. Isabelle silenced them with a curt command. 'Sybilla, go above,' she said. 'Make sure no one enters the room. Elizabeth, fetch your husband here immediately. Rohese, find Father Walter and tell him he is needed.'

'What's happened?' Looking frightened, Elizabeth Avenel rose to her feet. 'Is the lady Alais . . .'

Grimly Isabelle shook her head. 'There has been foul murder done, here at the heart of our keep,' she said. Her voice was as hard as stone because if she had not encased herself in a protective shell, she would have been unable to cope. 'By whom I do not know, but my son's wife and their unborn child are dead . . .'

Isabelle was not to remember the next few hours with her conscious mind, but what had happened and its aftermath were to give her nightmares for the rest of her life. The guard was doubled and the castle secured, with no one permitted to enter or leave. Although her orders were carried out immediately, there had still been a leeway of opportunity for an assassin to make his escape. The murder weapon was searched for and not found – but since every man carried a knife at his belt, it was like hunting a forest for trees. Isabelle was frighteningly aware of the suspicious glances being cast her way. Everyone knew of the frictions between her and Alais; and she had gone up alone to talk with her. No one who knew her well believed for one moment that Isabelle had anything to do with the death, but those less familiar looked and wondered.

Isabelle didn't have to wonder. She knew herself responsible. She should never have allowed Alais to go to the chamber alone. She should have had more care for the domestic security of the keep. The thought of Will's reaction to what had happened made her feel ill with worry, guilt and grief. That someone could have so much hatred in them, enough to murder a young, heavily pregnant woman in such a shocking manner, was sickening. Few candidates came to mind, but her husband and son were fighting for the foremost one and the fear and loathing added a deeper blackness to the cloud hanging over her.

In the royal camp at Gloucester, Will had been drinking hard. William had noticed, but said nothing. His son was a grown man and responsible for his own mistakes. Lecturing him would be counter-productive because he was already on a knife-edge.

'It's war, isn't it?' Will pushed his dark brown hair off his forehead. 'John never had any intention of looking at the terms put to him.'

William shrugged. 'He looked but he didn't like what he saw. There's still room for negotiation on both sides.'

'You think so?' Will looked sceptical. 'I reckon the only speaking to be done now is on the edge of a sword.' He tossed down the rest of his wine and reached for the flagon to find it empty too. 'Christ, where's it all gone?'

'In your belly, all but the one cup that's in mine.' William pointed towards the pallet set up in a corner of the room. 'You're drunk. Go to bed.'

'It'll all look better in the morning?' Will's upper lip curled.

'I didn't say it would look better,' William replied with laboured patience. 'I said that you were drunk. Of course, you might be able to think clearly on a bucket of wine, but I always find—' He broke off and looked up as Jean D'Earley entered the chamber, followed by Isabelle's chaplain, Walter.

'My lord, there is news from Pembroke,' Jean announced in a blank voice.

William knew it wasn't good news, not delivered by a senior knight and a chaplain when everyone was on the verge of retiring. Walter looked exhausted, miserable and frightened. He bowed to William, but it was to Will he turned. The latter sat as if frozen to his seat, like a man watching his doom approach and unable to do anything about it.

'Sir . . . my young lord . . .' He fell to his knees before Will. 'It grieves me beyond expressing to be the bearer of dreadful tidings, my lord, but your wife the lady Alais is dead . . . and the child with her.'

Will stared at him. 'Dead?' he said blankly.

Walter put his hands together as if praying. 'My lord, no one knows how it happened. The lady Alais was . . . was . . . Oh, Holy Christ have mercy . . . murdered in her chamber.' The final words emerged as if a sudden hard blow had forced them out from where they had become stuck. 'Your lady mother found her, but by that time it was too late and she and the child were dead.'

'Murdered?' William demanded, horror crawling over him.

The chaplain gave a frightened nod. 'Stabbed. No one knows who or why . . . or they didn't when I set out to bring you the news. It was in the heart of the keep . . . the top room. The Countess has put every guard on duty and none of the keep ladies is to be left on her own.'

Will drew a tearing breath and lurched to his feet. 'No!' he snarled. 'You lie!' And he lunged at Walter, seizing him by the throat and shaking him like a terrier with a rat. William stepped forward to try to separate them, but Will's choke hold had the strength of trauma behind it. Jean D'Earley had to punch Will in the stomach before he would release his grip. Will doubled over, retching, and the chaplain staggered backwards, clutching his throat, wheezing for breath, his eyes almost popping out of his skull. William folded his arms around his son and drew him on to the bench. Will shuddered, spasms rippling through him as his body reacted to the news even while his mind rejected it.

'I have ridden three good horses into the ground getting to you,' Walter croaked. 'The Countess fears for your lives. She begs you to be on your guard. She herself is bearing the lady Alais to the abbey at Tintern.'

William's own mind was numb, but less so than his son's. He had picked up the implication that Isabelle believed the death to be political rather than the work of a deranged person or someone with a personal grudge against Alais. 'Tell me what happened . . . all of it,' he said.

'My lord, I am not sure it is wise,' said Walter, casting a hesitant look in Will's direction.

'Even so, I would know, rather than let the details come out in festering drips. We will have to hear sooner or later. Apply the cautery and make it now.'

Hesitantly, with long pauses between his words like a

man on his deathbed, Walter told father and son the tale inasmuch as he knew it.

Will vomited up the wine he had drunk; William's expression grew harsh and wintry. 'I have seen and heard much wickedness in my lifetime,' he said, his voice gritty with revulsion and grief, 'but nothing to match this.'

'It's John's doing.' Will lurched to his feet. 'He hates us. He's never forgiven you for paying homage to Philip of France for Longueville and for how you humiliated him in Ireland. He hates me too because I'm a Marshal!'

'John isn't stupid,' William snapped. 'He wouldn't turn against us when he needs us so badly.'

'You don't see it because you don't want to see it. What will it take? Will we all have to be murdered in our beds before you open your eyes?'

'Enough!' William said, his voice harsh with the effort he was making to hold on to control. 'You have said enough!'

'I haven't even begun,' Will retorted, but clamped his jaw and, heeling about, wove unsteadily towards the door. 'I'll ride by moonlight . . . be at Striguil by dawn.'

William caught his arm. 'Then in God's name sober up first. Your troop will need time to assemble. Take Bloet and Siward for escort. I'll bring the rest of them as soon as I can.'

Will nodded stiffly, wrenched himself free and, without looking at his father, stumbled from the room.

William sat down heavily and put his face in his hands. He was appalled that such a deed could have been perpetrated in the heart of his earldom. It was a violation that threatened to rip the soul out of his family and his dynasty. If not John, then who, or why? And the poor girl . . . the only child of his best friend. How could he stand at

408

Baldwin's tomb and tell him that she had been murdered at the core of the Marshal household where she should have been safe?

His blood froze as he remembered an incident in Ireland when he had been involved in a heated argument with Albus, Bishop of Fearns, over two disputed manors. The Bishop had cursed him, declaring that his sons would never have sons and that the name of Marshal would be obliterated within a generation. The Bishop might or might not have the power or the means to do such a thing in the physical sense, but a curse had its own terrible, unseen energy.

Isabelle was waiting at Striguil with the funeral cortège when Will arrived with his small escort of companions. She had only been there a few hours herself and was exhausted from the gruelling journey and her equally gruelling thoughts. The sight of Will flinging down from his tottering mount in the bailey filled her with dread. What was she going to say to him when the enormity of what had happened was too much for words to encompass?

She went to him, her arms outstretched, but he ignored them. 'Where is she?' he demanded in a ragged voice. His face was grey and gaunt and his eyes were wild.

'The chapel,' she said.

He thrust past her and strode towards the keep. Isabelle had to run to keep up. 'I tried to save her, but there was nothing I could do – nothing anyone could have done. I'm so sorry, I . . .'

He said nothing, gritted his teeth and increased his pace.

Striguil's small chapel was ablaze with expensive wax candles, their light clear and hot, redolent with the scent

409

of clover and honey. Incense too filled the spaces and haltered his breath. Before the cross on the altar stood a bier covered in silk cloths of scarlet and gold, fringed with tassels, and upon that bier, in cold state, lay Alais, hands clasped together in prayer, eyes closed as if she slept. Four household knights stood in vigil around her, swords drawn, and Father Roger, another of the family chaplains, was kneeling at prayer.

Gasping for breath, Isabelle caught up with her son and tried to take his arm, but he shook her off and, making a perfunctory reverence to the altar, approached the bier. The knights on guard flickered their eyes to him then looked away into the middle distance.

He stared for a long time, still now after his rapid move-ment. The baby lay at Alais's side, swaddled in linen, features perfectly formed even down to the feathery pale gold eyebrows and lashes. Until that moment he hadn't quite believed it was true. There had still been a faint chance it was a mistake, or a lie, but such mercy was now gone. Grief and rage gathered within him, hot as molten lead and as brittle as midwinter ice. Between the two extremes, he was immolated and shattered. All the promise, all the joy, all the future: it was nothing, a barren wasteland.

'She's to be borne to Tintern tomorrow,' his mother said. 'It's green and peaceful there and the monks will say daily masses for her soul and that of the baby.'

'Boy or girl?' he asked in a husky voice. His fists opened and closed.

'Boy . . .' she whispered, her eyes swimming with tears.

'My son . . . my wife . . .' His voice cracked. 'In the heart of Pembroke, Mother . . . how could it happen? Tell me, how could it happen?'

She shook her head and swallowed. 'We don't know.

There were no witnesses. I found her . . . I was going to talk with her and she was . . . she was lying on the floor by the window . . . She wanted to be on her own awhile, you see. It never entered our heads that she might be in danger.'

Will moved away from her. He couldn't bear to stand at her side and listen to her talk. In a moment he was going to seize her as he had seized Father Walter, and there would be no way back from that . . . but then as matters stood there was no way back and no way forward for him anyway. He was trapped for ever in limbo with his dead wife and child. 'Go,' he said to her. 'Leave me be.'

'Let me at least—'

'Go!' he half sobbed, his voice lifting towards a snarl. 'I cannot bear you in my presence. Do you not understand? You always say you do, but you have no idea!'

Isabelle took a backstep and gasped at the blaze of rage bordering on hatred in her son's eyes.

'I blame you,' he spat out of the depth of his anguish. 'You were there, you could have done something. Perhaps you even knew!'

'What! Jesu God!' she cried. 'Grief has sent you mad. I would have protected her with my life!'

'But you didn't!'

'He was my grandchild too.' Isabelle's voice quivered with shock. 'Do you think I'd have stood by and let someone take a knife and rip out his life?'

'I don't know what I think. I only know that she is dead and I do not want you near me. I want her, but I cannot have her, can I?'

Isabelle drew a deep breath and felt her entire body ache as she inhaled. There was no point in staying to argue. She was reeling from the accusations he had hurled

411

at her and felt so unwell that she couldn't have remained even had she wanted to. She needed William, his wisdom, his guidance . . . although she had a suspicion that William would have struck Will to the ground for what he had just said.

On unsteady legs she left the chapel. She was vaguely aware of the staring, appalled faces of servants and retainers. Sybilla D'Earley took her arm, whispering that Isabelle should pay no heed, that her eldest son was overset and that he would come to his senses by and by.

'I don't see why he should,' Isabelle said brokenly, 'when the entire world has gone mad.'

It was a beautiful spring morning, bursting with life, when Alais's funeral mass was held at Tintern and her body laid to rest before the choir at Aoife's side. The sun shone through the high glass windows, creating streamers of clear light on the tiled floor. The chanting of the monks rose in plaintive melody to mingle with the incense smoke.

Hollow-eyed, savage with grief and anger, Will held his place only to honour Alais and his son. He had barely spoken to his mother. It was her fault and it gave him a sense of stability to have someone immediately to blame. He had not apologised for his wilder accusations. The way he felt, he would rather set the world alight than conciliate. It had to be John's doing. A man who could murder his own nephew, hound vassals into exile, starve their wives and children to death and hang little children was unlikely to cavil at getting his own back on the Marshals for the humiliation he had suffered over Ireland and Normandy.

His father had arrived from Gloucester in haste with the main troop. Will had scarcely exchanged a word with him, and did not intend to do so once the funeral mass was over. All he wanted to do was escape. He couldn't bear the notion of a family conference with his parents united in their compassion and concern. He would feel backed into a corner, would have to fight, and he didn't know what would come out of that fight, only that it would be deep, bitter and black.

As they emerged from the chapel, the usual gaggle of beggars and poor folk were waiting to receive alms. Will was aware of his mother giving them, of having a kind word for each person . . . as if she were genuinely caring of their plight. His father stood with her, supporting her with his hand at her arm and with the solid strength of his presence. Biting the inside of his cheek, Will turned towards his groom who was holding his horse ready.

As he set his foot to the stirrup, his father strode over to him, bidding him wait, calling out that they had matters to discuss.

'We have nothing to discuss,' Will answered as he gained the saddle.

'FitzWalter and de Vesci have left Gloucester and declared open war. I know you are shocked and grieving, but I need you and your men in the field.'

Will gathered the reins. 'I am taking my men to join FitzWalter and de Vesci. I renounce John as my King and I swear I will do everything within my power to bring him down.'

'Don't be a fool,' William said gruffly. 'It's the grief in you talking.'

Will vehemently shook his head. 'It's the sense of decency I've been holding down in deference to you. You have sworn your oath to John and you are fettered to it, but I have given him no such allegiance and I never will. Even if I have to end my life as an outlaw or take service in Outremer, I will not bend my knee to such as him – ever!'

'You are speaking out of your backside.'

'Well, perhaps my backside has more integrity than John. If you want to save the hide of your grandson's murderer, then so be it, but do not expect me to ride at your side!'

'You do not know that—'

'I know enough.' Will heeled his horse around and spurred to a canter, scattering the alms-seekers and pilgrims.

William palmed his face. 'Christ,' he muttered through his fingers. Isabelle came to his side and took his arm, clinging to him for support.

'Is this it?' he asked bleakly. 'Have I lived this long and fought this hard to see it all end in strife and downfall? Am I to spend my last years warring with my sons the way that King Henry warred with his until they killed him?'

Tears trickled down Isabelle's face. Her family was unravelling before her eyes and so fast she was unable to turn in time to meet each fresh assault. From being invulnerable, she was suddenly laid open wide. 'You told him not to be a fool, but you talk like one yourself,' she said in a grief-shaken voice. 'He has the same integrity as you, and you are no Henry. At least if John does founder, we have our heir in the other camp, and if John keeps his throne, you will be a buffer between him and Will . . .' Her voice steadied as she strove to find a way out. Keep busy; keep searching. 'If it comes to the worst, there is always Outremer, as he says.' She sniffed and wiped her eyes. 'Do you think he's right?' she asked after a moment. 'Do you believe that John had a hand in this?'

William gave an exhausted sigh. 'We have made more enemies than John in our lives. Yes, I think him capable, but whether he gave the order is another matter. If I had

414

proof he had done this to Alais . . . to us, I would bring him down, even if I had to harrow hell to do it, but without witnesses and unless someone admits to the deed, how are we to know?'

'Like Prince Arthur,' she said bitterly. 'How are we to know indeed?'

35

Caversham, Berkshire, June 1215

Isabelle cuddled her three-year-old grandson in her lap, taking comfort from his solid weight and warmth. His brother Roger, aged five, was deeply absorbed with Joanna and Ancel in a game of pretend with toy wooden knights.

'They are just like you were at that age,' Isabelle reminisced with a smile.

'I still have my *poupées* in a chest,' Mahelt replied. 'If I bear Hugh a daughter, then she shall have them when she is old enough.'

'You will have plenty of new ones to add.'

Mahelt looked wry. 'Yes, but I wouldn't be able to decide whether to give Hugh and my father-in-law ass's ears or the tail of an ox . . . and the same for Will.'

'And your father?' Isabelle asked. 'How would you have him?'

Mahelt screwed up her face. 'Not in a hauberk,' she said. 'I would have him here with you and taking his ease by the hearth as he ought to be.'

Isabelle laughed sourly. 'When has your father ever taken his ease? It's not about to happen. Even if peace is agreed between the King and the barons, there's trouble brewing in Wales. Your father says that holding every-thing together is like trying to keep water inside a sieve.' She heaved an anxious sigh. 'I worry about him. He might be hale and fit, but he should not be burdened in this fashion. Your brother ought to be taking on some of the responsibility but there is no hope of that as matters stand.'

Mahelt bit her lip and looked uncomfortable. Her own husband and father-in-law were numbered amongst the rebels. It was only through the respect the Bigods had for her father that she was permitted this visit to Caversham. 'If there is peace today . . .'

Isabelle nuzzled her grandson's soft blond hair. 'Even if everyone agrees to a truce, I doubt we will see much of your brother. The most we can hope for at home is a truce too.'

Mahelt gave her a piercing look. 'It's because of Alais, isn't it?'

Isabelle nodded. 'Will thinks John planned her death for revenge on us and blames me for not keeping a close enough watch on the household. His hatred and anger are all that keep him fed and none of us can reach him.' Her voice was bereft of emotion because all emotion had been wrung out of her in the six weeks since she had found her daughter-in-law expiring on the floor in a pool of blood and Will had ridden off to join the rebels. William as usual had shown an impassive face to the world, but in the privacy of their chamber, he had wrapped his arms around her and, taking her to bed, had loved her with a shuddering fierceness that had left her gasping, breath-less and weeping enough tears for both of them.

Mahelt laid a comforting hand on her mother's sleeve and Isabelle wondered if the tide was turning. Was she becoming the child instead of the mother? 'I will always feel guilty,' she said, 'and it has nothing to do with Will.

417

No, don't argue with me. You'll have more chance of changing your brother's mind than mine. She should have been protected; she wasn't. As to John . . .' She set her grandson down on the floor as he began to struggle in her arms. 'I always said I would put nothing past him, but he would have to be mad to set upon us in this fashion when we are one of the few props he has remaining, and whatever else I lay at his door, he is not mad.' She leaned against the cushioned back of the bench and rubbed her temples where a dull headache was beginning to throb. 'Had John wanted to destroy us, he would have done so in Ireland. In our position it is as easy to make enemies as friends and suspicions are nothing without proof. The best we can do is be vigilant.'

In the meadows of Runnymede on the banks of the Thames, William drank the King's Gascon wine. It was as smooth as a courtier's tongue, but with an underlying sharpness hinting that it wouldn't last much longer in the cask. The scribes were busy at their portable lecterns, quills scratching across vellum sheets as they made copies of the charter of liberties that John had agreed to put his seal to that afternoon.

Stephen Langton, Archbishop of Canterbury, a man who had had a long and bitter tussle with John over his appointment, removed his mitre and scratched his pate. The linen lining of the gorgeously encrusted headwear was dark with grease and sweatily crumpled. Everyone was sweltering in their court robes as the sun beat down. The King had retired to the shade of his great pavilion and dropped the flaps for a private discussion with Pandulf, the Papal Legate.

'Well?' said Langton to William, who was stirring the

lush grass with the toe of his boot. 'I am uncertain whether to call that a success or an unmitigated disaster.'

William found a smile. He liked Langton, indeed preferred him to any of the previous Archbishops of his acquaintance. Hubert Walter had been expertly efficient but lacking in humanity; Richard of Dover had just been filling a gap; and Becket . . . well, let Becket rest in his blessed sainthood. 'At least it is a document with points set down for all to see, and copies to be sent around the country. That much is well done.'

'Indeed, Marshal, but when some lords leave while the words are still wet on the parchment, saying they do not trust the King to stand by the charter, and when the King closets himself with the Papal Legate, then it does not bode well for peace. You know he will try to avoid obeying the clauses because they will curb his excesses.'

William conceded the point with a shrug. 'That is his nature, but I believe he now has a notion of how strongly his barons feel about them. Granted, some men are natural troublemakers who will nail their blazons to any kind of disruption, but there are many decent and honourable men also.'

'Your son and your son-in-law among them?' asked Langton with an acerbic smile and looked towards another pavilion outside which stood a group of young men including Will and Hugh Bigod, deep in conversation.

'Yes, them too.' William gazed at them. He had spoken to Will a couple of times during the sessions, but it had been like talking to a stranger.

As if sensing his father's scrutiny, Will looked up and across, and for a moment their eyes met. It was like sword clashing upon sword and William almost flinched, but, being a veteran, held his ground until Will dropped his stare. A young man, short of stature, dark-haired and tawny-eyed, leaned to murmur in Will's ear and Will responded in a monosyllable.

William eyed Baldwin's stepson William de Forz with dislike. The young man had arrived in England to claim his maternal inheritance and had been heaped with so many favours that no one could doubt whose son he was. Even so it was not enough for his overweening ambition and he had chosen to bite the hand that fed him and join the rebels. Despite their earlier dispute over Alais's dowry, de Forz and Will had become bosom companions. De Forz had been scathing about the security at Pembroke, which had allowed an assassin the liberty to walk in, murder his half-sister and escape. He had slighted William for continuing to support John and his attitudes were very much to Will's taste at the moment.

'Your son grieves deeply for his wife,' Langton said with perceptive compassion.

'Yes,' William murmured, 'we all do.' Excusing himself, he walked over to the group of young men. Will regarded him with a shuttered expression. Hugh Bigod looked discomforted. De Forz wore a supercilious smile.

'There is food and lodging for you at Caversham if you wish it,' William addressed his son. 'I will not hold you to anything save a family visit. Hugh will be coming anyway, to fetch Mahelt.'

A flush crept up Will's neck and mantled his face. 'I have urgent matters to attend to in London.'

'Should you change your mind, the door is open,' William said with a trenchant nod. He was not going to beg.

'I won't.' Tight-jawed, Will delivered William a formal bow before turning away to the groom who was holding his horse. Still half smiling, de Forz followed him.

Hugh continued to look worried. 'I'll watch out for him,' he said gruffly.

420

William gripped his son-in-law's shoulder in gratitude. 'I know you will.'

Hugh's brow furrowed. He was plainly trying to think of something positive to say. 'At least with you in one camp and him in the other, you're keeping a balance.'

'Is that what it is, Hugh?' William asked bitterly. 'If so, it's doing nothing for my peace of mind.'

Hugh's frown deepened. 'I don't remember what peace of mind is either,' he said, 'except when I'm with Mahelt and my sons. That's why I'm coming to dine with you at Caversham.' He tried to make a jest. 'Besides, the food's better than in London.'

'And the company?' William found it in him to tease his son-in-law.

'Any company bereft of de Forz will do me,' Hugh said in a heartfelt voice. 'It's like dining with the King – not because he looks like him, but because he acts like him. Will's going to see it too – the sooner the better, I'd say, for his own good.'

36

Pembroke Castle, South Wales, Spring 1216

'France?' Isabelle stared at William in shock. 'You're going to France?' She heard her voice rising and abruptly closed her mouth.

William nodded and showed her the letter, the royal seal dangling from its base. 'John wants me to lead a delegation to treat with King Philip.' His voice held an eager note that Isabelle had not heard in a long time.

'Can't he send someone else?'

He looked at her askance.

'Why does it always have to be you?' she demanded. 'You have done enough. You have sufficient burden on your shoulders keeping the Welsh in check.'

William sat on a cushioned bench, winced and raised one haunch to remove the toy wooden horse that had almost been his undoing. 'Because I am the one King Philip is most likely to heed,' he said patiently. 'I have known him all of my life. We have often dined together in friendship as well as having faced each other across a battlefield. Besides, I owe him homage for the Longueville lands. It won't be for long – a fortnight or three weeks at the most.' He gave her a half-amused, half-impatient look. 'I may be growing old, but I am not yet in my dotage.'

Isabelle sighed at him. 'No, but sometimes I feel as if I am. William, I cannot keep up with you, and half the time neither can your men.'

His amusement increased. 'You're being diplomatic.'

'I just worry that you have too much to do already. The Welsh . . .'

He made an irritated sound. 'The Welsh will have to wait. They've bitten off all they can chew for the moment, and even if that includes Cilgerran, I can't afford the time and men it would take to push them back. Pembroke and Striguil are not seriously threatened. That is the best I can hope for now.' He gave her a sombre look. 'It's a case of doing first what must be done first and leaving the rest until there is time . . . and we both know I am borrowing it hand over fist these days.'

'William . . .' She spoke the word as an entreaty, then again closed her mouth and folded her arms tightly around herself. 'Don't.'

'What?' He met her gaze with clarity. 'Three score and nine,' he said. 'I don't need an exchequer cloth to do the sums.'

'Then you should be hoarding the flame, not going all out to burn it down.'

He laughed and shook his head. 'I doubt that hoarding it would make a difference. What would I do except get under your feet and spend my time reminiscing in the hall about my days on the tourney field when I could take out a crow's eye on the point of my lance? My wits would grow dull and my belly would overgrow my belt like a bag pudding.' He pinched his midriff, where the muscle was still taut from hard exercise. 'It's not as if I can yield responsibilities to Will and spend less time in the saddle, is it?'

423

Isabelle winced as if salt had been sprinkled into an open wound. Going to his travelling coffer, she threw back the lid. It had got wet last time out, and although it had been dried out, oiled and polished, it still smelled musty. She made a mental note to put some cinnamon bark amid the folds while she was packing his clothes. 'I wrote another letter to Will this morning,' she said, 'wherever it may find him.' She had made it her task to write to their son through her scribe once a week. The letters were brief notes of family matters: what his brothers and sisters were doing; how everyone was faring; how they missed him. She knew that on balance he was probably burning them unread, but it helped her to feel less powerless. There was always the minor chance that he was reading them, in which case she was keeping the connection alive.

'London, no doubt,' he said neutrally. 'The rebels have scarcely moved from there all season while they wait for an answer from the French.' He turned the small wooden horse between his fingers. 'It's my brief to try to persuade Philip not to allow his son his chance at England.'

'Are you likely to succeed?'

William spread his hands. 'I don't know. Philip would dearly like to add England to his territories. On the other hand he doesn't want to risk his heir in a war on English soil – a war that defies the Pope. And Louis's claim to John's crown holds as much water as a leaky bucket so he's unlikely to win his petition to Rome.'

'Then there is a chance.' Isabelle went to his clothing coffer and began sorting through his tunics, shirts and hose in search of garments suitable for the French court.

'Well, yes, but never underestimate the pigheadedness of young men. Those in London have invited Louis to be England's King, and if Louis wants it badly enough, his father is more likely to yield to him than he is to listen to the pleadings of myself and the Bishop of Winchester.'

Isabelle ran her fingers over the cloth of silver he had worn in Ireland as lord of Leinster. Too ostentatious, she thought; he would outdo Philip in that one. The blue would be better, with the garnet grape clusters embroidered at the cuffs.

'I want you to come with me,' he said.

Isabelle's heart gave a sudden kick. She turned from the coffer and gazed at him.

He shifted under her stare and she sensed uncertainty – almost, she would have said, the hesitancy of a suitor unsure of the response he was going to receive and beginning to regret opening his mouth. 'You will be an asset to me at the court, and when that is done, we can go to Longueville for a day on the way home. It will be good to see the place again, especially when I had not thought to do so . . . and Richard will either be there, or at court.'

When she said nothing, he cleared his throat. 'I know we cannot go back to the past, but I'd like to pay homage to my memories.' He gave her a teasing look to rescue the moment from the danger of becoming maudlin. 'It'll be an excuse to wear your court gown and those shoes with the gold embroidery and pearls that you only ever wear at Christmas.'

Isabelle swallowed. She had been saving them for her funeral, but she wasn't going to tell him that. Besides, thinking about it now, there was no point in hoarding them for an event she wasn't going to experience. She could always have another pair made. 'You are right,' she said. 'Better the King of France admires them than the moths.'

He returned her smile. 'No, wear them for your husband. Let him do the admiring as you dance.'

Turning to him, Isabelle threw her arms around his neck. 'Oh, William,' she said, and laughed, although deep inside she felt a poignant sadness.

At the French court, Isabelle wore her gilded shoes almost every day. Now that she had changed her mind about their purpose, she was determined to wear them out and they took her to formal feast, informal dancing and personal exploration of the booths, market places and churches of the Île de France. She saw little of William, closeted as he was in delicate negotiations, but she was far from bored. The obligatory social round involving the wives and daughters of the French nobility kept her well occupied and she gleaned almost as much information from them as she would have done sitting in council with William.

She was ecstatic when Richard arrived at court from Longueville. William's second cousin, Thomas, Count of Perche, rode in from his lands too, and insisted on offering hospitality to her and William at his lodging on the banks of the Seine.

'Your son is a fine young man,' he told Isabelle and William one evening after vespers as they drank wine and the river flowed past his lodging house like a dark stained glass window. He lifted his cup off the shelf of his belly and toasted the broad-shouldered young man at his side. 'Although I should not be saying so to his face, especially in front of his proud parents. I wouldn't want to make him big-headed.'

Richard flashed a white grin. 'And that would be a disaster for the tourney field. I need to be able to get my skull in and out of a helm.'

Isabelle gave him a sharp look. 'You tourney?'

Richard shook his head. 'Not like my father used to

426

do, if the tales are anything to go by,' he said with a mischievous look at William, 'but on occasion I enter the lists. Besides, I don't have the time with the Norman estates to tend.'

Thomas snorted. 'What he doesn't tell you is that he took the prize at Saint-Damme at Christmas – and faced down William des Barres, who is the best tourney knight in France.'

'I had some good fortune,' Richard said, flushing but obviously pleased. In his mid twenties, the fleshiness of adolescence had yielded to height and muscular strength. What had emerged from the chrysalis was an extraordinarily attractive young man with ruddy-gold hair and smoke-grey eyes. Just looking at him made Isabelle feel proud and terrified.

'It was more than that,' grunted Thomas. 'You ride like your father.' He saluted William with a cup that waved precariously in his hand for he had been drinking steadily for much of the evening. 'There haven't been any tourneys of late because of Lent, but they'll be starting up again soon. Good practice for the battlefield.'

Isabelle choked on her wine and Richard laid a solicitous hand on her sleeve. 'Don't worry, Mother. Even if Prince Louis does take an army to England, I won't be in the ranks. I'm not obliged to serve him across the Narrow Sea.'

'For which I thank God,' she said vigorously. 'I suppose you know about your brother – that he is amongst the rebels.'

The grin left Richard's face. 'Yes,' he said, and leaned back from the table as if withdrawing a little from the conversation. 'I am sorry. I am also glad I'm out of it.'

'I am too,' Isabelle said.

An uneasy silence fell and was broken by Thomas. 'If

Prince Louis gets his way, half the French lords will be crossing to England, but no point worrying about it tonight. Not worth spoiling good wine and company, eh?' He gestured to his minstrels and entertainers who had been playing quietly in the background during the meal, ordering them to strike up a lively tune and perform feats of tumbling. The manner of his doing so made it plain that while he was happy to discuss old times, the future was a different matter.

A week later, the conference with the French over and to no purpose, William and Isabelle spent a night at Longueville before embarking for England.

Isabelle walked the rooms where she had spent her young motherhood. Ghostly echoes of family laughter rang from the walls and haunted the corridors. Many of her children had been born here. Will, her first, on a morning in late April after a long night's labour. She stood in the great bedchamber, remembering lying against the bolsters, the baby's soft weight resting along her arm as he nestled at her breast. Richard and Mahelt were both English born, but this room bore the imprint of Gilbert and Walter's first cries too. Her eyes misted over. The years had flown with the swiftness of summer swallows on the wing.

Longueville was now a bachelor's home, but Richard had furnished the dwelling rooms with curtains and hangings from Flanders in the latest fashion. Woven reed matting covered the bedchamber floor, topped with the luxury of richly coloured rugs either side of the bed to comfort the feet on rising. Isabelle supposed that he had learned these touches of luxury at John's court. Either that or he had a mistress about whom he was keeping quiet. Isabelle had noticed many women giving him looks at court, but he hadn't returned any of them except in the most general of ways, so she suspected not.

Running her fingers over a coffer painted with shields bearing the arms of Marshal and de Clare, Isabelle wondered if they should have remained in Normandy when the lands were split – done homage to Philip in full and abandoned the rest. They would certainly have led more peaceful lives as lords of Longueville and Orbec. But then they would not have achieved so much either, especially in Ireland.

In thoughtful mood, Isabelle returned to the great hall. William was sitting before the fire, holding the hand of a frail, elderly man – his brother, Ancel, namesake of their youngest son. Isabelle had never met him and if William had not told her that this was his sibling and younger than him by several years, she would not have believed it. The noses were the same, strong and bony, and perhaps the line of the jaw, but there the resemblance ended. Ancel was cadaver-thin, yellow of complexion and so unsteady that he could barely walk. In his prime he had served in the mesnie of Count Thomas's grandfather, Rotrou, but now, wasting away, he had come to his nephew's keep at Longueville to end his days.

'I knew you would come back,' he was saying to William, his speech slow and careful as he harboured his strength. 'I prayed to God to see you before I died and He has been gracious enough to grant my wish.' He gave a sad shake of his head. 'I thought about returning to England, but it was too far for me to travel. Besides, I'm glad I didn't if all the rumours I hear are true.'

'I told you never to listen to rumours,' William said with great sadness in his eyes, although his lips were smiling for the benefit of his brother.

Ancel gave a wheezy laugh. 'Hah, I remember all the

429

ones about you and the Young Queen Marguerite. Nearly your downfall, they were.'

'They weren't true though.' William shifted on the bench as if pricked by a thorn.

'No, but they ruined your reputation for a while.' Ancel leaned towards Isabelle. 'He was accused of having an affair with King Philip's half-sister, did you know that?'

'Yes, I knew,' Isabelle said, unperturbed. 'But it was long before our marriage, and nothing but the petty scheming of jealous rivals. I have ever known the difference between dross and gold.'

Ancel nodded his approval. 'So have I, my sister,' he replied with a pained smile. 'Marguerite was a great lady, but she couldn't hold a candle to you.'

Isabelle thanked him for the compliment with a courtly dip of her head.

Ancel was silent for a while, then looked thoughtfully at William. 'So,' he said, 'Louis is still intending to invade England?'

William gave a resigned nod. 'His father would rather not have him go, but he will agree eventually. It's too much of a prize not to.'

'And you'll resist him when he invades?'

'I have no choice.'

Ancel held out one trembling hand and looked at it. 'I'm glad I can no longer fight. I don't envy you . . . but then I suppose you do not envy me.' He gave a brief, cracked laugh, and his breathing caught, but when Isabelle gave a murmur of concern, he waved her aside. 'I'm all right,' he said. 'Best I've been in an age.'

He retired to his chamber soon after that to sleep. William stood a long time, watching him, then quietly left the room. Isabelle made to follow her husband, then changed her mind and left him alone. She had seen the way his fists were clenched, and knew from the set of his jaw that what he needed most was solitude. His need for company would come later, and she would be there for him then.

37

London, Spring 1216

'I don't know why you are bothering to meet him,' said William de Forz as Will checked and recinched the double girths on his bay courser and prepared to mount. 'It won't make any difference, will it? What are you going to say?'

'I'll cross that bridge when I come to it,' Will answered, deliberately busy with his task so that he did not have to meet his companion's scornful amber gaze. 'My father has asked to see me and I'm not going to refuse him.'

'I would.'

'I'm not you.' Will's friendship with de Forz had cooled considerably over the months they had spent in each other's company in London. At first de Forz had been a bolster to Will's fury and grief over Alais's death, and a tenuous connection with her since he was her half-brother, but as Will began to find a modicum of balance, he had started to notice things about de Forz that made him uneasy. He was always aggrandising himself at the expense of others. He clad himself richly but doled out alms and charity from a grudging fist, and he was casually cruel. If a dog got underfoot, he kicked it out of the way with enough force to make it yelp. A pargeter's lad had accidentally spilled limewash on de Forz's cloak yesterday and de Forz had cut him across the cheek with his riding whip, inflicting a vicious wound.

As Will swung into the saddle and prepared to leave, de Forz detained him with a hand on his bridle. 'Your father is new returned from France. You'll tell us everything that he tells you.'

'I'll think about it,' Will said and used his spurs, forcing de Forz to release his grip and leap back. Will clattered out from the lodging yard into the road with an escort of two knights and two serjeants. The streets were moderately busy with folk going about their business, but at the sight of armed men, they hurried past or stood to one side with heads down and eyes lowered. The city of London had opened its gates to the rebels, but its inhabitants were wary. Only two days since a young wine merchant had been stabbed to death in a brawl with one of de Forz's henchmen. De Forz's man had slipped away before he could be arrested and hanged, leaving behind a lingering taint of suspicion. The rumour ran that de Forz had given him funds for his escape on a French-bound galley, and de Forz was known to have a grudge with the vintner over unpaid debts.

Will left the city by way of Ludgate, crossed the Fleet river, swollen dirty brown by recent rain, and continued along Fleet Street until he arrived at the precincts of the Temple Church. Word had gone ahead and Aimery de St Maur, master of the Templars in England, had come from his lodgings on the east side of the church and was waiting before the ornate arched doorway to greet him. The lord Aimery was to be his escort and safe conduct from the Temple to Caversham. No one from either faction would dare to attack a conroi of Templar knights going about their business.

Will gave his mount to a lay brother and knelt to kiss the lord Aimery's ring. The knight greeted him with warmth and gravitas and Will felt his burdens lighten a little. Side by side, without a word, he accompanied the Templar into the church and, reverencing the altar, knelt to pray. As always when in this place, he felt the atmosphere raise the hair on his nape and bring gooseflesh to his arms. This was where his father would eventually lie, and probably himself too. The round nave, designed to replicate the Holy Sepulchre in Jerusalem, had been consecrated by the Patriarch of that city during a visit several years before Will's birth. The tranquillity and grandeur provided by the great glossy columns of Purbeck marble supporting the vaulted roof raised his eyes to heaven and at the same time made him realise his own insignificance, but not in a detrimental way. The church possessed a special air of sanctity. Men who were buried within its hallowed precincts were blessed.

'I have considered taking Templar vows,' Will admitted to the lord Aimery as he rose from his prayer and the men returned outside. An escort of knights in their familiar pale woollen mantles was waiting and a groom had brought Aimery's stallion from the stables.

Aimery gave him a penetrating glance as he reached to his bridle. 'You are the heir to the earldom of Pembroke,' he said. 'It is beholden on you to further your line.'

Will mounted the bay. 'And so I did, but it was taken from me, and perhaps it was a sign from God? I have four brothers, all with the hammers and anvils to provide offspring. Gilbert is in minor orders, but has not taken full vows and there is no bar whatsoever on the other three.'

Aimery's brows drew together in concern. 'The grief

still rides you close,' he said. 'In time you may well change your mind.'

'I won't,' Will said with finality and spurred his horse.

The river at Caversham was steel blue, reflecting in a darker hue the changeable April skies. Standing on the bank, the numerous buildings of the manor behind him, acutely aware of each draw and release of breath from his lungs, William wondered how many spring seasons were left to him. He had no doubt that his brother Ancel was living his last one.

The swans were nesting on the far bank as they had always done, the female brooding a clutch of five eggs, the male guarding their patch of river with wings arched in graceful angel symmetry. Further along the bank, watched by the women, his three youngest children were playing tag, five-year-old Joanna's skirts kilted up to show her thin ankles and narrow calves. She was squealing with delight, her hair flying like a banner.

His eldest son was standing at William's side, feet planted apart, arms folded and expression closed, in contrast to the carefree mood of the little ones. 'You won't persuade me to return to the King,' he said coldly.

William concealed his irritation. 'I know that. You're more stubborn than my old pack mule. I asked you to come here for a discussion, not because I thought I had any hope of changing your mind.'

'What's to discuss? I thought it had all been said.'

William watched coins of light sparkling on the river. 'There is always room for words.'

'Even when no one hears them?'

'Said aloud, they help me to think, and I don't believe that they go entirely unheard.' He glanced shrewdly at his heir, who still looked mutinous. 'King Philip is not keen to have Louis aid your cause because, like all fathers, he fears for his son's safety – but he will not refuse him. The offer of a crown and the possibility of destroying John are too tempting to resist. As a father, Philip heard me very well, but as a king, he will take the risk.'

'So Louis is going to invade?'

'In all likelihood. And it is my task to stand in his way.'

'You can't do it on your own and you don't have many allies left, do you?' Will challenged.

William was unperturbed. 'Those who remain loyal are of such calibre that they will never break and run.' He cast his son a cautioning look. 'Don't underestimate us, Will. We have you pinned down in London and we've retaken Rochester. Whatever his enemies say, John is no softsword.'

'Everything will change when Louis arrives with his troops,' Will parried. 'You won't hold us then.'

'Perhaps, and perhaps not. There are factors other than strength of numbers. Men who oppose John might decide that at least he's the devil they know. If the French are undisciplined or if Louis takes away English lands and gives them to Frenchmen, how long will the honeymoon last?' Hands clasped behind his back, William started to walk along the riverbank, thereby forcing Will to walk with him. 'It's not why I asked you to come here. I'm not going to plead a lost cause; rather I'll make the best of it. At least our family has a foot in each camp and that is no bad thing.' He cleared his throat. 'What I do not want is to have to face my own son across a battlefield. If you are going to give your oath to Louis, I want your word that you will not deliberately seek confrontation with me. In my turn I will do the same for you.'

Will frowned. 'Yes,' he said after a long hesitation.

'It makes sense and it's not a dishonourable compromise.' He watched his younger siblings. 'Is that all you wanted?'

'No, it's not.' William stopped before a jetty and studied the small moored boats. Sometimes he and Isabelle would take one downstream but it had been a while since they had had time. Perhaps this evening, he thought. If they didn't make the opportunity now, perhaps they might never have another one. He faced his son. 'I need to make other preparations too. Pembroke will be yours when I die, and its welfare will be in your keeping. I want to speak with you on the matter.' He gestured that they should walk back to the manor.

'You're not dying,' Will said sharply.

William's smile was grim. 'Not at the moment, but who knows what will happen when Louis lands and I have to be constantly in the field. Added to which the miles left of my life's journey are dwindling. I must be practical.'

'You will not make me feel guilty.'

'That was not my intent,' William said wearily. Although his son was a grown man, he still felt in many ways as if he was dealing with a difficult adolescent. They should have had everything in common and yet they stood on opposite sides of a divide.

Will looked at his feet. 'Then I apologise. It is hard to know what is and is not intended these days.'

Squealing as she was chased, little Joanna ran up to her father. 'Sanctuary!' she shrieked, clinging to his legs. 'I claim sanctuary!'

William lifted her in his arms and swung her round. Her hair was warm with sunshine as it whipped against his cheek, and scented like new grass. The blue ribbon that had tied it back was wrapped in a silken flash around her small clenched fist.

'Granted!' he laughed, although his eyes were sad. The juxtaposition of youth and age – the innocence of his smallest daughter and the world-weariness of his eldest son – made him ache to the marrow.

38

Gloucester Castle, Summer 1216

A pack-pony train had recently arrived from the Marshal warehouses at Charing. The sturdy bay ponies stood in the courtyard, silver bells jingling as they tugged at nets of hay while attendants unloaded supplies from their panniers. There were sheets of vellum, parchment and green sealing wax for the scribes. Bolts of linen and wool spilled from one pony's baskets, furs and skins from another's. The candle supply had been running low and eight panniers of these had been delivered, plus wax and linen wicks to make more. Then there were spices, candied fruits and barrels of silver pennies to pay the retainers' wages.

One of the serjeants escorting all this bounty was young and stunningly attractive, with glossy dark hair and sleepy, fox-coloured eyes. Belle and Sybire were giggling in his proximity, sending him coy looks through their lashes and generally acting like silly young hens in the presence of a cockerel. Rolling her eyes, Isabelle intervened and sent the young man away to the guardroom where meat and ale had been set out for the escort. Her wayward daughters she chivvied back to the private chamber, ignoring their pouts and protests.

'Not the least problem with this war is that our daughters are ready for betrothal, but half the families we would consider appropriate are on the opposing side,' Isabelle said in exasperation to William when he entered the chamber a moment later. 'Sometimes I don't know what to do with them.' She was so distracted herself that she didn't immediately notice the look on his face.

'Just half the families?' he asked sourly. 'There are so few of us left that our daughters have almost no choice at all. Chester, Derby and Warwick are the only ones, and Chester doesn't have sons.'

His tension belatedly reached beyond her preoccupation and she looked at him. 'What's happened?'

'Louis has advanced on Winchester and taken the submission of Arundel, Warren de Warenne and Salisbury. Hywel's just ridden in with the news.'

'Salisbury?' Isabelle's voice rose a notch, causing her daughters to look up like startled deer, and her women to stop what they were doing. 'But he's John's half-brother! What's he doing with Louis?' Alarm shot through her. John's supporters really were being pared down to the bone.

William glanced around the chamber and he lowered his voice. 'There's a rumour circulating that John despoiled Ela whilst Salisbury was a prisoner after Bouvines.'

'Holy Virgin!'

William's nostrils flared with disgust. 'It's not true. I wouldn't put it past John to be cruel to Ela or frighten her, but he wouldn't seduce her or resort to rape. She's his sister-by-marriage – she's family.'

'Knowing the things he's done to others, including his kin, that's no protection,' Isabelle said tartly.

William made an impatient sound. 'He enjoys marking other men's territory, but he wouldn't do it to his little brother.'

'But Salisbury believes he would.'

'I'd say he's more worried about his earldom than his wife with the French all over the south. I suspect he's reached the end of his halter and is looking for an excuse to rebel. His reasons don't matter just now. The point is that he and the others have given their oaths to Louis.'

Isabelle sat down abruptly on a cushioned bench and looked around her comfortable, well-appointed chamber. 'So where does that leave us? Where do we go now?'

William sat down beside her and took her hand in his. 'Back to Wales for the moment to keep an eye on the borders,' he said. 'And from there it's a fast retreat to Ireland if necessary. I doubt the French will come there in a hurry. John is at Corfe but planning to strike across the Midlands.'

There was also the path of bowing to Louis as others had done, but Isabelle knew William would rather die than yield. It was an issue of honour. It didn't matter what John had done to him, it was his own oath that weighed in the balance.

'Hywel also said that Louis has granted Will the title of Marshal of all England,' William said. 'He is my counterpart in Louis's camp.' He laughed cynically. 'I am not certain anyone in his right wits would desire such a title at the moment, but at least he's been given a glimmer of recognition.'

She looked down at their linked fingers. She had seen Will when he came to Caversham with Aimery de St Maur. He had been remote but courteous, doing his filial duty by her but holding aloof and staying in the company of the Templar as much as he could until it was time to leave. It had cut her to the quick, although she had not shown it to the world. She prayed for him daily.

'Of course it's all piss in the wind,' William added.

'What Will really wants is Marlborough, but Louis has given it to Robert of Dreux – he prefers a Frenchman to have custody. That can only work to our good. The more he gives to his countrymen and the less to his English supporters, the better it suits us in the long term – if we have a long term left.'

Will stared. 'Worcester,' he said to Louis, as if the word was snake venom. 'You want me to take Worcester?'

Louis looked up from the maps and sketches filling his campaign trestle. He drummed his fingers, then laid his palms flat on the wood. 'You're capable, aren't you, Marshal?' There was a touch of scorn in Louis's voice, and the hint that if Will was not prepared to do as he asked, there were plenty of others who were.

'Yes, but it is in my father's jurisdiction . . .'

Louis raised a dark eyebrow. 'And are you not "Marshal of all England"?' he asked coldly. 'How can you be that when your father claims the same? Perhaps you are afraid of him.'

'I do not fear my father,' Will replied stiffly, 'but I respect him. I do not see why you are sending me into the heart of his territory when you would not give me Marlborough.'

'Does Marlborough really mean so much to you?' Louis enquired with a scornful smile.

'More than it does to Robert of Dreux,' Will said brusquely. 'It belonged to my grandfather in the days of King Stephen and my uncle was its castellan.'

Louis looked down at his maps and plans and shuffled them between his hands. 'If you want the place and my trust you will have to earn it. Take Worcester for me and we'll talk again about Marlborough.'

'Sire.' Will pressed his lips together, bowed and flung from the room.

William de Forz followed him out. 'Your father won't be pleased,' he said, a note of relish in his voice.

'I cannot help that,' Will snapped. 'What am I supposed to do – refuse?'

'I could go in your stead.' De Forz's eyes held a lupine glint.

'No, I'll do it,' Will said savagely. He knew de Forz's appetites and capabilities well enough by now not to want him anywhere near Worcester. 'Prince Louis appointed the task to me.'

'Well then, I wish you good hunting.' Smiling, de Forz held out an elegant, well-tended hand. Will ignored the gesture and, putting his head down, strode off to the stables. On his way he had to negotiate Gilbert de Clare, Earl of Hertford, and William of Salisbury, who was still agitating about whether he had done the right thing in joining Louis. He said as much to Will, but Will had neither the patience nor inclination to chew on that particular bone. 'You must do as your conscience sees fit,' he snapped as he sent his squires in search of his senior knights.

Salisbury looked bitter. 'Easier said than done . . . unless you happen to be William Marshal.'

As Will made preparations to ride, he found himself pondering Salisbury's words and wondering how easy it was for his father. Was honour the same as conscience? If not, how did one choose between them? And was the choice, when made, bitter as gall?

At Striguil, Isabelle was busy with the travelling chests brought from Caversham when a loud scream made her jump out of her skin. A terror of memories flashed through her like the keen cut of a blade as she ran into the antechamber, followed by her women. Sybire was clutching the side of her head and howling like a banshee. Belle was standing over her, flushed with distress. When she saw her mother, her eyes filled with guilt.

'Holy Virgin, what on earth's the matter?' Isabelle demanded. 'Let me see!' Hurrying to the girls, she took Sybire's hand away from her head and saw that her ear was covered in blood from a ragged, welling hole in the base of the lobe.

'It's Belle's fault,' little Joanna volunteered, her eyes as wide as goblet rims with the shock of the screams. 'She did it.'

'It's not my fault!' Belle burst into tears. 'Sybire made me do it!'

'Do what?' Isabelle asked, striving to keep her voice level.

Belle opened her closed hand and showed her mother the ornate Byzantine earring on her palm, its wire glistening with Sybire's blood. 'They were in the jewel box, and Sybire said she wanted to wear them. She told me to—'

'I didn't know you were going to make such a mess of it!' Sybire gasped, tears pearling down her cheeks. 'I should have known. You can't sew to save your life!'

Isabelle took the earring from Belle and prayed for patience. The jewel was part of the earldom's portable treasure. At some time it had been traded by a returning crusader, and had found its way to the Marshal counting house at Charing, and from there to the strongbox in their chamber. 'Sweet Mary, you are not Greeks! When you are grown women you will cover your hair and ears except in the bower and the private presence of your husband. Nor is it appropriate for you as unmarried virgins to wear such trinkets.'

Recovering from the initial stab of pain, Sybire lifted

444

her chin. 'I saw a lady in London with them in her ears once and my father says that the women of the tourneys often wore jewels in their ears.'

Isabelle wiped the earring hook on her skirt and returned it to the jewel casket, which she then took into her custody whilst holding out her hand for the key the girls had purloined. 'None of my daughters is about to become a tourney follower,' Isabelle said tersely. Later, she would probably laugh, but for now her sense of humour was struggling with the handful that her daughters were proving. Giving the casket to Sybilla D'Earley for safekeeping, she fetched a cloth and a vial of rose water to dab the wound. 'I can find a lot more for you to do than play at vanity,' she threatened as Sybire flinched and protested through clenched teeth. 'Let this be a lesson to you and you had better say extra prayers to the Virgin. You don't want to take the wound poisoning and end up with your father's field chirugeon having to slice off your ear.'

Sybire suddenly looked worried. Isabelle returned to unpacking the chests, thinking it a good thing William had never mentioned in front of his daughters the dancing girls who frequented the tourneys and the vicinity of their anatomical piercings!

She was sorting through his shirts and braies, the girls now virtuously helping her in atonement for their prank, when he stormed into the room, his expression thunderous. 'Louis has sent troops into Worcester!' he snarled.

'Worcester!' Isabelle's eyes widened in shock.

'And he's sent them under Will's command.' The look he shot her was filled with fury, and more than that – pain. 'It's a step too far, Isabelle; I won't stand for it.' He strode to one of the chests yet to be unpacked, slammed back the lid and heaved out the leather sack protecting and containing his hauberk. 'The whelp's seized the town and occupied the castle.'

Isabelle's heart began to pound with fear. 'What are you going to do?'

'Go there, of course. I won't have him encroaching on my domain. We made a pact at Caversham to leave each other's interests alone inasmuch as we were able, but obviously he's chosen to break his word.'

She swallowed. 'Don't go,' she said in a voice tight with panic. 'Send one of your knights . . .'

William gave the sack to a waiting squire and directed another one to take mail chausses, gambeson and surcoat from the chest. 'If I don't do something about it, Chester and Warwick will. Besides,' he added, 'he has broken his word to me and I will know the reason why.'

'Perhaps he was backed into a corner.' Isabelle followed him as he and his squires headed for the bailey.

'Well, he's backed me into one now,' William said grimly.

Ralph Musard was holding William's courser, saddled up and ready. Aethel was clipped on a lead rein and tended by a groom.

'Come back whole,' Isabelle said unsteadily, 'and be careful with Will.' She felt helpless, unable to find any soothing words or gestures to smooth the path and make things less jagged. Her son was out of reach and so was William, his kiss perfunctory before he swung to horse.

'I'll make no promises,' he said and, turning from her, gave his courser the spur.

Will took a swallow of the rich red wine and felt it burn down his gullet, leaving a tannic coating on his tongue. His men had taken it from a vintner's shop near the guildhall together with several casks of mead and a large cheese from his larder.

Worcester had yielded to Will and his troops after a token resistance, as he had suspected it would. He was the 'Young Marshal' and therefore the weight of his father's reputation allied to his own standing had made the populace amenable to his entry into the town. What resistance there was had been swiftly put down. Will had kept a rein on the troops. No houses had been burned and no violence offered to the people who did not resist. Looting had been selective and controlled.

The wine lay on Will's stomach like molten lead. Grimacing at his goblet, he set it aside. He wasn't thirsty and knew if he continued to drink for the sake of it, he would be violently sick. Nor would drink do anything to alleviate his state of mind except by way of granting him temporary oblivion. 'God on the Cross,' he muttered and, hot-eyed, removed his boots and went to lie down. His squire had made up his pallet with clean linen sheets, pulled crisp and tight. The blanket was of undyed wool and the coverlet of a simple striped weave – the bed of a monk, not the heir to an earldom. He found sleep came more easily in such a bed these days.

The door opened on a cold draught of air and then closed again firmly. Expecting his squire, Will started to say he desired to be left alone unless the matter was urgent. Then he laid eyes on the tall cloaked figure and dived for his swordbelt instead.

'Leave it,' his father snapped and, straddling a camp-stool by the bed, put down his hood.

'How did you get past my men?'

William snorted. 'Your pickets are lax and Worcester has long been in my authority. The townsfolk might have let you in, but it doesn't mean they're overjoyed about it. There are plenty of stout English men out there who object to having their city occupied by the supporters of a French prince. They were happy to guide me in and the knights of your mesnie are too sensible to interfere between a father and son.' He gave a sardonic smile. 'Despite your title, it seems that my own name still stands for something.'

Will flushed. 'I didn't ask to be given this task.'

'No, but I'm sure your heart didn't bleed when Louis awarded it to you – save that it wasn't Marlborough. You try my patience, you know that.' His eyes were bright with anger within their shadowed sockets. 'Why in God's name come to Worcester when you know full well it's right under my nose?'

The headache Will had thought to avoid by not drinking any more wine began to throb at his temples. 'You didn't have to come. If it is under your nose it is because you have made it your business to come sniffing around. What did you expect me to do: sit on my backside in Louis's camp and do nothing?'

'Let me turn that around and ask you the same. Did you think I was going to skulk in Gloucester or Striguil and let you take Worcester from me unchallenged?' William helped himself to wine from the flagon Will had abandoned. 'Let me speak plainly as I should have done long ago instead of holding my peace.

'You blame your mother's lack of vigilance for what happened to Alais, and she abets you by blaming herself. You are fettered together like prisoners in a dungeon and the tragedy is that neither of you needs to be. Your mother can be forgiven for thinking Alais was safe at the heart of Pembroke.' He stabbed a forefinger at his son. 'Forgiven, Will. That's the word you both lack. Grieving and remembering is right but not when it is twisted like this.' He took a gulp of wine, then rested the cup on his knee. 'I know you think John is behind Alais's death, but you have no proof and there are others who could as easily be accused. Albus of Fearns cursed our line to die out within a generation. I would not put it past him to help the prophecy along. Then there's William de Forz. His envoy was at Pembroke the day before Alais died, supposedly bringing messages of conciliation. I know how hard de Forz tried to reverse the ruling about Alais's dowry before your wedding and how angry he was at having to give up the lands. And there are many more candidates in the race and nothing you can prove.'

Will swallowed nausea. 'You won't twist me back to your side by this,' he said in a voice thick with revulsion.

His father's gaze was sombre and compassionate. 'Good Christ, son, I am not trying to twist you either way. You've already wound yourself up tighter than the rope on a mangonel.' He finished the wine and set the cup aside. 'Ranulf of Chester and Henry of Warwick will be here by first light. I am drawn up a mile away with all the men of Gloucester and my Welsh levies. We are coming in at dawn and God help you if you stand in our way. It's up to you whether you fight or retreat, but either way you are going to leave Worcester. It's mine; if you hold on to it, it will be over my dead body.'

'You will not fight me.' Will jutted his jaw. He felt like a scolded child and resentment burned in his breast.

'I hope not, but I will do as I must. I pray you have the great good sense to leave before such a calamity happens. We'll be riding in as soon as mass has been said and the men have broken their fast.' His father rose to his feet and went to the door, then paused, his hand to the latch. 'You have an unfair advantage of me, Will. If you choose confrontation, I have given you a few hours' grace to prepare yourself. I hope you make the right choice.' With a dip of his head, he opened the door and was gone on another waft of cold air.

Will stared at the door as the latch dropped back into place. A part of him was utterly numb, but try as he might, he couldn't make that numbness spread to obliterate everything. He imagined coming face to face with his father on the morrow. Had the jousting session at his wedding been a premonition? Would he be able to raise his sword against his father or take him prisoner if the situation arose? His nausea intensified and he had to dive for the chamberpot. He knelt over it, retching until his throat was raw, but even when the spasms subsided, he felt no better. What his father had said about Albus of Fearns and William de Forz made dreadful sense. It didn't mean John was innocent, far from it, considering he was de Forz's unacknowledged father. There was no proof, only a yawning black chasm of uncertainty and suspicion.

Will sat down on the edge of his pallet and pressed the heels of his hands to his eyes until red stars burst across his vision. If he chose not to hold Worcester, he could not return to Louis. At best he would be humiliated and made a laughing stock, at worst branded a traitor and ostracised. He refused to contemplate returning to John. That at least was immutable. He wished he was Richard. It was so much easier for his brother, administering Longueville, attending the French court and sporting at the occasional tourney. Richard didn't know he was born, and Will was beginning to wish his own life uncreated.

He donned his shoes and left the bed at an aching walk to open the door. The grey-bearded guard on duty brought his spear to attention, met Will's gaze, then stared into the middle distance.

'You let my father enter and leave,' Will said coldly.

'Yes, my lord. He was alone and I deemed him no threat.'

450

Will nodded. 'And he has so great a reputation and is so venerated that you would not lay hands upon him.'

'It would have been dishonourable, sir.'

Will found the travesty of a smile. 'Then you are of my father's ilk,' he said. 'Go and make yourself more useful than you are here. Rouse the men. We're leaving before dawn.'

The soldier's focus shortened to Will. 'Leaving, my lord? What about the town?'

Will clenched his fists. 'Perhaps you would like to stand in my shoes since you're plainly incapable of taking an order,' he snapped.

The guard shuffled his feet and reddened. 'No, my lord . . . Where shall I say we are going?'

Will shrugged. 'Anywhere . . . Away from the fight. Not to Louis, not to John. A murrain on the pair of them.'

39

Gloucester, October 1216

Isabelle awoke in the dark and for a while lay listening to the sound of William's breathing. Finally, putting out her hand, she parted the enclosing bed curtains and saw the weak glow of daylight filtering through the high windows. Rain was spattering against the lead-encased glass, driven by an inclement autumn wind. She let the hanging drop back into place, pulled the fur coverlet up to her shoulders and snuggled down into the warm den of the bed. William muttered and moved closer to her, setting his arm across her waist and nuzzling her neck. Isabelle made a soft sound and turned into his arms, pressing herself against the welcome heat of his body.

'Give me an excuse not to rise and be about my duties,' he murmured.

Isabelle laughed throatily. 'It's cold and it's raining,' she teased. 'The moment you rise your clerks and chamberlains will be at you. Your knights will be making their reports and the couriers will be waiting with their budgets of news – probably none of it good.'

He chuckled. 'Well, the first's an excuse, yes, but the others are reasons to be up and about. Have you nothing more compelling in your armoury?' He nibbled the tender skin beneath her ear and Isabelle felt the burn of his morning stubble, prickly, but pleasurable nonetheless. She stretched luxuriously like a cat.

'How compelling do you want?' she purred. 'A glance through the door, or the complete inventory?'

He closed the bed curtains against the grey streak of morning and in the warm darkness kissed her with leisurely thoroughness and stroked her body with his fingertips until she arched and gasped. She was five and forty, still of childbearing years, but her fluxes were sometimes erratic these days. She knew that she might conceive – after all, Queen Eleanor had done so with John at a similar age, but on balance she thought not. On two occasions since Joanna was born she had harboured suspicions, but they had come to nothing.

They made love slowly in a tender exploration of touch that made her skin tingle, her breath shorten and her loins flood with exquisite lust. At the end, he took her hand and meshed her fingers through his and somehow the fierce grip of crisis was more intimate than the surge of his body within hers.

They lay together in the centre of the bed regaining breath, kissing, touching. Isabelle willed her husband to doze off and sleep for a while longer. She didn't want the world outside their bed curtains to intrude just yet. 'A few more moments of peace,' she pleaded with God. William's hand lay upon her breast, his lips moved softly at her shoulder and then ceased as his breathing deepened.

A sudden banging on the door roused them both with a shock.

'My lord, my lady, there is grave news!' shouted Jean D'Earley from without.

William groaned. Rolling to the edge of the bed, he

parted the curtains. Isabelle sat up, reaching for her chemise. Grave news could come from all quarters at the moment and it was knowing where to turn to face it that was their greatest challenge. So much for her recent plea to God. William pulled on his braies and, tying the drawstring, went to unbar the door.

Jean was dressed, but his hair was sticking up in untidy spikes and his face was puffy with slumber, revealing that he too had been roused from his bed. 'My lord, King John is dead – at Newark of a flux. Jack was at his deathbed and he's sent a messenger.' Jean indicated the man standing beside him, drenched from his hard ride, shivering, grey-faced and looking close to collapse.

William's mind had yet to assimilate the news, but experience took command. 'A few moments will not matter. Get this man some dry clothes and meet me in the lower chamber. Find Walter and summon the mesnie.'

Jean bowed and left, the tottering messenger in tow. William returned to the room, leaving the door open to admit his squires and Isabelle's women. Inside the privacy of the bed hangings she had already donned chemise and undergown and was now pulling on and gartering her stockings.

'You heard what he said?'

Isabelle nodded. 'This changes everything.' She didn't say whether for better or worse. Like William she was stunned and trying to grapple with the implications. John's heir was a child of nine years old; his rival a grown man in his twenties with more than half the country backing him.

William stared at the wall as his squire knelt to wrap braid bindings around his hose and fasten the ends with ornate gold hooks. When the youth brought William's soft kidskin shoes to finish the toilet, William waved the choice

454

away. 'No, lad, my riding boots. It'll save time later and I'm going to need them.'

Isabelle suppressed her instinctive protest. He had to leave Gloucester, but at this point she hadn't been thinking that far ahead. Obviously he had. 'At least you have a thick new cloak,' she said courageously with a glance towards the rain-spattered window glass. 'We finished stitching it two days since.'

'I might be needing my hauberk too.'

Fear squeezed her heart. 'I pray not . . .'

William shrugged at her. 'I pray not too – the rivets are the devil to prevent from rusting in autumn and winter. Best to be prepared though.'

It was typical of him to make light of the moment, but she could see the serious worry in his eyes.

Once dressed, Isabelle and William attended mass, made a hasty breakfast of bread, cheese and ale, and talked to Jack's messenger. The latter, a tinge more colour to his face now, had been furnished with a dry tunic and shirt and was finishing a bowl of hot gruel. Hastily spooning up his last mouthful, he bowed to William and Isabelle, swallowed, and told them about John's death. The King had spent the night at Lynne and had complained of feeling unwell with a rolling stomach and a flux of the bowels. He had recovered sufficiently to eat a dish of fruit and drink some newly pressed cider from the local orchards but, during the night, his condition had deteriorated.

'Then we heard his baggage train had got bogged down in the Wellstream estuary at tide-turn.' The messenger dolefully shook his head. 'Men and horses drowned, carts buried to the axles, pack animals sucked under by quicksand. Half his book chests gone, the Empress Matilda's crown, his personal chapel, pieces of regalia and many

455

barrels of silver.' Fuelled by the hot food, his voice gained the relish of a storyteller.

Isabelle exchanged worried glances with William. Depending on how much had been lost, the accident to the baggage could be either a minor upset or a complete disaster.

'The King rode on to Newark Castle,' the messenger said, 'but his strength gave out and everyone knew he was dying. The Abbot of Croxton was with him at the end and heard his confession, and the Bishop of Winchester.' He looked at William. 'My lord, the King requested before witnesses that you and the Legate govern the realm on his son's behalf. He asked that you protect his son and keep him safe from French hands and he sent you this ring in token.' He unfastened a leather cord from around his neck. Threaded on to it was one of the King's favourite rings: a large balas ruby set in clawed gold. William took it from the man and cupped it in his hand. 'Go on,' he said impassively.

'There is little more to tell, my lord. When the King had made his will and the Bishop of Winchester had heard his confession, he spoke no more and, at the hour of vespers, his soul left him.' The messenger crossed himself, as did his audience. 'Some said they could hear it keening as it flew away, but the Abbot said not to be foolish, it was only the wind beating against the castle walls, and indeed the weather was very stormy. The Abbot took the King's entrails to Croxton but, as the King wished, his body is to be brought to Worcester. Your nephew is escorting the cortège and says he will meet you in the city two days hence.'

'One step at a time,' William told Isabelle as he prepared to go to Worcester and meet John's funeral train. 'I've

456

sent to Hereford for the shroud cloths. Thomas Sandford will bring Prince Henry from Devizes and, as soon as the King is buried, I'll ride to escort them here.' He rubbed his forehead as if doing so would quicken his thoughts. 'Chester and the Legate will already have messages from the deathbed at Newark, but I've written again, bidding them come to Gloucester.'

Isabelle touched his sleeve. 'But how can you carry on fighting if Henry has no money and all the south and east is in Louis's hands?'

He gave a heavy sigh. 'I can only hope the situation is better than it looks. Until I have taken an inventory, I am working blind; I don't know what resources might be else-where. Devizes and Corfe might yield revenue if we're fortunate. I'm hoping now John is dead some of the barons will return to our camp. It was John they hated, not his son. Henry's an innocent child; I can use that in our favour. Louis rewards his Frenchmen with lands and ignores many of his English lords. It's one of the reasons Will turned his back on him and I suspect others will take little persuasion to cease their allegiance. As soon as I've had time to assess the situation I'll have letters written and safe conducts issued.'

Listening to him, Isabelle's fear increased, but so did her pride. 'Many years ago,' she said, stroking his sleeve, 'you saw an assault on a keep foundering, and you climbed the siege ladder and seized the battlements yourself.'

'Milli.' He gave a lean smile. 'Richard was angry because I was first on the ladder and his men pulled him back because they wouldn't risk both of us together.' The smile vanished. 'But Richard's gone now . . . and it's a long way up that ladder.'

Isabelle pulled his head down and kissed him hard. 'I am glad we had this morning,' she said.

He squeezed her waist. 'So am I. Perhaps we should have bolted that door and stayed abed. My love, I'll be returning with Prince Henry and we'll have to hold a council here. I leave it to you to make preparations.'

'It will keep me from worrying . . . about you, anyway. Sorting out sleeping places and provisions for an unknown number is a different matter. What of the Queen?'

'She's safe at Corfe with the younger ones, and staying there for the moment,' he said. 'The last thing we need is for her or her other children to be kidnapped by the French.'

Isabelle could not help feeling relieved. Finding secure and comfortable accommodation for the household of the Queen of England as well as the Earl of Chester would have taken prodigious organising, not to say a miracle.

He kissed her again, hard, and swept out.

Isabelle touched her lips where the imprint of his mouth on hers lingered. Despite their lives being more uncertain than ever, she felt as if John's death had lifted a great weight from her shoulders. Another burden had settled in its place, but it was considerably less onerous. John's heir was a child and someone was going to have to rule in his stead. The vultures would be gathering for their share of the control and William would be in their midst. What happened in the next few weeks was in the hands of God and a few powerful men, including her husband. It was frightening, but at the same time she felt a touch of exhilaration and perhaps inevitability. All of his life, William had been travelling towards this point.

As requested at his deathbed, John wore the cowl of a Benedictine monk. The hood was buckled beneath his chin to keep the bearded jaw firm and the mouth closed.

A dalmatic of heavy red wool clothed him from neck to ankle and his right hand gripped his scabbarded sword. William had provided silk shrouds to cover the bier and enough silver for the poor waiting outside the church that they would not go away empty-handed. John's tomb was to lie in the cathedral's chancel, with Saint Oswald on his left and Saint Wulfstan on his right.

Kneeling and standing, his joints aching with cold, the Latin words of the funeral mass flowed over William's head. The ritual was comforting and here and there a word he recognised stood out, but his mind was not so much on the ceremony as his own chequered life. He had been born when Stephen was on the throne: a lifetime ago. Perhaps more than a lifetime; there were few remaining who remembered those days and the vicious civil war that had torn England apart. He had served King Henry and Queen Eleanor, the Young King, then Richard and John. Now the heir to the kingdom was a nine-year-old boy and civil war was again devouring the land. His life had come full circle. He had almost lost it at five years old when taken hostage by King Stephen. If it ended now, it wouldn't matter. He had had more than his share of years. But still he prayed the candle had a little longer to burn – enough at least to see the country out of crisis.

After the funeral, William took a brief respite to eat and drink in the Bishop's rooms at the cathedral and then, accompanied by Jack and the knights of the mesnie, set out in the direction of Devizes to greet the nine-year-old heir to England.

'The reports are true about what the King said on his deathbed,' Jack told him as they rode. 'I was there and he said he wanted you to govern until Henry comes of age. He wasn't delirious; he was aware almost to the end, God rest his soul.' He crossed himself.

William crossed himself too. 'John knew how to torture me even until the last,' he said darkly. 'The Earl of Chester is twenty years younger; let him take up the reins.' He kicked his horse, urging it ahead at a rapid trot.

Jack gazed at William's straight posture and easy seat in the saddle. Frowning, he pinched his upper lip.

'Daydreaming?' Jean D'Earley enquired with a half-smile as he rode past him.

Jack shook his head. 'I hope not,' he replied.

Standing in the courtyard of Gloucester Castle Isabelle watched William's troop arrive. William was riding his bay courser and young Prince Henry sat before him on the saddle, bundled up in the folds of William's cloak. The boy's thin face was wan from the long journey and his eyes heavy with blue smudges beneath. William leaned over and murmured to him and Henry answered with a nod, then wriggled upright.

Isabelle knelt, as did the knights, clerics and various household retainers assembled behind her. Henry looked a little nonplussed, but at another murmur from William, gestured everyone to rise. His eyes widened when everyone did. Henry was accustomed to deference because he was the heir to the throne, but full obeisance had always been for his father and mother.

Isabelle exchanged glances with William as he lowered the Prince to the ground and dismounted. 'It has been a long journey,' he said. 'In more ways than one. I think my lord the King would like to bathe and rest.'

She nodded. 'Will you come to the private chambers, sire?' she said to Henry, gesturing towards the keep.

'Thank you,' Henry replied in a stilted voice, pitched high with strain and the natural treble of childhood. His hair was the pale gold of fresh straw and his eyes the same startling aquamarine blue as his mother's. His mouth was hers too, hinting at a sulky droop, but just now held firmly straight as he strove to play his role and not appear afraid or unnerved.

When Isabelle ushered him into the castle's domestic chamber, he seemed relieved when the door closed behind them, shutting out the world. He eyed the Marshal children warily and they eyed him back with similar reserve, having been warned by their mother that this was England's future King and they were to behave themselves.

Henry was too tired to eat more than a few morsels of sops in cinnamon milk and Isabelle didn't press him. She had Ancel show him the privy and when he returned gave him warm water scented with rose oil to wash his hands and face. Removing his day clothes, she had him don a warmed nightshirt. He was a narrow slip of a child with milk-white skin and none of his father's stockiness. His pale complexion showed no trace of outdoor play and his fine frame had none of Ancel's hard wiriness, developed from days of rough games and weapons practice.

Thoughtfully, Isabelle saw him to the bed that had been readied for him. It was screened from Ancel's by a woollen curtain. The straw mattress was topped by a second one stuffed with feathers. The sheets were soft bleached linen and the coverlet was made from green silk, powdered with moons and stars in gold and silver threads, as were the bolsters. She had bought the fabric from a charming, persuasive Bristol cloth merchant, who swore it had come from a sultan's treasury in Damascus. Henry was as captivated by the design as Isabelle had been, and ran his fingers over it with tactile, covetous pleasure.

'One day, I am going to have a chamber with a ceiling like this,' he said, a determined, almost avaricious note entering his voice.

461

'I am sure it will look very fine,' Isabelle said, wondering if the child would survive to manhood and have the funds for such a project. Had he been one of her own, she would have gently pushed the hair off his smooth, white brow, but she wasn't familiar with his upbringing and was uncertain whether such a move would be welcomed. 'This must all seem strange to you,' she said.

Henry looked at her through his lashes. In the candle-light, his eyes had darkened, their startling daylight blue quenched. 'I didn't want to leave my brother or my sisters or my mother,' he said.

'I know you didn't,' Isabelle murmured. 'You have been very brave.'

He considered this, a flush tinting his pale cheeks. He was clearly not immune to flattery. 'Will I still be able to see my brother now I've to be King?'

It was the slight wobble of his chin before he controlled it that tipped Isabelle's resolution over the edge and she reached out to stroke his golden hair. 'Bless you, child, of course you will – and very soon.'

'I miss them,' he said in a forlorn voice that made Isabelle ache with maternal tenderness.

'It would be strange if you did not. I know we are not your family, but we will do our best to make you feel at home.'

He looked at her and withdrew a little into himself, stroking the shiny coverlet over and over. 'You won't blow out the candle out, will you?' he said. 'I . . . I don't like the dark.'

'No, it'll burn all night,' she soothed, wondering how much it had cost him to admit to that. 'Ancel is only behind the curtain and someone will be listening all the time. Do you want me to sit with you a while longer?'

'Yes,' he said, his whisper so soft that it barely stirred the air.

He was asleep when William arrived from the hall where he had been talking to the men. Isabelle pressed her forefinger to her lips as William came to gaze at the sleeping child. Henry's delicate features were cast in shadowy gold by the candlelight. After a moment William sighed and moved away into the main part of the room.

Isabelle tiptoed after him. 'He is a beautiful child,' she said. 'No one could look at him and not melt.'

'It's one of the few advantages he has,' he replied, sitting down and easing off his boots with a groan of relief. 'The Legate is going to anoint him King in the cathedral on the morrow. It'll be a long day for the child . . . and everyone else.'

'You are not going to wait for Ranulf of Chester?' Isabelle asked sharply.

'It would be more diplomatic, I admit, but we dare not. Louis will know by now that John is dead. This is the best opportunity he will have to seize the country for himself – while he thinks we are in disorder. We have to make Henry's coronation a fait accompli before Louis seizes the title for himself. Chester's a realist. He'll understand why we couldn't delay. As soon as he does arrive we'll smooth his dignity and discuss what to do next. Even though we crown Henry King, we can do nothing more without Ranulf's support.'

'Then come to bed,' Isabelle coaxed. 'I know you have more worries than there are eel traps in the Severn, but there is no need to dwell on them tonight. If you are to see Henry crowned and make important decisions, then you must rest.' She was filled with concern for him, but as they prepared to retire for the night, she felt a glimmer of optimism too. With John dead, the road to the future was open again, and the possibilities endless, including those of reconciliation, both the far flung and the closer to home.

The coronation in Gloucester Abbey was a dignified but forlorn affair, bereft of much of the pomp and ceremony of Westminster, although the barons present did their best with what they had. Henry's crown belonged to his mother and thus had not been lost in the Wellstream estuary. It also had the advantage of fitting his head. It was a gold circlet with simple gold finials, set with pearls interspersed with sapphires. Henry's robes were of cloth of gold that had travelled with him from Devizes and his hose were woven of scarlet samite, bound with gold garters. His throne was the Bishop's chair, the back draped with a silk cloth. The Papal Legate placed the crown on Henry's head, his hands trembling as he lowered the diadem on to the child's golden hair.

Henry was trembling too, Isabelle noticed, and judged that it was part excitement and part the result of the cold. There was a keen easterly wind and the abbey stones seemed to have absorbed its chill.

Following the ceremony, Henry was borne in procession back to the castle. The townsfolk lined the streets and cheered, but their numbers were small when compared with London and there were no flowers to strew in the path of the royal party as there had been at John's coronation on a May morning, or Richard's in sweltering August heat. Nor was there much in the way of alms to scatter among the crowd. William had donated silver from his own coffers for the event, but given the current situation, he literally could not afford to distribute too much. Isabelle had provided food for the poor in the outer ward, and seen to the distribution of cloaks and blankets to the most needy, but it was a far cry from the largesse and splendour of a coronation at Westminster.

Once within the castle, Henry's gilded regalia was replaced with lighter garments, although he insisted on keeping on the red silk hose and gold ties. A coronation feast of sorts was held, again lacking in numbers and elaboration, but at least with a variety of courses including roast boar, haunch of venison, swan, peacock and great silver salmon seethed in verjuice. The new King was very taken with the gilded nuts and the almond sugar subtlety in the shape of a crown, complete with edible gems of coloured sugar paste.

Once the formal feasting had ended, Isabelle saw Henry and Ancel to the domestic chamber above the hall. Ancel took a chess set out of one of the coffers and the boys went to sit in the window embrasure and play. Glancing at the newly anointed King as he assembled his pieces, Isabelle was reassured. Henry was still pale and heavy-eyed, but he had weathered his coronation and eaten well at the feast. From her contact with him thus far, he seemed a fastidious child, strongly aware of his rank but sufficiently disturbed by the recent turmoil in his life to be rendered more humble than was his natural wont. She hazarded that given different circumstances he could be petulant and sulky. For the moment he was being so sweet and obedient that her women adored him, and the barons were relieved, if a little wary. The word 'backbone' had not been said aloud, but she had seen it mooted in more than one pair of eyes. Personally Isabelle thought the boy had plenty of backbone. Indeed, she hazarded that he could probably outdo a mule for stubbornness on the wrong day, if he chose.

The door opened and William entered, accompanied by his nephew Jack, by Jean D'Earley, and by Ralph

Musard, a senior knight of the mesnie. The latter had a spectacular auburn moustache that looked as if Musard had frightened a cat, stolen its tail and attached it to his upper lip. William's expression was gravely thoughtful as he gestured the men to be seated on the benches set around the hearth and beckoned Isabelle to join them. She shot him a look filled with question and fear, but he shook his head at her and pointed to the bench. Mystified, anxious, she moved to sit down at the end beside Jean.

Folding his arms, William faced his audience and said, 'Derby, Aubigny and Warwick have approached me saying they will back me to govern the country on our young King's behalf.'

Isabelle's breath hissed through her teeth. Jean, Jack and Musard exchanged rapid glances with each other, then stared at William.

Jack leaned forward, his hands clasped between his knees and his gaze intent. 'What did you reply?'

'Nothing,' William said. 'I told them I needed time to think and consult with my advisers and my wife.'

An eager light appeared in Jack's eyes. 'You are a man of high reputation and great honour. Everyone trusts you and knows you will be even-handed. There's a saying that a man who does not finish what he sets out to achieve has reached only the point where his efforts are in vain. Perhaps this is what God meant you to do. I say take the post and trust in His guidance.'

William nodded impassively. He had expected Jack to urge him to the regency. 'Ralph?'

Musard stroked his bristling ginger moustache with the fondness of a besotted pet owner. 'I agree with Jack, my lord. It will increase your standing amongst the barons and I believe it will be of great advantage to the house of Marshal and all its retainers. Benefits are bound to filter down to all.'

'A valid point,' William said. Musard could always be relied upon for fiscal plain speaking – the reason he had asked him to the council. If made regent he could indeed advance his own retainers. It would only be natural to give high positions to men whom he knew and trusted. 'What do you say, Jean?'

The latter glanced at Isabelle, then straightened his spine and cleared his throat. 'My lord, I think you should let the Earl of Chester and the Bishop of Winchester take the burden. You have enough to do already. It's true you will be able to benefit your men, but others will think this too. You'll be plagued by people clamouring for patronage and privileges – and much of it at your own expense because we all know the royal treasury is nigh on empty.'

Jean's words confirmed William's own doubts and anxieties. 'You have given me both sides of the coin as I knew you would, for which I am grateful. There's a lot to think about. I need to talk with my wife, who has also heard your advice, and to sleep on the matter. We'll know better where we stand when the Earl of Chester arrives and we hear what he has to say.'

When the knights had gone, William turned to Isabelle, who was still sitting before the hearth, gazing into the flames, her cheeks heat-flushed. 'Jean's right,' she said. 'If you choose to steer the ship, you will have a difficult passage and to very little gain.'

William sighed and held out his hands, palm down, to study them. His fingers were long and firm, with no sign of a tremble, even if the skin upon them was shiny and freckled. The seal ring of the earldom adorned his left middle finger, and a sapphire ring, given to him by old King Henry, his right. 'How much strength do I have left in these?' he asked. 'Governing England is a task for a younger man such as Chester.'

Isabelle gave him a troubled look. 'Chester might have the strength to undertake the task, but men relate better to you. They are more likely to cooperate if you ask than if he does.'

He sat down beside her. 'So you too think I should take it on?'

Isabelle shook her head. 'I think the same as Jean. You have done enough. Jack and Ralph want you to put yourself forward because they see wealth and prestige for themselves, but Jean is thinking of you, the man, and so am I.' She looked at him with her heart in her eyes. 'I don't want to be the wife of England's regent if it's going to make me a widow. I don't give a fig for all the wealth and prestige in the world. It's useless without you.'

He pulled her to his side. 'Do you remember our wedding day?' he murmured. 'You didn't know me beyond a glimpse, nor I you. You were a slender girl with enormous blue eyes, hair the colour of a cornfield and a mouth that drove me to distraction because all I wanted to do was kiss it.'

Isabelle laughed through her anxiety, and gently nudged him. 'I thought you were struggling to find the courtesy to cope with a naive adolescent.'

'Innocent yes; naive no. From the moment you gave me that look, I knew you were as sharp as an awl.'

'I gave you a look?'

William chuckled. 'As shrewd and assessing as a wool merchant at a fleece auction. "Do I go with him willingly? Do I trust him? How soon is he likely to die if I don't like him?"'

Isabelle blushed because it was indeed what she had been thinking at the time.

He sobered. 'I was hoping you weren't shrewish, or vain and simpering with feathers for brains. I was worried about how you would respond to marrying a man more than twice your age and well used by life.'

Isabelle bit her lip. 'You are not more than twice my age now,' she said.

Now there was no humour in him at all. 'What I would give to have back the years we have spent,' he said.

'They have not been wasted years.' Isabelle managed to keep her voice steady. She wasn't going to cry again. 'I value every one more than gold.'

'But you can keep gold, whereas time slips through the fingers like grains of sand. If there was a way to stop the march . . .' His breathing caught. 'Ah, enough,' he said brusquely. 'I need to sleep. It's going to be a long day tomorrow whatever decision we come to.'

Isabelle knelt before him to unfasten his boots. 'Back then, at our marriage, I was ambitious,' she murmured. 'Now we are well in the saddle, I suddenly find I have no great desire to ride that particular horse.'

William gave her a wry look. 'You can't change your mind at full gallop, my love. First you have to draw in the reins, and that is as great a decision as climbing astride in the first place.'

Ranulf of Chester arrived the next morning as the barons were leaving the castle chapel after morning mass. He was greeted with due ceremony and furnished with a position at the head of the high table on the dais while the assembly breakfasted on bread, cold bacon and ale.

Chewing, Chester scowled at William, his air one of indignation bordering on petulance. 'You could not wait, one day,' he grumbled.

William returned his look equably. 'We could not afford

to let the opposition take advantage of any hesitation. With the boy made King, it strengthens our stance and weakens Louis's. We could have waited one day for your arrival, we could have waited three. I hope you understand the necessity of our action.'

Chester didn't answer. He took a sip of ale and screwed up his face. 'I don't know how you drink this muck, Marshal.'

William shrugged. 'It suits me in the morning. If you'd rather have wine . . .' He gestured a squire to replace Chester's cup with a brimming goblet.

Chester took a long drink. He ate the bread and bacon and grew noticeably more sanguine as the sustenance worked on him. William judged that half of the Earl's irritation was caused by riding hard on an empty stomach. To have missed the coronation would have ruffled his feathers too. Chester enjoyed his rituals and ceremonies.

Breakfast finished, the trestles were cleared away and deliberations upon the future rule of England commenced. Goblet in hand, Chester leaned against the high back of his chair, his dark gaze assessing and inscrutable. Peter des Roches, Bishop of Winchester, played with the ornate gold and garnet cross around his neck. He had removed his mitre and placed it on the trestle, where the gold thread in it made it twinkle like a piece of the gilded marchpane subtlety from the coronation feast. The Legate kept his on. William had never seen him without it, nor his robes of office, even late at night.

The men deliberated, arguing this point and that. Now and then William glanced towards the new King, who was not taking part in the discussions, but being kept close enough to be summoned. He and Ancel were playing with Ancel's toy wooden castle and the carved figures of the garrison knights and horses. From the snippets of conversation William overheard, Henry was fascinated by the interior rooms of the castle rather than the 'men' on the walls, and was not impressed when Ancel began piling up straw and dust to build defensive embankments.

The discussion circled back on itself. Several hints had been dropped in William's direction, and Chester's too, without conclusion. Everyone was watching everyone else. Impatience rippled through William. This was getting them nowhere. Someone had to do something. He placed his hands flat on the trestle and pushed to his feet. 'My lords, if we did not have the time to wait for a coronation, we certainly cannot afford to procrastinate here like a frightened bride running away from the bed on her wedding night. I say that my lord of Chester should accept the regency. He is young enough to give the task his full vigour, but old enough to be wise.'

Chester snorted and raised one eyebrow in ironic reply. 'I will gladly follow his lead and do everything in my power to assist him for as long as God grants me the strength to do so.'

Chester rubbed his forefinger consideringly across his top lip. After a moment he too stood up, adjusting the miniver collar of his cloak. 'Marshal, I would accept if I thought you incapable, but you're not.' He looked wry. 'Men will follow you who would baulk at taking orders from me. I have seen you keep your temper when even angels would have raged. You have Ireland which is far out of Louis's reach and from which to draw resources. I am content for you to govern the realm and in my turn I will give you what aid I can.' He bowed deeply towards William and extended his right palm, conceding him the rule.

William felt the words settle their weight on him like an invisible mantle. Heavy with expectation. Suffocating.

471

For a moment he couldn't breathe and his heart was pounding so hard he thought it might burst from his chest or beat itself to a standstill. He wondered if he was going to survive the moment. Chester would have no choice but to take over if he suddenly dropped of an apoplexy before the entire company.

'My lord Marshal?' Chester looked at him in concern.

William shook his head and drew a difficult breath, sucking it over a larynx tight with pent-up emotion. 'You hand this thing to me,' he said, 'but I hesitate to take it on.'

'There is no one better,' Chester replied unequivocally. 'In God's name, Marshal, put on the harness and be done.'

The Legate raised his voice, his French bearing the heavy accent of his native Tuscany. 'My lord Marshal, you seem reluctant to accept the regency, but no one here disputes you are the best man for the charge. Perhaps if I offered you absolution for all the sins of your lifetime, it would settle your mind. No?' He raised a thick silver eyebrow, his stare knowing and shrewd.

William stared back, his breathing rapid and his heart still slamming against his rib cage. You spider, he thought. You cunning old spider. The Legate couldn't offer William gold and riches; it was not within his power to do so. The papal authority already had all its weight behind the boy playing castles at the side of the dais, but offering William a direct path to heaven at the end of his life was a bribe of genius. What man would not desire such surety?

William opened his clenched fists and bowed his head. 'Then on those terms and given that no one else has put himself forward, I accept.' As he spoke, he felt as if the marrow had left his bones. He managed to stay on his feet, but it was a triumph of will power over body. Chester handed him a goblet. William took it, realised that his hand was shaking and, without drinking, set it down. Wine slopped on to the trestle and gathered in a glistening red pool. Drawing on all his resources, William pulled himself together to address the practical business. He didn't want congratulations and he almost resented the way that all the men were now relaxing, the weight lifting off their backs as he took it from them and set it on his own.

'The King needs a guardian and stability in his life,' he said. 'By necessity I will be constantly on the road with a battle campaign to conduct. I cannot drag him from pillar to post and if he is to be King then he needs to continue to be fitted for the task. I would suggest that my lord the Bishop of Winchester takes on this role – if he is willing.'

Peter des Roches dipped his head. 'I will be pleased to do so, my lord.'

William could tell it was more than just a polite response. The Bishop of Winchester guarded his privileges jealously and would expect a prominent role in governing the country, even if William held the reins. Des Roches had been a close confidant of John and possessed a shrewd fiscal brain. He would be useful in government. As a tutor to the King, there was no man among the gathering better suited.

The rest of the day was spent discussing the finer points of detail with William in the midst, building the edifice and hoping that it wasn't going to fall down at the first challenge like a house of straw in a puff of wind. Sometimes he was aware of Isabelle by his side, supporting him, smoothing his path, setting men at ease. On occasion, she absented herself to supervise the provision of food for the company. He would glance up and see her talking to others, applying mortar to decisions, shaping the stones of agreement, but he had no time to talk to her himself.

Dusk came and went. William's larynx was worn to a husk with talking. He was so exhausted that he could barely set one foot before the other as he made his way to his lodgings in the bailey. Isabelle studied him with covert worry as she walked beside him. Behind, she could hear Jack and Ralph talking in muted tones, but there was no mistaking the excitement in their voices. She fought the urge to turn and glare at them. For them, William's acceptance of the regency was a triumph, but she was annoyed that they were not giving a thought to their lord's wellbeing. Jean, however, walked with his head down and bowed shoulders as if he too had taken a great weight upon himself.

Once within the chamber, William leaned against the wall and closed his eyes. The candlelight lent false colour to his complexion, but the shadows in socket and cheek-bone were as dark as bruises and made Isabelle afraid for him. If this was the first day, what were the next and the next going to do to him? She had prayed that Ranulf of Chester would show willing and decisive and take on the burden, but either God had not been listening, or He had other plans.

'Here, beloved, drink.' She pressed a cup into his hands, the fact that she called him 'beloved' in front of others a sign of her agitation.

William shook his head. 'I will be sick if I do,' he said huskily, returning the cup to her.

Struggling not to cry, Isabelle gave the wine to Jack instead, who raised it in toast. 'To the regent,' he cried, his voice reverberating with triumph. The salute was echoed by Ralph and Jean.

William stared at them like a dazed stag brought to bay before hounds. 'I am going to need all of your help,' he said in an exhausted, rusty voice that barely carried across the space between him and them. 'I have embarked upon an open sea so deep that no line could sound the bottom, and with no sign of land as far as the horizon. If I reach safe harbour, it will be a miracle, because God knows, we are this close to foundering . . . this close.' He held up his forefinger and thumb, brought so near to each other that they almost touched.

Isabelle's chin dimpled. William had always called her his safe harbour, but she could not protect him now; there was no shelter from this storm – for any of them.

William's voice choked on emotion. 'As you know, the child is almost penniless. Half the King's treasury was lost crossing the Wellstream and, with the country so divided, there are no revenues to replenish the coffers. None. God knows how we are going to raise money to pay the garrisons and the troops. I am too old to carry this burden . . . I cannot . . .' He swallowed and covered his face with his hands, his shoulders shaking.

Filled with shock and distress, Isabelle hastened to him, putting her arms around him, holding him fast. In nearly thirty years of marriage this was the first time she had seen him break and it almost broke her too. Her own eyes filled and flooded. She gripped his shoulders and whispered his name as she had done to their children when comforting them in the nursery. She was aware of the men staring, open-mouthed, almost as distressed as their lord. Jean's eyes were glistening too. Against her body, she felt William's breath shuddering in and out of his chest as he strove to gain control and she was filled with a vast wave of love, compassion and tender fury that he had been brought to this.

Slowly, he straightened, and it was like a wounded man rising up from the field of battle because he knows that if he stays down he will die. He eased her gently to one side and, still breathing convulsively, wiped his cuff across his eyes. 'Is that all?' he whispered hoarsely to the three men staring at him in frozen shock. 'Have you nothing to say?'

Jean gave a loud sniff. He pressed his clenched fist to his lips. 'My lord, I know you think you have been forced to take on something too great for you, but I say not. There is still all to fight for.' He cleared his throat and jutted his chin. 'What is the worst that can happen? Even if everyone who has pledged their support to you surrenders their castles to Louis, your honour will remain intact and – my lord of Chester was right – you have your Irish lands to fall back upon. They are far enough removed from England to deter Louis from following you there. What's to lose at this late hour?'

William wiped his eyes again on the heel of his hand and breathed out raggedly. 'You are right,' he said in a voice that was choked but recovering. 'Ireland is a haven should I be forced to retreat that far.' He straightened his spine. 'Even if I have to carry the boy on my shoulders from island to island and beg for my daily bread, I will keep him from Louis.'

Listening to him, Isabelle was unable to gauge whether he believed what he was saying or whether he was putting on a pretence for the sake of his men.

'It is late,' she said with a meaningful look at the knights, 'and everyone will be astir early in the morning. We should all seek our beds.'

She saw the three men out. On the threshold, Jean hesitated, his face grave with worry. 'Will he be all right?'

Isabelle nodded with more conviction than she felt. 'I think so,' she said. 'He is just very tired.'

'He didn't want to take it on.'

Isabelle looked at him, considering, grateful for his concern. 'A part of him didn't,' she said, 'but the young knight of the tournaments still lives within him, keen to try out a new horse on a new field. Come the morning, we shall see.'

After closing the door on the men, she fetched the flask of aqua vitae from her coffer. William, who was now sitting on the bed, eyed it and her through swollen, half-closed lids.

'I thought you only gave that to the badly wounded,' he croaked.

Isabelle wiped out a wine cup with the end of her trailing sleeve and poured into it a small amount of the clear liquid. It was difficult to obtain, but occasionally came their way through their merchant contacts.

'That's right, I do, but you seemed badly wounded to me a moment since.' She handed him the cup. 'Straight down in one blow.'

He laughed bleakly. 'My voice is almost gone. If I swallow this, I will never have one again.' After a moment when he was plainly summoning his courage, he raised the cup to his mouth and tilted the rim sharply.

The next few seconds were filled with the sound of wheezing and choking, but when he had ceased to splutter, he sat up straight and looked at her reproachfully. 'That was uncalled for,' he croaked.

'I beg to differ.' Isabelle removed shoes and wimple and climbed on to the bed beside him. 'It'll warm your humours and help to balance them.' She nestled up against him.

William set his arm around her shoulders and stroked her hair. 'It's bad, Isabelle,' he said softly.

'I know . . .'

He was silent for a long time, and then he said, 'I suppose it is always darkest before dawn. If I take it on trust that this is the blackest moment, then at least I can watch the horizon for the light and not lose my faith.'

40

Gloucester, March 1217

William tipped the contents of the leather pouch on to the trestle. Isabelle stared at the gems, which glistened like giant coloured droplets of rain. There were several sapphires ranging in hue from the summer sky at midnight to dark ocean blue. Rubies, spinels, topazes and emeralds flashed beside them, some simple stones, others set in rings, brooches and crosses. There were even some incredibly rare faceted stones – an amethyst with an intense core of purple light and a pale green jewel that glittered like shards of splintered glass. The gems had arrived from the royal treasury at Corfe together with bolts of silk brocade and cloth of gold. This wealth was the final reserve of the royal family and William was using it to pay the castle garrisons and the troops in the field. The apartments at Corfe had been stripped to the bone. Queen Ysabel had protested furiously until warned in no uncertain terms that either she sacrificed her wardrobe or her son's chances of being King.

Belle and Sybire peered over Isabelle's shoulder, drawn to the siren song of the treasure trove.

'They're for the garrison at Dover,' William said drily.

Isabelle gave her daughters a swift look. Their father didn't know about the attempted ear-piercing. There had been a female conspiracy of silence on that issue. Sybire sported a faint white scar from the incident and the earrings of Byzantine gold had gone to pay the wages of the troops.

Isabelle picked up a ring set with a ruby the size of a blacksmith's thumbnail and red as blood. The object was powerful, but far from attractive. Belle wrinkled her nose in distaste.

'Covetous, my love?' William asked with a smile.

Isabelle shuddered. 'Not of this. The only thing I covet is time alone with my husband, and I know it's a treasure I'm unlikely to receive.'

'You have me for a night and a day.'

She made a face. 'I suppose a piece of bread is better than none at all.'

'That's what I keep telling the men.'

The girls and their smaller sisters had turned their attention to the fabric. Isabelle let them admire and touch while they could. Even if they made marriages of the highest order wealth like this was unlikely to be theirs and on the morrow it was going south with William and his troops.

Isabelle linked her arm around William's in a gesture of affectionate support and he responded with a distracted smile. She could tell his mind was already miles away, wrestling with the details of the coming campaign.

'The south is vulnerable while Prince Louis is in France raising more support,' he said, biting his thumbnail. 'I know he'll return and mayhap with a vengeance, but if we can regain some of the ground, he'll have to waste his new supplies on fighting for what he's lost instead of pushing on to fresh territory. If we don't launch a counter-attack now, we never will.'

'You have to do it,' Isabelle agreed vigorously, not showing the fear she felt for him.

In the weeks following his appointment to the regency, Henry had returned to his mother and siblings at Corfe. William had immediately set to work, sending out promises of safe conduct to all who wished to come and talk to him about changing their allegiance. He had offered amnesties and favourable terms for rebels returning to the fold and had reissued the great charter of Runnymede in amended form. Thus far his efforts had yielded a desultory trickle, but no one of significance had been moved to join the young King's cause. Nevertheless, against the odds, William was managing to keep the troops paid, armed and in the field. Even after nigh on thirty years of marriage, Isabelle found space to be astounded at her husband's abilities and his sheer, stubborn determination to find a way. Following that single, private show of doubt and despair, he had rallied and set out to go down with the ship. Five months later, storm-tossed, battered, sails ragged, they were still afloat and that in itself was a testament to the calibre of the man at the steerboard.

At the chamber door, William's usher cleared his throat. 'Sire, my lady . . . the Earl of Salisbury is here to see you.'

Isabelle turned; so did William.

'Marshal . . .' Salisbury had been waiting on the usher's announcement and now he moved past him into the room.

Isabelle hastened to greet him, her hand outstretched, delight on her face. 'My lord, this is indeed a welcome surprise!'

Salisbury gave a shadowed smile. 'Welcome to you, and certainly a surprise to me,' he said, but kissed her warmly on either cheek before going to William. The men clasped each other hard. Isabelle hastened to plump the cushions on the bench near the hearth, and had Belle bring wine.

'Pray,' she murmured sidelong to her daughter, 'as if your life depended on it.'

The Earl took his seat, flipped his fine emerald-green cloak out of the way, and accepted the cup Belle gracefully presented to him. 'You have beautiful daughters, Marshal,' he said. Belle lowered her lashes and looked suitably demure.

'They take after their mother,' William replied, sitting beside Salisbury.

'Not betrothed yet?'

'Given the circumstances, no.'

'Ah.' Salisbury sipped the wine and fiddled with his cloak again.

'I am pleased to see you – you know you are always welcome in my house. Have you come alone?'

Salisbury looked pensive. 'If you are asking whether I have brought other barons with me, the answer is no. My decision to come to you is mine alone. If you are asking if I have brought troops, then yes; if you want them, they are yours.'

'I take it you have left Louis?'

'I was reluctant to join him in the first place,' Salisbury said sombrely. 'I always had my reservations about Louis . . . but then I had my reservations about my brother too, and cause to leave him.' He looked towards Isabelle. 'You've heard the story about him and Ela?'

She nodded. 'Several versions.'

'He frightened her badly. She irritated him, you see, and you know how cruel he could be. He thought she took my attention away from him and he didn't like that either . . . but he didn't lie with her. That part at least is untrue.'

'So you left him because of Ela?' Isabelle asked with a woman's curiosity.

Salisbury frowned. 'That was part of it, Lady Isabelle,

but it was the other things. God knows Maude de Braose had much in common with a viper, but the way she ended her life . . .' His mouth twisted and he looked down at his wine. When he raised his head again, his gaze was bleak. 'I saw my brother say and do things that no decent man could stomach, but I loved him despite all. Even if his soul was twisted, it hurt me to desert him, but I couldn't stay. When Louis threatened to invade my lands I didn't resist him, but now my brother is dead and I have no quarrel with my nephew.' Drawing a deep breath, he turned to William. 'If we can agree terms, I offer my support to our young King, my nephew.'

'You won't find me difficult.' William's smile was thin. 'I do not have so many allies that I can afford to turn men away and, in truth, I welcome you with open arms as a friend, as well as an ally.'

'I have never counted you my enemy, Marshal, even when we have been on opposite sides. I don't know how many more will come to you, though. It will depend upon how soon Louis returns from France, and what resources he brings.'

'And how determined we are in his absence,' William said.

'Yes, that too,' Salisbury agreed. 'I will not shirk whatever's to be done. I am here to build my nephew's future, not see it destroyed.'

A week later, William and Salisbury were riding along the coast road near Shoreham, on their way to lay siege to the French-held castle at Farnham, when the scouts brought news that another troop was advancing towards them at a rapid trot from the direction of the Downs.

'It's your son, my lord, the Young Marshal,' said the soldier, looking uneasy.

The news sent a flicker of optimism to William's core. He had been hoping for a long time and sometimes it had been very hard to keep faith. Of course, there were no guarantees even now.

'Ah,' said Salisbury with the glimmer of a smile. 'I thought he might come to treat with you now Louis has gone home.'

'He hasn't been fighting for Louis since Worcester,' William said sharply.

'But neither has he come back to you. He's been staying clear, hasn't he? He's a good young soldier – well taught. Besides, it's in his blood. We could use his help.'

William drew rein and tried not to let his tension show. 'We'll wait. No point in riding further.'

Salisbury eyed him shrewdly. 'You're not going to dismount, I take it?'

'No,' William said, tight-lipped. 'He may be my son, my own flesh and blood, but I won't yield him the advantage.'

'As you wish. You don't mind if I do?' Salisbury leaped from the saddle and walked to the beach. His boots crunched on the pebbles and shingle and the fresh sea breeze made his magnificent green cloak billow around his body like a frenzied lover.

Moments later, banners approached from the landward side, silks snapping in the wind. The scarlet lion of Marshal rippled across its field of green and gold and beside it, in symbolic tribute, the blue and gold diagonals of Béthune. Sensing William's anxiety, Aethel sidled and pranced. William increased his grip on the reins until his knuckles showed white.

When the distance had closed to twenty yards, his son halted his troop. Harness creaked and jingled. The soft shush of wave over shingle was an incongruous backdrop to the strained atmosphere enveloping the road. William nudged Aethel and rode forward. Will did the same so that father and son met between their lines.

William was shocked at the changes wrought in his son since the previous summer. Gone was the youth and even the young man. The slate-blue gaze was heavy and quiet – Isabelle's, but lacking her brightness and zest. Unable to pierce its surface, William was unnerved. 'God save you,' he said and had to clear the emotion from his throat. Holy Christ, he wanted to hug his son, but dared not. For the sake of all that was at stake, he had to be cautious.

'And you, my father.' Will inclined his head. His mouth remained tight and unsmiling. The wind ruffled his dark-brown hair. There was a long silence of stares, punctuated only by the tossing and champing of their horses, the gust of the wind and the crash of wave on shore. Usually eloquent and confident, William was floundering for words. He cleared his throat again. 'I assume you are here to commit yourself to King Henry's cause?'

Will raised an eyebrow. 'Your assumption is premature. It depends on what you have to offer.'

William stared at his son in astonishment and a touch of affront. 'You want me to give you something?'

Will shrugged. 'If I join you it will weaken the French. The rift between us was much to their advantage. I have troops I am willing to put at your disposal, so I ask again: what do you have to make it worth my while?'

Nonplussed, but trying to look impassive, William folded his hands on the pommel of his saddle and stared at his son until the blue gaze finally dropped. 'What do you want?' he asked brusquely. 'What do you expect me to offer?'

Will's expression turned bleak. 'I cannot have what I

want, you know that. Tell me what you are willing to give and I will tell you if it is enough.'

Inwardly William grimaced. This was going to be more difficult than he had anticipated. There was a steely quality in Will now. He had come to bargain as an equal, not a son and a supplicant. 'You could go to Lancaster,' William said, thinking that sending Will north would keep him out of the main fight.

'No, not Lancaster,' Will said shortly. 'I would only be kicking my heels up there.'

'Huntingdon then.'

Will's shrug of response was casual, but William noticed the way his eyes narrowed. De Forz was after Huntingdon too. It went unsaid, but both men knew the reason why it might appeal. 'And Marlborough,' Will added after a moment's deliberation. 'I want Marlborough; it's ours by right.'

'And Louis wouldn't give it to you, would he?'

'I didn't leave him because of Marlborough, and I'm not returning to you for that purpose.' Restrained anger flared in Will's eyes. 'I want fair compensation, but I am no mercenary. If I am joining the young King's party it is because John is dead and it is time to move on.' His nostrils flared. 'Also I intend keeping William de Forz where I can see him. I still don't understand why he had to have Rockingham and Bytham.'

'They were bargained for his offering the support of Aumale,' William said. 'I made the decision as the regent, not from personal choice. We need his men. Besides, I will not condemn a man without proof. For whatever he is responsible, God will bring him to book.'

Will said nothing, but the set of his body and the look in his eyes were more eloquent than words.

'So,' William said, urging a conclusion, 'you will fight

for King Henry on the understanding that Huntingdon is yours, and Marlborough if you can take it.' He kneed his horse closer and held out his hand.

Will hesitated, then gave a stiff nod. 'Agreed,' he said. They clasped hands formally but did not embrace. That might or might not come later, William thought, deciding on restraint. For now their skittish mounts gave them good excuse not to fall upon each other's neck. He hoped it was at least the beginning of the end of their estrangement, but what lay in front of them now was new territory, like a sea-scoured shore after a long night of storm. Seeing them clasp, Salisbury turned from wandering the beach and walked back to them, a broad smile fixing from ear to ear.

'What do you think of his latest cloak?' William asked in an effort to lighten the atmosphere.

Will's lips curved, as if unaccustomed to the expression. 'I like the colour,' he said. 'It suits him.'

Isabelle came to Marlborough in the spring, her grey mare pacing delicately through the soldiers' lines as the first stars pricked a turquoise sky. The perriers and trebuchets were still assembled, their leather slings hanging motionless in the still evening air. Their ammunition of boulders was piled at the feet of the machines and their crews were sitting around fires and cauldrons, eating their evening meals of stew and bread. There was a lot of laughter and camaraderie. Morale was high, as well it might be. Isabelle had heard on her way from Gloucester that Will had finally broken the siege and taken the castle.

'God save you, Countess!' cried one man, bolder than the rest, with a flourish of his doffed cap.

Isabelle inclined her head, smiled and had Eustace, who was leading her escort, toss him a handful of silver.

She could see as she rode into the yard that Marlborough would need considerable shoring up. The stink of scorched wood was pervasive and the masonry had been severely punished by the siege machines. The thatching on some roofs had burned away, exposing charred skeletal beams, and two blackened heaps on the ground were all that remained of two storage buildings.

'The Earl is here too, my lady,' announced the groom who came to help her dismount. 'He arrived at noon-tide.'

Isabelle felt a flutter of pleasant surprise. As far as she had been aware, he was forty miles away at Winchester, but then it was only a day and a half's ride – less if one changed horses. It explained the extra tents she had seen in the bailey.

William and their eldest son were in the chamber above the great hall, parchments unrolled on a trestle as they pored over maps and diagrams. A pang rippled through her to see father and son with their heads close together, their voices blending in amicable discussion. She had cried with relief when William had told her that Will had made his peace and joined Henry's party, but for herself such peace had been from a distance. This was the first time she had seen him since last year at Caversham.

Will glanced up and saw her. He didn't flinch, but she felt his shock, because it hit her too and almost made her recoil. She steadied herself, put a smile on her face, and continued towards him and his father. William asked a question and when it wasn't answered, raised his head.

'Isabelle!' He stared at her, then strode around the trestle and took her hands. 'What in the name of God are you doing here?'

Noting that his eyes were filled with both pleasure and censure, she leaned forward to kiss his beard-grizzled cheek. 'Visiting my son – and my husband too, it seems. You appear to have forced open the door so I don't have to sleep in a tent.' Making an effort, she kept her tone light and turned to their son. 'Perhaps I should have stayed at Gloucester but I thought it worth the risk.'

Will's throat worked and, for a terrible moment, she thought perhaps he was trying to swallow his gorge or find the wherewithal to be civil to her. But then he leaned forward and pecked her on either cheek. 'Mother,' he said, and then: 'You are welcome, although Marlborough is hardly fit for a lady's occupation. The privies are stinking, there are no wall hangings or candles and the floor rushes are bouncing with fleas . . .' He broke off, swallowing, clenching and unclenching his fists.

Her eyes blurred. 'You think I care about that?'

'You do in your own household.' Will's voice strained at the seams.

'I can make exceptions.'

There was a long hesitation, then he opened his arms and let her in, and they embraced, clinging desperately to each other like shipwrecked sailors to a spar. Tears of joy and pain ran down Isabelle's face. Will's grip was so hard it hurt, but she didn't care about that either.

'I know there was nothing you could have done; I understand that now,' Will said thickly. 'You were there; it was someone to blame.'

'It's over, finished . . . Hush now, hush now.'

She felt him stiffen in her arms, the man not the boy. He pulled back from her and wiped his gambeson cuff across his wet eyes. 'It'll never be finished,' he said stonily, 'not while there is breath in my body. Things will never be the same either, but at least I have the wherewithal to go on . . . like that three-legged dog Mahelt used to have.'

'Tripes.' She gave a tremulous smile. 'His name was Tripes.'

Will returned her smile. 'So it was,' he said. 'And a kindred spirit.'

'Will sent me a message to say that Marlborough was ready to fall,' William told her as they shared his camp bed in the chamber below the wall walk. 'I thought to help in the final assault but by the time I arrived the garrison had surrendered and Will had taken possession.' He pulled her close. 'What I hadn't bargained for was seeing you here too.'

'I wanted to talk to Will.' Lying against him, Isabelle played with the laces on his shirt. 'I knew he wouldn't come to Gloucester, so I came to him.'

'You're a brave woman, my love.'

She raised on one elbow to look at him, trying to decide if he was being wry, but despite the limewashed walls lending a pale gleam to the room and the shutters being open to an outside world of deep-blue sky and full, high moon, his features were difficult to read. 'No,' she said, 'just a mother. I can no more walk away from that than I can from myself.'

'No,' he agreed, 'and I meant it.' He rubbed her arm and sighed. 'I have to return to Winchester on the morrow. I wish I didn't.'

'I will come with you,' Isabelle said. 'The children do not need me at Gloucester and they have carers and attendants aplenty.'

William grunted with irritated humour. 'And you consider I need more care than my offspring?'

'Of a certainty,' Isabelle said. 'And before you say it is too dangerous and you do not want me travelling in the army's tail, I will forestall you with Ireland and Kilkenny.

I will remind you how I followed you to Normandy when I was carrying Will in my womb.'

The bed shook as he silently chuckled. 'Baldwin used to worry for me – do you know that? – God rest his soul. He said that he admired you, but you were in danger of not knowing your place. He said I indulged you too much.'

Isabelle considered indignation and decided against it. 'And I was fond of Baldwin,' she replied. 'He was a good man, but he wore a blindfold when it came to women. Had I been wed to him, either he would have strangled me within a year, or I would have put hemlock in his dinner. I do know my place, and it is at my husband's side.'

'I was not going to refuse you for it would be a waste of time. Ride with me if you will, but be prepared to ride hard, live out of a tent and eat pottage every day.'

'It sounds idyllic,' she said lightly. 'I will wash your clothes and lie with you under the stars every night.'

He laughed at that and set his arm around her. 'A laundress. Now there's a whimsical notion. I've never lain with a laundress before.'

41

Winchester, April 1217

Florence the laundress puffed into the tent and piled a heap of folded shirts, chemises and sundry linens on to William's campaign trestle. ''Ere we are, my lady. Good fresh breeze today. You can smell the sun on 'em.' She thrust one of William's shirts under Isabelle's nose.

Isabelle nodded. All she could smell was a strong but not unpleasant aroma of lanolin and lye from the Bristol soap Florence used in solution to pummel the washing, but she had learned from experience it was best to agree.

Florence had been King John's washerwoman, but she had been dismissed by the Queen who viewed her as one of John's little idiosyncrasies that need not be indulged now he was dead. Taking pity on her, William had given her employment in his household and Isabelle was gradually becoming accustomed to her sudden appearances, as blustery and swift as a bright windy drying day. William's comment at Marlborough about never having lain with a laundress had greatly amused Isabelle when she first laid eyes on the woman. Florence was at least six feet tall and as wide as a barn. The size of her hips would have put the rump of the strongest destrier to shame; her breasts were doughy mountains that could have smothered a giant and her forearms were like a pair of prize hams. A mass of frowsy black hair was constantly escaping the decency of the kerchief supposed to conceal it and her complexion was so red and coarse she looked as if someone had used her face to scour pots.

''Eard some interestin' news over by the 'orse lines, my lady,' Florence said as she refolded the shirt with a delicacy and dexterity belied by her large, rough fingers. The loving way she smoothed the garment made Isabelle bite her lip as she wondered if Florence had touched John's underwear in so intimate a fashion.

'Did you?' Isabelle half suspected Florence's usefulness to John had been as much for her knowledge of who was sleeping with whom and plotting what than it was for washing his underclothes.

'I reckon we'll be on the move soon enough.' Florence licked her lips and eyed the dish of stuffed dates on the trestle.

Taking the hint, Isabelle gestured to them. Predictably Florence took two. 'What did you hear . . . ?'

Florence contemplated the first date, then nibbled it with a dainty lasciviousness that would have brought most men out in a sweat. 'The French 'ave landed at Sandwich, 'aven't they? Messenger was givin' 'is 'orse to a groom an' I 'eard 'im say so. Masses of ships filled with 'orses an' men an' barrels o' supplies. They'll be marching on Winchester to take it back, that's what I reckon.'

The news was a blow. Isabelle didn't need to ask if Florence was certain. If she had heard a messenger say so, then it was true. She thought of all their hard work to retake Winchester and the ports of Winchelsea and Rye. If Louis had indeed brought a massive army across the Narrow Sea, then Henry's forces would be unable to hold.

493

Florence popped the remainder of one date in her mouth, put the other in her apron and, chewing vigorously, made to leave. 'Better pack me mule,' she announced stickily. 'We'll be movin' before the day's much older . . . my lords.' She dipped a coy curtsey to William as she deliberately squeezed her way past him and Jean D'Earley in the tent entrance.

Isabelle saw from the expression on William's face that Florence was right. 'I've heard.' She pre-empted him.

Removing hat and cloak, William flung them over a stool. 'All we needed was a few more days,' he said in a voice gritty with frustration and anger. 'Just enough to turn the tide. Instead, the tide has turned for Louis and blown him back to us with more men and supplies than we can withstand.' He poured himself wine, drank and banged the cup down on the trestle, causing the wood to vibrate. 'I've called a council of the senior commanders, but the only matter to discuss is how far we pull back and to where. We can't hold Winchester and he'll move straight to retake it. God's life, we'll have to abandon all this.' He gestured towards the battle-camp outside the tent flaps. As he spoke, Florence wallowed past with her mule, its panniers laden with her washing cauldrons.

'Do you know their numbers?' Isabelle asked.

'Not yet, apart from enough to sweep us to kingdom come if we ride to meet them. I've sent out my scouts and spies and I'm liaising with the garrison at Dover. That's the plum Louis really wants, but whatever the cost, he can't be allowed to pluck it, or else whatever we do it's the end.'

Isabelle bent over William's open palm and in the light from the window attempted to dig the splinter of wood out of the fleshy part with one of her sewing needles.

494

The sliver had entered slant-wise and was visible as a thin dark line under his skin. The culprit was a rough tent prop he had grasped while doing the rounds of the troops who were encamped in the bailey of Northampton Castle.

'At least it wasn't on a privy seat,' Isabelle said as she probed and dug. 'Have you seen them? They're terrible!' Then she laughed to herself. 'Not that matters like privy seats are of much importance just now.'

Her remark brought a preoccupied smile to his lips. 'They would be if I had splinters in my arse. Instead I have Louis and his reinforcements.'

Isabelle made a face. Messengers had been coming and going all day and William had scouts out seeking the French and trying to gain intelligence of their movements. Louis had moved swiftly on Winchester and Farnham, retaking them in the face of little resistance. Then, supposedly, he had turned his attention to the siege of Dover. However, at dawn this morning, William had received reports that French troops were in Leicestershire and had driven the Earls of Chester and Derby away from the castle of Montsorrel which they had been besieging, forcing them to retreat in the direction of Nottingham. Information was badly muddled and William needed more detail before he decided where to commit himself. For the moment he was in Northampton, covering as many cross-roads as possible, and waiting.

Isabelle teased the end of the splinter from the entry wound and, with the tips of her fingernails, succeeded in pinching it out. 'If Louis has brought his men to Montsorrel, does that mean Dover has fallen to him?' she pondered.

William sighed at her question. 'That I don't know. If Dover has fallen and he has moved north en masse, then it is bad for us. I cannot see Louis breaking camp and riding to break the siege of Montsorrel without having secured Dover, but I must be certain of the reports before I move.'

Isabelle rubbed the splinter wound with salve and looked at him from beneath her lids. He could have had the chirugeon or one of his men dig it out had he been so minded; their eyesight was probably much better than hers. The fact that he had come to her meant he needed her company and her counsel. She felt warmed by the knowledge, but worried too. He didn't bring niggling anxieties to her, only the greater ones. What if Dover had indeed been taken? Could they weather such a drastic setback? She smoothed in the last of the salve and looked at his hands. His fingernails were grimed from handling his greasy hauberk. There was a smut of oil on his cheek too.

'Hubert de Burgh would have fought to the last and Dover is heavily fortified,' she said as she gently wiped away the latter with the side of her thumb. 'I do not believe Louis would have taken it in so short a time. Either it was an isolated band at Montsorrel, or the reports are exaggerated. The French must still be in the south.'

'Mayhap. I'll find out soon enough.' He rose to his feet and went to look out of the window. 'I am hoping against hope,' he said softly, 'that Louis has done the unthinkable as a commander and split his troops.'

Seeing the tension in his shoulders she realised why he had come to speak to her. It was a hope so brave, so tenuous, that it was also a huge fear. Without concrete knowledge, it was as much speculation as the other scenarios.

'And if he has?' She returned her needle to its ivory case and dropped it in her sewing casket.

'Then we stand a fighting chance.'

Isabelle gnawed her lower lip. 'It will depend where he has deployed himself and how he has arranged the split,' she said.

'Yes, it will, but even so any kind of division goes some way to our advantage.' Turning from the window he paced the room to release the congestion of energy and frustration building inside him. 'We should know by noontide at the latest.'

'And if he has divided his army, where will they go after Montsorrel?'

That answer came slightly later than William had predicted, in the middle of the afternoon as the main meal of the day was being eaten in the great hall. William's appetite seldom suffered, whatever the situation, and he was determinedly forcing his way through a slice of pigeon pie and a dish of wild fungi when Hywel arrived, sweat-drenched and staggering from his hard ride. William forced down the mouthful he had been chewing and urgently beckoned him to the high table.

'Yes, my lord!' Hywel gasped, bowing to William, his expression ablaze with the tidings he bore. 'Prince Louis has divided his army. He remains in Dover, but has sent a thousand men north with the Count of Perche. They've retaken Montsorrel and gone on to Lincoln to aid the rebels besieging the castle.'

Isabelle saw the colour come up in her husband's face and the glow in his eyes. She felt his triumph with him, but she knew fear too. She had no delusions about the 'fighting chance' of which William had spoken. He meant it literally.

The tower room in Newark Castle where John had died held no ghosts, for which Isabelle was grateful. She had half expected to be disturbed by the King's unquiet spirit wandering the nocturnal watches, but the atmosphere was quiet and if she had not slept particularly well the previous night, it was owing to spectres of her own rather than those left by the departed.

It was the Wednesday eve before Whitsuntide, the air soft and poignant with the green scents of late spring. Beyond the river and the towering castle walls, the town itself heaved with activity as the young King's army rested for a day and prepared to march on Lincoln. Escorted by her chaplain, a household knight and two of her women, Isabelle went among their men and spoke to them, finding their mood tough and resolute. There was anticipation and nervousness, but no talk of defeat. The Legate had promised every man full remission and pardon for his sins if he fought for King Henry. The French, on the other hand, had been excommunicated and thus were bound for hell.

Florence had taken advantage of the day's rest and the fine spring weather to scrub a pile of linens at the riverside with other washerwomen from the camp. Isabelle saw her from a distance, her heavy arms pounding the dirt from the garments as mercilessly as the troops swore they were going to evict the French from Lincoln. Her wimple was bound with a red ribbon today and Isabelle could hear her voice raised in a raucous washing song. Her high spirits were infectious and Isabelle began to smile.

'You find the sight of washerwomen amusing, my lady?' Ranulf of Chester asked, joining her. His tone was brusque and she thought he seemed irritated. She knew he had been chagrined at being forced to retreat from Montsorrel. Folk were treating him gingerly at the moment. Ranulf had many fine qualities, but was renowned for his sulks and his fierce pride. He too had obviously been inspecting

498

his men for two of his senior knights were with him and a couple of serjeants from the lower ranks.

'Entertaining when it's Florence,' Isabelle said, nodding towards the woman. 'A dozen of her in our front ranks and the French would not stand a chance.' She had made the remark in jest, so was taken aback when Chester scowled and reddened. 'Have I spoken amiss, my lord?'

He eyed her narrowly, then sighed out hard, his tension easing. 'No, Countess, or not that you would know. I have been talking matters of protocol with other members of your family concerning our march on Lincoln.'

'My lord?'

'Your eldest son desired to be in the front rank with the men of Normandy.'

'I see.'

'Do you, my lady?'

Knowing Chester's character, Isabelle laid a hand on his sleeve. 'Indeed, my lord, I do,' she soothed. 'It is only right that more experienced men should take the lead, but you cannot blame the younger ones for their eagerness. As Countess of Pembroke, I am glad that my heir is keen and bold, but as a mother, I would rather not have him the first to charge out.'

Chester grunted and looked slightly mollified. 'Well, you have your wish,' he said. 'It has been agreed I will deal the first blows – as it should have been from the start.'

'Then I am glad, my lord,' Isabelle said sweetly. 'It is only fitting a knight of your prowess and experience should do so.'

Following her encounter with Chester, Isabelle made her way thoughtfully back to the castle. She knew William would be busy about his concerns as battle commander and did not expect to see him for most of the day, but shortly before the dinner hour, he came to their chamber to change into his court tunic.

As he washed his face and hands, Isabelle told him about her encounter with Chester.

William blotted his face on a towel and sighed at her. 'Ranulf is suffering from an excess of bile,' he said. He thrust his arms into the shirt of fine bleached linen his squire held out for him, and pulled it over his head.

'Did Will say he wanted to head the troops?'

'In so many words. The Norman contingent came to him and said that since he was born in Normandy they would be pleased to have him lead them and deal the first blows. As soon as Chester heard, he objected.' William took his tunic from the youth, his Irish one of cloth of silver, Isabelle noticed. Obviously he was intending to show Chester at dinner there was more than one magnate who could throw his weight around if he chose. 'In fairness I can understand it from Chester's point of view,' he said judiciously. 'He's still smarting over having to retreat at Montsorrel. He was willing to let me take the brunt of the responsibility for the country because he knew men would follow me more readily, but he won't have my son, a former rebel, taking precedence when we reach Lincoln.' He laughed but with annoyance. 'I've even heard rumours that he thinks I should stay back and let him command the men – phrased diplomatically, of course, and mouthing concern for my age.'

Isabelle refrained from saying it might be a good idea. Chester was not the only one to have his pride. And more than pride: William was wholly competent to perform the task. Indeed, perhaps his whole life had been leading up to this moment. 'It would be a disaster,' she said quietly.

He smiled as he latched a belt at his hips. The braid was woven with thread of gold and decorated with rows of overlapping bezants. 'I wouldn't go so far as that, but if Chester had wanted this task, he should have taken on the regency himself. Let him ride at the front if that be his wish, but I will not relinquish the reins . . . not yet. He keeps threatening to leave us – to go on crusade – but I will not be browbeaten and he knows it.'

'And Will?' she asked. 'What does he say of Chester's words?'

His smile faded. 'Will has been through the fire. To him it is no more irritation than a stray spark. He knows what's at stake is not worth a petty quarrel over who strikes the first blow.'

'Then I am glad for his good sense.' She had been tidying her own garments while they spoke, changing her outdoor wimple for a veil of fine lavender-coloured silk, which her maid had secured to the delicate net beneath with gold pins, and now she was ready to accompany him to the hall. However, he made no move towards the door.

'What?' she asked. Her unease increased when he came to her and took her hands in his.

'I don't want you travelling on to Lincoln with the baggage train.'

Isabelle shook her head, feeling fear, pushing it down. 'I have come this far; you will not put me aside now. It is my right to be with you.'

He gazed down at his hands upon hers. 'If it goes badly for us and we must run, I need you to be free and clear. You will know what to do to rally our vassals. Perhaps it is selfish of me too, but I do not want to be worrying about your safety when I am in the thick of the battle. If I know you are not in danger, then my mind will be better fixed upon what I have to do.'

She stared at him with indignation. 'But it will be all

right for me to worry about you and Will from a distance, unable to be there if you are hurt or in need?'

He was silent for a time and when he spoke his voice was hoarsely soft. 'It is what will help me the most. God help me, I can bear to part from you here, two days' ride from battle, but I think it would break me if I had to do so before going in to fight. You may be strong enough, but I am not.'

His words melted her, even while she knew he was being diplomatic. 'Do not be so sure about my strength,' she said tremulously. 'I need you to sustain it.'

Giving her a tender look, he stooped to kiss her. 'And you have me, even at a distance. You have been further away than this – much further.'

She held him tightly, knowing he was right. During the fight for their Irish lands, they had been separated not only by the sea, but by differences of opinion that had threatened to shipwreck their marriage. But they had survived both and emerged the stronger for the tempering.

A squire arrived at the chamber door to announce that the dinner horn had sounded and that the gathering in the hall awaited their presence.

Isabelle released William and wiped her eyes on the absorbent cuff of her linen undertunic.

He smiled ruefully. 'We had better make haste,' he said, 'otherwise Ranulf of Chester will think we are deliberately being late to make a grand entrance and steal the attention.'

The following morning King Henry's army assembled outside the castle and made ready to leave. The Papal Legate was riding to the royal fortress at Nottingham, which was more secure than Newark, and Isabelle was accompanying his entourage. She had already bidden farewell to William, who, as senior commander, was occupied among the men, but she still had their eldest son to wish on his way.

'Have a care, Will,' she said as she clasped him beside his stallion. 'Don't do anything rash.' Under her hands, the rivets of his mail shirt were cold. All the men were riding in armour as they drew nearer to the enemy. Those who couldn't afford the protection of mail were wearing tunics of padded leather and linen.

Will smiled gravely. 'I think I'm beyond rash now, Mother.'

'Well then, guard your father and don't let him over-reach himself!'

He gave her a steady look. 'I will let him do as he wishes,' he said. 'He has the right, don't you think? Don't fret. We'll look out for each other. He'll have Jean and Ralph and my cousin Jack around him. It is what he wants to do.'

Isabelle found a wan smile. 'I know that. He is on familiar ground and it is what he was trained to do. I am not afraid for him . . . but for myself.' She gestured with her hand as if releasing a hawk into the air. 'Go with God, both of you.'

'I pray so.' Impatient to be away now, he hitched his scabbard to one side and turned to his stamping stallion.

'Will . . .'

'Mother?' He gained the saddle and leaned to adjust his stirrup. Someone started to speak to him but he gestured them to hold.

'Just tell him to remember the woman who waits. Send to me as soon as you have news, whatever its nature.'

His expression softened. 'Immediately,' he replied. 'Hywel has his instructions on that score already, and a good fresh horse.'

Isabelle stood with the castle garrison, the men, their wives and children, to watch Ranulf of Chester lead the troops out of Newark, followed by her husband and son riding side by side with the Earl of Salisbury on their right, and Peter des Roches, Bishop of Winchester, bringing up the rear with his three hundred arbalesters. The street vibrated to the clop of hooves, the rumble of carts, the tramp of feet. Her vision filled with the sight of mail and weaponry, blurring and blending as she stared too hard and her eyes began to water. She wanted to imprint the image of William and her son on her mind as a keepsake, but when she tried, all she could see was the hard carapace of their mail and accoutrements.

After they had gone Isabelle was left staring at the empty road, the settling dust, the piles of manure which enterprising townsfolk were rushing to scoop up. At the back of her mind was the terrible thought that she might never see them alive again and all she would remember of this day were the heaps of dung in the road.

42

Lincoln, May 1217

The flat plain to the north of Lincoln had been a battle-field over seventy years ago when the forces of the Empress Matilda had defeated King Stephen in vicious, hard-fought combat, and it was here, on the same blood-haunted field, that William and Chester halted the troops and drew up their ranks.

Lincoln itself stood on a ridge above the River Witham, with the castle and the cathedral at the high northern edge and the town running down from the high ground to the river in a steep drop, all surrounded by the city wall. On the west side, the castle and town shared the wall. The French held the town and were currently besieging the castle. Its female constable, the indomitable Nicolaa de la Haye, was mounting a spirited defence. Despite a harsh pounding by trebuchets and constant assault from the French, the castle remained unbroached and defiant.

William dismounted from his courser and sent the lighter horse back to the baggage lines, replacing it with Aethel, knowing if it came to a hard fight, his life might depend on the stallion.

'We want twice as many men,' Will muttered, exchanging his own palfrey for his chestnut destrier. 'Even split as they are, the French have more soldiers. I know God is on our side, but even so we will have to deal with two of them to every one of us.' He took the costrel of wine handed to him by William of Salisbury, removed the stopper and drank deeply.

William studied the grooms and squires bringing destriers through the lines to their owners and looked thoughtful. 'The French may have seen our approach, but they don't know how many we have.' He took the costrel from his son and put it to his lips. The wine was smooth and rich, and had travelled remarkably well, given that most vintages usually turned to vinegar in less time than it took to cart them out of the vineyard.

'What are you thinking?' Salisbury asked.

William handed back the wine. 'We might be able to fool them into thinking our numbers are greater than they are.' He wiped his mouth. 'Raise the banners in the baggage camp, have every squire and groom don what spare armour there is. Make it look as if we have a strong reserve.'

Salisbury pouched wine in his cheeks, considered and slowly nodded. 'It could work. Certainly it'll cost nothing to try.'

William had the word passed back and soon a forest of banners and spears sparkled and rippled amid the baggage lines. The Earl of Chester cantered up to William on his destrier, its coat the colour of hoar frost, mail barding jingling on the breast-band. The horse stood almost sixteen hands at the withers. Chester, being of modest stature, used every advantage he could get.

'Good strategy, Marshal,' he said with a stiff nod towards the reserve 'army'.

506

'Wine, my lord?' offered Salisbury.

Chester hesitated, then accepted the costrel and drank. As he swallowed, a horn blared the alarm.

'They're coming!' bellowed a knight on lookout detail, his voice high and breaking with strain. 'The French are coming!'

Men scrambled to mount horses and grab weapons. Spears rattled to attention; shields were braced on left arms. The Bishop of Winchester arrayed his crossbowmen in a long line to the right of the English troops, ready to shower arrows on the French should they charge.

A glittering array of mounted knights was emerging from the north gate, the banners of Poissey, de Quincy and Perche fluttering at their head. William stared at them. Thomas, Count of Perche, was his kin and last time he had seen him was at the French court. Now they were facing each other across a battleground and each would do what he must.

The silence and the tension drew out as the French made no move to engage, and William held his men in abeyance. He glanced towards Chester's contingent and was reassured. The Earl might desire to strike the first blow but he had himself and his troops under control. No one was about to charge out and get picked off.

There was a stir of activity at the head of the French line and de Quincy and the Count of Perche rode forward, each accompanied by heralds bearing banners. William signalled to Chester and together they rode out with their own heralds to the middle ground between the armies. When a few yards apart, the men drew rein and faced each other. A warm summer wind rippled the horses' barding and billowed the knights' surcoats. William's hair blew about his face. Thomas of Perche was wearing an arming cap and Saher de Quincy's blunt features were framed by a mail coif. All set for battle, William thought, and aiming for intimidation. He almost smiled at the ruse.

'God's greeting, my lords,' he said.

De Quincy muttered a less than gracious response into his ventail, but Perche answered courteously. 'And to you, Marshal, and my lord of Chester. This is a sad day when I find myself facing kin in battle, especially a battle that can be avoided.'

'Indeed so, my lord,' William replied. He was aware of de Quincy eyeing up the royalist troops, gauging strength, numbers and morale. William was tempted to glance over his shoulder and see if the baggage wains looked sufficiently convincing, but held his gaze steady on his cousin.

'You know you cannot win this battle,' Perche said.

'You are wrong,' Chester retorted scornfully. 'You have been excommunicated by the Papal Legate and stand in peril for your souls. How many of your men want to go to hell today?'

The Count flushed and anger sparked in de Quincy's eyes.

'The castle is held against you,' William said on a more diplomatic note. 'If you surrender to us now, we will deal leniently with all.'

De Quincy laughed. 'By Christ, Marshal, has old age withered the single wit you have left? You must have pushed your horses to get here but ours are as fresh as the dew.'

'Do you want to take that risk?' William asked impassively.

Perche waved his hand. 'You cannot win, my lord. If we choose not to fight in the open, all we have to do is retreat behind our walls and wait for Prince Louis to bring up reinforcements. Sit out here and besiege us for as long as you dare; it won't do you any good.'

'If I am not master of Lincoln town by nightfall, then may God abandon me,' William retorted. 'I give you one last chance to surrender.'

Thomas of Perche smiled. 'You know I have to decline and in my stead offer the same to you.'

'Ach, this is a waste of time,' growled de Quincy, turning his horse around.

William and his second cousin looked at each other, then briefly clasped hands. 'As God decides,' Perche said. He held out his hand to Chester too, who accepted it briefly, gripped and withdrew.

Perche cantered after de Quincy and William and Chester returned to their lines where William's captains were waiting.

'They won't fight on the plain,' William said to the gathered men. 'They'll depend on the city walls to keep them safe.'

'How do you know?' demanded the mercenary captain Faulkes de Breauté.

'Because they were both counting our men and noticing our "reserve",' William replied. 'They won't charge with the numbers so equal because for all their talk there is no assurance of victory.'

'And if they retreat behind the walls? We don't have the grace of time to set up siege machines. Louis will be upon us within a couple of days.'

'No,' said Peter des Roches, joining the discussion. In place of his gilded mitre, he wore an iron cap and the mail and surcoat of a knight. 'There's an entrance to the west of the castle that's been blocked up since the trouble began and never properly sealed. If we can draw the French away by feints and ruses, we may be

509

able to break into the town at that point and unite with the castle garrison.'

William eyed des Roches keenly. 'Just how good is your information, my lord bishop?'

'Good enough.' Des Roches's breathing had quickened. 'Let me take one of my knights and reconnoitre. There's another gate further along at the corner of the castle. If I make contact with those within and tell them what we intend, they can give us archery cover.'

'Go then,' William said with a rapid gesture. 'And I'll send others out to inspect the walls for gaps we might use.'

The Bishop turned swiftly to his horse. William looked round at the other commanders. 'If the Bishop is right and we can break through that blocked gate, we will need to concentrate attacks at other parts of the wall to draw off the French.'

'I'll take the North Gate,' Chester said immediately. 'It's the main thoroughfare from that side of the city, and it wouldn't just be a ruse. I would hope to break through.'

William nodded. 'As you see fit.' He swung to de Breauté. 'You enter the castle with your men and penetrate the town through the East Gate. Put the arbalesters on the castle walls to shoot down at the besiegers. The French will be forced to split themselves between defending the North Gate and their position outside the castle. While they are doing that, I, my son and the Earl of Salisbury will break down the West Gate – if the Bishop of Winchester is right about it being easily broachable.'

De Breauté gave a warped smile. 'You make it sound simple, Marshal.'

'It is,' William said. 'It is what we must do and we have to succeed.' He handed the wine to de Breauté. It was a gesture of acceptance, something that seldom came de Breauté's way. He was not born of the aristocracy,

510

had had to fight his way up from lowly beginnings and often that fight had been bloody, dirty and underhand, but through it all he had remained loyal to King John. It was because of that loyalty now that William offered him a drink.

The mercenary took the costrel, gulped and wiped his mouth. 'Thank you, my lord Earl,' he said, holding William's gaze as an equal before he turned to his stallion. 'I'll go and ready my men.'

Within the hour, the Bishop of Winchester returned from his reconnaissance with the information that the blocked-up gateway could be broken down. 'It's filled with rubble and mortar,' des Roches said, 'but it will yield to a good battering ram or a few blows from a well-aimed trebuchet. The French have got more siege machines than Agamemnon had before the walls of Troy. One of the garrison knights managed to guide me into the castle, but stones and masonry are falling all around and there are many dead and wounded. They're in perilous straits and I fear if we don't take the town soon, the castle will fall.'

'Did you speak to Lady Nicolaa?' William asked.

Des Roches nodded. 'The lady is in fighting spirits, but needless to say relieved to see us. She says she will do all she can, and if the French break through, she will take up weapons herself and fight on the battlements.' His expression was slightly disapproving. Whilst Lady Nicolaa's defence of the castle was laudable, there was a fine line between being doughty and acting the termagant.

William looked wry. 'I do not doubt she would. She has the stoutest heart of any woman I know . . . saving my wife, of course.'

'I doubt your wife would ever need saving, Marshal,' Chester remarked without expression.

William grinned. 'From herself sometimes,' he said. Although the humour lightened the moment, his thoughts were not upon the jest, but the task in hand. The success of their assault on Lincoln depended on luck, timing and their ability to stand hard. And their success or failure would decide England's sovereignty. It was like being on the siege ladder at Milli, he thought: run for the battlements and don't look down, because looking down meant taking eyes and mind off one's goal and realising how great the drop was.

The leaders mounted up, spoke to their seconds and organised their contingents. Chester was the first to go, bringing up the siege ladders and great ram towards the North Gate, behind the protection of great circular targes fashioned from woven withies. De Breauté followed with the Bishop of Winchester, taking the detail of arbalesters and cutting towards the entrance where the castle and city wall met on the western side. William rode with de Breauté, but did not intend following him and the crossbowmen into the castle. A crash of stone shattering on stone came from within the compound as yet another missile from a French trebuchet struck its target.

'Godspeed,' William said to de Breauté, clasping his hand.

The mercenary gave him a broken-toothed grin. 'In through the jaws of hell and out through the Devil's arse,' he quipped. 'Don't be too long about breaking through that wall. I don't want to fry my cods in the heat of battle.'

The castle defenders opened the gateway to admit de Breauté and his troop. Moments later the crossbowmen appeared on the battlements and the first quarrels began spitting down on the French besiegers. Cursing and yelling the French drew back; the instant they did, de

Breauté sallied into the town through the eastern gateway. Horns blew the advance, battle cries rang out and the clash of sudden, intense fighting carried back to William and his men. For the moment the stretch of wall over the West Gate was bereft of defenders as the French raced to deal with the assaults on the north and east sides.

William signalled for the battering ram to be brought up and applied to the blocked gateway. 'Hard as you can, lads!' he urged the men.

'Don't worry, my lord!' the team leader shouted back irrepressibly. 'We'll swive like sailors fresh in port after three months at sea! There's no barrier we won't breach!'

The ram snout smashed against the mortared stone with a dull boom and a cloud of dust and rubble puffed around the iron head, spiked with larger slivers of stone. 'Fetch my helm!' William commanded his squire as the ram withdrew and thudded again, releasing another shock of stone and cement. Cracks appeared, striating the work in the centre of the wall like jags of petrified lightning. The men took up a rhythm, shouting and pounding, their chants cheerfully obscene.

On the walls a lone French arbalester saw them and, bellowing the alarm, shot at the soldiers on the ram. The quarrel thudded into the oak trunk, burying deep, the feathered end trembling. The arbalester stooped to load his bow for another attempt and the ram struck up against the wall. Stone shuddered and broke, mortar crumbled and at the next blunt thrust the ram burst through and the soldiers rushed to clear cut stone and rubble from the entrance. The arbalester on the walls rose to shoot again, but was forced to duck as one of William's Welsh bowmen retaliated.

William fretted Aethel. His heart was pounding and

his mouth was dry. A lifetime ago, he had fought the French in the streets of the Norman town of Drincourt. He had lost his horse that day and been wounded during the battle. It had been his first taste of blade-on-blade combat and the occasion when he learned that beyond the practice bouts of squirehood, beyond the play jousts on the training ground, he had a natural, deadly talent at his fingertips. Even now the surge tingled through him and the blood in his veins remembered. There was a fresh horse beneath him and he felt as if he were one and twenty again. It wouldn't matter if he died today.

The arbalester had been joined by two companions. Bolts whizzed overhead, one bouncing off the iron face of the ram, another striking into a shield and splintering through to the other side. William threaded his arm through his own shield straps and prepared to charge.

'No, my lord,' said the Bishop of Winchester urgently. 'We should wait. Who knows how many are waiting through that gap? De Breauté may not have drawn them all off yet. We dare not risk it. At least send in a few men to reconnoitre.'

'No,' William snarled as another crossbow quarrel sang overhead. 'By the time they've done so, French reinforcements will have arrived. I will tarry no longer.'

'My lord, your helm!' cried the squire as William made to spur Aethel into the gap. The youth dashed forward with William's helmet.

'Jesu God,' William hissed through his teeth with self-irritation as he snatched the helm from the youth and jammed it on his head. The squire hastened to help him lace it to his hauberk.

'You'll be forgetting your head next,' Will said laconically, his own voice emerging muffled through his visor guard.

514

'Losing it more likely,' William retorted with self-deprecating humour. 'A good thing Chester isn't here to see it.' He saluted his son with his sword. 'God be with us.'

'Amen.' Will kissed the hilt of his own sword and flourished the cross guard at his father.

Abruptly William turned, lashed the reins down on Aethel's neck and plunged through the dusty gap into the town of Lincoln. There were few to meet them in the initial charge, for the French were engaged either in defending the North Gate against the Earl of Chester, or battling with the contingent led by Faulkes de Breauté in the streets around the east side of the castle. Easily sweeping aside the small resistance they met, William's force galloped down Westgate Street, swung right and met the French who were still engaged in assaulting the castle's southern wall.

'Marshal, Marshal, God is with the Marshal!' roared the Bishop of Winchester at the top of his lungs, as if by doing so he could win the Almighty's ear. William felt Aethel's fluid power beneath him and the stallion's strength and vitality seemed to flow into him too. He dug in his spurs and the destrier hit full stride, the mail breast-band swishing like a silver curtain as they struck the French besiegers. William's sword sang and descended, silver light flashing off the honed edge before it bit flesh. He felt the jolt of the first blow shudder up his arm, and with it came tingling exhilaration as he relinquished himself to the terrible beauty of his God-given talent. Even at seventy years old, it felt almost as good as it had done at twenty and thirty.

The fighting split up into hard, individual combats. A master of the mêlée, William handled sword, shield and destrier in perfect coordination. The Bishop stayed close behind him, roaring his battle cry, and Jack and Jean were

515

at either shoulder in the positions they had held as his squires in the days of the old King Henry. Will and Salisbury had broken away to tackle a group of French knights who were putting up a stout and skilled resistance, the silver and red shield of Perche showing at its centre.

A French trebuchet team was still in position, launching stones at the castle walls, its crew plainly mistaking the English knights for their own men returning from the North Gate. They rolled the boulder into the sling and cranked the tension. The crew leader raised his arm and counted down the launch. 'Three, two—' The final shout never came as a sword flashed like the flank of a fish in shallow water and took off his head. As the body toppled, the rest of the crew fled, yelling the alarm.

The fighting bubbled through the streets of Lincoln like yeast frothing on top of new ale, churning up afresh as pockets of English and French met and clashed. The Count of Perche had made a stand before the cathedral and, in its shadow, was fighting so fiercely that it looked as if he might turn the tide. William pricked Aethel towards the knot of fighting men, intent on reaching Perche in the hopes of making him yield.

A French knight tried to strike William with a mace and he deflected the blow on the side of his shield. Another came at him with a spear but Jean caught the haft on his sword and forced it away; pushing under the man's guard, he cut him down.

The ground was bloody underfoot. Men fell and were trampled. Horses screamed as they were slashed. The clash of battle deafened William's ears. He spurred through the fray, aiming inexorably towards his cousin. Perche thrust off an assault from the left. Reaching him, William roared at him to yield, but Perche was in the grip of battle fever. Turning, he struck out at William, hitting him fiercely on the helm. At William's side a knight thrust his sword through the eye slit of Perche's helm, then wrenched it free, blood damascening the steel. Perche's arm continued in motion for a second blow and then a third. On the downstroke, his fingers lost their grip and the sword fell from his hand. He slumped sideways from the horse and hit the ground with a thud like a sack of wet flour, and didn't move again. There was a sudden hiatus in the fighting, the Count's supporters pulling back, the English holding their blows.

William gestured Jean to dismount and remove the Count's helm and it became immediately plain he was dead. The wound through his eye slit had pierced to his brain; his final two blows had been naught but reflex. His good eye stared frozenly; the other was a ruined red cavern. 'Cover him,' William said in a parched voice. 'And mind that he is afforded full honour.' He swallowed, trying to moisten his battle-dried throat before he raised his voice. 'Your lord is dead. Let all those who desire to yield, lay down their swords and cry quarter!'

Some did, but many fled the scene in search of the other French forces in the town who were fighting on near the river. William was enjoining two knights and a detail of serjeants to take custody of those who had surrendered when more knights arrived at the gallop, the wheatsheaves of Chester blazoned on their shields.

'My lord, the North Gate is breached!' one cried, drawing rein before William. 'The Earl of Chester has broken through!'

'Great news!' Triumph blazed through William. He wouldn't think of his cousin's death. There was no time. Besides, Thomas had died in fierce battle, which was no bad way to make an end. 'Return and tell him to come to the lower end of the town. The French are trying to rally there!'

The knights saluted and spurred back the way they had come. William turned for the next onslaught and was joined by Will. He noticed a trickle of blood running down his son's right hand, and the red rims to his finger-nails.

'You are not wounded?' he asked sharply.

Will shook his head. 'Most of it's not mine,' he said. 'I've taken scratches, nothing more. If I was afraid, it was for you in the thick of it all.'

William smiled behind the mask of his helm. 'I've taken ten times worse on the tourney field. But the danger is always the sword through the eye slit. God rest Thomas's soul.'

'Amen,' said Will, signing his breast.

William echoed the gesture, gathered his reins and spurred on.

At the South Gate of the town the fighting grew fierce again as the French regrouped and attempted to fight back up the hill, their efforts bearing a desperate edge. The moment came when their ranks broke on the granite of the English resolve and fragmented into individuals fleeing for their lives, but their escape from the town was prevented by a jammed portcullis. Picked off, hewn down, captured, the French were annihilated. Saher de Quincy, Earl of Winchester, was taken prisoner, and with him Robert FitzWalter and Gilbert de Clare, English leaders crucial to the opposition.

'Victory!' The cry arose in a single English throat and was taken up, man by man, until it was a full-blown triumphant roar. William felt the words surge through him in a tangible vibration. Aethel snorted and sidled, ears flickering. The gamble – the greatest gamble of his life – had paid off. One half of the French army and the senior English rebels had been brought either to destruction or to surrender on the battleground. With fingers that were suddenly unsteady, he sheathed his sword and fumbled to unlace his helm.

Jean was swiftly at his side, helping him as he had once done as a squire. Sweat trickled down William's cheeks, mingling with tears. He wiped his face on the oily cuff of his gambeson. 'You know the first thing I have to do?' he croaked.

'No, my lord?' Jean was breathing hard from his own exertions.

'Find Hywel and send him to my wife with the news that we're all safe. If she doesn't hear, then no matter the victory, I won't live to enjoy it beyond the first moment of reunion.' A tremulous grin broke across his face.

'Yes, my lord.' Jean returned the grin.

William pushed down his coif and, unfastening his arming cap, dragged it off his head. 'I'm still not sure I believe it,' he said. 'I knew we had to take the victory, and I knew we could do it, but . . .' He blotted his brow. 'There's still many a slip, but for the first time I can see the harbour lanterns.'

43

Nottingham, May 1217

Two hours after his arrival at Nottingham Castle with the soldiers who had defeated the French at Lincoln, Isabelle finally got her husband to herself – more or less. Servants and retainers still occupied the room like worker bees in a busy hive, but she paid them no attention; her focus was all on William. The Legate had wanted to suck every drop of information out of him like a leech draining blood from a victim's body. Even now, bloated with detail, he was not satisfied, but had reluctantly conceded William needed to refresh himself before the dinner hour.

When William entered the room, her heart turned over when she saw how fatigued he looked, his eyes bleary and the hollows beneath dark as ink. He walked heavily too, as if there were weights attached to his feet. The victory at Lincoln had been decisive, but there came a time when the heady mix of triumph and exhilaration no longer had its effect on the exhausted body.

'You need to sleep,' she said as she helped him to disrobe, dismissing the squires and her women – reserving that right to herself.

'I am looking forward to it,' he admitted. 'I knew the

Legate was a hard taskmaster, but I hadn't expected to fight the Battle of Lincoln all over again.'

Isabelle inspected his body as she removed the layers. Bruises of varying shades discoloured his upper arms and from the careful way he had moved when entering the room, she knew he was suffering from strained muscles at the very least. Jean had told her he had performed in his usual manner, refusing to stay back among the ranks. His throat and wrists bore dark streaks from the places where the grease and steel from his hauberk rings had rubbed against his skin.

'You should not have yielded to him.'

William shrugged. 'It's politic to keep him sweet. Once he's dissected the situation to his satisfaction, he'll be less demanding.' He stepped into the tub, sat down, and leaned back with a soft groan.

Isabelle fetched a piece of white soap and set about washing him with a soft linen cloth. William closed his eyes and surrendered to her ministrations. It was another indication to her of how tired he was, for usually he would opt for independence and wash himself – unless he was inveigling her into love-play, and this obviously wasn't one of those moments.

'I was sorry to hear about Thomas of Perche,' she murmured.

His closed eyelids tightened. 'I was there,' he said. 'There was nothing to be done; it was in the press of battle, God rest his soul. At least it was a quick, clean death, and the way he would have chosen.'

Isabelle made a non-committal sound. She could imagine that William would choose the same, and didn't want to think about it. 'What next?' she asked after a moment's soaping and rinsing.

He replied without opening his eyes. 'I've ordered a

muster at Chertsey in a couple of weeks, and in the meantime we wait to see what Louis does. Half his army has been destroyed and I am confident that as well as the men we captured at Lincoln, others will return to the fold. While Louis was winning it might have seemed worth their holding on, but now I believe we'll see a steady trickle away from his service.'

'You think he'll sue for peace?'

'He might. I don't suppose it will be easy, nothing ever is, but at least we're making progress instead of going backwards.' He raised his lids to slant her an amused look through his weariness. 'My love, you stand in danger of interrogating me more fiercely than the Legate.'

Isabelle flushed with chagrin and his smile widened. 'Then again perhaps not. I can't see a priest of Rome soaping my back whilst I sit in my bathtub.'

The image made Isabelle splutter and then giggle. 'I won't be able to sit near him at the table and not think of that now!' she admonished.

He laughed and almost began to look like himself instead of a shadow. 'He'll just think that the return of your husband whole and victorious has turned your wits and made you as flighty as a girl.'

'He would probably be right,' Isabelle said ruefully and handed him a green glass cup filled with wine.

He arched his brow without comment, drank and made an appreciative sound. Isabelle told him about the caves beneath the castle and throughout the town that made the Nottingham vintners the envy of all their neighbours, because of the perfect storage conditions. She spoke of everyday trivia while she continued to attend to him and by the time he stepped from the tub, the first measure of wine drained and the second one halfway down, the dark smudges beneath his eyes had lessened and his gaze was no longer lifeless. Even so, once he was dressed, Isabelle made him lie on the bed.

'I will call you when the dinner horn sounds,' she murmured persuasively. 'It will do you no harm to rest awhile.'

For a moment she thought he was going to be stubborn and refuse, but then he capitulated with a sigh and lay back, closing his eyes and folding his arms behind his head. Isabelle leaned over to free the bed hangings and draw them shut so that he could have some privacy in the chamber.

'You might have a word with Gilbert de Clare and tell me what you think,' he murmured.

'Why?'

'It would be useful to bind him to us and Belle is of an age to wed.'

She looked at him for further elucidation, but he was either asleep, or feigning it. Frowning, Isabelle closed the bed curtains and signalled the others in the room to go about their work quietly whilst William snatched at sleep. Gilbert de Clare, Earl of Hertford and Gloucester, had been one of the rebel barons captured at Lincoln. She did not know him well, although she was his distant kin. He had recently come into his father's earldom and, with the Gloucester lands as well, was both rich and powerful.

Thoughtfully Isabelle went from her chamber to the one that had been allotted to Earl Gilbert and his immediate retinue and where he was being guarded under informal house arrest. He had pledged his word and, given the circumstances, it was unlikely he was about to make a wild dash for freedom. As soon as ransom terms were agreed, he would be welcome to leave or stay as he chose.

De Clare unfolded his long body from the window-seat when Isabelle entered the chamber and gave her a courtly bow. He possessed handsome, regular features. His brow was broad, his cheekbones high. He had curly hair of strong de Clare red and his complexion was dappled with the freckles common to such colouring.

'My lady.' His voice was so deep that it seemed to rise from his boots, but it had a pleasing quality.

Isabelle inclined her head to him. 'My lord. I came to see if you have everything you need.'

Wintry humour lit in his eyes which were the hue of Baltic amber, stranded with green. How old was he? Late thirties, she thought. An earl of the highest rank and great-great-grandson of the first King Henry. 'Perhaps not everything I want, Lady Marshal, but that is not the fault of your hospitality.'

'Since you have surrendered your sword to my lord husband, you are our guest, not our enemy,' she said graciously, 'and even were you still our enemy, we would treat you with honour.'

'In your husband's household, I do not doubt it, my lady.' He gestured to the stone bench in the window embrasure. 'Will you be seated?'

Isabelle hesitated, then acquiesced. He took his place on the opposite bench and folded his hands between his parted knees. She noticed that his fingernails were short and cared for and his clothes, although creased, were clean. Around his neck he wore a gold cross set with precious stones and there was a matching brooch pinning his cloak at the shoulder.

'My lady, forgive me for speaking plainly, but I receive the impression that I am being eyed up the way a horse-coper would study the points of a stallion at a country fair.'

Isabelle flushed at his words. Shrewd, she thought. Very shrewd indeed, or perhaps she had been too obvious. Her cheeks burned as she suddenly realised that he might think she was flirting with him. She drew herself up and, hands folded primly in her lap, said, 'My lord, you are one of my husband's most important hostages. My father and your grandfather were cousins. Now you are Earl of Hertford and Gloucester, you and my husband are bound to cross paths. It is always good to know the doings of one's neighbours.'

'Especially when they have been fighting on opposite sides,' he said astutely.

'We have to look to the future.'

'Ah, the future.' His gaze was knowing. 'You have something in mind?'

Isabelle shook her head. 'Not at the moment, my lord, but my husband might . . . depending on circumstances and the responses of those involved.'

'Ah,' he said again and leaned back, crossing one leg across the other. 'Then if I am involved, I hope I have offered you the right responses.'

'Certainly food for thought,' Isabelle replied, in her own turn giving nothing away.

44

Striguil, Welsh Borders, August 1217

In the stultifying August heat everyone at Striguil had taken to the cool shade offered by the castle's thick stone walls. Even dressed in the thin silks of summer, Isabelle could feel sweat in her armpits and at the back of her neck where her hair was plaited up beneath her wimple. It had been a week of fierce, burning sunshine when even the coolest points of the day at dawn and retiring yielded no relief.

The great hall bulged with allies and family, gathered to witness and celebrate the betrothal of Belle to Gilbert de Clare, Earl of Hertford and Gloucester.

'He certainly sets store by his own worth, Mama.' Mahelt joined her mother in one of the embrasures lining the great hall. She nodded towards her future brother-in-law, who was accepting the congratulations of Striguil's constable.

Isabelle was warily amused. 'That doesn't sound like a compliment. Do you not like him?'

Grimacing, Mahelt pressed one hand into the small of her back, and the other on her belly, seven months round with the next Bigod infant. 'He seems to me a man who will weigh things up and measure his response before he acts,' she said in the same diplomatic way her father used when he was trying to be fair but had his doubts.

'Is that not to the good?'

'Oh yes,' Mahelt said. 'And I am sure it is a match that will help to heal the wounds of this war.'

'But?'

Mahelt shook her head impatiently. 'But nothing, Mama. Belle is resourceful and strong. So is he. There are good seeds for germination. You know how passionate I was about Hugh when I married him. I suppose I want to see my sister feel the same.'

'Some things come at once, others need time to grow,' Isabelle said. 'We have done our best.'

'I know that.' Looking contrite, Mahelt kissed Isabelle's cheek. 'Have you and my father set a wedding date for them?'

Isabelle sighed. 'No, but soon we hope – before the year's end. Your father wants Louis out of England first.'

'Is that likely?'

'Your father thinks so.'

'Even though negotiations have broken down?'

Isabelle's expression closed. 'Louis's supporters desert him daily,' she said defensively. 'Surrey, Arundel and de Braose's son Reginald changed allegiance last month and John de Lacy at Oxford last week. Dover's still under siege, I admit, and Louis hopes for reinforcements, but his situation is precarious. Your father says that Lincoln was the turning point. We're not out of the woods, but at least they have thinned enough to show chinks of daylight.' Puffing out her cheeks, she lifted her veil away from the back of her neck. 'Of course, the moment the threat from Louis lessens the Welsh decide to attack. Your father has done what he can, but he can't give the situation the full attention he'd like.'

Mahelt laid her hand on her mother's sleeve. 'It'll be all right,' she said.

Isabelle made a face. 'That's what I used to tell you at bedtime when you were frightened of the wind roaring around the walls at Longueville.'

'And you were right. The morning always came, and more often than not the wind had died and the sky was blue.'

Isabelle pressed her hand over Mahelt's. 'It has been a very long and stormy night this time,' she said. 'When it's over, I'm going to take your father to Caversham and refuse to see anyone but our sons and daughters for . . . well, for a month at least.'

'You think he'll let you?' Mahelt was sceptically amused.

'That is why I said a month,' Isabelle said and, smiling, gazed into the middle distance. 'When we were first wed, he was recovering from difficult times. We were married at Saint Paul's Cathedral and on the next day, he took me away to a friend's manor in the middle of nowhere and spent the next four or five weeks lazing about doing naught but eat and sleep.' Her smile became laughter and her complexion grew rosy. 'Well, that and beget your eldest brother,' she said. 'I had been told he was a man of great prowess – a champion of the tourneys who had once unhorsed King Richard, yet all he wanted to do was lounge abed and eat enough for ten men.' She gave her daughter an eloquent look. 'Then he woke up and I began to realise what I really had on my hands.' She gazed in William's direction. 'He needs that kind of peace and quiet now; I can feel it in him.'

As if sensing her scrutiny, William glanced in her direction and smiled in the way she knew so well by now, but which still made her vital organs melt.

Later, in the purple dusk, she walked with him along

the battlements. There was dancing in the hall, but William had only stayed to tread an obligatory measure with his newly betrothed daughter and had then retreated outside. He said it was to let the younger element enjoy the moment without the constraint of his presence, but Isabelle sensed the departure was for himself – that he was seeking solitude. In consideration, she walked beside him, companionable, but silent.

Thunder rumbled in the distance and lightning flickered on the horizon. The air was as heavy as a new cloak. Leaning against a merlon, William gazed at the river below, purple-grey like the sky. Isabelle joined him. Boats bobbed at the jetty, just visible in the darkening dusk. She set her arm around him, leaned her head against his shoulder and watched the storm come in. He had always been exhilarated by such spectacles, seeing them as one of God's miracles, and Isabelle had come to love them too, although she was still apprehensive of their great power.

The first spots of rain were splashing like ink blots on the wall walk timbers when Will joined them, his chest heaving from his rapid climb. 'Hywel's ridden in,' he said brusquely. 'The French are preparing to sail for England with more supplies and men for Prince Louis. As soon as the wind is right they'll be across the Narrow Sea. Hubert de Burgh begs you to come with all haste before it is too late.'

William braced his spine, as if withstanding a blow. 'I suspected this would happen,' he said. 'It's the reason Louis has been dragging his heels over negotiating for peace.' He cast his gaze towards the storm. 'Let's pray the weather keeps them in Normandy for a couple more days. We'll muster tonight and ride at dawn.'

As the wind strengthened and the rain stabbed down in silver spears, Isabelle followed her husband and son off the battlements and back to the great hall. William summoned the barons present, made the necessary announcements, assembled scribes and messengers. Hywel was seated at a trestle gobbling down bread and meat, full knowing he'd be on the road again in a matter of hours, storm or no storm.

Mahelt joined her mother, asking if there was anything she could do, adding on a wry, but uplifting note, 'You had better make sure that Caversham is well stocked, Mama. You will both surely deserve it after this.'

Isabelle rode with William to muster the men of the Cinque Ports. By the time they reached Sandwich, her buttocks were sore from straddling a horse and keeping pace with the knights, but she was determined to accompany her husband and this time refused to go and lodge elsewhere and wait.

She was at his side as he called a gathering on the quayside to persuade the ships' masters and crews to put to sea for the sake of the young King. There was a deal of reluctance from men who remembered what King John had done to them in the past and who, having heard about the penurious state of the royal treasury, wanted reassurances that they would be paid for their labour.

'Whatever you lose will be made good,' William said firmly, 'and you will be richly rewarded from the booty of the French ships you capture.'

'Words are much cheaper than silver,' growled one of the more outspoken men, a Kentish ship's master who usually spent his time hauling wool between England and Flanders. 'How do we know you'll keep yours?'

'You don't, but I hope you'll trust my honour and weigh it against how far a French prince will console English interests if he wins.'

There was some muttering amongst his audience. Isabelle looked at William. His expression was calm and good-humoured, even though there was no guarantee that he could get these men to fight for him. They were hardly eating out of the palm of his hand just yet.

'We've heard that the French have employed Eustace the Monk to pilot them into English waters and lead their assault,' spoke up a helmsman from Chertsey. 'And their best knights are coming – Robert de Tournelle and William des Barres.'

William folded his arms and nodded, acknowledging their fears rather than dismissing them out of hand. 'I expect the rumours are right, but such men can be defeated. Eustace is a pirate and serves whoever bids highest for his services. Yes, he's skilled at what he does, but that does not mean he is invincible. Men were stamping me into my grave before the Battle of Lincoln, but I'm still here to ask how daring are you? Are you going to let French ships sail into our English harbours and take them? Do you want a French backside on England's throne and preference given to French shipping? What if their best knights are on board their ships? They have to land them first, and even if they do, they have the best knights in England to greet them on the beaches.'

There was more muttering and consultation. William sent around the wine he had provided and took a cup himself. He handed one to Isabelle and gave her a swift half-wink.

'Where will you be, my lord?' asked the Kentish captain, wiping his mouth and hitching his belt in a businesslike manner.

William turned. 'With the shore knights,' he said. 'While I would gladly board a ship and lead you at sea, I am not the man best suited. I have been known to puke crossing the Thames on a rough day and someone will have to muster the men on dry land. Hubert de Burgh will command at sea, assisted by Richard FitzRoy and the Earl Warenne. De Burgh is easily the equal of des Barres, and quite capable of outwitting even so wily a devil as Eustace the Monk.' He smiled at the men. 'It takes one to catch one.'

They responded with muted laughter. Isabelle watched William dig deeper than a miner in search of ore and, as the afternoon darkened into dusk, woo his audience from scepticism to capitulation and finally, as the wine sank down the barrel, to an eager agreement that had seemed beyond reach at the start of the talks. Seeing him thus, Isabelle realised anew why William held the regency over and above any other baron, magnate or bishop in the land.

'They are ready to follow you into the jaws of hell,' she said when they retired to his lodging in the town.

He gave her a tired smile. 'Ah, well, that comes of an apprenticeship longer than I care to remember, my love,' he said hoarsely. 'I've had to stir up men and change minds far more stubborn than theirs in my past.' He allowed her to ease off his boots and flopped down on the bed. 'I'd have talked to them all night if necessary. If the French fleet puts to shore, we'll be in difficulties. We must stop them in the water because a head is no good without a backbone and they are Louis's backbone.'

'But without the head to find the words to stiffen that backbone, the body wouldn't walk,' Isabelle said, joining him. 'There would just be spineless marrow.'

He snorted with sleepy amusement. 'Then let us hope my words last out the day,' he said, 'and prove stronger than their fear of Eustace the Monk.'

* * *

532

The morning of the Feast of Saint Bartholomew dawned fine and clear. Sky and sea were as smooth as a child's brow and the wind no more than a sigh. At Sandwich the motley collection of ships composing the English fleet rode at anchor, their crews hastening to make their vessels seaworthy and battle-ready. Amongst them rocked the royal nef, the lion banner of England rippling at her prow, her strakes painted blood red. Her crew bustled about her deck, checking blocks, lines, halyards and warps. Hubert de Burgh, constable of Dover Castle and commander of the fleet, stood at the prow, directing operations.

William's own men had embarked upon the great cog commanded by senior ship's master Stephen of Winchelsea. She rode high in the water, her rotund build making her much slower than the sinuous nef, but increasing her cargo-bearing capabilities. Apart from the usual weaponry, her soldiers were armed with clay pots of powdered lime. They were packed in rush baskets along her bulwarks, ready to be seized and hurled at the French when they came within range.

Isabelle rode down to the shore to watch the preparations, but stayed apart from William now, remaining in the baggage camp and allowing him to give his full attention to preparing for engagement should the French gain the shore.

Tension hung in the air like a summer heat haze as everyone waited for the first sighting of the French fleet. Men made jests and laughed too loudly while others kept watch in silence. Priests were busy with their portable altars, praying for victory and shriving men who were joining the ships and going to battle. A couple of brightly striped tents were doing very brisk business indeed. Soldiers emerged from them hitching their hose and braies then, scratching their groins, headed straight for the confessional.

Isabelle had ridden in the baggage train sufficiently often to know the kind of business conducted inside those tents. It was a man's last opportunity to perhaps leave something of himself behind should he die in battle. Once the customers had gone to meet whatever fate awaited, the women would emerge, straddle-legged and frazzled, to breathe clean air and count their takings.

Her own chaplain had set up an altar beside William's tent and Isabelle came with her women to kneel and pray to God and Saint Bartholomew for an English victory and her husband's safekeeping.

The French sails hove into view on the high tide and, eagerly but without fuss, the English ships hoisted anchor, slipped moorings and sailed out to engage with them and prevent them from beaching. It soon became clear that the French intended to fight, as many of their ships were clewing up their sails, and the soldiers crowding their decks were brandishing their weapons.

Hubert de Burgh's sleek, swift nef harnessed the breeze, which was stiffer once out of the harbour, and ploughed towards the French ships as if intending to take them on alone; but de Burgh heeled away at the last moment, drawing jeers in his silvering wake and hot pursuit by the French ships that hadn't furled their sails.

'He's luring them to break their ranks,' William said to Will and chewed on his thumbnail. 'I'd have done the same.'

Will clenched his fist on his sword hilt. 'Reports say there're three hundred of them – far more than we have.'

'Yes, but ours are all fighting ships and many of theirs are supply transports. No vessel laden with grain or horses is going to be much use in a sea battle.'

'No,' Will said, but continued to grip his hilt and William still worried at his thumb until the nail end was ragged. He wanted to be in the thick of it, commanding, and was agitated not to be, even though Hubert de Burgh was a formidable leader.

A large French cog still under canvas manoeuvred to engage de Burgh, but her track was intercepted by a lighter English galley under the command of Richard FitzRoy. The English swung boarding grapnels towards the French, but did not have sufficient strength of numbers and were repulsed, the French retaliating as if swatting gnats.

'Isn't that *The Bayonne*?' Will asked. 'Eustace the Monk's ship?'

William narrowed his gaze. 'By Christ, it is,' he said, his voice hoarse with tension. 'If she was any lower in the water, the sea would be up to her wash strake. She can't manoeuvre like that!'

Stephen of Winchelsea's great cog arrived to join the fray, cutting through the water like a huge butcher's knife. She hove to alongside the lower-lying French ship and more grapnel ropes shot out like an eruption of snakes. Jars of powdered lime were lobbed to smash on the French cog's deck, shedding their eye-destroying white powder in the breeze. Moments later, William saw soldiers leaping down on to the Frenchman's deck. The clash of battle wafted to those on shore, fading in and out with the wind. All around the French ships were unfurling their sails, but they had lost the weather gage and the English arrivals stalked amongst them like wolves in a flock of sheep, biting, tearing, seizing by the throat. More clouds of lime puffed in the air as another French ship was boarded. Now there was panic, the French striving to escape and run for free water and the English chasing hard and pinning them down.

The battle moved further out from shore and sight, except for those English ships engaged in securing victims already snared. Stephen of Winchelsea brought Eustace the Monk's great French flagship *The Bayonne* into port to ecstatic cheers from the soldiers waiting on the quay.

A vivid scarlet splash stained *The Bayonne*'s topsides near the trebuchet she had been carrying as part of the provisions for Louis's reinforcements. A wide grin in the space between his beard and moustache, Stephen of Winchelsea held aloft to William a severed head by its grey-salted locks, the neck plopping gore on to sun-heated stone.

'Eustace the Monk, my lord!' he declared exultantly. 'I gave him the choice between having his head struck off on the trebuchet or on the ship's rail. Being a seafaring man, he chose the ship – may his soul rot in hell for eternity.'

An enormous and sustained cheer rose from the crew and was taken up by all, for Eustace the Monk had been a scourge to shipping for many years and no one voyaging in the Narrow Sea had been safe from his depredations.

'And by the faith I owe, may yours be blessed in heaven, Master Stephen,' William responded with a grave bow.

'Amen to that, my lord, but I will tell you the Monk's ship is stuffed bow to stern with treasure. If you ask me, the bastard brought all his wealth to the fight – didn't want to leave it behind, but you can't take it with you when the Devil seizes your soul, can you, eh?'

William decreed that the goods were to be shared out among the crew. He reserved the ransoms of the knights on board to himself and took them into his custody. In gratitude to Saint Bartholomew, he commanded that once every man had had his fair share of booty, a portion was to be set aside to found a hospital in the saint's name.

By dusk, as the English ships returned to harbour, it

became clear that the French supply fleet on which Louis had rested hopes of keeping his fight in England alive had either been captured, sunk or scattered to the four winds. Hubert de Burgh had seized two French ships for himself and many a merchant captain returned from the sea battle with his ship laden to the wash strake with plunder. For the next several days, the sailors roistered in the taverns, decked in finery, spending their share of the booty like patrons at a tourney and vying with each other as to who had secured the most spoil.

Louis was forced to sue for peace and this time sat down to negotiate the terms with more humility, his hubris destroyed by a second, decisive English victory and the worrying possibility that God was indeed with the English.

William greeted him pleasantly enough, but could not help rubbing a little salt into open wounds. Louis had told his knights they had nothing to fear with an old man at England's helm – that he respected William Marshal, but he had had his day. In his turn, William welcomed Louis and with a smiling remark about the Prince being a young-ster still wet behind the ears sat down to settle a peace that would free England of the French.

Now the rebuilding could begin.

45

Striguil, Welsh Borders, November 1218

Coming fully awake, Isabelle realised she was alone, although the mattress still bore the warm imprint of William's body. Pulling on a loose robe, she rose and left the bed.

He was sitting before the dying fire, a cup of wine clasped between his hands as he stared into the embers.

'What's the matter?' Joining him on the cushioned bench, she gathered her hair and tied it back with a length of braid. 'Is it your stomach again?'

He shook his head. 'It's nothing,' he said.

Isabelle eyed him narrowly, not entirely convinced by his dismissive tone. He had been suffering from bouts of pain ever since Eve's wedding to William de Braose's grandson at Bramber in the autumn. He had made light of the affliction, dismissing it as something to be expected of advancing age. Tisanes of camomile and ginger helped and it appeared to be an intermittent nuisance and discomfort rather than anything more acute. Even so, she was worried. 'Are you sure?'

'As certain as rain in Ireland,' he said with a weary smile, 'and believe me, I would know. It's the thought of returning to London on the morrow when I'd rather still be here.'

Isabelle watched a log fall and settle, soft grey flakes feathering the hearth stones, flickering hems of red winking and dying. During the last year, William had continued to push himself to the limit while at the same time making arrangements to ease back and delegate now the French had left English soil. He was preparing to have a great seal issued in the King's name rather than continue to use his own for the business of government, so that others of the ruling body would be able to issue writs and commands in the boy King's name. He had also reinstated the judicial courts and the exchequer sessions. The country was still impoverished; there were still petty disputes and private wars continuing as a result of the earlier war with Louis, but matters were slowly inching on to a stable footing. She and William had squeezed out sufficient time to make a progress of their estates at Usk, Hamstead, Caversham, Marlborough, Crendon and now Striguil. They had seen Sybire and Eve married into the houses of Derby and Braose. With Gilbert in minor orders and set upon a career in the Church and Will and Walter constantly absent acting as their father's deputies in the earldom, only ten-year-old Ancel and eight-year-old Joanna remained in the household.

Isabelle knew she wasn't being fanciful; of late there had been a definite change in William – a drawing in like a winter's evening, a husbanding of resources and taking stock, ready to move on . . . and there could only be one kind of moving on now. She was frightened this progress through their estates was William bidding farewell to familiar and beloved territories. Striguil had always been one of the places of his heart. Hot-eyed from the fire, she looked at him. 'You don't have to go to London.'

'Unfortunately, I do,' he said with a grimace. 'There are matters of government to attend to, and the ride isn't beyond me yet.'

She heard the defensive sharpness in his tone. 'I did not say that it was, but the Tower of London will not fall down, nor Westminster lose all of its windows should you choose to linger in the Marches for a few days more.'

He smiled at that. 'Mayhap neither tower nor abbey, but the Legate will not wait for time and tide and I need his goodwill. I owe him the courtesy of a prompt appearance.'

'Then if it is set in stone that we go to London, I want some new shoes for court. I wore out the last pair at our daughters' weddings, and the pair before that in Paris.'

William's smile deepened with genuine amusement. 'Everyone should wear their shoes threadbare,' he said.

'In which case, you will need more yourself judging from the state of your riding boots.'

His eyes widened in alarm. 'They're old friends!'

'Well, you need to make the acquaintance of new ones very soon.'

He pursed his lips thoughtfully. 'I wonder how many cows' worth of shoe leather a man wears out in a lifetime.'

'Depends how big his feet are and how many steps he takes . . . and also the size of the cows.'

He grinned. 'Now I know why you win so often at chess. I tell you what, we'll call at the warehouses at Charing and see what they have in store. With good fortune they will have finest kidskin slippers for you and Cordovan hide for me.'

She shared his jesting whilst well aware he was functioning on two levels. The light-hearted banter was genuinely meant but it was what existed on the surface.

Beneath the sunlit shallows lay serious, darker thoughts that would take more than the heat of a dying fire to brighten.

William and Isabelle spent the winter months in London, lodged at the Tower from which he conducted the business of the regency, tying up loose ends, only to discover that others had unravelled and needed his attention. Isabelle watched him and worried, knowing that he needed to lay down his burdens, for the sake of his health if nothing else.

The February morning was bitterly cold and damp, rain lashing upon London from a sky as dark as charcoal. Although it was mid-morning, the world was little more than twilit and folk huddled round their fires. Those obliged to be out splashed through the muck in their pattens, heads down, cloaks and hoods wrapped tightly around their bodies, teeth chattering. On the banks of the churning, sullen Thames, the Tower of London's whitewashed walls gleamed like a sugar confection at a royal feast. Behind its arched windows, candles and lamps lit the winter-dark chambers and logs burned in every available hearth.

William lay on his bed in his chamber whilst the third black-robed physician of the morning poked and prodded him, examined his urine and asked various intimate questions concerning his diet and bodily functions. He answered the man with growing irascibility, while Isabelle stood to one side, hands clenched into fists with worry and exasperation.

'He has no appetite,' she told the doctor. 'All his life until now he has eaten heartily.'

William glared at her. 'Is a man not allowed to dine in peace without his wife watching and noting his every mouthful?'

'Do you not wish me to notice you?' Isabelle returned his glare. 'Why would the doctors be here unless you were ailing? I am not some panic-stricken ninny who runs for the physician at the first sign of a sneeze or a belly gripe and well you know it.' Aware that she was breaking the code of manners before the doctor, who was diplomatically looking away, she compressed her lips and lowered her gaze.

William said nothing, but his own jaw tightened. He suffered the rest of the exploration in taut silence and, as soon as he could, dismissed the man. Isabelle saw him to the door, waving away the maidservant who came to the task.

The physician gave her a compassionate look that filled her with dread. 'I will make up a tincture for the pain and have my assistant bring it to you,' he said, 'but I fear that the Earl is strong-willed and resistant to what he sees as the interference of a doctor's arts.'

Isabelle nodded wry agreement. 'Very strong-willed indeed,' she said. 'But then he has never been ill in his life before, not even with the toothache or joint stiffness.' She drew a deep breath. 'You speak of relieving the pain, not of effecting a cure?'

The compassionate look remained. 'My lady, I would be giving you false hope if I said I knew of a cure. That is in the hands of God and the Earl may yet make a full recovery . . .'

It was a platitude. At least he was being tactfully honest. The previous doctor had suggested cold baths and a rigorous application of leeches to balance the humours. That William had not thrown him from the room head over tail was a testament to her husband's control under extreme provocation.

'Yes,' she said. 'I pray so.'

542

After closing the door behind him, she returned to William and found him sitting on the edge of the bed, his expression as tight as a sealed chest.

'He said he will mix you something for the pain,' she said, trying to keep her voice level. 'You should let him help you.'

He turned his head towards her and his gaze was bleak. 'I am beyond that, Isabelle. I am not a fool and I have seen enough death in my time to know the signs. I have no intention of being clystered, plunged in a freezing tub or stuck with leeches. The doctors could do nothing for King John, or for Richard, or their father. You make the best end you can when God decrees it is your time.'

Isabelle made a small sound in her throat and went to the window where she stared out on the sward and the freezing rain that was almost sleet. 'We met here for the first time,' she said in a tremulous voice. 'I saw you crossing the courtyard – the way you walked, how tall you were and how straight your spine . . . and all unknowing I envied the wife you might have at home.'

She heard him exhale on a long breath that was marred by a slight catch of pain. Then she felt him behind her. 'And I remember seeing you and thinking that the man who took you in marriage would be fortunate indeed.' He rested one hand lightly at her waist, thickened from its girlhood slenderness in the bearing of ten children. 'I have been the most fortunate of men, Isabelle . . . and I still am.'

A great wave of desolation washed over her. 'I don't envy your wife now,' she whispered, her throat constricting. 'William, you cannot leave me; I will not survive.' Tears spilled down her face and she began to sob.

'Hush now.' He pulled her round into his arms. 'We have had thirty years – thirty good years, which is more

543

than most people are given. Even without me you have our sons and daughters and you will still be lady of Leinster and Striguil.'

'Do you think it matters to me?' she wept, shaking her head.

'It will matter to our . . . to your people. You must make it matter to you.'

She said nothing but pressed herself against his tunic, drawing in the scent of wool and the lingering ghost of cedarwood from the chest in which it had lain before he donned it.

'We have time before us yet,' he murmured. 'Order the barges prepared and we'll go to Caversham. The air is better than here in the city and it will do me good . . . and if it doesn't and I am certain of my death, then I will do it, God willing, my way, with dignity and on my own ground. People can come to me there at need. The King and his tutor are only across the river at Reading, and we can send for our children.'

Isabelle swallowed against the choking lump of grief in her throat. She should be comforting him, not the other way around. This moment was as bitter as gall, but there was a sweetness in it too, so poignant as to be near unbearable, yet bear it she must. She had no choice.

46

Caversham, Berkshire, Spring 1219

April sunshine gilded the floor of the great chamber at Caversham, picking out the colours in the tapis by the bed, striping the woollen coverlet with pale gold and glinting on the cushioned oak benches assembled around the bed where William lay. The sky through the open window was duck-egg blue, patched with a few torn wisps of grey cloud, hinting at later showers. For now, though, the day was fair and new, and William's pain was not debilitating.

He had been busy for a month issuing writs, preparing to relinquish the government of the country into other hands. Now the moment had arrived and he was relieved. This morning he had had his attendants wash and shave him with care and even though he was confined to bed, he had donned his court tunic and pinned it with a magnificent gold and sapphire brooch.

Isabelle sat on the window-seat, looking out, her cheek and the line of her body illuminated in the good morning light, her hands quiet in her lap. William watched her, the intensity of his gaze driven by the knowledge that he would not have this gift for much longer. It was one of the hardest parts of bidding farewell and preparing to move on. He wasn't ready to detach himself, but knew the time was riding in fast whether he willed it or not.

'They are here,' she said, 'and the young King with them as you requested.' She rose from the window-seat and faced him. He saw the anxiety in her eyes and knew she was assessing whether he was up to the task of dealing with the Papal Legate, the Bishop of Winchester and the assorted earls and barons who had come from Reading at his summons.

'Good.' He forced a smile. 'Everything is ready; let them come.'

Isabelle stooped to kiss his cheek and went from the room. Expression contorted, William pulled himself to a higher sitting position. Immediately Will, who had been standing in the background, moved to help him, his brow puckered with concern. William swallowed his pride and accepted his son's strength. He needed to husband what remained of his own for the coming interview.

King Henry had grown since Candlemas when William had last set eyes on him. He had not yet begun to develop adult muscle and his features were still those of a child, but he was taller and his skin had a slight sheen, harbingers of adolescence. In the two and a half years since his coronation at Gloucester, he had acquired a polish of poise and assurance, although the aquamarine eyes, his mother's legacy, guarded the thoughts behind them and the line of his mouth still hinted at petulance. He greeted William with indifferent courtesy. His fastidious nostrils flared and he looked towards the door as if he would rather be anywhere else.

William knew he was being shrewdly assessed by the men who came to his bedside to greet him, all of them considering how much strength he had left; how far gone he was and what they should do about it. That was what they were here to decide. Ranulf of Chester was absent on crusade, but Salisbury was present and the King's tutor, Peter des Roches, Bishop of Winchester. William could sense the tension in him, taut as a mangonel rope. He sat with his arms tightly folded across his chest, which William knew of old was not a good sign. The Papal Legate Pandulf showed a calm, implacable face, but beneath his heavy eyelids, his obsidian gaze was fierce. Derby and Warwick were present, Arundel and de Warenne. In the great hall many more waited to hear the decisions of the meeting in the bedchamber.

Once his audience had settled and those who wanted had been furnished with cups of wine, William gathered himself, cleared his throat, and addressed the juvenile King.

'Sire, when your father died, it was decided at Gloucester in the presence of the Papal Legate and many here today that your realm and yourself should be handed into my care. I have served you faithfully to the best of my ability and I would continue to do so if I could.' He paused to draw breath and tried to ignore the pain that knifed through the centre of him. He had not drunk the potions that would have dulled its edge, for they would have dulled his mind too, and for this meeting he needed to be as sharp as a blade. With a wave of his hand he added, 'It is plain for all to see that I can no longer fulfil the role. If it please you, sire, your barons must elect someone else to protect you and your lands. God grant that you find a governor who will serve you in such a way as to bring you honour.'

Des Roches, who had scowled ferociously throughout William's speech, leaped to his feet, his complexion ruddy with anger. 'I agree that it was given to you to take charge of the land and safeguard the realm, but the King was specifically given into my care!'

William had known des Roches might be difficult and try to take advantage. Although the pain was savaging him, William raised his voice and forced his will to dominate the other man's. 'Come now, my lord,' he said sternly. 'None of that. You and the Earl of Chester agreed I should be regent of England and governor of the King and realm. A host of witnesses, many here today, heard you. They also heard me accept the post in the name of the Legate and everyone. The single reason I handed the King into your keeping was so I did not have to drag him about the country-side in an army's baggage wain, and in truth you know it.' He paused for breath and found it difficult to draw. Pain had turned to agony and the effort required to impose his authority on des Roches had left him sweating and nauseous. He couldn't go on, but knew he must for the sake of a future he was not going to see, but which his family would have to live in. Isabelle had started to move towards him and Will had half risen from his seat, but he gestured them back and summoned his reserves one last time.

'I . . . I have thought about this for a while, my lords. When one's world closes down to a room and a bed, one has time for consideration. It is my decision to hand over my charge to the Legate since he represents the Pope who is England's overlord.'

Pandulf inclined his head. The way he made the gesture was all gracious humility, but his eyes were those of a hawk. 'A wise decision, my lord Marshal,' he said.

'I hope so, although I sometimes wonder at the nature of wisdom.' William beckoned to Henry, who rose from the bench and somewhat reluctantly stepped up to the bedside.

'Sire, give me your hand,' William said.

After a hesitation, Henry did so. William was not surprised. At that age he would not have wanted to stand by a sickbed and take the febrile hand of a dying man.

Unlike his father's, which had been short, square and energetic, Henry's hands were fine and languid, the skin pale, almost translucent, with delicate blue veins on the tender inside of the wrist. Not a warrior's hand, but then he didn't need to be in the flesh. Just as long as he had the strategies in his head when the time came.

'Sire, I beg the lord our God that if ever I did anything in my life to please Him, He grant you grow up to be a worthy man. But should you follow in the footsteps of some wicked ancestor and become like him, then I pray that your life is cut short. Do you understand?'

Fear and disgust widened Henry's eyes. The youth tried to pull away from William, who immediately increased his grip. 'Do you understand?' he repeated.

White-faced, Henry nodded. 'Yes, my lord,' he said in a frightened voice.

William knew the boy had spoken out of a desire to be free of the engagement, but he had needed to hear the words. Breathing shallowly to counter the pain, he opened his hand and let Henry go. 'Good then,' he said. 'I want you to remember.'

The Legate rose to his feet. 'We should leave you a while, my lord,' he said tactfully. 'I can see you need to rest.'

William managed a short nod. 'Thank you,' he said with a look of gratitude for Pandulf. 'Perhaps you will return later.'

The company filed from the room, escorted by William's ushers and two of the senior household knights. William beckoned urgently to Will. 'Go with them,' he gasped. 'Go and hand over the King to the Legate in the presence of all the others in the hall. I don't want anyone to say that it was done in secret and the Bishop of Winchester may yet make trouble . . . Return to me when you have done and tell me how it falls out . . .'

Will nodded and departed purposefully. William sank against the bolsters, exhausted and consumed by pain. Isabelle was swiftly at his side, a cup in her hand.

'Drink,' she said.

The familiar smell of the contents almost made him gag and he waved her away. 'No,' he gasped. 'Give me plain wine. I need a clear head for when Will returns. I would rather have sharp wits and suffer – for the moment anyway.'

She looked anxious, but did as he asked, replacing the wine containing syrup of poppy with a cup of plain red. When she made to tilt it towards his lips William took it from her. 'I still have the strength to hold my own cup,' he said tetchily. Isabelle said nothing. She looked at his hand, which was shaking, then turned away, pretending she hadn't seen. William took several unsteady sips and prayed not to spill the wine. And strength to hold his cup did not mean the strength to reach out and set it on the coffer.

'Isabelle . . .'

She looked round, took the cup from him and sat on the bed. 'I know I should not coddle you,' she said with self-irritation. 'I always do, and you have always resented it . . . even from the first. I know how you hate this . . .'

He leaned back. He was so tired. The world was turning to grey shadows, splintered with agonising red lances, but he needed to stay awake and aware. 'Whether I hate it or not, I have no choice but to accept God's will, but the most difficult thing I have ever faced is letting go and bidding farewell.'

She leaned over and kissed him, her face wet with tears, but the salt she tasted on her lips came from him.

Will returned from the hall and bade the chamberlain close the door. 'It's done,' he said, coming to William. His hands gripped his belt and his posture had an air of authority that William was pleased to see. It hadn't just been for the sake of openness he had sent Will to make the exchange. It had also been a symbolic transferral of the power of the Earl of Pembroke. Will would have the title before the long days of summer clad the trees in their full spread of green.

'Problems?' he asked, being economical with his words for the sake of his failing strength.

'Only what you would expect,' Will said with a shrug. 'The Bishop of Winchester tried to overturn what you said in this room, but no one would pander to him and he was put in his place. Most men were relieved at your giving the King to the Legate. That way, none can claim to be higher than his peer.'

William nodded. 'Then it is good. I will not say it is perfect, but in the circumstances, the best I can do.' He closed his eyes. 'Now the matter is settled, I can put my own affairs in order and take thought for my soul.'

Isabelle watched William's slumber. The meeting with the King, Legate, barons and bishops had so exhausted him that even without the syrup of white poppy to deaden the pain he was able to sleep. 'I feared for him when he was talking to them,' she murmured to Will, knowing her voice would not disturb her husband. He seemed to rest easier when there were people around. 'His face turned so grey that I thought he might . . . might die there and then.' She gave an involuntary shiver.

'He's stronger than that,' Will said. 'Even with all their

faculties, other men would not have been able to do what my father did just now when he is so ill.' His voice rang with pride and it brought fresh tears to Isabelle's eyes to hear him.

'At least now, as he says, he has given up the mantle of governance. The rest of the time is for him.' Will went to the flagon and poured wine. 'I have been thinking that we should keep vigils round his bed. Three for the night watch, three from dawn until the afternoon, and three until the midnight hour. I know all will be willing to do so. It will show how much we honour him and mean that he is never alone.'

'I think it an excellent idea,' she said tremulously, 'and one he will appreciate, providing you tread softly on his pride.'

'I will do all that is needful, and I will do it out of duty, out of honour . . . and for love.' He took a deep drink of the wine and she saw the dark beard stubble move upon his jaw and throat. 'I have not always understood him, nor him me, but we stand on common ground now.'

That evening, as the spring dusk was falling, Mahelt arrived with Hugh and their three offspring. Isabelle kissed her grandchildren, embraced her son-in-law, then opened her arms to her eldest daughter.

Mahelt gave a soft gasp and hugged her mother fiercely. 'It's not true!' she said in a voice raw with pain. 'Tell me it is not true!'

Isabelle patted Mahelt's back. They had ridden through a shower and the dark green wool was damp under her palms. 'With all my heart I wish I could, but I cannot. He is sleeping just now, but when he wakes, he will want to see you all. Your sisters are on their way too . . .'

Mahelt pulled away wiping her cheeks with the heel of

her hand. 'Mama, I am sorry. I should have asked after you, not wailed on your breast like an infant.'

Isabelle smiled tenderly at her daughter. 'But you are my infant,' she said. 'Even if you are a full-grown woman with infants of your own.'

Mahelt laughed unsteadily. 'Even so, I am here to help. Mama, are you all right?' She stood back and held her mother's upper arms, her gaze anxious and assessing.

Isabelle sighed and shook her head. 'No,' she said desolately, 'I am not all right, but for the moment I am coping, and that is all I ask . . . to cope.'

Mother and daughter embraced again, and this time the exchange was of equals, woman to woman.

Isabelle was leaving Caversham's chapel after mass when Jean D'Earley arrived. His horse was blowing from being hard ridden. Sweat shone on its dark hide; salty tide marks streaked the line of breast-band and saddle. There was no sign of his escort, so Isabelle assumed he had outridden them. William had sent him into Wales a fortnight ago to deal with matters in Netherwent and she was surprised to see him back so soon.

Jean dismounted and strode over to her, a linen package grasped in one hand and his gaze filled with anxiety. 'My lady, is all well with the Earl?' The manner of the question, the way he did not greet her first, revealed his fear and the reason for his haste.

'His condition is no better.' She touched his mud-splashed sleeve. 'But he yet lives and he will be glad to see you.'

Jean's shoulders sagged with relief and he rubbed one hand over his face. 'Thank Christ. All the time I was travelling, I was praying I would not be too late.' He looked down at the linen package in his hand.

'What is that?' Isabelle asked curiously.

He shrugged. 'I do not know, my lady, but he was insistent I should bring it to him. It was at the bottom of his great coffer at Pembroke.'

Isabelle eyed the package and frowned. She vaguely remembered seeing it, but had never paid it much attention. Apparently, though, it was important. 'I will see if he is awake,' she said. 'Go and refresh yourself, and then come to his chamber.'

Like a man newly woken, Jean blinked owlishly at his mud-stained clothing, then gave a surreptitious sniff in the direction of his armpit. 'Forgive me, my lady. I had no thought but to return to Caversham as swiftly as I could.'

'Nothing to forgive.' She gave him a gentle push. 'Go to.' She watched him leave, staggering with tiredness and a little bow-legged from being so long in the saddle.

'What do you think it is, Mama?' asked Mahelt.

'I have no idea,' Isabelle replied, 'but obviously it means much to your father.'

The package proved to contain two pieces of plain silk cloth, but exquisitely wrought, the weave so fine that it was a marvel to behold. The sight of them, unfolded across his bed, made William quite loquacious and brought a spark to his eye that Isabelle had not seen in several weeks. He rubbed the cloth between his fingers, a faraway look on his face. 'I bought these lengths of cloth more than thirty years ago in Jerusalem,' he said to the gathering of family and knights surrounding the bed. 'They are a symbol of the covenant I made with God that I would strive to be worthy of Him. I made a vow that my body would be given to the Templars for burial. I still remember the heat, the flies, the dust between my teeth . . . and the promises

I made. I've tried to keep them, even if I haven't always succeeded.' For a while he was silent, contemplating the cloth. Isabelle wondered if he was becoming exhausted, but his colour was still good, without the waxen shadows she was coming to dread.

'Jean,' he said quietly at length, 'in the name of the love you bear me and by the faith you owe me, take these into your keeping, and when I am dead cover me with them and cover and surround the bier on which I am borne.'

'Yes, my lord,' Jean said hoarsely.

'Good. I also want you to buy some lengths of plain grey cloth; the quality does not matter. All it needs to do is protect these silks from the rain and mud should my final journey be undertaken in foul weather.' He spoke in a prosaic and matter-of-fact fashion as if dictating a routine letter to Walter or Michael and his even composure as he gave such exquisitely painful instructions made Isabelle bite her lip. Beside her Mahelt was openly weeping.

'It shall be done, my lord,' said Jean in a wavering voice, his eyes glassy with tears.

William nodded briskly. 'After I am buried, give the ells of grey to the brothers of the Temple and let them do with them as they wish.'

Jean swallowed. 'My lord,' he choked and started to refold the lengths of silk.

William watched him for a moment, then looked at Isabelle. She pressed her lips together and returned his stare, her throat working. 'Now,' he said quietly, 'I would like a little time alone with my wife. There are things I have to say to her . . . and she to me.'

Somewhat subdued, the audience left the room, Jean holding the pieces of fabric with great respect and yet as if he did not want to be anywhere near them. The door closed behind the last person, leaving William and Isabelle alone.

She moved slowly to the bed as if she had been struck a mortal blow. 'In all our years of marriage, you never told me,' she said in a grieving, hurt-filled voice.

He held out his hand towards her but she didn't take it. 'The matter was between myself and God,' he replied with an air of gentle patience that made her want to strike him and then feel guilty for harbouring such anger. 'You always knew of my links with the Templar order.'

'Yes, but not this . . . It is one thing to conceal yourself from others, but not from me.'

He looked at her steadily. 'I have shared more with you, Isabelle, than anyone in my life. When we were wed I told you that there were parts that were mine alone to me and you accepted it then, so why can you not accept it now?'

She shook her head, feeling numb. 'I do accept it, but I wish I had known.'

'Then while it is time for truths, let us have it all out,' he said. 'If I am to die a Templar, I must renounce all worldly matters, you must know that.'

Isabelle nodded wordlessly.

'Go into the garderobe yonder, and bring out the cloak you will find in the third coffer along.'

Isabelle bit back a stinging retort asking what other 'surprises' he had concealed in chests around their various castles and manors and went to do as he asked. The anger and hurt were a raw pain in her breast. She had thought, after thirty years together, to know everything about William, but was discovering that she didn't know him at all, and time had almost run out.

The cloak was made of heavy, expertly finished but undyed wool and the weight of the garment made her forearms ache as she lifted it. Embroidered in red silk upon the left breast was the blood-red cross of the Templar order. Isabelle drew a shuddering breath and fought for composure, knowing if she began to scream and rage at him out of her own pain, she would be unable to stop. Trembling, she returned to him and laid the mantle upon the bed.

'When did you have this done?' she asked unsteadily.

He hesitated then said, 'Before we set out on the tour of our lands last May. It was part of setting things in order. Once it was done, I did not have to think on it again. I wanted to be prepared.'

Isabelle sat on the bed and looked down at her hands. 'When we went to Paris,' she said shakily, 'I wore my court shoes, do you remember? I attended King Philip in them; I walked and danced until the soles were worn through. I didn't tell you then, but I had intended them to be for my own burial – but I changed my mind. And now you show me shrouds that you have kept for thirty years and this mantle . . . I cannot . . .' She shook her head, overwhelmed.

He sighed with resignation. 'I knew if I told you, you would not take it well. I have never made any secret of the fact that I would take Templar vows at my death. It settled my mind to have this mantle made while I was still in good health. Like those shrouds it is part of my own preparation – private to me. I wish I could make you understand . . .'

'I do understand,' she said hoarsely, 'but it still hurts.'

He brushed one hand gently over the cloak. 'I wanted to tell you about this now because soon I will have to make it formal and public.'

She stared at him, beginning to feel a flutter of panic. 'Once I take the vows of a Templar, I may no longer embrace you, nor you me. It is forbidden by the rule.' His tone was gentle but inexorable.

A part of her had always known this was coming, but knowing and preparing from a distance was not the same as having the moment arrive on the threshold. She thought the word 'No!' but clenched her teeth and pressed her lips together so that it would not escape.

'Isabelle . . .' He was gazing at her in concern.

She looked at the rafters and bit her lip. Tears spilled over her lashes and ran down her face. 'This is what you want?'

'Yes,' he said. 'I vowed myself to the Temple thirty years ago, and the time has come to fulfil the promise I made to their order. For my honour, for my soul, this is the way it must be.'

She wanted to stamp and rail, to throw things and shriek that this was not the way it must be at all, but she controlled herself. It was his choice and she had to abide by that. She had loved him for all of her adult life and for that love she would go down his road.

Slowly she rose from the bed and, removing her wimple, unpinned her braids and let them tumble down. Her hair was still thick, although more silver than gold these days. She unfastened the blue ribbons wound through the plaiting and combed out the twists with her fingers. Then she took off her belt and her shoes, and climbed on to the bed beside William. 'I know you are in pain and I know that all things carnal and of the body are past,' she said hoarsely, 'but I want to lie beside you one more time, as your wife. If I have this, then I can face the rest.'

Moving gingerly because of the discomfort, he made room for her and then curved his arm around her shoulders, under her hair. 'Isabelle,' he said, and now she heard the anguish in his voice. 'What I would give to push back

558

the wheel of time and have this a different spring season with you a young wife in my arms and myself whole and strong . . .'

She laid her hand to his cheek and he turned his head and kissed her fingers. 'I too,' she said.

There was a long silence in which she thought he had fallen asleep. He did a lot of sleeping these days when the pain allowed him respite, but then he spoke. 'This bed,' he said with a smile in his voice. 'Do you remember, I had it made by a carpenter in London.'

'Yes, I remember,' she murmured. 'From an oak tree felled at Hamstead. Its pieces have travelled wherever we have gone . . .' Their marriage bed, the heart of their home, where they had slept, made love, talked and quarrelled, and mended such quarrels in the time-honoured fashion. Their ten children had been begotten and born within its hangings. Made up with different covers, the curtains tied back, it had served as a day couch and witnessed the comings and goings in the chamber, the scratching of the scribes' quills, the robust discussions of knights and vassals, the gossip and laughter of informal assemblies, the closeted intimacy of private discussion. Now it waited to perform the final service.

'The tales it could tell,' he said.

'Then perhaps for decency's sake it is a good thing that beds do not have voices.'

He laughed, but the laughter was curtailed by a spasm that stiffened his body and drew an involuntary gasp from him. Isabelle was immediately attentive. Leaving the bed, she hurried to bring him a cup of the syrup-of-poppy mixture prescribed by the physicians. On this occasion he did not refuse the offer, but drank the laced wine with something close to desperation.

When she took the cup from him, he closed his eyes,

and it made her ache to see the dark shadows beneath them.

'I never thought to say it, Isabelle, but I am weary for the end of the road,' he said after a moment. 'I grieve to leave you behind, but each mile now is a burden. I would have done.'

She returned to the bed and lay down again at his side. There was nothing to say, and besides, she was so close to tears again that replying was impossible.

Three days later, William prepared to take the vows of a Templar knight in the presence of Aimery de St Maur and other Templar brethren who had travelled from London for the ceremony. The knights of his mesnie were present too, and Isabelle and their children, saving Richard who was in France.

Isabelle knew her part and had steeled herself to it. At the appointed moment, she approached the bed. William was propped up by a pile of bolsters and pillows. The coverlet was turned back, showing a neat border of embroidery. He was wearing a shirt and tunic of unbleached linen, the colour of dirty snow, and his skin, tight over his bones, stripped of flesh, was the same hue.

She stooped to kiss him for the last time, and was suddenly very glad that they had had the time together three days ago, for otherwise she could not have borne this dry simulacrum, performed in front of others.

'*Belle amie*,' he whispered, and stroked her face.

She had been prepared for the embrace, but not the word and the caress, spoken with such aching tenderness. The defences she had built could not withstand such an assault and they crumbled. She had sworn she would not cry, but her eyes filled. She was aware of Mahelt's arm about her, gently drawing her back from the bed, and Mahelt too was sobbing.

William's almoner, himself a Templar, stepped up to the bed and gravely laid the white mantle upon it. Covering her mouth, Isabelle fled the room and ran to her chamber. Sitting on her solitary bed, she drew the curtains and, behind their flimsy privacy, broke her heart.

'Mama? Mama, are you awake?'

Isabelle raised her head from the pillow. The linen was saturated under her cheek. Her head felt as tight as a drum; her eyes were sore and swollen. Mahelt, puffy-faced and red-eyed herself, had parted the curtains and was looking at her with anxiety.

'Yes,' Isabelle croaked and sat up. Through the gap in the bed hangings, she could see one of her women lighting candles. The sound of shutters being closed came to her ears. 'What hour is it?'

'Nigh on compline. I've looked in on you once or twice, but you've been asleep and I haven't wanted to disturb you. I've had the servants bring food to the chamber . . .' She gestured into the room.

'I'm not hungry,' Isabelle said. A savoury smell drifted through the gap in the curtain. Something with cumin by the scent of it, and new bread. Her mouth watered and she half thought she was going to be sick.

'You must try and eat something. You have to keep up your strength,' Mahelt said practically.

Isabelle looked up at her daughter. She was tall and robust, William's in every way with his long bones and dark, winter-river eyes. 'What for?' she said.

'For us . . . for Ancel and Joanna – for the earldom. I know my brother is competent, but you are still its heart, Mama.' Her voice almost cracked.

561

Isabelle sniffed. 'You will make me weep again,' she warned as she eased to her feet. Her body ached all over as if she had aged forty years in a few hours.

Mahelt took her arm. 'Come, at least try and eat. It might make you feel better. I'm not hungry either but taking a meal together will help, I think.'

Isabelle doubted that anything would make her feel better, but she allowed Mahelt to bring her to the trestle. It had been laid with a good white cloth and set with the best silver platters and green glass goblets from the sideboard. Two steaming bowls of chicken and cumin stew had been set in the middle of the table, with baskets of new bread to accompany them. Cushioned benches had been drawn up to the trestle and Isabelle's chair positioned at the head of the table.

There was a sense both of routine and occasion and Isabelle felt it unfurl through her misery like a twist of bright ink through water. Father Walter arrived to bless the meal and inform her the Templars were dining in the guest chamber while Will, the knight Henry FitzGerold and Jean D'Earley were watching over William, who was asleep.

Isabelle dipped her spoon in the stew and stirred it round, wondering if she could manage a mouthful. A glance showed her daughters all doing the same. Even Mahelt, who had urged her with such brave words, was breaking bread with vigour, but conveying very little to her lips.

Summoning her will power, Isabelle tasted the food. It was warming, pungent and spicy, full of flavour, but it might as well have been sawdust in her mouth. She made herself chew and swallow, to reach for bread, dip it in the sauce. Eat.

She had just forced down a third mouthful with a

swallow of wine, when Jean D'Earley was announced to the chamber, his breathing swift with the haste of his stride.

Isabelle looked at him and shot to her feet, the chair crashing backwards on to the floor and fear flooding through her. 'William!' she gasped.

Jean hurried forward, waving his hands in negation. 'No, no, my lady, it is not what you think, I am sorry for frightening you.'

'Then, what – what is the matter?' She pressed her hand to her breast and felt her heart galloping like a runaway horse.

'The Earl has woken, and he is in good spirits, my lady. He has asked for his daughters and he wants them to sing for him.' Jean stooped to pick up the fallen chair and guided her back into it with a solicitous hand.

'Sing!' Isabelle stared at him, wondering if her hearing was defective. 'He wants them to sing?' Perhaps William had been given too much poppy syrup and was delirious.

Jean's smile was a travesty. 'Henry and I were sitting with him and he said that it was strange, but he felt an urge to sing – perhaps because he was relieved at having set his affairs in order, I do not know. I told him he ought to do so – that it might gladden his heart and give him strength, but he told me to be quiet, that everyone would think he had gone mad. So Henry suggested perhaps it would be more fitting if his daughters should come and sing for him, and I said I would bring them.'

Isabelle gestured to the wide-eyed young women. 'What are you waiting for?' she demanded. 'Your father has asked for you. Go – go!'

Looking bemused and a little frightened, they left the trestle ushered by Mahelt, who took Joanna's hand.

Jean sat down on the bench beside Isabelle. 'I am sorry,

I did not mean to frighten you. The Earl is very weak, but still in his senses.'

Isabelle pushed the food aside, all glimmer of appetite gone. Jean covered her right hand with his own. 'It is very hard,' she said. 'He is letting go, but I am still clinging, still hoping, but for my own selfish sake, not his.'

'He was the father I barely knew,' Jean murmured, 'then a mentor, friend and companion. There will be a great hole in the fabric of my being when he is gone, but not as great a hole as the one had I not known him.'

'Ah, Jean,' she said as his words touched her to the quick. 'You know.'

'Yes.' He squeezed her fingers, then rose and left the room.

Isabelle sat for a while, the back of her hand pressed to her lips, the smooth gold of her wedding ring a harder pressure than that of flesh and bone. Then she left the trestle and, bidding her women remain where they were, took the path to William's chamber.

Henry FitzGerold was sitting outside, playing chess with his squire. Both leaped to their feet when they saw her, but she motioned them to be reseated, and quietly slipped through the door which had been left slightly ajar.

Mahelt was standing before the bed, her sisters at her back, singing in a clear, pure voice without trace of a tremor. The song was a rotrouenge that William had taught her when she was a child at his knee. Her voice lifted the hair on Isabelle's nape and raised in her feelings too intense, too sharp for tears. William's eyes were alight as he listened to his daughter sing and he was smiling. Isabelle moved unobtrusively to a bench at the side of the room and sat down, hands folded tightly in her lap. One by one the girls took their turn singing for their father, and although Mahelt had by far the best voice, they all did their best to please him. Joanna was shy and William helped her, raising his own voice in song. Isabelle's throat closed with emotion, for despite all the debility and suffering, William's voice remained deep and fine. The effort, however, of breathing and singing drained him. Seeing the colour leach from his face, Isabelle rose and shooed the girls from the room. In the aftermath of maintaining her composure to sing, Mahelt was weeping now, bitterly, but Isabelle left her in the hands of her younger sisters, closed the door and returned swiftly to William.

His eyes were shut, but as she trod across the rushes to the bed, he opened them again and, despite his dreadful colour, gave her a fatigued smile.

'And what song shall I sing for you?' she asked unsteadily.

'The one of Solomon,' he said. '"Set me as a seal upon your heart . . . for love is strong as death." Ah, I am tired now of singing. Come and sit with me awhile.' He held out his hand.

'Will your new vows allow a woman to sit upon your bed?' she asked and managed not to sound bitter.

His smile remained. 'As long as she does not climb into it and seduce me into carnal lust,' he said. 'We must needs control ourselves.'

Despite herself, she laughed through her anguish and sat upon the coverlet, taking the hand he had held out in hers.

'Our daughters . . .' he said after a while when he had recovered a little. 'Even as much as our sons, they carry our bloodline and I am glad to see them together. Make sure Will finds a good man for Joanna when the time comes.'

Isabelle murmured assent.

He smiled ruefully. 'And that she practises her singing.'

'Daily.'

He closed his eyes and she thought that he had fallen asleep, but he had been summoning his strength. 'Last night I saw two men robed all in white standing either side of the bed. I know I was not dreaming, even though my son and the others sitting in vigil plainly saw nothing.' He let out a sigh. 'It will not be long now, Isabelle . . .'

The Tuesday after Ascension Day dawned bright and clear. Trees were in pale green leaf, bursting with life, and the birdsong had begun early in the morning and scarcely abated from the dawn chorus. Isabelle had gone down to the riverbank with Ancel, Joanna and her grandchildren to feed the swans and cygnets. As they had done every year of her marriage, the birds were nesting on the far bank. She liked to imagine they were the same pair but knew she was being fanciful. Bishop Hugh of Avalon had had a pet swan for thirty years, but those in the wild were not so long-lived.

'They mate for life,' she told Mahelt, who was walking with her. The women's skirts were soaking up a dark hem of dew and their feet were wet, but neither minded.

'How do you know that?'

'One of the gamekeepers told me.'

'What happens if one dies?'

'I didn't ask him that.' Isabelle divided the bread they had brought between the youngsters, and saving half a loaf to herself, broke it in her hands and threw pieces to the adults. They dipped their graceful necks and shov-elled up the softened morsels. The fluffy youngsters imitated their elders. Under the water their webbed feet looked ridiculously large for their bodies. Fish rose to gobble their share – great tench and chub, and red-finned rudd.

'Don't go too close to the water or you'll fall in. Rohese, watch them!' Mahelt called across to the nurse keeping an eye on her two sons and her toddling daughter. 'They're daredevils, the boys. Heaven help me when they leave my skirts for the training ground!' There was pride in her voice as well as anxiety.

Isabelle eyed her grandsons with poignant amusement. The chubbiness of infancy had melted away leaving active, wiry little boys of nine and six, dark like their mother and with her eyes – William's eyes. 'It doesn't seem a minute since you were that age. You'd have been in one year if your father's reactions hadn't been so swift. He grabbed you and nearly fell in himself. The mud and water came over the top of his boots.'

'I don't remember . . . I wish I did. Will my children be the same when it comes my turn?' Mahelt blinked hard and she threw the last of her bread into the water. 'What of their memories?'

Feeling a flood of tender warmth, Isabelle hugged her. 'You know the important parts, as do they,' she said. 'That they are cherished and well loved. I do not suppose the details matter in God's scheme. I—' She looked up as Father Walter came puffing across the grass towards them, waving his arms as he ran. 'Countess, Lady Mahelt, come quickly, it is the Earl!'

Isabelle's heart kicked and started to pound in swift, hard strokes. Raising her skirts above her ankles, she dashed towards the manor.

The door to William's chamber stood wide, the windows too, allowing the full flood of the May sunlight to brighten the chamber and dazzle the whitewashed walls. Tears streaking his face, Will was supporting his father in his arms. A weeping Jean was trying to revive his lord by splashing his face with rose water, but to no avail; although he yet lived, as attested by the laboured rise and fall of his chest. William's executor Richard of Notely had placed a cross in William's hands and was praying over him with the Abbot of Reading and the household chaplains.

Her breath sobbing in her lungs from distress and the urgency of her run, Isabelle knelt at the bedside and clasped her own hands in prayer and supplication. '*Maria, Mater gratiae, Mater misericordiae, Tu nos ab hoste protege et mortis hora suscipe. Maria, Mater gratiae, Mater misericordiae, Tu nos ab hoste protege et mortis hora suscipe.*' A part of her was screaming 'Don't leave me!' but another part was praying with desperation, 'Holy Mary, release him. By your great mercy, let him go!'

The sun moved across the window space, shining in full benediction on the bed and those standing around it. William's gaze was open, fixed upon the arch of light. Isabelle followed its path. The dazzle of sun on lime-washed wall and bleached coverlet was blinding and for an instant she thought she saw the figures of whom he had spoken to her, perhaps even the ruffle of feathers like the arch of a swan's wings. When she looked back at William, half in awe, half distrusting, he had ceased to breathe and his parted lips were curved in the faintest hint of a smile.

Epilogue

Striguil, Welsh Borders, August 1219

Isabelle had had her tapestry frame moved into the bailey to take advantage of the warm summer's weather and the good, clear light. These days her eyes needed help to see to make the fine stitches and since this was an altar piece for the abbey at Tintern, she wanted it to be the best she could do.

Her women sat with her, quietly plying their needles, working in companionable silence that no one felt the need to break. A refreshing breeze, neither too cold nor too strong, blew across the walls from the river far below. Isabelle paused to rest her eyes for a moment. The embroidery displayed the resurrection and its border was edged with alternating shields bearing the arms of Marshal and de Clare. At Mahelt's insistence she had embarked upon the project in the first days and weeks following William's death. The endless repetition of stitches had given her something to do, day in, day out, while she was desolate with grief and nothing mattered.

At first Isabelle had felt numb inside and as solid as the shields she had spent hours embroidering, but gradually, as she worked, the colours, the symmetry and beauty of the patterns had begun to open her feelings to the world around her again. She had started to take notice, although it was a gradual process and there were still days when the world was grey and overcast with sorrow. She had not yet reached a state of happiness, but today she was content, and it was a step forward.

As he had desired, William had been laid to rest in the Temple Church in London. The funeral had been attended by a vast throng of barons and magnates, and conducted by the Archbishop of Canterbury. So great was the crowd that the alms-giving in honour of William's soul had had to take place at Westminster where there was sufficient space. Now a skilled master stone carver was preparing the effigy to lie upon the tomb, and when it was done, she would go to London and see that it met with her approval. Even if it was not her fate to lie beside her husband, she would have him fittingly represented.

She had pondered long on the nature of death and found comfort in the fact that even the Christ had had to die, and that it was an honourable estate that all must come to. She prayed that when her own time came, she could leave the world with as much honour as William had done. She had asked for God's blessing on the time that remained to her, and upon her family and children, especially Eve, who was carrying her first child.

Richard had not been in time to attend his father's funeral, but had come to her from France and stayed for a week at Caversham before escorting her here, to Striguil. He was so much like William, except rendered in the rich auburn colouring of de Clare, that his presence had given her great joy, seasoned with great pain. A month ago he had returned to France and for a brief while the grieving had begun again, but not as deep and she was past it now.

A joyous shout made her raise her head and look across the bailey. Two young knights had set up a quintain on the sward and were preparing to tilt at the ring, as William had so often done. Now and then they glanced covertly towards the women. Seeing Isabelle watching, one of them saluted her with his painted lance, then made his horse side-step and caracole, his grin as bright as the sun.

Above the young man's head, the banners fluttered on the battlements, proclaiming her residence; the red chevronels of de Clare and beside it the blazon that William had taken for his own on the tourney field of Lagny-sur-Marne before she had known him. The scarlet lion snarled out from its background of emerald and gold, blowing in the direction of the Welsh hills to the north-west.

As long as there were young knights to break lances and women to watch their prowess, as long as there were men who would temper their desires and ambitions with honour and integrity, William's presence would still be felt.

After a moment of watching the knights train, Isabelle picked up her needle and began to sew, a poignant smile on her lips and a tentative feeling of peace in her heart. Whatever the future held, she was ready to face it.

Author's Note

The Scarlet Lion is my second novel about William Marshal. My first, *The Greatest Knight,* covers his early career and climb up fortune's ladder, from household knight and tourney champion to magnate and co-ruler of the realm during Richard I's absences on crusade.

As I have continued to research the story of William Marshal, his family and familiars, I have been privileged to be drawn into a life that by the standards of any age would be amazing and inspiring. Perhaps the only modern hero who comes close is Sir Winston Churchill and indeed the lives of the two men share many parallels, not least that of taking the helm at a time of national crisis.

William Marshal's name is a byword for chivalry. He is the dashing knight, the champion of the tournaments, contemporary of the Lionheart, flawless paragon. The man behind the legend, however, is somewhat more complex and occasionally flawed, but that only serves to make him more of a hero. He was easy-going and courteous, and enjoyed the simple pleasures of life when they came his way, but could play the great magnate to the hilt when it suited his purposes. He was an accomplished soldier and commander with a natural talent for the battle-field, but hand in hand with such skills came the dextrous ability to negotiate and seek diplomatic solutions rather than plunge into all-out war. He was generous to his men and open-handed, but fiscally astute – King John often borrowed money from him. By various, often hand-to-mouth stratagems, William kept the country from bankruptcy during the period of his regency despite the limited resources at his disposal. He set great store by his honour and his oath of fealty, but was prepared to blur the lines when his lands were threatened as in the case of his estates in Normandy and Ireland.

At a time when women's voices were not always heard, his wife, Isabelle, Countess of Pembroke, was very much William's partner and equal. Although she does not feature often in the primary sources, when she does appear, her presence is telling and reveals that she was no retiring flower. She did indeed object to her sons being taken hostage and said so. Heavily pregnant she did take on Meilyr FitzHenry and rule Leinster in William's absence, as she ruled their other estates when he was in the field. William said of her that '*Ge n'i rien si par lui non.*' 'I have no claim to anything here, save through her.' She was present at his councils. Wherever he was, Isabelle was not usually far away. She was his '*Belle amie*' and it is what he called her at their final embrace before he took the deathbed vows of a Templar. When he died, she was distraught and she herself only survived him by a year, despite the age gap of more than twenty years separating them.

I am grateful to Catherine Armstrong at the Castles Wales website for her lead suggesting that Isabelle's mother, Aoife, Countess of Hibernia, was laid to rest at Tintern Abbey. Further personal research of my own appears to bear this out, and it would go part way to explain William and Isabelle's fleeting visit to Ireland in 1201.

I have tried to stay as true to the facts and the characters as I can, whilst acknowledging that this is a novel, not a reference work. If the edifice is built with solid building blocks of research, then it is bound together by the mortar of imagination.

Readers will not find the murder of Alais de Béthune in any reference work. All they do say is that she died about nine months after her marriage, but I firmly believe, although cannot prove beyond circumstantial evidence, that her half-brother William de Forz had her murdered and got away with it. That's the thing with history. Loose ends are not always neatly tied up. The death of Prince Arthur also remains open to conjecture. It is my personal belief that John did kill him, but that it was as a *coup de grâce* after French agents forced his hand.

Where possible, the minor characters are drawn from life too. Readers might notice that the names of the chaplains serving William's household change but this is because there were several of them, who worked in rotation, or came and went as years and circumstances dictated. Chaplains named in the Marshal's charters include, among others, Eustace, Roger, Nicholas and Walter (who was chaplain to Isabelle).

I have included a select bibliography of the main primary and secondary sources I used in the writing of *The Scarlet Lion* so that readers who are interested in knowing more about William Marshal, Isabelle de Clare and their children can explore them and their world in greater detail. I found the Anglo-Norman Text Society's translation of the *Histoire de Guillaume le Maréchal* invaluable for an eye-witness account of William's life and death.

The piece was commissioned shortly after he died, and told to its composer by the people who had known him best, and thus the man himself shines through in much of the content. The *Histoire* itself is also remarkable for being the first secular biography of an Englishman.

For readers feeling adventurous, William's tomb effigy can be visited at the Temple Church in London. The effigies of his sons William and Gilbert are also present in the round nave. Isabelle lies with her mother, Mahelt and Walter at Tintern, but their graves have long since been lost. Visitors to Chepstow Castle (known as Striguil in *The Scarlet Lion*) can see the great castle doors that William commissioned when he became the Earl. A large replica of Isabelle's seal can also be viewed at Chepstow Castle together with information about the Marshal family. Pembroke Castle still retains the shell of William Marshal's great keep and there are exhibitions concerned with the Marshal family and their descendants. The town that William founded in Ireland, called Newtown in the novel, is today known as New Ross.

It has been a wonderful journey for me as an author to share the lives of such extraordinary people. It is with great respect, a touch of sadness and a tremendous sense of inspiration that I move on.

> *E Dex en perdurable glorie*
> *Dont que la sue ame soit mise*
> *Et entre ses angles assise!*

> *Amen*

Select Bibliography

Carpenter, D. A., *The Minority of Henry III* (Methuen, 1978, ISBN 0 413 62360 2)

Church, S. D., *The Household Knights of King John* (Cambridge University Press, 1999, ISBN 0 521 55319 9)

Coss, Peter, *The Lady in Medieval England 1000–1500* (Sutton, 1998, ISBN 0 7509 0802 5)

Crouch, David, *William Marshal, Knighthood, War and Chivalry, 1147–1219* (Longman, 2nd edn, 2002, ISBN 0 582 77222 2)

Flanagan, Marie-Therese, *Irish Society, Anglo-Norman Settlers, Angevin Kingship: Interactions in Ireland in the Late Twelfth Century* (Clarendon Press, 1989, 0 19 822154 1)

Gerald of Wales, *The History and Topography of Ireland* (translation of 12th-century manuscript, Penguin, 1981)

Hardy, Thomas Duffus, FSA, *A Description of the Patent Rolls of the Tower of London to which is added an Itinerary of King John* (Printed by command of His Majesty King William IV under the direction of the Commissioners of the Public Records of the Kingdom, 1831)

History of William Marshal, Vol. II, ed. by A. J. Holden with English translation by S. Gregory and historical notes by D. Crouch (Anglo-Norman Text Society Occasional Publications series 5, 2004, ISBN 0 905474 45 7)

Johns, Susan M., *Noblewomen, Aristocracy and Power in the Twelfth Century Anglo-Norman Realm* (Manchester University Press, 2003, ISBN 0 7190 6305 1)

Labarge, Margaret Wade, *Mistress, Maids and Men: Baronial Life in the Thirteenth Century* (Phoenix Press, 2003, ISBN 1 84212 499 4)

Painter, Sidney, *William Marshal, Knight Errant, Baron and Regent of England* (Johns Hopkins University Press, 1933)

Painter, Sidney, *The Reign of King John* (Johns Hopkins University Press, 1949)

Powell, F. York, ed., *English History from Contemporary Writers: Strongbow's Conquest of Ireland* (Putnam, 1888)

Tyerman, Christopher, *Who's Who in Early Medieval England* (Shepheard Walwyn, 1996, ISBN 0 85683 132 8)

Other bestselling titles available by post:

☐ The Champion   Elizabeth Chadwick   £6.99

☐ The Love Knot   Elizabeth Chadwick   £7.99

☐ The Conquest   Elizabeth Chadwick   £6.99

☐ The Marsh King's Daughter   Elizabeth Chadwick   £6.99

☐ Lords of the White Castle   Elizabeth Chadwick   £6.99

☐ The Winter Mantle   Elizabeth Chadwick   £6.99

☐ The Falcons of Montabard   Elizabeth Chadwick   £6.99

☐ The Greatest Knight   Elizabeth Chadwick   £6.99

The prices shown above are correct at time of going to press. However, the publishers reserve the right to increase prices on covers from those previously advertised, without further notice.

———————————————— sphere ————————————————

SPHERE

PO Box 121, Kettering, Northants, NN14 4ZQ
Tel: 01832 737525, Fax: 01832 733076
Email: aspenhouse@FSBDial.co.uk

POST AND PACKING:

Payments can be made as follows: cheque, postal order (payable to Sphere), credit card or Switch Card. Do not send cash or currency.

All UK Orders   **FREE OF CHARGE**
EC & Overseas   25% of order value

Name (BLOCK LETTERS) . . . .

Address . . . .

. . . .

Post/zip code: . . . .

☐ Please keep me in touch with future Sphere publications

☐ I enclose my remittance £ . . . .

☐ I wish to pay by Visa/Mastercard/Eurocard/Switch Card

Card Expiry Date | | | | | Switch Issue No. | | |

Warren, W. L., *King John* (Eyre & Methuen, 2nd edn, 1978, ISBN 0 413 45510 6)

Woolgar, C. M., *The Great Household in Late Medieval England* (Yale University Press, 1999, ISBN 0 300 07687 8)